Praise for *Syndrome E*

"Compulsively readable . . . An eerie psychological mystery with a truly stunning resolution."
—*Pittsburgh Post-Gazette*

"A crackerjack story that most readers will devour in one sitting . . . Spare evocative prose propels French author Thilliez's stellar U.S. debut."
—*Publishers Weekly* (starred review)

"Blending science and neurology into the intrigue of his excellent thriller, Thilliez takes us into the maze of the human brain, with all the evils it can unleash."
—*Elle* (Paris)

"With a fascinating blend of noir procedural, espionage flavor, and an eerie setup that makes the video from *The Ring* seem harmless, it is no surprise that *Syndrome E* has already been an international sensation. Beneath its dazzling, byzantine plot are menacing questions of what lurks at the intersection between the new and chilling capabilities of neuroscience and the ancient but more chilling capabilities of human evil."
—Michael Koryta, *New York Times* bestselling author of *The Prophet* and *The Ridge*

"This terrific French thriller . . . boasts distinctive characters you want to spend time with, a lively plot, evocative settings, fun film references, and, icing on the cake, an enjoyable offbeat romance. Having achieved bestseller status in Europe, Thilliez is poised to do the same in the U.S."
—*Kirkus Reviews*

"Detective Lucie Henebelle is an overwhelmed single mother who doesn't need more trouble. Then she gets the call from a friend who has gone blind after watching an obscure film embedded with heinous images. It's her colleague, a profiler for the Paris police department, who makes the connection between the movie and the five men murdered at a construction site. Twisty neuroscience! Who can resist?"
—*New York Daily News*

"A tour de force . . . A captivating plot that keeps the reader in his seat until the final moments."
—*Le Monde*

"Franck Thilliez leads his story like a beating drum, multiplying the reverberations without ever losing track of the psychological development of his characters. . . . A reflection on the origins of violence that is as playful as it is erudite. Essential reading!"
—*Metro* (Paris)

PENGUIN BOOKS

SYNDROME E

Franck Thilliez is the author of many bestselling novels in his native France, where his books have sold almost two million copies. This is his first novel to be published in the United States.

Mark Polizzotti is a translator of more than thirty books from French. His articles and reviews have appeared in *The Wall Street Journal* and *The Nation*. He heads the publications program at the Metropolitan Museum of Art in New York City.

Syndrome E

Franck Thilliez

Translated by Mark Polizzotti

PENGUIN BOOKS

PENGUIN BOOKS
Published by the Penguin Group
Penguin Group (USA) LLC
375 Hudson Street
New York, New York 10014

USA | Canada | UK | Ireland | Australia | New Zealand | India | South Africa | China
penguin.com
A Penguin Random House Company

First published in the United States of America by Viking Penguin,
a member of Penguin Group (USA) Inc., 2012
Published in Penguin Books 2014

Originally published in French under the title *Le Syndrome E*
by Editions Fleuve Noir, Department d'Univers Poche, Paris.

THE LIBRARY OF CONGRESS HAS CATALOGED THE HARDCOVER EDITION AS FOLLOWS:
Thilliez, Franck.
[Syndrome E. English]
Syndrome E / Franck Thilliez ; translated by Mark Polizzotti.
p. cm.
ISBN 978-0-670-02578-7 (hc.)
ISBN 978-0-14-750971-0 (pbk.)
1. Detectives—France—Fiction. 2. Evil in motion pictures—Fiction.
3. Subliminal perception—Fiction. 4. Violence—Fiction.
5. Murder—Investigation—Fiction. I. Polizzotti, Mark. II. Title.
PQ2720.H58S9613 2012
843'.92—dc23
2012004718

Printed in the United States of America
2 3 4 5 6 7 8 9 10

Set in Minion Pro
Designed by Francesca Belanger

To my family

Syndrome E

1

*B*e *the first one there.*

   No sooner had he seen the classified ad than Ludovic Sénéchal hit the road at the crack of dawn, covering the 120 miles between suburban Lille and Liège in record time.

   For sale: old films, 16 mm, 35 mm, silent and sound. All genres, short and full length, 1930s and after. 800+ reels, including 500 spy thrillers. Make offer on site.

This sort of notice was pretty rare on a general-interest Web site. Usually, owners of such things sold them at trade fairs or put them up on eBay. This ad sounded more like someone trying to dump an old fridge. It boded well.

   In the center of the Belgian municipality, Ludovic parked after some effort, verified the number on the building, then introduced himself to its occupant: Luc Szpilman. Around twenty-five, Converse All-Stars, surfer shades, Bulls T-shirt, scattered body piercings.

   "Oh, right, you're here for the movies. Come this way—they're in the attic."

   "Am I the first?"

   "There should be others soon. I've already had a few calls. I didn't think they'd go this fast."

   Ludovic followed close behind. The house was typical Flemish: bland colors and dark brick. The rooms were all arranged around the stairwell, a kind of main area lit by a well of brightness.

   "Can I ask why you're getting rid of these old films?"

   Ludovic had chosen his words carefully: *getting rid, old* . . . The bargaining had already started.

"My father died the other day. He never told anybody what he wanted done with them."

Ludovic couldn't believe his ears: not even cold in the ground, and already the patriarch was being stripped clean. On top of which, his idiot son didn't see the point of hanging on to full-length movies that weighed a good fifty pounds each when you could store a thousand times more at a thousand times less weight. Poor sacrificed generation . . .

The staircase was so steep you could break your neck. Once up in the attic, Szpilman switched on a dim bulb. Ludovic smiled and his collector's heart skipped a beat. There they sat, completely protected from natural light. Variously colored canisters stacked in turrets of twenty. There was that wonderful celluloid smell, and the air barely circulated between the storage racks. A ladder on wheels provided access to the highest shelves. Ludovic moved closer. On one side were the 35 mm, a hefty stock of them, and on the other the 16 mm, which were his particular interest. The circular canisters were all labeled and arranged perfectly. Silent classics, feature films from the golden age of French cinema, and especially spy thrillers, easily filling more than half the shelves. Ludovic took one in his hands. *The Chairman*, a film by John Lee Thompson about the CIA and Communist China. A complete, intact print, preserved from humidity and light like a bottle of vintage wine. There were even pH strips in the canisters to monitor acidity. Ludovic struggled to hide his emotion. This treasure alone would have fetched five hundred euros on the open market, easy.

"I take it your father was a fan of spy films?"

"And how—you should see his library. Conspiracy theories, the whole nine yards. It was like an obsession."

"How much do you want for these?"

"I poked around on the Web. It's a hundred euros a reel, give or take. Mainly I want to clear all this out as quick as possible, 'cause I need the space. So the price is negotiable."

"I certainly hope so."

Ludovic kept rummaging.

"Your father must have had a private screening room?"

"Yeah, we're about to redo it. Getting rid of the old stuff and putting in all new equipment. LCD screen and the latest home system. Here's where I'm going to set up a practice space for my band."

Disgusted by such a lack of respect, Ludovic turned to his right, rearranged some piles of films, immersed himself in the celluloid aroma. He discovered features by Harold Lloyd, Buster Keaton, then, farther on, classics like *Hamlet* and *Captain Fracasse*. He wished he could take them all, but his functionary's salary at Social Security and his various monthly subscriptions—online dating, Internet, cable, satellite—didn't leave him much wiggle room. So he'd have to make choices.

He walked toward the sliding ladder. Luc Szpilman cautioned him:

"Careful on that. That's where my father fell and fractured his skull. I mean, really, climbing up there at eighty-two . . ."

Ludovic paused an instant, then rushed forward. He thought of the old man, so passionate about his films that he'd died for them. He climbed as high as he could and continued shopping. Behind *The Kremlin Letter*, on a hidden shelf, he discovered a black canister with no label. Balancing on the ladder, Ludovic picked it up. Inside was what looked like a short, since the film took up only part of the reel. Ten or twenty minutes' projection time, tops. Probably a lost film, a unique specimen that the owner had never managed to identify. Ludovic grabbed it up, climbed down, and added it to the stack of nine cult films he'd already chosen. Anonymous reels like this always added spice to the screenings.

He turned around, playing it cool, but his pulse was pounding.

"I'm afraid most of your movies aren't worth a whole lot. Pretty standard stuff. And besides, can you smell that odor?"

"What odor?"

"Vinegar. The films have been affected by vinegar syndrome. They'll be worthless before long."

The young man leaned forward and sniffed.

"You sure about that?"

"Absolutely. I'm willing to take these ten off your hands. Shall we say thirty-five euros apiece?"

"Fifty."

"Forty."

"All right . . ."

Ludovic wrote out a check for four hundred euros. As he was pulling away from the curb, he noticed a car with French plates looking for a parking spot.

No doubt another collector—already.

Ludovic emerged from his home projection booth and sat down, alone with a can of beer, in one of the twelve fifties-style leatherette seats that he'd scavenged when they closed the Rex: his own private movie theater. He'd created an authentic auditorium for himself in the basement of his house, which he called his "mini-cinema." Fold-up seats, stage, pearlescent screen, Heurtier Tri-Film projector: he had it all. At the age of forty-two, the only thing he was missing was a partner, someone to squeeze close while watching *Gone with the Wind* in the original English. But for the moment, those lousy dating sites had yielded only one-night stands or washouts.

It was nearly three in the morning. Saturated with images of war and espionage, he decided to round out his marathon screening with the un- identified, and incredibly well-preserved, short feature. It must have been a copy. These unlabeled films sometimes turned out to be veritable treasures or, if the gods were really smiling, lost works by famous filmmakers like Méliès, Welles, or Chaplin. The collector in him loved to fantasize about such things. When Ludovic unspooled the leader to wind the film into the projector, he saw that the strip was marked 50 FRAMES PER SECOND. That was unusual: normally it was twenty-four per second, more than suf- ficient to give the illusion of movement. Still, he adjusted the shutter speed to the recommended setting. No point watching it in slow motion.

Within seconds, the whiteness of the screen yielded to a dark, clouded image, with no title or credits. A white circle appeared in the upper right corner. Ludovic wondered at first if it was a flaw in the print, as often happened with those old reels.

The film began.

Ludovic fell heavily as he ran upstairs.

He couldn't see a thing, not even with the lights on.

He was completely blind.

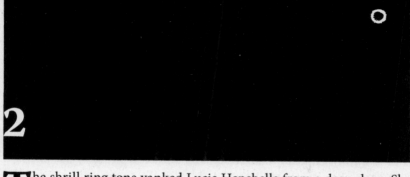

2

The shrill ring tone yanked Lucie Henebelle from a deep sleep. She jerked up in her chair and groped around for her cell.

"Hello . . . ?"

Pasty voice. Lucie glanced at the clock in the room: 4:28 a.m. Opposite her, her daughter Juliette, a glucose drip in her right arm, was fast asleep.

The voice on the other end of the line was shaky:

"Hello? Who is this?"

Lucie brushed her long blond hair off her face, her nerves on edge. She had finally managed to doze off. It was very definitely not the time for practical jokes.

"Who am I? Who the hell are *you*? Do you have any idea what time it is?"

"Ludovic—it's Ludovic Sénéchal . . . Is this . . . is this Lucie?"

Lucie Henebelle quietly left the room and found herself in a neon-lit hallway. She yawned and tugged at her shirttails, trying to look halfway decent. Distant babies' wails ran along the walls. In Pediatrics, silence was a pipe dream.

It took her a few seconds to place the caller. Ludovic Sénéchal. An e-dating fling, following several weeks of intense messaging, that had ended seven months later in a café in Lille, for reasons of "incompatibility."

"Ludovic? What's going on?"

In the receiver Lucie heard the sound of a crash, like a glass falling to the floor.

"Someone has to come get me. Someone has to . . ."

He couldn't speak, seemingly overcome by panic. Lucie urged him to calm down, talk slowly.

5

"I don't know what happened. I was in my cinema. Listen, Lucie—I can't see a thing. I turned all the lights on and it didn't make a damn bit of difference. I think . . . I think I've gone blind. I called a number at random and . . ."

That was just like him to be watching movies at four in the morning. A hand on her lower spine, Lucie walked back and forth past a huge window that looked out on the various hospitals of the Lille medical center. That crummy armchair had given her a stiff back. At thirty-seven, your body doesn't shrug things off so easily.

"Hold on. I'm sending an ambulance."

Ludovic might have bumped his head on something. A scalp wound or head trauma might provoke this kind of symptom and could prove fatal.

"Make sure you're not bleeding by feeling your head and licking your fingers. Skull, nose, and temples. If you are, cover it with ice cubes and press with a towel. The EMTs will bring you to the hospital right next door to here and I'll come check in on you. Whatever you do, don't lie down. You still live at the same address?"

"Yes. Please hurry!"

She hung up and ran to the emergency desk, from where she had them dispatch an ambulance. No doubt about it, her summer vacation was getting off to a rousing start. Her eight-year-old had just been admitted for viral gastroenteritis. Nobody ever had such crappy luck in the middle of summer! The illness had blasted through like a hurricane, dehydrating the poor girl in a mere twenty hours. Juliette couldn't swallow a thing, not even water. The doctors were predicting a stay of several days, with lots of rest and a special diet after she got out. The poor kid hadn't been able to go to her first summer camp with her sister, Clara. Being apart was hard on the twins.

Lucie leaned on the window. Watching the revolving light of an ambulance as it sped out, she reflected that in the police station or out in the world, on vacation or at work, life always seemed to land her in the shit.

3

Several hours later, 125 miles from Lille, Martin Leclerc, head of the Violent Crimes unit, pondered a three-dimensional representation of a human head on the screen of a Mac. You could clearly see the brain and several salient parts of the face: tip of the nose, outer surface of the right eye, left tragus . . . Then he pointed to a green area, located in the left superior temporal gyrus.

"So that lights up every time I say something?"

Half reclining on a hydraulic chair, head squeezed under a hood containing 128 electrodes, Chief Inspector Franck Sharko stared at the ceiling without moving a muscle.

"It's called Wernicke's area, linked to hearing speech. For you and me both, blood rushes there the moment you hear a voice. Hence the coloration."

"Impressive."

"Not half as much as seeing you here." Sharko spoke softly beneath the bonnet. "I don't know if you recall, Martin, but the invitation was for a drink at my place. The only thing you'll get here is watery coffee."

"Your shrink didn't have any problems with me sitting in on a session. And you'd suggested it yourself—or am I not the only one having memory lapses?"

Sharko flattened his large hands on the armrests; his wedding ring clanked against the metal. He'd been attending these "maintenance" sessions for weeks and still hadn't learned to relax.

"So what's up?"

The head of Violent Crimes massaged his temples, his face weary. In the twenty years they'd worked together, the two men had often seen each other in the darkest possible light: horrific crime scenes, family tragedies, health problems . . .

"It happened two days ago. Some dump between Le Havre and Rouen. Notre-Dame-de-Gravenchon—how's that for a name? Bodies unearthed on the banks of the Seine—you must have heard about it on the tube."

"That thing at the construction site, where they're laying a pipeline?"

"Right. The media was all over it. They were already there because the site itself is such a hot-button issue. They discovered five stiffs with their skulls sawed off. Criminal Investigations in Rouen is on the scene, working with the local cops. Their DA was about to send in the CSI boys, but in the end we caught it. I can't say I'm too thrilled—in this weather, it's disgusting."

"What about Devoise?"

"He's on a sensitive case. I can't pull him off. And Bertholet is away on vacation."

"What about *my* vacation?"

Leclerc straightened his narrow striped tie. A solid fifty years old, black rayon suit, shiny pumps, drawn, arid face: a top cop in all his splendor. Droplets of sweat pearled on his forehead and he mopped his brow with a handkerchief.

"You're the only one we have left around here. And they've got wives and kids . . . Shit, Franck, you know how it is."

The silence weighed on them like lead. A wife, children. Beach balls on the sand, laughter lost in the waves. All that was so hazy and far away now. Sharko turned his face toward the real-time animation of the activity in his brain, a fifty-something-year-old organ full of shadows. He jerked his chin, inviting Leclerc to follow the movement of his eyes. Despite the absence of speech, the green area on the upper part of the gyrus was glowing.

"If it's lighting up, it means she's talking to me at this very moment."

"Eugenie?"

Sharko grunted. Leclerc felt a chill. To see his chief inspector's meninges react to speech like this, when you couldn't even hear a fly buzzing, made him feel like there was a ghost in the room.

"What's she saying?"

"She wants me to buy a pint of cocktail sauce and some candied chestnuts next time I go shopping. She loves those miserable chestnuts. Excuse me a second . . ."

Sharko closed his eyes, lips pressed tight. Eugenie was someone he might see and hear at any moment. On the passenger seat of his old Renault. At night when he went to bed. Sitting cross-legged, watching the mini-gauge trains run around the tracks. Two years earlier, Eugenie had often shown up with a black man, Willy, a huge smoker of Camels and pot. A real mean son of a bitch, much worse than the little girl because he talked loud and tended to gesticulate wildly. Thanks to the treatment, the Rasta had disappeared for good, but the other one, the girl, came and went as she pleased, resistant as a virus.

On the Mac screen, the green area continued to pulsate for several seconds, then gradually faded. Sharko opened his eyes. He stared at his boss with a weary smile.

"You're going to have to get rid of your chief inspector someday, seeing him talk such crap."

"You're dealing with your problems and they haven't kept you from doing your job. I'd even say you're sometimes better at it."

"Yeah, try telling that to Josselin. The guy never lets up busting my chops. I think he's got it in for me."

"That's always how it is with a new boss. All they care about is cleaning house."

Dr. Bertowski, of the psychiatric department at La Salpêtrière Hospital, finally arrived, flanked by his neuroanatomist.

"Shall we get started, Mr. Sharko?"

"Mr. Sharko"—it rang funny, since "Sharko" sounded like the name of an advanced form of muscular atrophy: Charcot's disease. As if all the world's illnesses were his doing.

"Let's."

Bertowski leafed through his ever-present file.

"The episodes of paranoid persecution have become pretty scarce, from what I see here. Just a few lingering traces of distrust—that's very good. And your visions?"

"They've come back full force, maybe because I've been cooped up in my apartment. Not a day goes by without a visit from Eugenie. Most of the time she just sits around for two or three minutes, but she's kind of a pill. I can't tell you how many pounds of candied chestnuts she's made me buy since our last session."

Leclerc withdrew to the back of the room while they removed Sharko's hood.

"Have you been under a lot of stress lately?" the doctor asked.

"The heat, mostly."

"Your job doesn't help matters. We're going to shorten the time between sessions. Every three weeks seems a good compromise."

After immobilizing his head with two white straps, the neuroanatomist moved a figure eight–shaped instrument toward the crest of his skull—a coil that delivered magnetic impulses to a very precise area of the encephalon, so that the targeted neurons, like micromagnets, would react and rearrange themselves. Transcranial magnetic stimulation allowed them to attenuate, even eradicate, the hallucinations related to schizophrenia. The main difficulty was, of course, to target the right spot, as the area in question measured only a few centimeters, and being off by even a millimeter could make the patient start meowing or reciting the alphabet backward for the rest of his life.

Sharko lay there, a blindfold over his eyes, with just one order: don't move a hair. The only sound was the crackle of small magnetic pulses emitted at the frequency of one hertz. He didn't feel any pain, not the slightest discomfort, just the profound anxiety of knowing that, ten years earlier, they would have been treating him with electroshocks.

The session ended without incident. Twelve hundred pulses—or about twenty minutes—later, Sharko stood up, his muscles feeling a bit numb. He readjusted his spotless shirt and ran a hand through his brush-cut black hair. He was sweating. The sweltering heat of the hospital and the slight pudginess caused by Zyprexa didn't help. At the beginning of July, even the air-conditioning had trouble overcoming the hellish temperature outside.

Sharko jotted down his next appointment, thanked his psychiatrist, and left the room.

He joined Leclerc at the coffee machine at the end of the hallway. The

Violent Crimes chief felt like having a cigarette; those few minutes of observation had worn him out.

"That really gave me the willies, seeing them play with your head like that."

"Just routine. It's like sitting under the dryer at the hairdresser's for a perm."

Sharko smiled and raised the plastic cup to his lips.

"So go on. Tell me about the case."

The two men walked slowly.

"Five bodies, buried about six feet underground. Not a pretty sight. From what we know so far, four of them badly worm-eaten, the fifth in relatively good shape. All five missing the tops of their skulls, as if they'd been sawed off."

"What do the local cops make of it?"

"What do you think? They're in this provincial little town where the biggest crime up to now is not sorting your trash. The bodies must go back weeks, if not months. They're in it up to their necks, and the investigation is likely to get complicated. They could probably use a psychological leg up. Do what you usually do, no more, no less. You gather info, talk to who you gotta talk to, and after that we'll handle it in Nanterre. Two, three days, tops. Then you can get back to your miniature trains and go about your business. And I'll do the same. I don't want this to drag on. I need to go away pretty soon."

"Are you and Kathia going on holiday?"

Leclerc's lips made a thin line.

"I don't know yet. It depends."

"On what?"

"On a bunch of things that aren't anyone's business."

Sharko didn't push it. When they exited the hospital doors, a wave of heat crashed over them. His hands in the pockets of his linen trousers, the chief inspector looked back at the long, white stone building, its dome sparkling in the implacable sun. The establishment had become his second home these past few years, after the squad room.

"I'm a bit nervous about going out there again. All that seems so far away."

"You'll get used to it pretty fast."

Sharko remained silent for a moment, apparently weighing the pros and cons, then shrugged.

"Fuck it. Why not? I'm starting to look like a chair from spending so much time on my ass. Tell them I'll be there midafternoon."

4

Lucie was just finishing her coffee in the waiting room of Salengro Hospital when the attending physician in charge of Ludovic Sénéchal walked up to her. He was the tall, dark sort, with fine features and nice teeth, the kind of guy she might have crushed on in other circumstances. On his oversized scrubs she could read DR. L. TOURNELLE.

"So, Doctor?"

"No visible injuries, no scabs to indicate trauma. The ophthalmological tests didn't show anything abnormal. Ocular mobility, retinal exam—it's all good. His photomotor reflexes and pupil contraction are as they should be. That said, Ludovic Sénéchal can't see a thing."

"So then what's wrong with him?"

"We're going to run some more tests, especially an MRI to make sure he doesn't have a brain tumor."

"Can a tumor make you blind?"

"If it's pressing on the optic nerve, sure."

Lucie swallowed hard. Ludovic was no more than a memory, but even so they'd spent seven months of their lives together.

"Is it treatable?"

"It depends—on the size, the position, if it's malignant or benign. I'd rather not say anything before we do the scan. You can go see your friend if you like. Room 208."

The doctor gave her a firm handshake and quickly strode away. Lucie didn't have the strength to take the stairs and instead waited for the elevator. Between the tears and the vomiting, her two sleepless nights in the pediatrics ward had drained her. Lucky that her mother was able to take over in the daytime so she could get some rest.

After knocking softly at the door, she entered Ludovic's room. He was lying on his bed with a fixed stare. Lucie felt a lump in her throat. He hadn't changed . . . Hairline receded a bit, of course, but he still had the features of the mature man with the soft, round face that had first made her fall for him on the Web.

"It's Lucie . . ."

He turned toward her. His pupils didn't look at her directly but instead aimed at the wall just beside her. Lucie shivered and rubbed her arms. Ludovic tried to smile.

"You can come closer—I'm not contagious."

Lucie stepped forward and took his hand.

"It'll be okay."

"It's funny I dialed your number, isn't it? It could have been anybody."

"It's also funny that I happened to be in the neighborhood. At the moment, hospitals and I are old pals."

She explained about Juliette. Ludovic had known the twins, who were very fond of him. Lucie felt nervous, thinking of the horror that might have been growing in the head of her ex.

"They'll find what's wrong."

"I suppose they told you about the tumor?"

"It's just a theory."

"There is no tumor, Lucie. It's because of the film."

"What film?"

"The one with the little white circle. The one I found yesterday at a collector's. It was . . ."

Lucie noticed his fingers clutching the sheets.

"It was weird."

"Weird how?"

"Weird enough to make me lose my sight, for Christ's sake!"

He had shouted. Now he was trembling. He felt around him and gripped his visitor's hand.

"I'm sure it was this film the owner was looking for in his attic. He broke his skull as he was climbing the ladder. Something must have . . . I don't know, made him need to climb up those steep rungs to watch it."

Lucie sensed he was on the verge of a breakdown. She hated seeing friends or loved ones in distress.

"Why don't I have a look at this film?"

He shook his head energetically.

"No, no. I don't want you to—"

"What, go blind? Can you tell me how simple images projected on a screen can make me blind?"

No answer.

"Is the reel still on the projector?"

After a silence, Ludovic finally gave in.

"Yes. You just have to follow a few steps, the way I showed you. Do you remember?"

"Yes—with *A Touch of Evil*, I think."

"*Touch of Evil* . . . Orson Welles . . ."

He sank into a pained sigh. Tears had run down his cheeks. He pointed a finger at the void.

"My wallet must be on the nightstand. There are some business cards inside. Take the one with the name Claude Poignet. He restores old films, and I want you to bring him the reel. I want him to look it over, all right? I want to know where that footage comes from. And take the want ad—it has the name and address of the collector's son. Luc Szpilman."

"What do you want me to do with it?"

"Take it . . . take it all. You want to help me? Then help me, Lucie."

Lucie let out a silent sigh. She opened the wallet and took out the card and newspaper ad.

"Okay, done."

He seemed more at peace. He was now sitting up, feet resting on the floor.

"Aside from all this, Lucie, how are you?"

"Same old, same old. Still just as many murders and assaults. No danger of running out of work in the police."

"I meant you, not the job."

"Me? Oh, well . . ."

"Skip it. We'll talk later."

He held out the keys to his house and tightly squeezed her wrist. Lucie shivered when he stared straight into her eyes, his face mere inches from hers.

"Watch out for that film."

5

Midafternoon, Notre-Dame-de-Gravenchon. A small, picturesque town lost somewhere in the Seine-Maritime region. Cute shops, peace and quiet, greenery and fields as far as you could see, if you were facing in the right direction. Because if you looked southwest, not a mile distant the banks of the Seine were obstructed by a kind of giant steel vessel, which spewed so much grayish smoke and gas effluvia that it discolored the sky.

Sharko headed where he'd earlier been told by the police lieutenant, whom he was now hoping to find on site. Even though the bodies had been removed the day before—it had taken them a good day to dig them out of the ground without contaminating the crime scene, a real archaeology job—the chief inspector liked to trace his cases back to the start. Three hours on the road, with the sun smacking him in the face, had set him on edge—especially since he'd pretty much stopped driving years ago. These days he mainly took public transportation.

A road sign up ahead. He veered off, crossing the Port-Jérôme industrial zone with his windows shut and the AC going full blast. Even so, the air smelled viscous, heavy with metal shavings and acid. Here, embedded in nature, the big names parceled out the empire of fossil fuels and oils. Total, Exxon Mobil, Air Liquide. The inspector drove nearly two miles in this magma of smokestacks, finally crossing past it into a quieter area, a full-on industrial wasteland. Frozen bulldozers shredded the landscape. He parked just short of the construction site, got out, and loosened his shirt collar. To hell with his jacket—he abandoned it on the passenger seat, along with the sports bag that contained his effects for the hotel. He stretched his legs, which cracked when he bent them.

"Jesus . . ."

He slipped on his sunglasses, one arm of which had been reattached with glue, and took in his surroundings. The Seine on the right, a haze of trees to the left, the industrial site behind. Over it all reigned a vast impression of emptiness and abandonment. Not a house to be seen, just unused roads and barren lots. It was as if the area were dead, scorched by the fires of heaven.

In front of him, farther down, two or three men in hard hats were chatting. At their feet, a wide ocher scar split the earth in two, stretching along the riverbank for miles. It stopped dead right where the yellow-and-black tape of the national police flapped limply in the breeze. The air smelled of warm clay and humidity.

The cop immediately spotted his colleague from Rouen waiting for him, just from the holster on his belt. His piece shone in the sun like a beacon. The guy disappeared into a pair of low-waisted jeans, a black tee, and old canvas shoes. Dark, tall, lean; twenty-five, twenty-six at most. He was talking with a cameraman and what looked like a reporter. Sharko pushed his shades back into his short hair and showed his ID.

"Lucas Poirier?"

"You the profiler from Paris? Nice to meet you."

It would have taken too long to get into details and explain that his job, all things considered, had very little to do with profiling.

"Call me Sharko. Or Shark. No first and last names, no rank."

"I'm sorry, Chief Inspector, but I can't do that."

The newswoman came closer.

"Chief Inspector Sharko, we've been told about your visit and—"

"At the risk of seeming rude, kindly take your cameraman and get lost."

He gave her his darkest stare. Journalists were one thing he couldn't abide. The woman retreated a few paces, but nonetheless told her partner to get some footage. They'd no doubt cobble together some bit of fluff, with lots of continuity shots, stressing the fact that a real, live profiler was on the case. It would be a sensation.

Sharko pushed them farther away with his eyes and turned to Poirier.

"Do you know if my hotel room has been reserved? Who takes care of that at your place?"

"Umm, I have no idea. Probably the—"

"I want a large one, with a bathtub."

Poirier nodded, like most people from whom Sharko demanded something. The chief inspector gazed over his surroundings again.

"Right, let's not waste time. Explain the situation?"

The young lieutenant downed most of the mini water bottle he held in his hand and waved toward the Algeco prefab in the background.

"The site started up last month. They're building a pipeline to carry chemical products from the factory in Gonfreville to the Exxon refinery over there. Twenty miles of underground piping. They had only about five or six hundred yards to go, but with what they've just dug up the work's been shut down for now. They're not happy about it, and that's putting it mildly."

In the distance, a man in a tie—probably the site foreman—was pacing back and forth nonstop, cell phone glued to his ear. This kind of discovery must have been the last thing he was expecting. Even though he had no control over it, the poor slob still had to account to Financial.

Sharko mopped his brow with a handkerchief. Wide circles had formed under his arms. Poirier started to walk to the scene.

"Over there's where the workmen found them. Five bodies, buried six feet under. The backhoe operator didn't do too much damage—he stopped the minute he saw an arm appear."

Sharko ducked under the boundary tape and walked to the edge of the deep trench. He turned his face away, wrinkling his nose. Poirier stood next to him, nostrils buried in his T-shirt.

"Yeah, it's still pretty rank. They were soaking in muck, and the heat didn't help. You can imagine how much CSI and the ME are digging this."

The chief inspector drew a sharp breath, then studied the bottom of the pit.

"So what were they? Men, women, children? Any clue to their ages?"

"All men—you'll get all that from the forensic anthropologist. Four of them in pieces. The dampness of the ground and proximity of the Seine must have sped up the decomp. They were practically just skeletons, though there was still some putrefied flesh, fluids, you get the—"

"And the fifth?"

Poirier nervously squeezed his water bottle. Beneath his T-shirt, he was drenched. His forehead was dripping, his skin releasing ounces of water and salt.

"Also male, fairly well preserved. Comparatively speaking. With the other bodies above and below, it must have created a kind of insulating layer."

"Any body bags or special wrapping around the bodies?"

"No. No clothes either. They were completely naked. The guy who was better preserved had been . . . had scrape marks over part of his body. Arms, chest. Shit, I saw it with my own eyes . . . He was like a peeled orange. You can't imagine."

Actually, he could. He sighed. The case promised to be a tricky one, another file that would stack up with so many others in Nanterre, and that they'd churn through the computer now and then. He held his hand out to the lieutenant.

"Help me get down."

The detective did as asked. Sharko had the feeling the young man had already seen too much, so early in his career. He was in the quagmire from which he wouldn't emerge unscathed a few years down the road. All cops followed the same trail, the one that hurtled toward the abyss and didn't let you turn back. Because this bitch of a job chewed you up and ground you down, guts to nuts.

The chief inspector let go of Poirier's grip and stood in the pit. He brushed some soil from his shirt with the back of his hand. The air reeked of morgue drawers, the sun was fading, and over it all floated a sickly swelter. The cop squatted down and crumbled some dirt between his fingers. It had been sifted so as not to miss the slightest clue: small bones, bits of cartilage, insect pupae. CSI had done a thorough job. Sharko stood back up, lifting his eyes toward the ocher dirt walls. Six feet deep meant some serious digging to bury these corpses. Meticulous fellow . . .

"My chief mentioned something about skulls sawed open."

Poirier leaned over the top. A bead of sweat pearled on his forehead and dripped into the trench.

"That's true, and the press has been on it like white on rice. It's been causing quite a stir. They're talking about a serial killer and the whole shebang, pure craziness. We couldn't find any of the skull tops. Just vanished."

"What about the brains?"

"There wasn't a thing in the skulls. Except dirt. The medical examiner is still working on it. Seems the brain and eyes are the first things to decompose and disappear after death. So for now, we have no idea."

He stuck out his tongue and dripped the last dribble of water onto it from his bottle.

"Fucking heat!"

Feeling edgy, the young man crushed the container in his palm.

"Listen, Inspector, how about if we get out of here? I've been hanging around for two hours and I could use some fresh air. We can talk on the road—I have to go back with you anyway."

Sharko looked around the place one last time. For now, there was nothing left to see or discover. The crime scene photos, the close-ups and aerial views of the surroundings, if there were any, would certainly tell him more.

"Anything else peculiar about the bodies? Had their teeth been pulled out?"

A pause. The young man gave a nod, amazed.

"You're right. No teeth. And the hands had been cut off too. How did you—?"

"All five?"

"I think so, yeah. I— Excuse me a minute."

Poirier disappeared from Sharko's field of vision. A hell of a day for him, no doubt about it. The chief inspector slowly paced along the trench. In the distance, he could see the two nitwits from the TV news most likely zooming in on him. They discreetly moved away toward their rental car. The cop remained alone, staring at the empty space. He imagined the corpses, stacked five high . . . One had been skinned over part of his body—why? Had he been shown special treatment? Pre- or postmortem? All the questions inherent to a crime scene rushed to his lips. Had the victims met each other? Did they know their killer? Had they died at the same time? Under what circumstances?

Once again Sharko felt the first shivers of a new investigation, the most exciting part. It stank of death, backhoe fuel, and humidity, but he still caught himself loving those nauseating odors. There had been a period when he got off on adrenaline and shadows. When he lost count of the times he returned home in the middle of the night to find Suzanne sleeping on the couch, huddled up and in tears.

He loathed that past life as much as he missed it.

Farther on he found a construction ladder leaning against a wall of the trench and easily climbed out. A blacktopped road ran about thirty yards beyond it—no doubt the one the killer or killers had taken to dump the bodies. Rouen police must have started making inquiries in the area, questioning the factory staff just in case. But given the spot, they'd have had to figure they'd come up empty-handed.

A ways over, Lucas Poirier was sitting beside the Seine, cell phone at his ear. He was probably calling his wife to say it was looking like he'd be home late that evening. Soon he wouldn't bother calling at all, and his prolonged absences would become just part of the job. And years after that, he'd finally realize that what the job really meant was learning how to live alone with your demons. With a sign, Sharko let him know they were heading out. The detective from Rouen hung up and ran to join him.

"So how did you know about the teeth?"

"A vision. I'm a profiler, don't forget."

"Are you bullshitting me, Chief Inspector?"

Sharko favored him with a sincere smile. He liked the naivety of these kids. It proved they still had something pure about them, a glow you couldn't find in the old-timers, the ones who'd seen it all.

"The perp stripped his victims. He chose very loose, damp soil near the water to speed up the decomposition. Despite the fact that the spot is isolated and unsuited for building, he was afraid they'd be discovered, which is why he dug so deep. So with all those precautions, he certainly wouldn't have left identifiable bodies. These days, specialists can lift fingerprints even from wizened corpses. The killer might have known this, so he went at it with a vengeance. Without teeth or hands, these bodies will remain anonymous."

"Not entirely—we'll still get their DNA."

"DNA, yeah . . . You can trust that if you like."

They got into the car. Sharko turned the ignition and pulled out.

"Who should I talk to about my hotel room? I know I sound like a broken record, but I want a large one, with a real bathtub."

6

Ludovic Sénéchal lived behind the Marcq-en-Baroeul racetrack, in a calm town right next to Lille. Discreet neighborhood, "contemporary"-style single-family brick house, lawn small enough so you wouldn't spend your entire Saturday mowing the grass. Lucie raised her eyes toward the upstairs window, a wry smile on her face. It was in that charming little room that they'd made love the first time. A kind of online dating package: you meet for fake, then for real, you sleep together, and you see how it goes.

She'd seen. Ludovic was a good man in every respect—serious, attentive, with a heap of other sterling qualities—but he was definitely lacking in the thrills department. Quiet little life spent watching movies, putting in his time at the Social Security office, then watching more movies. Not to mention a real tendency to sink into moods. She had a hard time imagining him as the future father of her twins, the one who'd cheer them on at dance competitions or take them bike riding.

Lucie slid the key into the slot, but saw that the door hadn't been locked. It was easy to guess why: in his panic, Ludovic had left everything as it was. She entered the house, bolting the door behind her. It was large and handsome, modern, with all the room she and her girls lacked. Someday, perhaps . . .

She remembered where to find the cellar. Their private movie screenings, with beer and freshly made popcorn, seemed somehow memorable, timeless. Walking down the hallway, she came across broken or toppled objects. She could easily imagine Ludovic feeling his way upstairs, completely in the dark, knocking everything over before he managed to get her on the phone.

Lucie went down the flight of stairs that led to the mini-cinema.

Nothing had changed since last year. Red carpeting on the walls, the odor of old rugs, seventies ambience . . . It had its charm. In front of her, the pearlescent screen quivered under the white light from the projector. She opened the door to the minuscule projection room, which was hot as an oven, owing to the powerful xenon lamp. A loud hum filled the space, the take-up reel spun uselessly, the tail of the film clacked in the air at each rotation. Without thinking, Lucie pressed the fat red button of the power unit, a mastodon weighing 130 pounds. The rumbling finally stopped.

She flipped a switch and a neon light flickered. In the small room, empty film cans, tape recorders, and posters were stacked haphazardly. It was Ludovic to a T: an organized mess. She tried to remember how you went about loading a film: switch the feed and take-up reels by slipping them onto the projector arms, screw on the knobs to keep them in place, press MOTOR, align the film sprockets with the rollers . . . With all those buttons in front of her, the operation was more complicated than it appeared, but with a certain amount of luck Lucie managed to get the machine working. Through the magic of light and optics, the succession of still images would be transformed into fluid movement. The cinema was born.

Lucie switched off the neon light, closed the door of the elevated booth, and descended the three steps that led to the screening room. She remained standing against the back wall, her arms folded. This small, empty room, with its twelve green leatherette seats, had something profoundly depressing about it, just like its owner. Staring at the screen, Lucie couldn't help feeling a vague apprehension. Ludovic had talked about a *weird* film, and now he was blind . . . What if there was something dangerous about these images, like . . . like a light so sharp it could ruin your vision? Lucie shook her head—that was idiotic. Ludovic had a brain tumor, end of story.

The beam of light titillated the darkness and briefly lit up the white rectangle. Then an image of uniform black spread over it, followed, five or six seconds later, by a white circle that settled into the upper right-hand corner. Suddenly, music rattled the walls—a jolly tune, the kind you used to hear in old street carnivals, among the wooden merry-go-rounds. Lucie smiled at the awkward splutters that were plainly audible; the sound track must have come from an old 45, or even a 78.

No title or credits. A woman's face appeared in close-up in an oval that occupied the center of the screen. All around this oval, the image remained dark, a kind of grayish, almost black fog, as if the cameraman had put a mask over the lens. It made you feel like a voyeur peeping through a keyhole.

The actress struck Lucie as beautiful, hypnotic, with large, enigmatic eyes that gazed directly at the lens. She was about twenty, with dark lipstick, jet hair brushed back, a kiss curl on her forehead. One could glimpse the top of her checked suit and pure, immaculate neck. Lucie was reminded of those family photos, the kind you find inside austere pendants hidden in grandparents' jewelry boxes. The actress didn't smile and seemed a bit distant, the kind of femme fatale Hitchcock would have loved on his set. Her lips moved, briefly: she was saying something, but Lucie couldn't make out what. Two fingers—a man's fingers—entered the frame from the top and spread the lids of her left eye. Abruptly, jutting from the left, the blade of a scalpel slit the eye in two, rightward, in the throb of circus music and the clash of cymbals.

Lucie jerked her face away, teeth clenched. Too late: the image had struck her like a blow and it filled her with rage. She had nothing against B horror movies—she often rented them, especially on Saturday evenings—but she despised this method of suddenly splashing something horrific over the screen without any warning. It was cowardly and low.

Suddenly, the fanfare stopped.

Not a sound, other than the harrowing thrum of the projector.

Shaken, Lucie looked back at the screen. One more scene like that and she'd turn the whole thing off. After her time in the ER, she'd had quite enough of blood.

The tension had ratcheted up a notch. Lucie no longer felt quite so assured.

The projector continued to send out its cone of light. The next image was the soles of shoes. By a translatory movement, they receded into the distance. The sky shone reassuringly. A well-dressed little girl was on a swing, smiling broadly. It was shot in black and white, silent, even though the girl could be seen talking at various points. She had long, fair hair, blond no doubt, and she radiated liveliness. Her eyes caught the light; the shade patterns from the trees played over her skin. The lighting, the camera angles, and the expressions drawn from her childish face suggested that this was the work of a pro. Most of the time, tracking shots—he must have swiveled around with a handheld camera on his shoulder—stayed on the girl's eye: clear, pure, and full of life, it palpitated, the pupil contracting and widening like a diaphragm. The white circle did not budge from its position in the upper right, and Lucie found it hard to ignore. It wasn't that it attracted her—more like it irritated her. She couldn't say why, but she felt a prickling in her stomach. The scene with the slit eye had definitely affected her.

Next came some very quick cuts focused on the girl. A jumble of disconnected sequences, as if in a dream, which could be situated in neither time nor space. Certain images skipped, probably because of the quality of the film. It flitted from the slit eye to the swing set, from the swing to the little girl's hand playing with ants. Close-up of her childish mouth eating, of her eyelids opening and closing. Another, in which she petted two kittens in the grass for two or three minutes. She kissed them and held them tight against her, while fog—Lucie couldn't help wondering about the technique used here—closed in around her. When the girl raised her eyes to the camera, she wasn't acting. She was smiling in complicity, speaking to someone she knew. Once she came toward the camera and began spinning around and around. The image spun as well, accompanying the dance and, amid the fog, provoking a sensation of vertigo.

Next sequence. Something had changed in the little girl's eyes. A kind of permanent sadness. The image was very dark. All around her swirled the same drenching fog. The camera moved forward, then back, as if taunting her; the girl pushed it away, both hands in front of her, as if she were chasing away an insect. Lucie felt out of place as she viewed the film. She felt like an intruder, a voyeur secretly watching a scene that might be taking place between father and daughter.

Just as suddenly it tipped into another sequence. Lucie's eyes widened, taking in the scene: a stretch of grass surrounded by fences, the sky black, stormy, chaotic, and not quite natural—a special effect? At the far end of the pasture, the same girl waited, arms hanging along her body. In her right hand she held a butcher's knife, so out of proportion to her small, innocent fingers.

Zoom in on her eyes. They stared at the void, pupils visibly dilated. Something had shattered that child; Lucie could feel it. The camera, placed behind the fences, spun rapidly to the right to focus on a furious bull. The animal, monstrously powerful, foamed at the mouth, pawed at the ground, and butted against the barriers. Its horns pointed forward like sabers.

Lucie's hand flew to her mouth. They weren't really going to . . .

She leaned against the back of a seat, head bent toward the screen. Her nails dug into the leatherette.

Abruptly an unidentified arm entered the field of vision and lifted a latch. The person doing this had taken care to remain offscreen. The pen was opened. The overexcited beast charged straight ahead. Its body expressed power of the purest, most violent kind. How much did it weigh— a ton? It stopped in the middle of the field, pivoted around, and then seemed to focus its attention on the little girl, who remained motionless.

Lucie considered running back into the projection booth and shutting off the film. Playtime was over; it was no longer about swings, smiles, or complicity—this was sinking into the inconceivable. Lucie, a finger on her mouth, could not turn her gaze from that satanic screen. The film was sucking her in. In the sky, the black clouds swelled, grew darker, as if preparing for a tragic ending. Lucie suddenly had the sense of a staged battle: Good versus Evil. An outsized, all-powerful, unassailable Evil. David against Goliath.

The bull charged.

The silence of the sound track and the absence of music added to the feeling of suffocation. One could imagine, without hearing it, the sound each hoof made as it fell, the snorting from the animal's greasy snout. The camera now contained both subjects in its field: the bull on the left, the little girl on the right. The distance between the monster and the stationary child was growing shorter. Thirty yards, twenty . . . How could the girl not be moving? Why wasn't she running, screaming for her life? Lucie thought briefly of the kid's dilated pupils: Drugs? Hypnosis?

She was going to let herself be gored.

Ten yards. Nine, eight . . .

Five yards.

Suddenly, the bull came to a halt, its muscles twitching, while clumps of earth flew from the ground. It froze completely, barely one yard away from its target. Lucie thought it must have been a freeze-frame; she couldn't breathe. Inevitably it would start up again, and the tragedy would occur. But nothing moved. And yet, the monster continued to pant, frothing at the mouth. One could read in its enraged eyes the desire to continue, to kill, but its hulk refused to obey.

"Paralyzed" would be the best word to describe it.

The girl stared at it without blinking. She took a step forward and slid beneath the head of this beast forty or fifty times her weight. Without betraying the slightest emotion, she raised her knife and slit its throat with a clean swipe. A black cascade began to flow and, as if vanquished by a demented matador, the beast fell over onto one side, raising a cloud of dust.

Suddenly, a black screen, as at the start. Slowly the white circle at the upper right faded out.

And then flickers in the room, like applause of light. The film was taking a bow.

Lucie remained frozen in place. She felt shaken to the core, and very cold. She nervously rubbed her forehead. Had she really seen an enraged bull stop short in front of a little girl and let its throat be slashed without reacting, all of it in one continuous shot with no visible edits?

With a shudder, she returned to the booth and sharply flipped the switch. The rumbling ceased, the neon flickered on again. Lucie felt infinite relief. What twisted mind could have filmed such deliria? She could still see that dingy fog spreading over the screen, those close-ups of the eyes, the opening and closing scenes of such unspeakable violence. There was something in this short that classic horror films couldn't provide: realism. The girl, seven or eight at most, didn't appear to be acting. Or if she was, she did it exceptionally well.

Lucie was about to head back upstairs when she heard a noise above her head. The crunch of a shoe on glass. She held her breath. Had the tension of the film caused her to imagine things? She moved forward cautiously, step-by-step, finally reaching the entrance foyer.

The door was open.

Lucie rushed forward, certain she'd locked it when she'd come in.

No one outside.

Dumbfounded, she went back in the house and looked around. At first glance, nothing had been touched. She moved on to the main hallway and checked the other rooms. Bathroom, kitchen, and . . . study.

The study—where Ludovic kept his many films.

Here again, the door was open. Lucie ventured into the stacks of reels. Dozens of canisters lay scattered about the floor. Celluloid spilled out in all directions. The cop noticed that only the canisters without labels—the ones that indicated neither title, director, nor year of production—had been disturbed.

Someone had been in here looking for something specific.

An anonymous film.

Ludovic had told her he'd acquired some reels the day before from a collector, including the one she'd just been watching. She hesitated, studied the room. Calling in a team to make a report seemed pointless. There was no break-in or vandalism, no theft. She nonetheless went back down to the cellar and packed up the strange film, so she could bring it to the restorer whose card Ludovic had given her. She couldn't recall ever having seen such a psychologically taxing piece of work. She—who'd been used to autopsies and crime scenes for years—felt drained.

Back outside she thought to herself that, all in all, that glare of sunlight in her face wasn't such a bad thing.

7

"What did you do before going to Violent Crimes, Chief Inspector Sharko?"

"To keep it simple, let's say I put in a lot of time in CI."

"Very well . . ."

Georges Péresse, chief of the Criminal Investigations unit in Rouen, which had caught the case, was a hard-faced man. In the car, Lucas Poirier had described him as a rigid, tenacious fellow who hated any sort of intrusion on his turf. Floating in his gray suit, Péresse measured barely five foot three but could boom out a voice like Barry White. It felt like the air was vibrating when he blew his stack.

"We're not really accustomed to working with . . . behavioral analysts. I hope you'll be able to manage by yourself—we're understaffed as it is and my men are very busy."

Sharko sat opposite, hands on his knees. The heat was stifling.

"Don't worry, I'll be as quiet as an autopsy report. In two or three days I'll probably scram with a stack of Xeroxes under my arm. The main thing is for me to have access to the info"—he pressed his finger against the gleaming desk—"all the info, I mean, and for my hotel room to have a bathtub, because I like to take a cold bath when the temperature gets like this."

Chief Inspector Péresse let out a wild burst of laughter. He stood and turned up the fan, placed just in front of President Sarkozy's portrait.

"So you want all the info, do you? Well, canvas of the area—*nada* for the moment. Direct or indirect witnesses—*nada*. Apart from the rotting corpses, we didn't pick up a single clue at the scene, which is understandable given they've been buried for several months and with the storms we've had. The whole medical corps—the ME's office, forensic anthropologist, entomologist—are squabbling among themselves to figure out what belongs to who. It's worse than a jigsaw puzzle. They'll definitely be at it all night again. Our only certainty is that they're all human adults. Unfortunately, that's about all you're likely to leave with, Inspector. In other words, not much."

Sharko closed his eyes each time the breeze from the fan lapped at his cheeks.

"What does the missing persons file say?"

"Too early to tell. I'm waiting for the medical examiner's report for the ages and physical characteristics. One thing's for sure, we haven't had any specific reports of a group disappearance, either here or anywhere else in the country."

"And what about outside the country? What does Interpol say?"

"First things first. The investigation has only just got under way. First we've got to figure out exactly what we're dealing with here. I've got nothing against intel from Interpol, but first we have to know what information we're asking them for, don't you think?"

He crossed his arms and stared out through the smoked-glass window. The central police station, a glass and steel blockhouse, clashed with the rest of the city's left bank. Péresse turned back to his colleague from Paris.

"And what are *your* early deductions?"

Normally, working from thick dossiers, Sharko started with four basic elements to work up a profile: the crime scene itself, the MO, the killer's psychological state during the crime, and his psychological state overall. For the moment, he didn't have a precise starting point. The only plausible hypothesis was that the victims had not been killed on site—slicing open a skull wasn't the kind of operation you performed on the street corner.

"Frankly, I don't have much. It might be worth checking into the delinquents and violent criminals in the area. Recent parolees, for instance. Given the number of bodies, we can't exclude revenge killings. In most cases, criminals attack people they know. We're probably looking for somebody with a panel truck or SUV. You can't cart around five stiffs in a buggy. Maybe check with the local car rentals?"

"We'll take care of it."

Sharko snatched up his jacket from the chair and slung it over his shoulder.

"I'll look in on the ME tomorrow, once all the autopsies are done. Could you make sure they know to expect me?"

A vague sigh.

"As you wish. Will there be anything else?"

Sharko held out a solid hand.

"See you tomorrow, Inspector. Here's hoping the corpses are feeling talkative. I used to be in your shoes once upon a time. I know it's no cakewalk."

Half an hour later, Sharko was quietly dining at a sidewalk table outside a restaurant facing the magnificent Rouen cathedral. A trace memory from his school days told him that the crypt housed the ticker of Richard the Lionhearted. Sharko smiled. He still had excellent recall, which he regularly exercised with crossword puzzles. One of his few qualities that hadn't gone to hell. There, at that moment, he was content, almost happy. Getting out of the capital had done him a world of good. Here life seemed different, more leisurely and restful. To his great satisfaction, he'd discovered his room had a tub, on the fifth floor of a certain Hotel Mercure, behind the cathedral.

He ate pasta until he'd had his fill, followed it with a disgusting Camembert sorbet—clearly meant for tourists—and doused himself with water. This heat, even at night, was definitely going to wind up kicking his ass.

He went back to the hotel. After an ice-cold bath, he slipped into some undershorts, shined his shoes, and pulled a wrapped package from his duffel bag, along with an old battery-operated tape recorder. He delicately removed the bubble wrap to reveal an O-gauge Ova Hornby locomotive, with its black car for wood and charcoal. One of the front headlights had broken off, but the engine beat all speed records on the wide circuit set up in his apartment.

The chief inspector placed it on his nightstand, swallowed a Zyprexa with a glass of water, and lay down on top of the sheets, hands folded behind his neck. The hotel, the dampness of an anonymous room . . . all of that was so far away now, since he'd begun tracking down his suspects from the safety of his leather desk chair.

Today, he recognized his old self in the contact with the terrain, the blood, the guts. He still didn't know how it would affect him. He might well get off on it, but the past also threatened to rear its head big-time. Better to keep some distance. Remain procedural, do his job, and stay behind a pane of glass. Otherwise, Eugenie would make him pay. The little girl in his head hated it when he derailed.

When all the lights were out, he rolled onto his side and turned on the tape recorder. Tonight, Eugenie would certainly not come to visit. Those radiations in his brain would keep her asleep for a bit.

The rasp of miniature trains, cruising full steam ahead on their tracks, rumbled from the speaker. Sharko fell asleep with a smile on his lips, seeing the faces of his wife and daughter, whom he'd lost five years earlier in horrible circumstances.

He had come to Rouen to investigate an abominable crime, but no matter. Alone in the middle of his bed, with his trains and a bathtub nearby, he felt just fine.

8

After her misadventure at Ludovic Sénéchal's, Lucie had left that vile film with the restorer, Claude Poignet. Once he had absorbed the news of Ludovic's blindness, the septuagenarian specialist in film autopsies had taken the reel away with him, promising to look at it first thing.

For now, Lucie sat with her daughter. Heaving a long sigh, she brought the fork one last time to Juliette's mouth. The doctors had said to keep pushing; the girl needed to eat. Easier said than done.

"Come on, just take one bite, just for me."

The child shook her head and started to cry. Her complexion was sallow, her cheeks sunken. Lucie pushed away the tray holding the awful dish of pureed peas and held her daughter tight. She felt the little hands slip off her back, their strength gone. It was hard seeing such an energetic and happy kid disappear inside pajamas that were now too big for her, or move around with an IV in her arm.

"Never mind, sweetheart. It's okay."

"Mom, I want to see Clara." Her voice was a whisper.

For the past two days, Lucie had been gauging the breadth of her mistake. She hesitated to call back Juliette's sister from her first summer camp. Clara had so been looking forward to this vacation with her little chums.

"Soon, Juliette. Soon. She's going to send you a beautiful postcard. She promised."

Lucie verified that no staff was around and took some chocolate-covered cookies from her pocket.

"Want one of these?"

Juliette nodded limply. "Can I?"

"Yes, of course. But just don't tell anybody, okay? Cross your heart."

Juliette weakly crossed her chest and smiled, then finally swallowed some of the cookie. Her throat got stiff, making her veins and tendons stand out. Lucie made sure to get rid of the wrapper, happy that her daughter finally had something in her stomach.

Juliette climbed back into bed, exhausted by her illness. When the nurse came to take her vitals, she noted with a frown, "Two spoonsful of puree, half a biscuit, and no ham." In other words, they weren't about to take out her IV yet. Which meant bye-bye to even the hope of getting out of there soon.

Worn out, Lucie remained with her daughter until the little girl fell asleep; her eyes stared blankly at the TV screen.

The news talked of that sordid affair in Upper Normandy near a pipeline. A bunch of corpses, skulls sawed open . . . A profiler on the case, whose face she saw onscreen at that instant. A solid-looking guy, built like a cop and definitely not like a shrink. Where did he come from, which school? Had he already had experience with serial killers? In a way, Lucie envied him. This business of bodies with sawed-off skulls was the kind of case that would have got her revved up like nothing else. The thrill of discovery, tracking down a sick and dangerous criminal. But she was on vacation, for God's sake, and it was the middle of summer. A time when people were supposed to be enjoying themselves, letting go, giving their brains a rest. This evening, alone, with her kid in some lost corner of the hospital, she felt light-years away from people like that.

Lucie placed a new stuffed toy near Juliette—a blue elephant, brought by her mother—told the nurse she was leaving, then headed over to Salengro Hospital, a hundred yards from the pediatric wing. Dr. Tournelle had news about Ludovic Sénéchal.

The physician met her in a large room, in which a scanner and cutting-edge equipment were visible behind wide panes of glass. Facing Lucie on a luminescent wall was a spread of X-rays. On a table lay articles and anatomical diagrams of the eye, nervous system, and brain. The doctor was edgily rubbing his chin. Since she'd seen him that morning, his hair had shriveled on his skull and the bags under his eyes had swollen. He wasn't as seductive as before. Just some overworked guy like anyone else.

"We spent the day running tests. Ludovic Sénéchal was transferred to the psych ward in Freyrat about an hour ago."

Lucie was floored.

"Psych ward? What for?"

Tournelle removed his glasses and massaged his temples.

"Let me try to explain in layman's terms. Ludovic is not blind, in the physiological sense. As I told you this morning, our evaluation of his pupillary reflexes and ocular structures revealed no significant abnormalities. On the other hand, the patient presents with an unfocused gaze and absence of visual contact."

"You mentioned psychiatry. So it wasn't a tumor?"

The doctor turned toward the two dozen X-rays depicting Ludovic's brain and pulled one down.

"No. Look—it's all clear. Not the slightest anomaly."

He might just as well have been showing her the brain of a cow. Still, Lucie felt reassured: Ludovic wasn't going to die.

"I'll take your word for it."

"We also looked for lesions around the visual cortex, which might have explained a cortical blindness, but we didn't find anything there either."

"Cortical blindness?"

The doctor gave her a tired smile.

"We tend to believe that sight is in the eye, but that's just a tool, a kind of light well. Read this, you'll understand."

Lucie took the printed card that he handed her:

This txet will demonsrtate that yuor brian dose not trnaslate exaclty waht yuor eye sees. Intsaed, infulecned by waht it has laerend, it reocignzes wrods golbally, wihtuot paynig muhc attnetoin ot teh ordre of teh lettres.

"Impressive."

"Isn't it? The retina just lends its body, so to speak, to materialize a physical image, like a movie screen. It's just a passive object, a lens. The brain is what interprets life experience, the cultural context, according to its knowledge. It's the brain that makes the image what it is: a meaningful object."

He put the X-ray back in its place.

"The remarkable thing about this patient is that he can avoid certain obstacles without seeing them. A box we put in his path, for instance. A chair, a dresser. We filmed it—you can watch the recordings. It's really amazing."

"No, thanks. That's okay. So he sees without seeing. That's incomprehensible."

"Incomprehensible from a medical standpoint. But if we physicians can't find anything, it means the origin is psychological."

"Are you talking about something like . . . depression, or schizophrenia? Something along those lines, that's keeping him from seeing?"

"You'd be closer to the mark talking about neurosis, anxiety, phobia, or hysteria. Personally, we're leaning toward hysterical blindness. That's a sensory disturbance that falls under the conversion hysterias: imaginary paralysis, deafness, numbness of the limbs . . . Perhaps the best-known example is the phantom limb."

He shut off the lights and asked Lucie to follow him down the corridors of the neurology ward. The wan lighting gave the place an antiseptic, futuristic look.

"A psychiatrist could tell you more about this than I can, but hysteria is a defense mechanism meant to protect the psyche from a sudden shock. It can be triggered by an event that has something to do with the patient's childhood. Some element that was profoundly traumatizing."

"Could certain images cause this?"

"I know what you're talking about. That film that supposedly drove him blind . . . Mr. Sénéchal has not stopped talking about it. Yes, in theory that's possible, and given the circumstances I think the cause comes from there. His blindness occurred in the middle of the viewing. The only hiccup is that the patient claims he wasn't shocked by the images onscreen. He's used to watching movies, and the sliced eye he told me about at the beginning apparently didn't make him blink. As for the rest, nothing traumatic, according to him. He wasn't even able to see the end of the movie—he was already blind."

"So he didn't see the scene with the bull?"

"Bull? No, he didn't mention it. On the other hand, he talked a lot about a feeling of unease, increasing anxiety as the film went on. As if something had grabbed him by the throat and squeezed it until he'd lost his sight."

Lucie had felt exactly the same thing, the sensation of suffocating. She rubbed her arms. And yet, between the slicing of the eye and the beast getting its throat slit, which Ludovic hadn't seen, there wasn't anything really all that shocking. Just a little girl petting kittens and eating at a table.

"Is it possible that hidden images might have caused it?"

The doctor paused a moment to think.

"You mean subliminal? It's something to consider."

"And . . . what's going to happen to Ludovic? Is he . . . ?"

The doctor stopped walking. They had come to his office.

"He should regain his sight, little by little. The main thing is to try to understand the origin of his trauma and bring it out in the open. My colleagues in Psych are very good at that, especially using hypnosis. I can give you the contact info for the doctor who's taken over Mr. Sénéchal's case, if you like. Try to avoid going to see him before tomorrow afternoon. In the meantime, you can try to make some headway with that film."

Lucie jotted down the information and returned to her daughter's room, her interest piqued by this bizarre story. The traumatic shock, someone rifling through Ludovic's place, the feeling of malaise during the screening . . . What was hidden in that film? Who was trying to get hold of it, and why?

Careful not to make noise, she brushed her teeth in the ridiculous bathroom and put on her pajamas. She stood motionless, staring at herself in the mirror. No, not at herself: at her reflection, this yield of light projected onto objects. Dr. Tournelle was right: the eye discerned only a mass of colors and shapes, but the brain saw a woman of thirty-seven, features drawn from lack of sleep, starved for love and sex. It interpreted each luminous impulse, and tried to relate them all to life experiences.

Lucie thought of the various close-ups of the girl on the swing, of her face, during the film's short duration. The blinking eye, the movements of the iris. That feeling of incursion, voyeurism, behind an oval-shaped mask: the eye that takes in light and silently observes . . . And, especially, of that eyeball sliced in half, the first sequence of the film. She remembered turning away, proof that her brain had reacted violently, that there had indeed been interpretation.

At that point, her vision of the film changed. The director might have included that first brutal scene not as a pure display of horror, but to make a statement: "Concentrate, look carefully at what I'm about to show you." Or else: "Do as I've done with my scalpel—open your eye . . ."

Open your eye . . .

In the middle of the night, her cell phone vibrated at the foot of her chair. Lucie did not awake this time; she was much too exhausted.

The text message read: "Claude Poignet here. Come by late tomorrow morning. Some peculiar things about your film, to say the least."

9

The two Rouen medical examiners and the forensic anthropologist had spent all day and all night on the case. So their examinations were almost complete when Sharko arrived at the ME's office the next morning, full of questions. Later, back in Nanterre, he'd probably have to immerse himself in the hundreds of pages of technical data that spewed out of these buildings, so he might as well be as informed as possible and get as many explanations as he could.

Later . . . He was in no particular hurry to get home, even if it was no great pleasure to wander through this death-haunted complex. Far too many violent incidents and unsolved crimes crowded into his memory. A child found dead at the bottom of the Seine. Prostitutes with their throats cut in seedy hotel rooms. Women and men beaten, lacerated, hacked to pieces, strangled . . . Dramas that had swept away his life and forced him to run on Zyprexa tablets.

And yet here he was.

Before going to see the medical examiner, he let himself be waylaid by the bone and tooth specialist, Dr. Pierre Plaisant. The physician was about to head off for a lecture on Lowenthal's caries, which were typical of heroin addicts. The two men exchanged a few banalities before getting down to business.

"The bones had a lot to say for themselves. How should we do this—simple or complicated?"

Plaisant was tall and thin, around thirty. A brilliant brain beneath a high forehead, smooth as a coated pill. Behind him lay radiographs of the bodies, bone joints gnawed at by X-rays.

"Either way. Tell me enough to keep me from having to drag around the fifty pages of tech data that Péresse is going to shove at me."

The doctor led Sharko to some graduated worktables: stainless steel counters, with sliding rules running crosswise and lengthwise for measuring bones. The four partially reconstituted skeletons each rested on one of them. The room, which looked more like a kitchen than a lab, smelled of dried earth and detergent. The remains had been treated in a bain-marie to remove any soft tissue.

"The fifth cadaver, the best preserved of the lot, is waiting for you in the autopsy room before going into the fridge."

He picked up a pencil and slid it into the anterior nasal spine of the skeleton on the left, the smallest one.

"The point of the pencil touches the chin. The zygomatics are in front, the face is flat and rounded. No doubt about it, we've got an Asiatic. The other four are Caucasian."

First bit of good news, the presence of an Asian corpse would help them search through the computer database. Plaisant left the pencil in the stiff's nose, picked up a sliced skull, set it down on its jaws, and pushed it backward. It began to rock.

"You always get this rocking motion with men. Women's skulls don't move. Brains are too small—" He smiled. "I'm just kidding . . ." Sharko's face remained neutral; he was in no mood for jokes. His sleep had been disturbed by traffic noises and the buzzing of a fly he couldn't swat. The doctor thought better of his attempt at humor and fell serious again.

"I mainly verified with pelvic bones, which are more reliable. In every ethnicity, the bone that starts at the top of the pubis is taller in women. All our subjects are male."

"How old?"

"I was getting to that. Since they didn't have any teeth, I based my findings on the joining of the cranial sutures, arthritic degeneration in the vertebras, and especially the sternal border at the fourth rib. It—"

Sharko suddenly motioned toward the coffeepot.

"Could you pour me some? I didn't have breakfast this morning, and the odor in this place is making me nauseous."

His momentum interrupted, Plaisant paused in surprise for a few seconds before walking to the far corner of the lab. He spoke with his back turned.

"We've been lucky with our subjects here. The younger they are, the narrower the margin of estimation. After they hit thirty, it gets trickier. To determine ages, we use the pubic symphysis. In a young adult, this part is very rough, with ridges and deep grooves. Then the—"

"How old?"

The coffee was dripping, the coffeemaker gurgling. Plaisant came back toward his skeletons.

"Our men were all between twenty-two and twenty-six at the time of death. As for their height and other anthropometric details, you'll see all that in the report."

Chief Inspector Sharko leaned against the wall. All young, all male. That might have been an important criterion, a crucial element for the killer. Was he of their generation? Did he mix with them? In what context? University, sports club? The cop pointed to a half skull that showed a hole near the occiput surrounded by tiny cracks.

"Killed by gunshot?"

The forensic anthropologist picked up a knitting needle.

"Killed or wounded, though for these four it's most likely killed. The fifth one was probably just wounded in the shoulder—Dr. Busnel will tell you about that."

With his needle, he pointed to the Asian's spine.

"This one was shot in the back. His fourth vertebra is shattered from behind. These two were most likely shot and killed from the front. Some ribs are shattered, probably because the bullet ricocheted before finding a vital organ. My colleague in radiography is going to scan them to make a 3-D reconstruction and try to reproduce the entrance and exit points of the projectiles. But it won't be easy, given their condition. As for the last one . . . shot right in the head. The bullet didn't even come out the front."

He poured coffee into two cups and held one out to Sharko, who stared at the bodies without moving. There was no consistency in the way the men had been eliminated. From behind, from the front, in the head. No ritual: the killings looked scattered, random, whereas the concealment and dehumanization of the bodies displayed great mastery. What could this have been about? An execution? Revenge? Some kind of run-in?

Sharko took a sip of his java.

"I don't suppose you found any bullets?"

"No. Neither in the organisms nor at the scene. They were all recuperated—sometimes rather brutally. You can tell from the way the ribs were yanked apart on one of the skeletons."

Sharko had more or less expected the answer. The killer had given every indication of remarkable follow-through, covering all his tracks. No chance of going through ballistics and following the trail back to the murder weapon.

"Any projectile fragments at all?"

Uncoated bullets always left fragments, traces like comets' tails or snowstorms.

"Not a thing. Definitely jacketed bullets."

That in itself wasn't really news to Sharko. Most classic munitions were solid alloys, not hollow lead like for certain hunting rifles. The inspector ran a hand over his hair. He wanted something else, a way of following a serious, physical path. Then he remembered that he was there just as an observer. To get a sense of the killer's psychology and motivations, nothing more. He wouldn't give in to the demons of fieldwork.

"When were they killed?"

"Now that becomes more complicated. Open ground always makes for serious problems with dating. It depends on dampness, depth, pH, and soil composition. The ground was particularly acidic in that spot. Given the condition of these four, I'd say between six months and a year. Impossible to be more precise than that."

Might as well have said prehistory.

"All killed at the same time?"

"I believe so. The entomologist found just a few domestic fly pupae on each of them, from the first swarm. Which means the bodies were buried a day or two after death. No question they were transported to that place."

The intact portion of Sharko's brain was already processing the data. He'd have to attack the missing persons file from another angle, concentrating on date rather than geography. The anthropologist continued his explanation:

"I also believe two different individuals worked on the bodies postmortem. One who sliced off the skulls and another who took care of hands and teeth."

He handed the inspector a loupe.

"The skulls were sawed with surgical precision. On the face of it, it looks like a Stryker, or something like it, the kind they use in forensics or surgery. The work is professional. You can see for yourself with the loupe—it shows the characteristic striations."

Sharko took the magnifying device and set it on the table without using it.

"Professional. You mean someone in the field?"

"Someone who's used to sawing. The starting point, for instance, meets the end point exactly, and I can guarantee you that's no easy trick on a circular structure. As to profession, it could range from medical examiner to lumberjack."

"Still, I have a hard time imagining a lumberjack going at his oak trees with a surgical saw. And what about the other potential perp?"

"The teeth were ripped out savagely—there are still bits of root in the recesses. We used tweezers to get them. And for the hands, it looks more like a hatchet. If it had been the same person, he would have been more careful. And he would surely have used his saw."

Plaisant glanced at his watch and set his cup down next to the coffeemaker, which he switched off.

"Sorry, I've got to run. You'll have everything in—"

"Were the brains removed?"

"Yes. Otherwise we would have found traces of spinal fluid or dura, which is made of very dense collagen fibers that could have withstood a year underground. They also stole the eyes."

"The eyes?"

"It's all in the written report. The soil found in the ocular cavities showed no presence of liquid, such as vitreous fluids. For the rest, go see Dr. Busnel on the basement level. I've been up all night and I'd like to at least take a shower before my lecture, if you don't mind."

The two men parted company in the hallway. Sharko took the stairs, mulling over these revelations. A vague preliminary sketch was taking shape in his head, which led to two divergent paths. On the one hand, the shooting deaths and concealment suggested an execution: the men try to run away or attack; someone shoots them down and makes them disappear very "professionally." Deep burial, just in itself, is an excellent method, along with fire and acid. On the other hand, there was that business of brains and eyes being removed, which tended to suggest a ritualized, highly controlled undertaking, requiring a cool head and a large dose of sadism. The fact of five cadavers immediately pointed toward a serial killing or mass murder . . . but with two killers? Something out of the ordinary, in any case. Sharko was keenly aware that he couldn't afford to leave any stone unturned when it came to the killer's, or killers', deep motivations. There existed on this planet individuals who were crazy enough to murder human beings and then devour the contents of their skulls with a spoon.

The inspector arrived at the morgue. At the back, a door with a peephole opened onto a scialytic lamp. In a forensic institute, it was never hard to find the autopsy room: you just had to follow the stench, which was everywhere and nowhere. When Sharko arrived, Dr. Busnel was rinsing the tiled floor with a shower hose. The Paris cop remained at the threshold, waiting until the other finally noticed him and came forward.

"Chief Inspector Sharko, from Paris?"

Sharko held out his hand. A solid exchange of handshakes.

"I see Inspector Péresse circulated the right information."

"You've come after everyone else, and I'll admit I'm not thrilled at having to repeat the same thing over again. I've been at this for two days, I'm exhausted, and there are still reports to—"

Sharko pointed to a fly on the green sheet covering the body.

"There was a fly in my hotel room as well. Yet it's refrigerated here. Nothing stops them. I can't stand insects, especially the flying ones."

Busnel noted his annoyance. He moved toward the table and pulled down the sheet.

"Right. Would you come closer, please, so we can get this done?"

The inspector looked at the water calmly draining into a trench. He moved forward slowly, as if walking on eggshells.

"I'm just being careful of my shoes. They're made of Cordoba leather and—"

"May we talk about the best-preserved body, if it's all right with you? I suppose my colleague in anthro already filled you in?"

"He did, yes."

Busnel was a strapping fellow, about six foot three. With his square jaw and flattened nose, he would have fit in easily on a rugby team. Sharko looked down at the stiff. What greeted his eyes was an indescribable entity, a magma of flesh, earth, bones, and ligaments. So dehumanized that it wasn't even shocking. In his case, too, they'd sawed off the top of the skull.

The medical examiner indicated the left shoulder.

"Here's where he was shot. The bullet exited through the back of the deltoid. A priori, this is not the cause of death. I say a priori because, given the degree of decomp, I have no way of defining precisely what did cause his death."

Busnel now showed the bony portion of the arms, wrists, and torso.

"These areas were skinned."

"With what instrument?"

The doctor walked to a table and lifted a closed beaker. Sharko squinted.

"Fingernails?"

"Yes. They were stuck in his flesh. Analysis will confirm, but I believe these were his own nails. Thumb, index, and middle finger of the right hand."

"So the poor bastard clawed at his own skin before dying."

"Yes. So fiercely and violently that it's unimaginable. The pain must have been horrendous."

More and more, the cop had the impression of swimming in murky waters. These discoveries were more complicated than he'd expected.

"And . . . what about the other bodies?"

"Hard to say, given their condition. I imagine they were also skinned over certain areas, like the shoulders, calves, and back. But not with nails. The marks are clean, regular, and particularly deep. Like the kind made with a knife or cutting tool. Like some moron trying to get rid of a tattoo."

He pointed again to the fingernails.

"You can force anyone to mutilate himself by shoving a gun against his head. The trick is to find out why."

"Can I have the photos?"

"They're attached to the file. It's not a pretty picture. Trust me."

"I've always trusted MEs."

The doctor nodded toward a shelf, on which lay a small transparent baggie.

"There's also this. A tiny piece of green plastic, found under the skin between the clavicle and the neck."

Sharko approached the shelf.

"Any idea what it's from?"

"It's cylindrical, hollow in the middle. It's certainly a fragment of the sheath from a subcutaneous catheter, like the kind they use in surgery."

"What for?"

"I'll check further with a surgeon. But if I remember right, there are a bunch of possibilities. It might be a chemotherapy stent. But they're also used as a central catheter, to avoid having to stick the patient several times over. The tox screen and cell analysis should tell us a lot. Like if he had a particular illness, such as cancer."

"Anything else?"

"Not as far as I'm concerned. The rest has to do with forensic technique, not very important for you. For the next step, I've taken psoas samples for the DNA of each subject. Since they shaved their heads, the pubic hairs went to the guys from tox. Their turn to work now. Let's hope this all gets us some IDs, or else this business threatens to drag on forever and get extremely complicated."

"Don't you think it already is?"

The medical examiner began removing his spattered scrubs. Sharko rubbed his lips, eyes to the floor.

"Even back when I practically lived in morgues, I never thought of buying shoes like yours, in rubber. You can't imagine how many pairs of slip-ons I messed up. The odor of death seemed to be . . . encrusted in the leather. Where can you get that kind of shoe?"

The specialist looked at his interlocutor, then went to the back of the room to put away his final tools, a wan smile on his face.

"Go to Leroy Merlin, gardening department, you should be able to find them. And now, good luck to you, Chief Inspector. I'm going to catch some sleep."

Once outside, Sharko sucked in a lungful of fresh air and looked at his watch. Almost eleven . . . Most of the reports wouldn't come through until late afternoon. He squinted up at the cloudless sky and sniffed his clothes. Barely two hours in there and they already smelled. The Paris cop decided to go back to the hotel and change before heading over to Criminal Investigations, to see what was what and look at the computer files. He'd take advantage to smush that miserable fly that had eluded him all night long.

And then, if there was no concrete progress by two days from now, he'd pack up and deal with it back in Nanterre. He was already missing his miniature trains something fierce.

10

The film restorer Claude Poignet lived on Rue Léon-Gambetta, a mish-mash of unrelated businesses and brightly colored shops. At one end, the street opened onto the Wazemmes covered market, with its intermingling of ethnicities, and at the other it plunged into the students' quarter, bordering Rue de Solférino and Boulevard Vauban. In his diminutive dwelling, crushed between a Chinese restaurant and a smoke shop, the septuagenarian didn't look like much. Bifocals in cordovan frames, ratty burgundy wool V-neck sweater, wrinkled checked shirt: was he a restorer of old films or an old film restorer?

"I'd say an old restorer of old films. I quit about twenty years ago, because of my eyes. Light doesn't get through as well as it used to. And cinema is first and foremost about light, you know? No light, no cinema."

Lucie penetrated farther into one of those old buildings from northern France, with living room tiles cemented in place, high walls, and visible pipes. A kettle was heating on the gas stove, giving off an acrid stink of burned coffee. When Claude filled the two cups, Lucie thought he was pouring liquid coal. Though normally she took hers without sugar, she plunked in two cubes before even tasting.

"So? Were you able to autopsy our short?"

Poignet smiled. His teeth were like the décor: one hundred percent rustic. Still, behind his wrinkles he still bore traces of a man who must have been a real charmer, like a young Redford.

"That's a real policeman's term, 'autopsy.' How did a beautiful young woman like you end up chasing down criminals?"

"Probably something to do with thrills. You get yours from looking at films, me from looking at streets. When you get down to it, we're both trying to fix something that doesn't work."

She forced herself to swallow her coffee—truly vile, even revolting, even with all the sugar in the world. An Angora cat came to purr between her legs, and she petted it gently.

"Have you known Ludovic a long time?"

"His father and I were in the army together. I gave Ludovic his first projector, more than twenty years ago—a 9.5 mm from Pathé that I was getting rid of for lack of space. Already back then, he used to hold screenings on the walls of his father's house. It's really a shame what's happened to him. His mother died of an illness before he was nine. He's a good boy, you know?"

"I know, and I'm here because I want to help him. Can you tell me about the film?"

"Come with me."

They walked up narrow, creaking stairs that clearly showed the age of the house. Portraits by the dozens hung on the walls. Not of movie stars, but of an unknown woman, whose delicately made-up face caught the light magnificently. Clearly the traces of an obsession, a love lost much too soon. Once upstairs, they walked down a dimly lit hall with worn floorboards.

"To the left is the lab where I develop. I still occasionally film with an old 16 mm, just for kicks. I'll exit this world with a roll of film in my hands, believe you me."

He opened the darkroom, revealing movie cameras, reels of film stock, and jugs of chemicals, and gently pushed back the door.

"We're going in back."

The last room opened onto a veritable laboratory devoted to the world of cinema. An editing table, viewer, loupes, the latest computer equipment, and a film scanner. There were also a number of more archaic instruments: scissors, glue, splicer, adhesive tape, rulers. Lucie had been right to use the word "autopsy." He must have sliced up celluloid here the way they dissected bodies. There were even the delicate white gloves, which the restorer put on.

"Soon, none of this will exist anymore. Fully digital HD cameras will do away with good old 35 mm. The magic of movies is being lost, I can tell you that. Is a film that doesn't skip still a film?"

The reel in question was mounted on a vertical rotating axis, on the left side of the viewing monitor. About three feet of film stretched from there into a central housing that served as both magnifier and screen, then exited toward a take-up reel. The only light in the room was from a neon tube.

"Let's begin at the beginning. Come closer, dear miss. Permit me to say that you're quite lovely."

He wasn't exactly tongue-tied, this one. Lucie smiled and went to stand beside him, facing the viewer.

"How should we do this?" he asked. "Simple or complicated?"

"Feel free to go into detail—I'm new at this, even though I love movies. When you were giving Ludovic the projector, I was watching my first horror film, alone in the house at eleven at night. It was *The Exorcist*. My best and worst memory."

"*The Exorcist* . . . One of the most profitable productions in cinema history. William Friedkin, who directed the first one, had subjected his actors to abominable conditions. Sudden gunshots next to their ears, freezing cold rooms to get more out of them. These days, actors have to have their creature comforts."

Lucie looked at him affectionately. He spoke with passion, just like her father when he talked lures and fishing rods. She'd been so small then.

"So, our film . . ."

"Right, our film. First of all, the format: 16 mm. It was shot entirely with a shoulder camera. Probably a Bolex. Light, portable, the mythic camera of the 1950s. Oddly enough, filmed at fifty frames a second, as the loss leader indicates, when the standard was twenty-four. But the Bolex allowed for this sort of whimsy, and so could satisfy all sorts of requirements."

"Is this the original copy?"

"Oh, no, no. The original, what comes out of the camera, is exposed on film as a negative, just like a photograph. Here you've got the positive print, what the eye sees. You always work with positives, which also act as a backup copy. This way, you can cut them up and manipulate them without worrying."

He advanced the film by cranking a handle. On the screen they saw, at the bottom of the strip, the word "S Å F E T Y."

"This word written on the leader, 'safety,' indicates that the support of the emulsion is acetate, so no danger. Until the fifties, it was still mainly nitrate, which is flammable. You surely remember the scene where Philippe Noiret catches fire inside the projection booth in *Cinema Paradiso*, because he opens a canister containing a reel of nitrate film. Mythic."

Lucie nodded, though she'd never seen that film. Italian classics weren't really her style, unlike American thrillers of the 1950s, which she devoured with a passion.

"The black dot just above the A shows that the film stock was manufactured in Canada. It's the international symbol used by Kodak."

Canada . . . Ludovic had said he'd unearthed the reel in the attic of some Belgian collector. And today, that same reel turned up in France. These anonymous films must have had the same life as collectible stamps or coins, traveling from country to country. Lucie filed away in her mind that she should perhaps question the collector's son, if it turned out to be worth it. She had to admit that this minor investigation, undertaken for personal reasons and off the books, was starting to excite her. Claude seemed to tap into her thoughts.

"These films travel and get lost. More than fifty percent of the productions from before World War II have disappeared. Can you imagine? And among them are some pure masterpieces that are now probably rotting in some attic. Films by Méliès, Chaplin, a ton of John Fords as well."

"Do we know when this one is from?"

Claude Poignet turned the handle. When the very first image appeared, completely black with the white circle, he showed her the bottom of the strip. Lucie noticed the presence of two symbols, ✚ and ◼, just above the sprocket holes, like numbers.

"Kodak used a code composed of geometric figures to date its filmstrips. They reused the same code every twenty years."

He handed Lucie a laminated sheet, a kind of specifications chart.

"Look at this grid. The cross and the square show that the positive was printed either in 1935, 1955, or 1975. Given the condition of the film and the actress's outfit in the opening scenes, this is definitely from the year 1955." He jabbed his index finger at the screen. "This number, here, which shows up every twenty frames, is what we call the key code. It identifies the manufacturer—Kodak in this case—the type of film, the serial number of the roll, and a four-digit suffix that individualizes each frame. In short, one could know where and when this roll of film came out of the lab. However, I can guarantee you from the outset that you'll get nowhere with these numbers—it goes back too far, and chances are, as things go, that the original lab no longer exists."

He stared at Lucie with a satisfied look. His glasses considerably enlarged his eyeballs. Lucie smiled back at him.

"Shall we deal with the content?"

The man's face darkened. He immediately lost his good humor.

"I should have said so at the start, but this film is the work of a genius and a psychopath. Both united in the same twisted mind."

Lucie felt excitement grow within her; she couldn't help it. In the middle of her vacation, she found herself in the rear corner of a workshop, tipping into the same sordid world that she encountered every day in the squad room.

"In other words?"

"There are images in here that are . . . disturbing, to say the least. You must have felt it deep within yourself, without really understanding why."

"Yes. A feeling of unease. Especially the scene with the eye at the beginning, which gives you chills right from the get-go."

"Pure special effects, of course. The sliced eye is from an animal, maybe a dog. But that scene mainly shows that the eye, in itself, is just a common sponge that soaks up images, a smooth surface that doesn't understand meanings. And that, in order to see better, you have to pierce that smooth surface. Go past it. Get inside the film . . ."

Claude Poignet turned the handle until he could show under the loupe the image of a completely naked woman. Well-endowed bust, provocative pose—it was the same actress from the beginning of the film, the one who had her eye slit. She was standing in a dark décor, with little contrast. On this still image, dozens of hands jutted out from behind to grope her curves and her sex. You couldn't see the actors, who must have been dressed all in black, like the onstage accomplices of a magician. The restorer then nudged the film forward one frame by moving the handle. They returned immediately to the little girl, sitting on her swing. Her face was now in the exact place of the woman's, to the centimeter.

"The twenty-fifth frame, as they say, though here it would be more like the fifty-first. The movie's crammed full of them. It dates from 1955, even though the subliminal process was officially used for the first time in 1957, by James Vicary, an American publicist. I have to admit, it's pretty impressive."

Lucie knew the principle behind subliminal images. They flashed by so quickly that your eye didn't have time to notice them, even though your brain had "seen" them. The cop recalled that François Mitterrand had used the technique in 1988. The face of the presidential candidate had appeared in the credits of the evening news, but not long enough for viewers to perceive it consciously.

"So the man who made this movie was a precursor?"

"Someone very gifted, in any case. The great Georges Méliès had invented everything by way of special effects and image manipulation, but not subliminals. And let's not forget this was the fifties, when our knowledge of the brain and the impact of images on the mind was still fairly primitive. A friend of mine works in neuromarketing—I'll give you his address. On top of which, I'm going to show him this film, if it's all right with you. With the equipment he's got, he might be able to find some interesting things that my eyes missed."

"Absolutely, please do."

Poignet rummaged through a basket filled with business cards.

"Here, this is his card, just in case. He can tell you about subliminal images better than I can—the brain, imagery, its impact on the mind. Do you realize how much they manipulate us today, without our even being aware of it? Do you have children?"

Lucie's features softened.

"Yes. Twin girls, Clara and Juliette. They're eight."

"So you've probably already shown them Bernard and Bianca—*The Rescuers*."

"Like every other mom."

"That cartoon contains a subliminal image of a naked woman hiding in a window, at one point. A small personal quirk of the animator's, no doubt. Don't worry, it won't have any effect on your children's minds—the image is too tiny! The fact remains that no one ever saw it, in all the years that cartoon was being shown."

The conversation was turning dubious. Lucie stared at the image of the nude starlet. Provocative, open. A pure scandal for the time.

"How did the director insert subliminal images in his film?"

"Did you ever make collages in school? It's the same idea. He first shot the scenes of the nude actress on another roll. Then he took the frames he wanted from roll A and spliced them into roll B, simple cut and paste. When it's all done, you dup the film, and you end up with what we've got here. A ton of famous directors used this process to heighten the impact of certain scenes. Hitchcock in *Psycho*, Fincher in *Fight Club*, and a lot of horror movies as well. But all that was later. At the time, absolutely no one would have suspected the presence of these images."

"And what about the other subliminal images in this film? What are they like?"

"Salacious, pornographic, sticky with sweat and sex. There are also some rather nauseating and risqué lovemaking scenes, with men in masks. And toward the end, you come across some murders."

"Murders?"

Lucie felt a sudden tension in her muscles. She'd already heard about snuff movies. Murders captured on film, tapes passed around hand to hand in alternative circles. Could she be dealing with one of those—a snuff film more than half a century old?

Claude slowly cranked the handle. The time counters clicked forward. The restorer paused at each hidden image. Certain nude scenes were especially daring, not very appealing, approaching morbid. No question that at a time when a woman could scarcely show herself in a bathing suit, this would have been shocking.

"The bloodier sequences come more toward the end. The scene with the girl and the bull is crammed full of them. Excuse me, I need to turn this for a few seconds—my automatic rewind broke. This film lasts a good thirteen minutes, or more than three hundred feet of film. Tell me, did you and Ludovic use to go out? He's always been attracted to your type of woman."

"What type is that?"

"Kind of like Jodie Foster."

"I'll take that as a compliment."

"It is."

"Uh . . . About the scene where the bull stops dead in front of the girl—how did they do that? Special effects?"

Lucie clasped her hands behind her back. It was strange, but very few films had left so strong an impression on her. She felt she could describe every scene of this one in detail, as if they were etched in her gray matter.

"Probably. But the animal actually was slaughtered at one point. As for the kid facing down the bull, I'll have to analyze the images frame by frame. He might have shot the bull by itself, rewound the stock without exposing it, then shot the girl by herself, using superimposition. But that seems highly complicated, and if so, he did a damn good job for the time, given that computers didn't even exist yet and the equipment was still pretty rudimentary."

"And did you see how dilated the girl's pupils were? Could they have drugged her?"

"You don't drug actresses. There are special products for movies and special effects that can do that perfectly well. They already had them in the fifties."

He wound more slowly. Lucie saw images succeed each other on the viewer, the movement starting up and varying depending on the speed of the rotation. They got to the image of the pasture surrounded by its fence. Claude wound the film more slowly still, then stopped on a shocking image. Grass, the naked actress blatantly spread-eagled on the ground, her hair flowing around her like biblical serpents. A blackish, circular wound gaped from her belly like a well. Lucie's hand flew to her mouth.

"Oh, Jesus!"

"You said it."

Claude moved aside, picked up the filmstrip, and held it up to the neon light.

"Look . . . It's really well done, because, just like the pornographic frames, the subliminal image is in the same tones as the other images. The same dominant tints, the same contrasts, the same light. The pasture is different, but not flagrantly so. When the film ran at normal speed, there was no break in tone, so you noticed absolutely nothing. The brain, on the other hand, got the full impact."

Lucie leaned in as close as she could to the film. To think those images had crossed through her sight without her knowing it. A few feet later, on the translucent strip, she saw the same woman positioned like a corpse. Then again and again after that, as Claude unspooled the film between his fingers.

"At each of the actress's appearances, roughly every two hundred frames, there's an additional wound, spreading from the black circle on her stomach. As if in temporal continuity. Until it forms . . ."

He started cranking the handle again, halted on the unbelievable scene in which the bull stood facing the girl. The following image was completely different.

". . . an eye."

Lucie had trouble understanding what she'd got hold of. Little by little, someone had lacerated the woman in every direction, radiating from her navel like a sun of gashes. Open wounds on her white body frozen on the thick grass. In appearance, the slits formed a pupil with its iris. A hidden, malevolent eye that observed you, transfixed you, made you want to turn away. *To not see anymore.* Lucie felt as if she were looking at crime scene photos: the victim of a twisted, sadistic killer.

"That can't be trick photography," she stated. "It's so . . . real."

Claude removed his glasses and wiped them with a chamois. Without the magnifying lenses, his face regained its balance, its features refined despite the deep wrinkles.

"That's the very definition of trick photography when it's done well. I have no doubt it's the case here."

The black and white amplified the violence of the image, dissociated the mutilated body from its environment. Lucie still couldn't get over it.

"How can you be so sure?"

"Because we're dealing with the movies, dear miss, not with reality. The seventh art is an art of magic, subterfuge, optical illusion. The woman could very well be a model. In able hands, some makeup and a few staging effects would do perfectly well. Nothing is real. One thing for certain, our director seems to be obsessed with eyes and the effect of images on the mind. A precursor, as you said, when today we see to what extent images inhabit our lives and flood it with violence. Our children confront more than three hundred thousand images a day—do you have any idea what that means? And do you know how many of them are related to violence, death, and war?"

The eyes of the woman Lucie privately called "the victim" stared up at the sky, devoid of any sign of life. A bit shaken, the cop turned back to face Claude.

"Do you think this film was ever shown in a theater?"

"I doubt it. The condition of the sprocket holes, especially near the beginning of the film, is impeccable. This copy, at least, was never shown on a large scale."

"So why the subliminal images, then? Why all that staging?"

"Private projections, perhaps? A film that the director showed to a few select individuals? Who knows. A personal fantasy? You know, subliminals can be incredibly strong. They're a direct line between the image and the subconscious, unmediated by any form of censorship. They take an image and jam it straight into your brain—*bam!* An ideal way to convey violence, sex, and perversity by alternate routes. These days, that all happens online, in visual and audio. Bands that pass subliminal messages in their songs, for instance. Perhaps our director enjoyed that kind of wild idea? When I think that it was only 1955 . . . You've got to hand it to him—the guy's no lightweight."

Claude switched off the screen. Lucie couldn't take her eyes off the reel. Thousands of images one after the other, imprinting life or death. She imagined a gleaming, magnificent river that churned up in its depths a host of invisible, deadly parasites.

"Is that all we can get out of this film?"

Claude hesitated. "No. I think it's a vehicle for something else. For starters, why fifty frames a second? And what's the point of that white circle in the upper right? It's present on every frame. On top of which"—he shook his head, lips pinched—"there are those areas of fog, parts of the screen that are very dark, that omnipresent dullness, like a kind of film over the lens. The cameraman seems to be playing with contrast, light, things unsaid. I felt the same anxiety as you when I watched this. The porno images, or even the ones of the woman being tortured, aren't enough to create such a powerful unease. And besides, let's not forget that Ludovic is in a psychiatric ward because of this film. There must be something I've missed. I have to look at it all again very carefully. Every frame, every bit of every image. But that could take days . . ."

Lucie couldn't manage to shake the vision of that maimed woman. A fat, black eye, like a gaping wound on her abdomen. She might have been holding the proof of a murder. Even if the case was more than fifty years old, she wanted to get to the bottom of it. Or at least understand.

"How could we find that woman?"

Claude didn't appear surprised by the question. After all the films he'd handled, most of them lost or anonymous, he must have been used to this kind of request.

"I think you'd have to look in France. She's wearing a Chanel suit, the 1954 model, in other words one year before the film was developed. My mother had the same one."

Shot in France, developed in Canada? Or else, had the actress moved there—assuming she even was an actress? And why? How had someone convinced her to appear in this sick film? One more oddity to add to the pile, in any case.

"Large bust, pear-shaped hips . . . this is smack dab in the Bardot era, when filmmakers finally dared show women. Her face doesn't ring any bells, but I can contact a film historian who specializes in the fifties. He's in touch with all the film archives and revival houses in the country. The porno and erotica milieu was very closed off and censored at the time, but there was a circuit even so. If this woman ever appeared in any other films, my friend will find her."

"Can you make me photocopies of the subliminal images off the film?"

"I can do you one better—I'll digitize the whole thing for you. My 16-mil scanner can churn through two thousand frames an hour in low res. Don't worry, the quality will be excellent, as long as you don't try to show it on a movie screen. When I'm done, I'll put it on a server, and you can download it from your computer."

Lucie thanked her host warmly and dropped her business card in the basket.

"Call me as soon as you find out anything."

Claude nodded and squeezed her hand between both of his.

"I'm doing this for Ludovic. It was thanks to his parents that I met my wife. Her name was Marilyn, like the other one . . ." He sighed, a sigh full of nostalgia. "I'd really like to know why this damn film drove him blind."

Once outside, Lucie glanced at her watch. Almost noon. Her meeting with Claude Poignet had made her feel sick. She thought about those subliminal images, inside her now against her will. She felt them vibrating somewhere inside her, without knowing precisely where. The scene of the sliced eyeball had shocked her, but at least she'd been aware of seeing it. But the others . . . Just perverted filth that had been lodged in her brain, without any possible defense.

Who had seen this insanity? Why had it been made? Like Claude Poignet, she sensed that the cursed filmstrip still harbored sinister secrets.

Her head full of questions, she went to retrieve her car at the République parking garage. Behind the wheel, before turning the ignition, she took out young Szpilman's want ad, which Ludovic had given her: "For sale: old films, 16 mm, 35 mm, silent and sound. All genres, short and full length, 1930s and after. 800+ reels, including 500 spy thrillers. Make offer on site." The son might know something. It might be worth making the trip to Liège. But first, she was going back to the hospital to have lunch with her mother and Juliette—though calling that hospital food "lunch" was a stretch.

She was already missing her little daughter something fierce.

11

Sharko, beside himself, yanked open the toilet stalls at Rouen police headquarters one after another to make sure no one was inside. Sweat was pouring down his temples and the cursed sun streamed through the windows. It was awful. He spun around suddenly, his eyes full of salt and fury.

"Leave me the fuck alone, Eugenie, okay? I'll get you your cocktail sauce, but not now! I'm at work, in case you hadn't noticed."

Eugenie was sitting on the edge of the sink. She wore a short blue dress and red shoes with buckles, and her hair was tied with an elastic. She was taking mischievous pleasure in coiling a lock of it around her fingers. She wasn't sweating a drop.

"I don't like it when you do those things, dear Franck. I'm scared of skeletons and dead people. Eloise was scared of them too, so why are you starting up again and putting me through this? Didn't you like it in your office? Now I don't want to go away alone. I want to stay with you."

Sharko paced back and forth, hot as a pressure cooker. He ran to the sink and stuck his head under the freezing tap. When he stood up, Eugenie was still there. He tried elbowing her aside, but she didn't budge.

"Quit talking about Eloise. Get lost. You should have gone away with the treatment, you should have disap—"

"So then let's go back to Paris, right away. I want to play with the trains. If you're mean to me and go see those skeletons again, things won't be so easy for you. That big dummy Willy can't come bother you anymore, but I still can. And whenever I want to."

Worse than a pot of glue. The inspector held his head in his hands. Then he rushed out of the bathroom, slamming the door behind him. He veered into a hallway. Eugenie was sitting cross-legged in front of him, on the linoleum floor. Sharko walked around her, ignoring her presence, and straight into the office of Georges Péresse. The head of Criminal Investigations was juggling his landline and his cell. Papers had piled up in front of him. He put his hand over the receiver and jerked his chin toward Sharko.

"What is it?"

"Any news from Interpol?"

"Yes, yes. The form was sent to Central last night." Péresse returned to his conversation. Sharko remained in the doorway.

"Can I see that form?"

"Inspector, please! I'm busy."

Sharko nodded and went back to his desk, a small area they had allocated him in an open space where five or six police functionaries bustled about. It was July, blue skies, holidays. Despite the importance of the ongoing case, the precinct was running at half speed.

The cop sat in his chair. Eugenie had set his nerves on edge; he hadn't been able to channel her like at his office in Paris. She came back, her rucksack stuffed with old memories and obsessions that she loaded into his head. She knew perfectly well which buttons to push, and he knew what to expect: basically, she punished him the moment he became too much of a cop again.

He dove back into his files, pen in hand, while the little girl played with a letter opener. She was making noise incessantly, and Sharko knew there was no use stopping up his ears: she was inside him, somewhere under his skull, and wouldn't clear out until she was good and ready.

Naturally, Sharko did everything he could to make sure no one noticed anything. He had to appear normal, lucid. That was how he'd managed to keep his ass covered in the Nanterre office. When Eugenie finally beat it, he was able to study his notes.

The cops had made good progress in forensics and toxicology. Further analyses of the bones, notably under the scanner, had shown old fractures on four of the five skeletons—wrists, ribs, elbows—with signs of healing, which meant they'd been sustained less than two years previous, and before death, since they were colored. So these unidentified men weren't the type to rot behind a desk. The injuries might have resulted from falls or hazards of their trade, or from contact sports like rugby, or from fights. Earlier that day, Sharko had suggested cross-checking with the various hospitals and athletic clubs in the area. The investigations were under way.

Despite the lack of head hair, tox screens of the pubic hairs had been extremely fruitful. Three of the five individuals, including the Asian, had been users of cocaine and Subutex, a heroin substitute. Analyzing cross sections of the pubes after cutting them into sections had shown that, for all three, narcotics use had at first strongly declined, then disappeared altogether in the weeks before death. Crushing the insect pupae hadn't revealed anything: if the men had taken drugs in their final hours, traces of it would have been found in the keratin of the insects' shells. Given this, the chief inspector had made a note to check releases from detox centers and prisons, as Subutex was a common drug on the inside. Perhaps they were dealing with ex-cons, dealers, or guys who'd gotten mixed up in something to do with drug trafficking. He couldn't ignore any potential lead.

One final point: the small plastic tube found around the clavicle of the best-preserved corpse. Analysis had not shown the presence of chemo drugs. Alongside the ME's hypotheses, the report stated that the sheath might also have served to link fine electrodes implanted in the brain to a subcutaneous stimulator. They called this technique deep brain stimulation, and it was used to treat severe depression, limit tremors from Parkinson's disease, or suppress Tourette's. That was a key discovery, since the killer seemed to be interested in his victims' brains.

"Whatcha writing?"

Eugenie had returned. Sharko pointedly ignored her and tried to pursue his thoughts. The little girl tapped on the table with the letter opener, louder and louder.

"Eloise is dea-ead. Your wife is dea-ead. Eloise and your wife are dea-ead. And it shoulda been you instea-ead . . ."

The conniving little bitch . . . It was her favorite song, the one that wounded him to the depths of his soul. The cop ground his teeth.

"Shut the fuck up!"

Heads turned toward Sharko. He leapt out of his chair, fists clenched. He rushed over to a desk sergeant who was making photocopies and showed him his police ID.

"Sharko, Violent Crimes."

"I know, Chief Inspector. Can I help you with something?"

"I need you to go find me candied chestnuts and cocktail sauce. 'Pink Salad,' the two-pound jar. Can you do that? For the chestnuts, any brand will do, but for the sauce be sure to get Pink Salad, no substitutes."

The other man's eyes widened.

"Well, it's just that . . ."

The Paris cop put his hands on his hips and his shoulders swelled. With his added pounds, Sharko, who'd already had a stocky build, commanded respect.

"Yes, Sergeant?"

The young cop left his protest hanging and disappeared. Sharko returned to his spot. Eugenie smiled at him.

"See you later, dear Franck."

"Yeah, that's right. Stay home."

She started running and skipping, then disappeared behind a cork bulletin board. The inspector took a deep breath, eyes closed. His calm was finally returning. The hum of the computers, the creaking soles of his colleagues. He resumed his thoughts, quickly leafed through the technical data in the various reports. In the end, it was only a partial failure. The absence of records meant that these men might have been marginals, illegal aliens, or just foreigners.

Later, Sharko went to get a drink from the water fountain, feeling like his brain was mush. He imagined himself outside, at a sidewalk café. The sergeant had brought him back the jar of cocktail sauce and the glazed chestnuts, and since then Eugenie had left him blissfully in peace. In just a few, he'd head back to the hotel, check in with Leclerc, and probably hightail it back home in another day or two. Because the more time passed, the colder the trail got. Nothing from the hospitals. The detectives who'd returned from canvassing the locals had brought back squat. Out of the hundreds of employees and ex-employees who worked in the industrial zone, not one had seen a thing.

Sharko, plunging one last time into the files, suddenly felt pressure on his shoulder. He turned around. It was Péresse, who stared at the cocktail sauce and chestnuts, then finally said, "We've got a real lead. Come take a look."

Sharko walked with him to his office. The chief inspector from Rouen closed the door and pointed to his computer screen. It showed the scan of a handwritten document in English.

A telegram.

"We got it from Interpol. You won't believe how this telegram made its way here. Some guy from their shop, name of Sanchez, calls them from where he's vacationing, some campsite near Bordeaux. He was watching TV, just having a drink before dinner, not a care in the world, when he sees you where the bodies were discovered, next to the pipeline."

"I was on TV? Jesus, they don't miss a trick."

"So at that point, Sanchez calls headquarters to get the lowdown. He wants to know what you're up to."

"I know Sanchez. We worked a few cases together in the late nineties, before he swung over to Lyon."

"He hasn't been watching much TV these last few days and he missed the media hoopla. So his colleagues tell him about it, the sawed-off skulls and so on. And then something in his head goes tilt. He tells them to look into the Interpol archives, and guess what they turn up?"

"This old telegram."

"Exactly. A telegram sent from Egypt. Cairo, to be exact."

Sharko jabbed his finger on the screen.

"Tell me I'm seeing this right."

"You are. It's dated 1994. Three Egyptian girls, all violently murdered in Cairo. Skulls sawed off, 'with a medical saw,' as it says there, brains removed, eyes gone. Bodies mutilated, multiple stab wounds from head to foot, including the genital areas . . ."

Sharko felt a morbid giddiness grab hold of him. His rib cage tightened, his chest constricted. The monster of the manhunt reared its head. Péresse kept on reading.

". . . All within two days. And no underground burial this time. The bodies were dumped in the open. Our killer wasn't being particularly subtle."

The cop from Paris straightened up and lowered his eyes. He imagined the girls spread over the desert sand, covered in lacerations, innards exposed, prey to the buzzards. All these images in his head. He stared at the screen, short of breath.

"That was so long ago. When there are serial killings, they're normally closer together in time. And in space. Normandy and Cairo aren't exactly next door . . . Could we be dealing with an itinerant? Did Interpol turn up any other cases like this?"

"Nothing."

"Which doesn't mean anything. As little as ten years ago, this kind of telegram was pretty rare. Spending time on paperwork is the last thing most cops do, and only if they feel like taking the trouble. Our Egyptian colleague was a meticulous policeman. Which is almost a paradox."

Sharko paused a moment. His eyes continued to run over the telegram while his brain was already in overdrive. Three girls in Africa, five men in France. Lacerations, skulls opened, eyes removed. Sixteen years apart. Why such a long wait between the two series? And especially, why the two series? The inspector returned to the cursory description dispatched to Interpol.

"The author of the report is Mahmoud Abd el-Aal. The name of the Egyptian officer who cast the first stone?"

"So it seems."

"Is this paper the only thing we've got?"

"For now. We first got in touch with Interpol in Egypt, then International Technical Cooperation in Cairo, who shunted us over to an inspector at the French embassy, Michael Lebrun, who's in direct contact with the authorities over there. The early intel isn't exactly promising."

"Why not?"

"This Abd el-Aal apparently hasn't been active there since this business."
Sharko paused a moment.

"Can someone get us access to the file?"

"Yes. His name is Hassan Noureddine, and he's the chief of police in charge of the squad. Something of a dictator, according to Lebrun. The locals are keeping mum—they don't like having Westerners sticking their noses in their business. Torture of defendants and jail time for dissidents is still common coin in Egypt. We won't get anywhere on the phone, and they refuse to send their files here, electronically or by mail."

Sharko sighed. Péresse was right. The police in Arab countries, and especially in Egypt, were still light-years from the Europeans—corrupted by money and power, focused entirely on internal security.

With a click of his mouse, Péresse sent the telegram to the printer.

"I called your boss. He's okay with us sending you over there. Cairo is four hours away by plane. If you don't mind, start with the embassy. Michael Lebrun will get you into the Cairo police. He'll direct you to Hassan Noureddine."

Eugenie suddenly burst into the room, livid. Sharko turned his head toward the girl, who started yanking on his shirt.

"Come on, come on. Let's get out of here," she whined. "No way we're going to that horrible place. I hate all that heat and sand. And I'm afraid of flying. I don't want to."

". . . spector? Chief Inspector?"

Sharko turned back toward Péresse, hand on his chin. Egypt . . . Not quite what he'd been expecting.

"Sounds like a bad James Bond movie."

"We don't really have much choice. We handle the groundwork, and you—"

"The paperwork, I know."

With a sigh, Sharko picked up the printout of the telegram. Several lines sent haphazardly, lost between two continents, with which he was going to have to make do. He thought of Egypt, a country he knew only from travel brochures, back when he still looked at brochures. The Nile, the great pyramids, the crushing heat, the palm groves . . . A tourist factory. Suzanne had always wanted to go; he'd refused, because of his job. And now that same lousy job was tossing him onto the cursed sands of Africa.

Lost in thought, he stared at Eugenie, who was sitting in the captain's seat and playing with rubber bands, snapping them against Péresse's ass.

"What's so funny?" the Rouen cop asked, turning around.

Sharko raised his head.

"I suppose I'm to leave as soon as possible?"

"Tomorrow at latest. Do you have an official passport?"

"Required. I'm supposed to expedite international investigations, even though that never actually happens."

"Here's proof that it does. Watch yourself—in Cairo, you'll be bound hand and foot. The embassy will saddle you with an interpreter, and you won't get anywhere unless the locals want you to. You'll have to walk on eggshells. Keep me posted."

"Am I allowed to carry a weapon?"

"In Egypt? Are you joking?"

They shook hands politely. Sharko tried to slip out and leave the little girl behind, but Péresse called him back one last time.

"Chief Inspector Sharko?"

"Mmm?"

"Next time, try not to send one of my sergeants to do your shopping for you."

Sharko left the building and headed for his hotel, Xeroxes of the reports under one arm, the jar of Pink Salad and candied chestnuts in the other. He was heading into an especially unwholesome business, apparently.

And about to dive into the guts of a burning hot city that reeked of spices.

The mythic city of al-Qahira.

Cairo.

12

After a revolting lunch with her daughter—a slab of overcooked meat with no sauce and boiled potatoes—Lucie swung by her place, a small apartment surrounded by the student dorms of the Catholic university. The tree-lined boulevard overflowed with neo-Gothic buildings, including the university, which regurgitated its several thousand students through the city's arteries. With all those young people around her, and her daughters growing up, Lucie felt a bit older every day.

She unlocked the door, went in, and dropped her bag of dirty clothes in the laundry room. Quick, crank up the washing machine to get rid of those horrid hospital odors. Then she dove under a cool shower, letting the spray beat against the back of her neck, nibble at her breasts. Those two days away from home, eating mush, taking bird baths, and sleeping folded in half, showed her just how much she loved her little existence, with her girls, her habits, the movies she watched every evening, cozy in the rabbit slippers that her twins—and her mother—had given her for her birthday. It's when you veer away from the simplest things that you realize they aren't so bad after all.

Once dried, she chose a light, supple blue silk tunic that she let fall naturally over her hips, over calf-length pedal pushers. She liked the curve of her legs, toned by the jogging she did twice a week around the Citadelle. Since her daughters started going to school and eating in the cafeteria, she'd managed to regain some measure of balance between work, leisure, and family time. She had once again become, as her mother said, a woman.

She stopped at her computer to check her online dating account. Her failure with Ludovic hadn't soured her on that kind of relationship. In fact, she couldn't quite do without these virtual, neatly wrapped interchanges.

It was worse than a drug, and more than anything it saved time—which, as with everyone else, she found in short supply.

Seven new messages had accumulated on her profile. She looked them over quickly, rejected five off the bat, and put the other two aside: dark-haired men of forty-three and forty-four. The self-confidence a man gave off at around forty was what she was seeking first and foremost. A strong, dependable presence, who wouldn't drop her for the first airhead that came along.

She went out, the back of her neck nicely refreshed. It was then that she noticed the slight grating of her key in the lock. Something seemed to catch when she gave the second turn. Lucie leaned down, looked closely at the metal, tried again. Although she managed to lock the door, the trouble persisted. Annoyed, she opened up again, ran her eyes over her living room, checked in the other rooms. She explored the closets where she kept her DVDs and novels. *Apparently*, nothing had been touched. She immediately thought of the phantom presence at Ludovic's. Whoever had rifled through there could easily have noted her license number when he left and gone to her house. Anyone else would have thought the lock was just getting old, that it was time for a drop of oil. Lucie shrugged her shoulders with a smile and finally headed out again. She really had to stop worrying over nothing. Which didn't keep her from staring at length into her rearview mirror after driving off, and reassuring herself that the film, that weird-ass film, was perfectly safe at Claude Poignet's.

Getting to Liège in an old rattletrap with no air-conditioning, along the bone-jarring highways of Belgium, was no mean feat, but she managed it nonstop. Luc Szpilman opened up for her. An off-putting safety pin ran through his lower lip.

"Are you the one who called on the phone?"

Lucie nodded and showed him her official card. She had justified the visit with a version of the truth: the police were interested in one of the films Ludovic Sénéchal had made off with, owing to the violent nature of its imagery.

"That's me," she said. "Can I come in?"

He looked her over with a beady, porcine eye. His hair looked as if it had exploded on his head, like the guy from Tokyo Hotel.

"Come on in. But don't try telling me that my father was mixed up in some kind of trafficking."

"No, no. Nothing like that."

They sat in the spacious living room, reached by a series of steps that plunged the area below ground level. A glass roof opened onto a limpid, deep blue sky. It reminded Lucie of a kind of giant vivarium. Luc Szpilman uncapped a beer; his interlocutor opted for water. Somewhere in the house someone was playing a musical instrument. The notes danced, light and mesmerizing.

"The clarinet. It's my girlfriend."

Surprising. Lucie figured him for someone whose partner played electric guitar or drums. She decided not to waste any time and cut to the chase.

"Were you still living with your father?"

"Sometimes. We didn't really have much to say to each other, but he never had the guts to throw me out. So yeah, I alternated between here and my girlfriend's place. Now that he's not here anymore, I think the choice is made."

He downed half the bottle—a Chimay red with double the alcohol content—and set it on the glass tabletop, next to an ashtray holding the remains of a few joints. The detective tried to size him up: rebellious kid, probably spoiled as a child. His father's recent passing didn't seem to have left much of an impression.

"Tell me about the circumstances of his death."

"I already told the police everything, and—"

"If you don't mind."

He sighed.

"I was in the garage. Since the old man didn't have a car anymore, that's where we set up our instruments. I was working on a piece with a bud and the GF. It was probably around 8:25 when I heard this huge crash from upstairs. First I ran in here, because when the news is on, you can't budge my old man from his chair. Then I went upstairs and I saw the attic door was open. That was weird."

"Why's that?"

"My dad was over eighty. He still got around pretty well, sometimes he even went for a walk in town to go to the library or something, but he never went up there anymore—the steps were way too steep. When he wanted to stare at one of his movies, he always asked me."

Lucie knew she was on the right track. Something sudden and unexpected had triggered a reaction in the old man, pushing him to go up without asking his son for help.

"And after that, in the attic?"

"That's where I discovered his body, at the foot of the ladder."

Luc stared at the floor, pupils dilated, then got hold of himself in a fraction of a second.

"His head was in a pool of blood. He was dead. It felt weird seeing him like that, motionless, eyes staring. I immediately called emergency."

He grabbed up his beer with a firm hand, letting nothing show. Somewhere in all this was a late-born son who'd seen his father as just some clumsy geezer, a guy who could never play football with him. Lucie nodded toward the painting of an elderly gentleman, firm gaze and black eyes. A mug as severe as the Great Wall of China.

"Is that him?"

Luc nodded, both hands around his beer.

"Papa, in all his glory. I wasn't even born yet when he had that painted. He was already fifty. Can you imagine?"

"What was his occupation?"

"Curator at FIAF, the International Federation of Film Archives, and he went there regularly to poke around. FIAF's mission is to 'preserve the international cinematic heritage.' My father spent his life in films. It was his great passion, along with history and geopolitics of the past hundred years. The major conflicts, Cold War, espionage, counterespionage . . . He knew all about that stuff."

He raised his eyes.

"You said on the phone there was a problem with one of the films from the attic?"

"Yes, probably the one he was trying to get to that evening. A short from 1955, which opens with a scene of a woman getting her eye slashed. Does that ring any bells?"

He took a moment to think.

"No, not a thing. I never watched his movies. Those old spy chestnuts didn't interest me. And my father always watched them in his private screening room. He was nuts about cinema, a real fanatic, able to watch the same film twenty or thirty times over."

He gave out a nervous laugh.

"Dad . . . I think he pinched a lot of those reels from FIAF."

"Pinched?"

"Yeah, pinched. It was one of his little quirks as a collector. He couldn't help himself. Call it an obsessive tic. I knew he made deals with a fair number of his colleagues who did the same thing. Because, theoretically, those films never left the building. But Dad didn't want those reels to rot in some soulless corridor. He was the type who'd pet film cans the way you'd pet an old cat."

Lucie listened, then told him about the little girl on the swing, the scene with the bull. Luc continued to deny and seemed sincere. Then she asked him to show her the attic.

In the staircase, she understood why Szpilman Senior had stopped going up: the steps were practically a sheer vertical. Once at the top, Luc went to the ladder and slid it to the far corner.

"The ladder was exactly here when I found the body."

Lucie gave the place a good once-over. A fanatic's inner sanctum.

"Why was it moved?"

"A ton of people have been by here, and others will probably still come. Since yesterday morning, the movies have been selling like hotcakes."

Lucie suddenly felt a connection forming.

"Did all the visitors buy something?"

"Uh . . . no, not all of them."

"Tell me."

"There was this one guy who came just after your friend. He seemed kind of strange."

He walked one step at a time, not as sharp as before. The beer, apparently.

"Tell me more."

"He had really short hair. Blond, buzz cut. Under thirty. Solid guy, wearing combat boots, or something like that. He poked through everything in the attic. It was like he was looking for something specific among the cans. In the end, he didn't buy anything, but he asked if anyone had already been here or had removed any of the films. So I told him about your Ludovic Sénéchal. When I mentioned that film he'd taken, the unmarked one, the guy said he'd like to make a deal with this Sénéchal. So I let him have the address."

"You knew it?"

"It was on the check."

So it all started here. Like Ludovic, the mysterious individual must have come across the ad and rushed over. He'd come just a bit too late, and Ludovic, who lived close to the border, had made away with the prize. Did this mean the other guy had been haunting junk shops and combing through want ads for years, in secret hopes of getting his hands on the lost film?

Lucie grilled Szpilman further. The visitor had come in a classic car, a black Fiat, as he recalled. French plates, whose number the young Belgian couldn't recall.

They went back to the living room. Lucie gazed at the giant flat screen set into the wall. Szpilman had said his father was watching the news just before his death.

"Do you have any idea what might have caused your father to suddenly run up to the attic?"

"No."

"What channel was he watching?"

"Your national station, TF1. It was his favorite."

Lucie made a mental note to watch a tape of the news from that evening, just in case.

"Had anyone come here before he went upstairs? Perhaps in the morning or afternoon?"

"Not that I know of."

She cast a glance around the room. Not a phone jack in sight.

"Did your father have a cell phone?"

Luc Szpilman nodded. Lucie poured herself another glass of water from the pitcher, playing it cool. Inside, she was churning.

"Was he carrying it on him when he died?"

The kid suddenly seemed to get it. He stabbed his index finger onto the low table.

"It was here. I picked it up this morning and put it on the shelf, out there. The police didn't even ask about it. You think that—?"

"Can you show me?"

He went to get it. Battery dead, of course. He connected it to a charger plugged into a nearby outlet and handed it to Lucie. The phone was in crummy shape, but she was able to check the call history, with date and time. She first looked at the incoming calls. The last one was from Sunday afternoon, the day before his death. A certain Delphine de Hoos. Luc explained that she was the nurse who came periodically for his blood tests. The other calls were farther back in time, and according to his son were all normal. Just a few old friends or colleagues from FIAF, with whom his father shared the occasional vodka.

Lucie then tried the list of outgoing calls. Her heart skipped a beat.

"Well, well . . ."

The last one was dated from the famous Monday, at 8:09 p.m. About fifteen minutes before the fall from the ladder. But much more interesting than the date was the phone number itself—curious, to say the least: 514-555-8724.

Lucie showed Szpilman the screen.

"He called abroad just a few minutes before he died. Does this number or the area code mean anything to you?"

"Maybe the States? He called there sometimes, when he was doing research."

"I don't think so, no."

Lucie took out her own phone and punched in a number, an intuition in the back of her head. She couldn't swear to it, but . . .

A voice on the other end of the line interrupted her musings. Information. Lucie made her request.

"I'd like to know which country the phone number 514-555-8724 corresponds to."

"One moment, please."

Silence. The phone cradled between ear and shoulder, Lucie asked Luc for a pen and paper. Then she quickly jotted down the number. The voice returned in her ear.

"Ma'am? It's the area code for the province of Quebec. Montreal, to be precise."

Lucie hung up. A word crumbled on the tip of her tongue, while she stared intently at Luc.

"Canada."

"Canada? Why would he have called Canada? We don't know anybody there."

Lucie gave herself time to absorb that information. For some reason or other, Vlad Szpilman had suddenly called a person living in the country where the film had been manufactured. She scrolled through the earlier calls as far back as a week before. No other trace of that number.

"Did your father keep notes about films or his contacts? Index cards, notebooks?"

"I never saw any. These past few years, my father's life consisted of a few square yards, between here, his screening room, and his office."

"Can I have a look at his office?"

Luc hesitated and finished his beer.

"Okay. But you'll really have to tell me what's going on. He was my father—I have a right to know."

Lucie nodded. Luc led her into a clean, well-organized room, with a computer, magazines, newspapers, and a library. The cop glanced into the papers, the drawers. Just normal office material, a PC, nothing unusual. The library in the back housed a lot of history books, about the wars, massacres, genocides. Armenians, Jews, Rwandans. There was also a section on the history of espionage. CIA, MI5, conspiracy theory. And a bunch of books in English, with titles that suggested nothing special to Lucie: Bluebird, MK-Ultra, Artichoke. Vlad Szpilman seemed preoccupied with the dark underside of the world from the last century. Lucie turned to Luc, pointing at the books.

"Do you think your father was hiding some important secret from you?"

The young man shrugged.

"My father had a bit of a paranoid streak. Wouldn't have been like him to talk to me about that stuff. It was his secret garden."

After a spin around the room, Lucie let herself be accompanied to the exit door, thanked Luc Szpilman, and handed him her business card, on the back of which she jotted her personal cell number in case. In the car, she took out her phone and dialed the number in Canada. Four nerve-racking rings before someone finally picked up. Not a sound, not a hello. So it was up to Lucie.

"Hello?"

Long pause. Lucie repeated, "Hello? Is anyone there?"

"Who is this?"

Male voice, pronounced Quebec accent.

"Lucie Henebelle. I'm calling from—"

Abrupt click. He'd hung up. Lucie imagined a nervous type, on his guard, distrustful. Dazed by the brevity of the exchange, she burst from her car and went back to knock on Szpilman's door.

"You again?"

"I'll need your father's phone."

13

Refine her strategy. Take him unaware before he can hang up.

Lucie let a good fifteen minutes go by, then redialed the number with Vlad Szpilman's partially recharged cell. With a little luck, her interlocutor would recognize the contact and not hang up. Not immediately, in any case.

She paced anxiously in front of the Belgian's house. Even though he'd been fairly easygoing and cooperative, she didn't want Luc to hear the conversation—assuming there was one.

The phone was picked up after two rings.

"Vlad?" went the voice with the Quebec accent.

"Vlad is dead. This is Lucie Henebelle, a lieutenant in the French police. Criminal division."

She'd blurted it all out at once. This was the decisive moment. An interminable silence followed, but he didn't hang up.

"Dead how?"

Lucie squeezed her fist: the fish was hooked. She just had to reel it in gently now, without any sudden jerks.

"I'll tell you. But first tell me who you are."

"Dead how?"

"A stupid accident. He fell from a ladder and cracked his skull."

Several seconds passed. A host of questions burned Lucie's lips, but she was afraid he'd cut the connection. It was he who finally broke the ice.

"Why are you calling?"

Lucie played it straight. She sensed that the other man was under great pressure, and that he'd sniff out a lie in two seconds flat.

"After he called you on Monday, Vlad Szpilman immediately went up to his attic to get a film. An anonymous film from 1955, made in Canada, that I now have in my possession. I'd like to know why."

Apparently she'd hit a nerve. She heard his breathing become more labored.

"You're not with the police. You're lying."

"Call my headquarters. Lille police department, Criminal Investigations unit. Tell them that—"

"Tell me about the case."

Lucie flipped through her recall at top speed. What was he talking about?

"I'm sorry, I—"

"You're not with the police."

"Of course I am! Lieutenant in Lille, for God's sake!"

"In that case, tell me about the five bodies, the ones discovered near the factories. How far have you got with the investigation? Give me the technical details."

Lucie understood: the bodies at the pipeline. So that was what had triggered Vlad Szpilman's phone call. They were reporting it on the news.

"I'm sorry. We work by jurisdiction, and mine is the north. We're not the ones handling that case. You'd have to check with—"

"I don't give a damn. Get to know the people handling it. If you're really with the police, you'll get hold of the information. And in case you try to trace me, my phone is a cell registered under a false name and address. Because of you, I'll now have to destroy it."

He was about to hang up. Lucie decided to bet all her chips.

"Is there a link between that case and the film?"

"You know there is. Good-b—"

"Wait! How can I reach you?"

"Your number came up when you called. I'll reach *you*." A moment's pause. "I'll call you back at 8:00 p.m., French time. Have the info, or you'll never hear from me again."

Call ended. Silence. Lucie stood there, mouth agape. That had certainly been the densest and most intriguing phone call of her entire life.

After thanking Luc for the use of the phone, she settled deeply into the front seat of her car, hands on her forehead. She thought about that voice separated from hers by some thirty-five hundred miles. Clearly, her interlocutor was scared stiff of being identified; he hid behind stolen phone numbers and abbreviated any form of exchange. Why was he hiding? And from whom? How had he got in touch with Vlad Szpilman? But the question that nagged at her the most was to find out what invisible connection could possibly exist between the anonymous film and the bodies unearthed in Normandy.

That evil reel might have been the tree that hid the forest.

Caught up, Lucie knew at that moment that she had no choice. Her conscience forbade her to call it quits or drop the bone. It was always like that, in a snap, that she decided to pursue her cases to the end. That same relentlessness that had pushed her to wear the badge. And sometimes, to go too far.

As of now, time was of the essence. She had until eight o'clock to find the right contact in Paris and ferret out the info demanded of her.

14

A schizophrenic's apartment tends to be messy. The internal personality disorder—the mental fracture—often manifests in an external disorder, to the point where some schizophrenics engage the services of a housekeeper. On the other hand, the apartment of a behavioral analyst demands a certain rigor, mirroring a rectilinear mind accustomed to compartmentalizing pieces of information the way you'd arrange shoes in a storage cubby. As such, Sharko's apartment pulled in two different directions. While the coffee cups piled up in the sink and the wrinkled suits and ties amassed in a corner of the bathroom, various other rooms, all very neat and tidy, made it look like the residence of a peaceful family. A lot of photos in frames, a small plant, a child's room with old stuffed toys, the yellow wallpaper with its frieze of dolphins.

On the floor of this latter room, a magnificent railway sprawled out its vintage tracks and locomotives, bordered by landscapes made of foam, cork, or resin. Restoring life to this miniature world, which had once required hundreds—thousands—of hours of assembly, painting, and gluing, was the first thing Sharko had done on his return from Rouen two hours earlier. The locomotives sent joyous whistles into the air and emitted their good, steamy smell, mixed with his wife Suzanne's perfume, which he'd added to the water tank. As always, Eugenie sat amid the tracks, smiling; at moments like these, the cop was glad to have her around.

When she decided to leave, Sharko stood up and retrieved a dusty old suitcase from the top of a closet. The smells of the past poured out as he opened it, laden with nostalgia. Sharko's heavy heart felt a pang.

His departure for Cairo was scheduled for the next morning, on Egyptair out of Orly. Economy class, the bastards. By prearrangement, the police inspector attached to the French embassy would be waiting for him. Sharko had checked online for the local temperature: celestial fires torched the country, a veritable sauna, which wouldn't help matters. He packed his suitcase with plain short-sleeved shirts, two bathing suits—you never know—two pairs of twill trousers, and Bermuda shorts. He didn't forget his tape recorder, cocktail sauce, candied chestnuts, or O-gauge Ova Hornby locomotive, with its black car for wood and charcoal.

His phone rang the moment he shut the valise, left half empty to make room for presents. It was Leclerc; Sharko picked up with a smile.

"Some cartons of cigarettes, Egyptian whiskey whose name I already don't remember, perfume burner for Kathia . . . So what else do you want now, a cardboard pyramid?"

"Have you got time to swing over to Gare du Nord?"

Sharko glanced at his watch: 6:30. Normally he'd be having dinner in a half hour, reading the paper or doing the crosswords, and he hated disrupting his routine.

"Depends."

"A colleague from Lille CID wants to meet you. She's already on the TGV."

"Is this a joke?"

"Supposedly it has some bearing on our case."

A pause.

"What kind of bearing?"

"A rather strange and unexpected kind. She called me, on my direct line, if you can believe the nerve of this one. Go find out if it's just a load of crap. You've already got something in common: you're both supposed to be on vacation."

"Some coincidence."

"Her train gets in at 7:31. She's blond, thirty-seven. She'll be wearing a blue tunic and tan pedal pushers. Anyway, she'll recognize you—she saw you on TV. You've become something of a star."

Sharko rubbed his temples.

"Thanks for nothing. Tell me about her."

"I'm sending you some background. Print it out and get moving."

Sharko had his electronic plane tickets in front of him.

"Aye, aye, Chief. At your service, Chief. By the way, two measly days in Cairo is a bit short, don't you think?"

"The locals don't want us there any longer than that. We have to follow protocol."

"Why are you sending *me*? Protocol isn't exactly my thing. And besides, what if I backslide? You remember that little green light in my brain?"

"It's when that little green light goes on that you're at your best. Your illness does some funny things to your head, a kind of stew that lets you grasp things nobody else can sense."

"If you wouldn't mind saying that to the big boss, he might treat me a little better."

"The less we tell him, the better off you are. By the way: Auld Stag."

"What?"

"The Egyptian whiskey—it's called Auld Stag. Write it down, for goodness' sake. For Kathia, find the most expensive perfume burner you can. I want to give her something nice."

"How's she doing? It's been a while since I've been to see her. I hope she doesn't hold it against me too much and that—"

"And don't forget the bug spray, or you'll really be sorry."

He hung up sharply, as if to cut the conversation short.

Fifteen minutes later, Sharko settled into the commuter train at Bourg-la-Reine, printed sheets on his knees. He pored over the brief report his boss had sent. Lucie Henebelle . . . Single, two daughters, father died from lung cancer when she was ten, mother a homemaker. Police sergeant in Dunkirk in the early 2000s. Assigned a desk job, she'd found herself caught up in a sordid case, the "death chamber," which had shaken the northern part of the country. Sharko was all too familiar with the hierarchic barriers back then between the rank of sergeant and that of detective. How had a simple paper-pusher managed to become the lead on such an investigation, which involved psychopaths and rituals? What inner forces had driven this mother of two to the *other side*?

After that, she'd been transferred to Criminal Investigations in Lille, with a rank of lieutenant. Nice promotion. She'd opted for the big city, where she'd have many more opportunities to come face-to-face with the worst. Spotless record so far. A driven, punctilious woman, according to her supervisors, but with an increasing tendency to go off the rails. Rushing in without backup, frequent shouting matches with the brass, and a worrisome habit of zeroing in on violent cases, especially murders. Kashmareck, her superior officer, described her as "encyclopedic, possessed, a good psychologist in the field, but sometimes out of control." Sharko dug deeper into the file. It was like reading his own story. In 2006, she had apparently taken a tumble: an intense manhunt to the far end of Brittany that in the end had put her on medical leave for three weeks. The official reason was "overwork." In cop speak, that meant depression.

Depression . . . And yet this woman seemed fairly solid, at least on paper. Why had she fallen so far down the hole? Depression grabs hold of you when an investigation kicks you in the teeth, when other people's pain suddenly becomes your own. What had happened to her that was so personal? Could it have anything to do with her two girls?

Sharko raised his eyes, a hand gripping his chin. She was only in her thirties, and the darkness already had such a hold that it was controlling her life. How old had *he* been when he'd started to tip over? Possibly well before that. And this was the result. Anyone watching could have guessed his situation in the blink of an eye: a guy bloated on meds who'd grow old alone, marked with the stamp of a fragmented life, encrusted along his wrinkles like a river of sorrow.

He stepped off the train at Gare du Nord at 7:20, less sweaty than usual. In July, the commuters were replaced by tourists, better behaved and much less sticky. The pulse of Paris beat more slowly.

Platform 9. Sharko waited among the pigeons, in a current of sullen air, arms crossed, in tan Bermudas, a yellow polo shirt, and docksiders. He hated station platforms, airports, anything that reminded him that every day people left each other. Behind him, parents were bringing their children to trains, packed for holiday camp. That kind of separation had its good side, promising the joy of reunion; but for Sharko, there would be no more reunions.

Suzanne . . . Eloise . . .

The mass of passengers surged like a single entity from the TGV arriving from Lille. Colors, a tempest of voices, and the noise of suitcases dragging along on wheels. Sharko craned his neck among the taxi drivers holding up signs with names on them. Making the obvious connection, he immediately spotted the right party. She came up with a smile. Small, slim, hair to her shoulders, she struck him as fragile, and without her damaged smile and that fatigue you see on certain cops, he might have taken her for just some broad coming to Paris to look for seasonal work.

"Inspector Sharko? Lucie Henebelle, Lille CID."

Their fingers met. Sharko noted that in their handshake, she looped her thumb on top. She wanted to control the situation or express a kind of spontaneous dominance. The inspector smiled back at her.

"Is the Nemo still on Rue des Solitaires in Old Lille?"

"I think it's up for sale. Are you from the north?"

"For sale? Damn . . . The best things always disappear. Yes, I come from the north, but that goes back a way. Let's go to the Terminus Nord—not very glamorous, but it's nearby."

They left the station and went to the large café, finding a sidewalk table in the shade. In front of them, the taxicabs lined up in an endless colored queue. It was as if the station were regurgitating the entire world: whites, Arabs, blacks, Asians were dispatched in an indistinguishable swarm. Lucie set down her backpack and ordered a Perrier; Sharko, a Weissbier with a slice of lemon. The young lieutenant was impressed by the fellow, especially his bearing: trim hair, eyes of an old vet, and a solid build. He gave off the ambiguity of a composite material, something indefinable. She tried to keep any of this from showing.

"They tell me you're an expert in criminal behavior. It must be fascinating."

"Let's cut to the chase, Lieutenant—it's getting late. What have you got for me?"

The guy was direct as a boxer's fist. Lucie didn't know who she was dealing with, but she knew he'd never give without getting something in return. That's how everyone worked in this profession: you scratch my back, I scratch yours. So she took her story from the top. The death of the Belgian collector, the discovery of the film, the violent, pornographic images buried in it, the fellow in the Fiat who seemed to be hunting for the same film. Sharko betrayed not a hint of emotion. He was the kind of guy who must have seen it all in his career, withdrawn behind his thick shell. Lucie didn't forget to tell him about the mysterious phone call to Canada that afternoon. She jabbed her finger on the table as the waiter brought their drinks.

"I went online and watched all the newscasts from that week. Monday morning, the builders find the five bodies, and that evening it's the lead story on the news. They talk about several bodies found buried with their skulls open."

She pulled a memo book from her backpack. Sharko noted her attention to detail, and the dangerous passion she harbored. A cop's eyes should never shine, and hers gleamed way too much when she talked about her case.

"I wrote it down: that Monday night, the report on the corpses started at 8:03 and ended at 8:05. At 8:08, old Szpilman placed a call to Canada. I got the length of the call from his phone log: eleven minutes, which means he hung up at 8:19. At around 8:25, he died trying to get hold of that film."

"Were you able to check Szpilman's other calls?"

"I haven't yet put my unit on the case. It would have taken forever to explain it all. The most urgent thing was to meet you first."

"Why's that?"

Lucie put her cell phone down in front of her.

"Because the mysterious caller is supposed to ring back in less than fifteen minutes, and if I don't have something meaty for him by then, that'll be it."

"You could have gotten info from headquarters over the phone. But you wanted to see a real one, right?"

"A real what?"

"A real profiler. Somebody who's been there."

Lucie shrugged. "I'd love to flatter your ego, Inspector, but that has nothing to do with it. I've told you what I know. Now it's your turn."

She was a straight shooter, with no tricks. Sharko liked the unspoken contest she was proposing. Still, he had to needle her a bit.

"No, seriously, you think I'm going to just hand over confidential information to some stranger from the land of the caribous? Shall we put up notices at the bus stops too, while we're at it?"

Lucie nervously emptied her Perrier into a glass. *Skinned alive*, thought Sharko.

"Listen, Inspector. I've spent my day on the road and I pissed away almost a hundred euros in train tickets to come drink a Perrier. A friend of mine is locked away in a mental hospital because of this nonsense. I'm hot, I'm tired, I'm supposed to be on vacation, and to top it off, my daughter is very ill. So with all due respect, spare me your lousy jokes."

Sharko bit into his lemon slice, then licked his fingers.

"We've all got our little woes. Some time ago I had to stay in a hotel without a bathtub. Last year, I think it was . . . Yes, last year. Now *that* was a real problem."

Lucie couldn't believe her ears. A round-trip from Lille to Paris just to listen to this shit?

"So what am I supposed to do? Just get up and go home?"

"The brass has been briefed on this case of yours, at least?"

"I just told you no."

Good lord, she was just like him. Sharko tried to get a bead on her.

"You're here because you feel life has overtaken you. In your head, pictures of corpses have replaced the photos of your children, am I right? Turn back, or you'll end up like me. Alone amid a population that's slowly wasting away."

What tragedies had sucked him in and stirred up so many shadows? Lucie recalled the pictures on the news when she'd first seen him, at the pipeline construction site. And that horrible impression he'd left her with: that of a man at the edge of a cliff.

"I'd like to feel sorry for you, but I can't. Pity isn't my strong suit."

"I'm finding your tone a bit blunt. Have you forgotten you're talking to a chief inspector, Lieutenant?"

"I'm sorry if I—"

She didn't have time to finish. Her telephone started ringing. Lucie glanced at her watch—the man was a bit early. She snatched up the cell apprehensively. A number with area code 514. She gave Sharko a somber look.

"It's him. What do I do?"

Sharko held out his hand. Lucie clenched her teeth and slapped the phone into his palm. She swung over to his side to listen in on the conversation. The inspector answered the phone without speaking. The voice at the other end of the line demanded abruptly: "Do you have the information?"

"I'm the profiler you might have seen on TV. The guy with the shirt that should have been green and who'd had it up to here with reporters and the heat. So, about the information, yeah, I've got it."

Lucie and Sharko exchanged a tense glance.

"Prove it."

"And this I do how? You want me to take a photo of myself and mail it to you? Let's quit playing hide-and-seek. The lady cop you talked to on the phone is with me. The poor thing pissed away a hundred euros in train fare because of you. Now tell us what you know."

"You first. This is your last chance, or believe me, I'll hang up."

Lucie tapped on Sharko's shoulder, urging him to accept and soften his tone. The inspector acquiesced, taking care not to reveal too much.

"We discovered five male individuals. Young adults."

"That much I saw on the Net. You're not telling me anything."

"One of them was Asian."

"When were they killed?"

"Between six months and a year ago. Now you. Why are you so interested in this case?"

There was a palpable tension in the crackling of voices that passed from ear to ear.

"Because I've been investigating this for two years."

Two years . . . Who was he? A cop? A private detective? And what was he investigating?

"Two years? The corpses were only dug up three days ago, and at worst they've been dead for no more than a year. How can you have been investigating for two?"

"Tell me about the bodies. The skulls, for instance."

Lucie didn't miss a word. Sharko decided to let out a bit more line: negotiations often required concessions.

"The skulls had been sawed off, very cleanly, with a surgical tool. Someone had removed their eyes, as well as . . ."

". . . their brains."

He knew. Some guy nearly four thousand miles away knew what was going on. Lucie made the connection with the film: the stolen eyes, the iris-shaped scarring. She murmured something to Sharko. He nodded and spoke into the phone:

"What's the connection between the bodies in Normandy and Szpilman's film?"

"The children and the rabbits."

Lucie strained to remember. She shook her head.

"What children, what rabbits?" asked Sharko. "What do they mean?"

"They're the key, the start of the whole thing. And you know it."

"The start of what, for Christ's sake?"

"What else about the bodies? Any chance of identifying them?"

"No. The killer eliminated any possibility of identification. Hands cut off, teeth pulled. One of the bodies, better preserved than the others, had large areas of skin missing from his arms and thighs, which he'd torn off himself."

"Do you have any leads?"

Sharko decided to play it coy.

"You'll have to ask my colleagues. I'm officially on leave. And I'm about to head off for a little ten-day trip to Egypt, near Cairo."

Lucie threw up her arms, furious. Sharko gave her a wink.

"Cairo . . . So then, you . . . No, it couldn't have gone so fast. You . . . you're one of them!"

He hung up. Sharko crushed his mouth against the speaker.

"Hello! Hello!"

A horrible silence. Lucie was virtually glued to his shoulder. Sharko smelled her perfume, felt the dampness of her skin, and couldn't bring himself to push her away.

It was over. Sharko put the phone back on the table. Lucie stood up, fit to be tied.

"I don't believe it! Jesus, Inspector! Holidays in Cairo! What are we going to do now?"

The inspector jotted the caller's number on a corner of his napkin and put it in his pocket.

"We?"

"You, me. Are we playing it solo, or do we eat from the same plate?"

"A chief inspector never eats from the same plate as a lieutenant."

"Please, Inspector."

Sharko took a gulp of his beer. Something cool, to clear his mind. The day had been particularly freighted with emotion.

"Okay. You drop the film restorer and get the reel to the lab. You bring your unit up to speed. Let them do a full workup. And have them send me a copy. Have them also get in touch with the Belgians, to check out this Szpilman. We absolutely have to find out who this Canadian was who just hung up on me."

Lucie nodded, feeling like she was crumbling under the weight of her responsibilities.

"And what about you?"

Sharko hesitated a moment, then began telling her about the telegram sent by a policeman named Mahmoud Abd el-Aal. He told her about the three girls, skulls sawed off just like here in France, and the mutilations. Lucie hung on every word; the case was burrowing deeper under her skin.

"He said, 'You're one of them,'" Sharko added. "That confirms that the killer I'm looking for isn't working alone. There's the one who cleanly saws off the skulls, and the butcher, the one who chops them up with a cleaver."

Sharko thought for a few seconds more, then handed her his business card. Lucie did the same. He pocketed it, finished his beer, and stood up.

"I need to go find some bug spray before I turn in. To say that I hate mosquitoes would be an understatement. I hate them more than anything in this world."

Lucie looked at Sharko's card, turned it over. It was completely blank.

"But . . ."

"When you find somebody once, you always find him again. Keep me posted."

He left the exact amount of the bill on the table and held out his hand. At the moment Lucie went to shake it, he blocked her thumb and slipped his own on top. Lucie clenched her jaw.

"Nicely done, Inspector. One to nothing."

"Everyone calls me Shark, not Inspector."

"Forgive me, but—"

"I know, you can't quite do it. In that case, let's stick with Inspector. For now."

He smiled, but Lucie noticed something deeply sad in his dark eyes. Then he turned away and headed off toward Boulevard de Magenta.

"Inspector Shark?"

"What?"

"In Egypt . . . be careful."

He nodded, crossed the station, walked through the entrance, and disappeared.

Alone. It was the only word that Lucie retained from their meeting.

A man alone, terribly alone. And wounded. Like her.

She looked at the blank card, which she held in her fingers; she smiled and wrote, diagonally across one side, "Franck Sharko, alias Shark." For a few seconds her fingers espoused the letters of that name with its harsh, Germanic consonance. Peculiar fellow. Slowly, she pronounced, stretching out each syllable, "Fran-ck Shar-ko." The Shark.

Then she slipped the card into her wallet and stood up in turn. The burning red sun was setting on the capital, ready to set it ablaze.

She headed for the Lille medical center, 125 miles away. The great divide, as always, between her work and family life. Her daughter needed her back.

15

It was after ten when Lucie slipped into Juliette's room. The antiseptic surroundings were becoming almost familiar. The nurses in the hallways, the carts loaded with diapers and bibs, the hum of neon . . . Her mother was at the console, neck leaning casually against the headrest of the large brown armchair.

Marie Henebelle hardly fit the stereotype of a grandmother, or even a mother. Short hair bristling with bleached blond locks, trendy clothes, fully conversant with the latest kids' gadgets: Wii, PlayStation, Nintendo DS. Moreover, she spent long hours playing *Big Brain Academy* on DS and *Call of Duty* on PlayStation, a game in which you had to kill as many enemies as possible. The contamination of the virtual world no longer had any age limit.

Marie greeted her daughter unsmilingly, stood up quickly, and grabbed her red leather handbag.

"Juliette threw up two more times this afternoon. Be prepared for a scolding from the doctor."

Lucie kissed her sleeping daughter, fragile as an ivory needle, and turned back toward her mother. On the screen, *Call of Duty* was on pause. Marie had just riddled three soldiers with a pump-action shotgun and seemed frankly annoyed.

"Scolding? How come?"

"The chocolate cookies you give her behind his back. You think they don't know? They see parents like you every day of the week. Parents who don't listen."

"She won't eat anything else! Seeing the face she makes at that disgusting mush makes my heart ache."

"Don't you get it? Her stomach won't stand even an ounce of fat. Why do you always insist on breaking the rules?"

Marie Henebelle's nerves were on edge. Spending her day shut indoors, the TV, the tears, those video games that hammered on your brain. This kind of hospital was nowhere near as restful as a three-star ocean spa in Saint-Malo.

"You're on vacation, you could spend a little time with your girls. But no—you ship one off to camp and you go running around Belgium and Paris while your other daughter pukes up her guts."

Lucie had had enough; the last few hours had already pushed her to her limit.

"Mom, I've got more time off coming in August and the three of us will go on vacation together. It's already planned—that's going to be our real family time."

Marie headed toward the door.

"All time is real family time, Lucie. I thought you had priorities in life, but I guess I was wrong. And now, I'm going home to bed. Because, if I'm not mistaken, I have to be back here in a few hours. Good thing Gramma Marie is here, right?"

She left. Lucie ran a hand over her face, exhausted, and turned off the television. The image of the pixilated soldier immediately vanished. Lucie thought of what Claude Poignet the restorer had said: violent imagery could strike anywhere, even in this children's room in the depths of a hospital. Wasn't there enough hostility on the streets, without having to bring it into the heart of a family's privacy?

Darkness fell, for once bringing peace.

In her pajamas, Lucie pulled the chair up to the bed and gently settled next to Juliette. Tomorrow morning she'd stop by the station to inform her superiors about this business with the film, even if no DA would launch an official investigation over a fifty-year-old movie. That Inspector Sharko was full of big ideas: send the reel to the lab, search Szpilman's place! As if it were all so easy. Where did they find him, that odd duck of a cop with his Bermuda shorts and docksiders? Curiously, Lucie couldn't shake the impression he'd left her with: of a guy who had more crimes under his belt than she'd see in a lifetime, but who didn't want to let anything show. What horrors were lurking in the back of his head? What had been his worst case? Had he already run across serial killers? How many?

She finally drifted off to sleep, her head filled with dark images, her hand resting in her child's.

Her awakening, yet again, was sudden: neons snapping on and tearing through her lids. In her half-sleep, Lucie didn't bother opening her eyes. It was probably a nurse, coming in for the nth time to make sure all was well. She was curling up tighter in her chair when a heavy voice yanked her from her slumbers once and for all.

"Get up, Henebelle."

Lucie grumbled softly. Could it be . . . ?

"Captain?"

Kashmareck was standing in front of her. Forty-six, stiff as a crowbar. The stark light chiseled his features and etched areas of shadow into his juglike face. He nodded toward the still-sleeping child, nestled under the blankets.

"How's she doing?"

Lucie covered herself with a sheet, embarrassed at being seen by him in such a scanty outfit. Too much intimacy.

"Oh, well . . . You didn't come here just to hear about her. What's going on?"

"What do you think? We've caught a murder. Something rather . . . unusual."

Lucie still couldn't figure out the reason for his visit. She sat up a bit and stuffed her feet into the rabbit slippers.

"What sort?"

"Bloody. This morning, a newspaper deliveryman calls us. He was in the habit of going to his customer's house every morning at six for a cup of coffee. Except this time, he finds the customer hanging from the kitchen chandelier, hands tied behind his back. And gutted, among other things . . ."

Lucie was talking to herself. She still couldn't understand what was going on.

"Forgive me, Captain, but . . . how does this relate to me? I'm on vacation and—"

"We found your business card in his mouth."

16

Police cars and the CSI van were still parked along Rue Gambetta when Lucie arrived. She had waited for her mother to show up, at nine o'clock, and taken a half hour to spend with Juliette, telling her that very soon they'd be going to the Vendée together, just the three of them, that they'd build hundreds of sand castles right near the ocean and eat ice cream cones until the sun went down.

But for the moment she had to let go the sand castles and ice cream cones. Make way for something sticky and twisted: the stench of a crime scene.

Kashmareck was already at the scene. At the hospital, Lucie had explained to him about the film, as she'd done with Inspector Sharko. But her meeting with the Paris cop the evening before, along with her call to Violent Crimes without clearing it upstairs, had made her boss livid. They'd settle this one later.

Lucie walked into Claude Poignet's living room, a lump in her throat. The room was lifeless, powerfully lit by the crime lab's halogens to leave no clue undetected. The man or men who had shown up at Ludovic's, then at Szpilman's, had finally managed to get hold of their film. According to the colleagues who were combing over the upper floor, there wasn't a trace of the mysterious reel. Lucie shook her head, lips pinched.

"He's dead because of me. I'm the one who threw him into the lion's den. He was living here in peace, and today . . ."

She knelt down and petted the cat, which came to rub against her leg.

"Who's going to take care of you now?"

Kashmareck stuck some photos in front of her face.

"What's done is done. We're not here to get all weepy."

With regret, Lucie didn't pick up the cat and instead turned her attention to the crime photos. Dozens of morbid rectangles, enough to make you vomit. Kashmareck was talking to her all the while, pointing to the photos.

"He was tied up, gagged, and hanged, there, from the chandelier hook, using filmstrips. I can't imagine somebody managing that all by himself. Given the ceiling height, I think there must have been at least two of them. One to lift him up and the other to attach him."

"Inspector Sharko advanced the hypothesis of two killers for the Gravenchon case. That might confirm that we're dealing with the same perps."

The captain pointed his finger toward the armchair.

"We found an empty film can on the cushions. The film they used to hang him with was *Good Day for a Hanging*, an old western. The victim had collected a hundred westerns in his closets upstairs. *Good Day for a Hanging*, can you imagine? You have to admit these killers have got some sense of humor."

Lucie had had only a cup of coffee and felt nauseated. Something the victim had said echoed in her mind: *I'll exit this world with a roll of film in my hands, believe you me.* He hadn't known how true that was. On top of which, her personal problems with her daughter and her mother weren't making her feel any better. Fortunately, the body had already been removed, which made the crime scene more impersonal, less difficult to stand.

The CSI team had cordoned off the areas of interest. You could walk around the house, but only via the swept paths. On the floor, under the chandelier, spread a pool of blood. Drops had fallen from everywhere like rain, spattering baseboards, tiles, feet of the table.

"Once they'd hanged him, they gutted him like a fish. Then they stuffed him with film, in place of his intestines. The ME was clear on that point: the victim was already dead by then, judging from the petechial hemorrhaging in his eyes. Death by strangulation. We still don't know if it was from the hanging."

The cat sidled up to the entry door and meowed to be let out. Lucie opened it for him, then looked at one of the photos. The old man, slit open from neck to pelvis. His entrails spread over the floor, having fallen more than three feet. His eyes were missing. Enucleation, once again. In their place, two little pieces of celluloid stuffed into the sockets, which made him look like he was wearing dark glasses.

"His eyes . . ."

"Gone."

Lucie absorbed the blow. One more point in common with Sharko's case and the bodies in Gravenchon. The importance of the eye, like in the film . . . It was becoming more and more likely that the same people who had buried the five vics in Normandy had also killed the film restorer. Kashmareck ran a hand through his close-cropped hair and sighed. He grabbed up a sealed bag and held it out to Lucie, who put on latex gloves. Inside the transparent bag were two nearly identical images, cut from the celluloid strip. Lucie knitted her brow and held the rectangles under the light.

"I can't make out much. It looks like . . . a close-up at ground level. Have we been able to identify the film these frames came from?"

"Not this time. We're sending them to our tech guys, who'll blow them up. We'll check with film scholars if we have to. They must mean some-thing."

Lucie stared again at the perforated rectangles.

"Sixteen millimeter. Just like the stolen film."

With his index finger, the captain pointed to the corpse's mouth.

"Your business card in his mouth doesn't bode well. We'll have to put a team on your building for a few days."

Lucie shook her head.

"There's no point. They're like a pack of wolves. They tracked us, me, Ludovic—they followed in our wake. My lock was sticking yesterday. They probably broke into my place the same way they did at Ludovic's or here."

The thought made her shiver. What might have happened if she'd been at home just then?

"Then they finally managed to get their hands on the film, and they wanted us to know. They marked their territory. Now that they've got what they wanted, they could just as easily vanish and fall back into oblivion."

She looked at the CSI technicians bustling about with their tweezers and powders.

"Did they pick up any traces or fingerprints?"

"Just the victim's. Nothing too definite for the moment. We don't have much hope for the neighbors; the street's got too many shops, with ridiculously few residents. Not many people around at night."

"What's the estimated time of death?"

"Between midnight and three a.m., from the preliminary findings. The lock was barely forced. The victim wasn't asleep yet, most likely, because his bed was still made."

In the living room, everything was still in order, no sign of a struggle. Lucie clearly imagined two beefy giants attacking that defenseless old man. They could easily have taken their film and left. But they'd wanted to "clean up" after themselves, leave no traces, no witnesses. And even grant themselves a little bonus, with their staging like something out of a David Fincher film. Killing someone in cold blood is not easy. You have to control your impulses, fight off everything that society, religion, and conscience forbid. Push away the very foundations of the human spirit. But these two had eliminated, enucleated, and eviscerated a man, even taking time to rummage through his westerns to create an effect. What sort of lunatic was hiding behind this crime? What motive had pushed them to go so far out of bounds?

Lucie went upstairs. The pictures in the stairwell hadn't moved. The cop avoided looking that woman in the eye, on the photos. Marilyn . . .

Some cops were poring through the rooms. Lucie glanced into the developing lab. On one shelf were some old cameras, reels, developing chemicals. She then went into the restoration studio, followed by her boss. The chair in front of the Moviola had been knocked over.

"Three in the morning, you said. What could Poignet have discovered to keep him working so late?"

She stood next to the viewer, careful not to penetrate into the area cordoned off by the yellow-and-black police tape. A tech continued to place numbered cards in front of objects and photograph them.

"The time counter on the viewer says zero. They must have rewound the film to take it with them. Poignet must have been studying it carefully."

Lucie turned to the back of the studio. Ripped-out cables, smashed scanner.

"Shit!"

"What?"

"Claude Poignet was going to digitize the film for me—I was still hoping to find it. But the laptop is gone."

She snapped her fingers.

"He might have had time to send me the file or a Web link where I could download it. I have to check my e-mail. Do you have Internet access on your phone?"

"It's the latest iPhone."

He handed her the device. Lucie sent up a silent prayer that Poignet had sent her the film. She wanted to prolong her journey with the mutilated woman, the girl on the swing; she wanted to go beyond what the images had shown. To dig deeper into the filmmaker's mind, understand his artistic madness, and maybe his very real madness. She logged in to her account. A few messages from the dating service, but nothing else. The sense of powerlessness washed over her.

"Nothing." She sighed, and in a pale voice said, "We have to reach out to the Belgians. We have to interrogate the son, make a composite sketch, search Szpilman's house from top to bottom, and find out where he first came across that film. Trace it to the source. For now, it's about the only way we're going to pick up the scent of that goddamn reel."

"We'll get on it."

Her eyes fell on the viewer, on the empty take-up reel, on the little basket with the business cards that the team would soon pack away.

"Unless . . ."

She turned toward the phone in back.

"I know what you're thinking," said Kashmareck. "We've already checked the LUDs for the victim's incoming and outgoing calls. We're following procedure. We'll follow up, contact all those people, but all in good time."

"Fine. Among them there's a film historian. We might still catch a break if he was able to identify the actress who gets her eye slit open. And also—" She took a card out of her pocket and handed it to her commanding officer. "This guy, Beckers. He specializes in the effect images have on the brain. Poignet was going to contact him."

Kashmareck pocketed the card.

"We'll get on it."

"This goddamn film. It's brought harm to everyone who's come in contact with it. Vlad Szpilman, Ludovic Sénéchal, and now Claude Poignet. We have to get it back."

"What about your vacation?"

"It's over. I'm going home to change and then I need to tell Ludovic Sénéchal his friend is dead. After that, I'm all yours. I want to find the pigs who did this to him."

17

When the front door of the A320 opened onto the tarmac of Cairo's international airport, Sharko felt a wave of fire slap his face. Suffocating air, laden with smoke and kerosene, gripped his throat. The steward had announced a ground temperature of ninety-seven degrees, which had provoked a huge groan from the passengers, tourists for the most part. From the second he set foot on Egyptian soil, the inspector knew he was going to loathe this country.

As arranged, Michael Lebrun was waiting at the end of the passageway. The man was imposing. Planted in light tan slacks and a colonial-style shirt, his face as square as the base of a pyramid, he meticulously sifted through the colored flux that scattered into all corners of the airport. Swarthy, tanned, and short haired, he could easily have been mistaken for a formidable customs officer. The two men exchanged a solid handshake—Sharko's thumb on top—then Lebrun pulled slightly back.

"I hope you had a good flight. Let me introduce you to Nahed Sayyed, one of the interpreters from the embassy. She'll accompany you on your travels around the city and help facilitate your dealings with the police."

Sharko greeted her. Her hands were soft and delicate, her nails cut short. Her long black hair, fine and buoyant, framed an enchanting pair of eyes. She must have been in her early thirties and didn't look anything like Sharko's image of Egyptian women: veiled, obedient, living in their husbands' shadows.

Along the endless air-conditioned hallways, they talked paperwork before anything else. Lebrun advised him to withdraw Egyptian pounds from the airport cash machines, because in town it would be hard to get small bills—tourism oblige. After a few preliminaries—including a customs officer's interrogation regarding the presence of a miniature locomotive and a jar of cocktail sauce in his luggage—the inspector could finally claim his belongings. As they talked, he began to understand the role Michael Lebrun played in this country. The French ambassador's right arm in matters of security in Egypt, he also served as technical adviser for the head of the Cairo police, a starred general. His specialty oriented him mainly toward matters of international terrorism. As for Nahed, she listened, a few paces behind, almost effaced.

The explosion of noise, the hubbub of the crowds, and the heat almost made the French cop fall over. He prayed that Eugenie would stay in her little corner, far in the back of his head. But given the circumstances and her lack of interest in architecture, it seemed obvious that she'd waste little time before coming out to make his life hell.

They climbed into a Mercedes Maybach, the largest model available in the country. Despite Inspector Sharko's insistence, Nahed had wished to sit in back. The powerful car left Heliopolis and dove into the Salah-Salem highway, which would propel them into the guts of Cairo. Ahead of them, the black mass of the center vibrated beneath a copper-colored sky.

On the way, Lebrun handed Sharko a bottle of water as he regained his strength by absorbing lungsful of air recycled by the car's cooling system.

"Your superior, Martin Leclerc, evidently doesn't want you to spend too much time, since your return flight is scheduled for tomorrow evening. He suggested you go to the police station today. Personally, I would have preferred to wait a bit, to give you time to rest up and enjoy the city, but—"

"Martin Leclerc doesn't know the meaning of the word 'rest.' So how do we do this?"

"I'll drop you off at your hotel, on Mohamed Farid Street, not far from headquarters. Nahed can wait in the lobby. She'll accompany you, in any case, anywhere you want to go. Take some time to freshen up. Then you head over; it'll be around four, I imagine. Police Chief Hassan Noureddine, the head of the brigade, will be there to receive you."

"At headquarters, will I have full access to the information?"

Michael Lebrun made a pinched face. Around them, the traffic became heavier. Crowded buses and taxis passed each other on all sides in a deafening cacophony.

"Right now we're in a delicate situation because of the pig slaughter. With the spread of swine flu, a bunch of deputies in the People's Assembly won approval to eradicate the animals. Since the end of April, I can't tell you how many outbreaks of violence there have been between the breeders and law enforcement. You're not coming at a very good time, and unfortunately my relations with the chief of police aren't the best in the world. He wields supreme authority over the governorate of Qasr el-Nil, which he rules with an iron fist. Noureddine is ex-Egyptian military, after all. But believe me, Nahed will help you as much as she can. Noureddine knows her extremely well."

Sharko glanced at the rearview mirror. Nahed sat rigid as a sphinx, framed between the leather headrests. When their eyes met, she turned away toward the window. In an instant, Sharko thought he understood what Lebrun meant by "extremely well."

Cairo finally revealed its burning heart, that pulsating muscle that Suzanne would so have loved to squeeze in her hands. Sharko ran a sad eye over the minarets with their ornate architecture bordering the universities, the gold-roofed mosques gleaming in the dust raised by the growling tires, the fields reserved for soccer clubs, hidden behind outsized fruit stalls. A fiery urban chaos reigned over it all, making Paris look like a mere village. Twenty million inhabitants who gave the impression of swarming in a pocket handkerchief. Hawkers of automobile parts jutted out into the crowded lanes, people crossed the roads every which way, sometimes assisted by "crossing helpers." Here, all work was indeed honorable. People pushed wheelbarrows full of bricks; worn-out mules dragged mountains of cloth and rubbed against old black Nasr 1300 taxicabs. On the dangerous sidewalks, veiled creatures ran and spoke on the phone at the same time, their cell phones wedged between their cheeks and their soiled hijabs.

"As you can see, the pedestrian is always right," said Nahed, smiling. "The pedestrian in the car, that is. You can't drive in Cairo without a horn. And if you don't have good ears, you should never cross the street."

It was the first time Sharko really heard her voice, a lovely blend of French and Eastern savors.

"And how do you live in such an environment day after day?"

"Oh, Cairo has many other faces! In its deepest arteries is where you'll hear its heart beat."

"The same arteries where they found the three murdered girls sixteen years ago?"

Sharko had always had a talent for casting a pall on the conversation; diplomacy wasn't his strong suit. He jerked his chin at Lebrun.

"Can you tell me about that case, since that's why I'm here?"

"My posting in Egypt only started four years ago. This job requires us to move around a lot. And I haven't yet seen the file. That's all I can say."

Sharko immediately understood that the other man didn't want to take sides. A diplomat.

"Will this Noureddine bring me to the crime scenes if need be?" the French cop insisted.

"There's one thing you have to understand, Chief Inspector. The country is moving forward, and the Egyptian authorities hate looking back. What are you hoping to find after all this time?"

"Would *you* do it, if it comes to that?"

Inspector Lebrun honked in turn, for no good reason. The guy was stressed out, but how could you help it in this whirlwind of noise and steel?

"It's out of the question for us to run our show without Noureddine's consent. For one thing, we don't like that type of solo op at the embassy, since the organization and the cases handled by the Egyptian police are under the seal of defense secrets. On top of which, you won't have enough time."

Sharko gave him a tight smile.

"Hence the reason for my quick round-trip, no doubt. And I suppose Nahed isn't by my side simply to interpret." He turned around. "Isn't that right, Nahed?"

"You have a vivid imagination, Chief Inspector," Lebrun answered in a dry voice.

"You have no idea."

Mohamed Farid Street. The Mercedes halted in front of the Happy City, a three-star hotel with a pink-and-black facade.

"Clean and stereotypical," said Lebrun, "given that most of the other hotels in the city were jammed. July in Cairo isn't exactly devoid of tourists."

"As long as there's a bathtub . . ."

The embassy inspector held out his business card.

"I'll expect you this evening at 7:30 at Maxim's restaurant, across Talaat Harb Square, not very far from here. You can listen to Édith Piaf songs and drink French wine. You can tell me all about your meeting with Noureddine, if you wouldn't mind."

Clearly they were leaving nothing to chance. Once he stepped outside, Sharko was engulfed by the sweltering heat and instantly drenched in sweat. The grumbling of motors, the strident shriek of horns, and the odors of exhaust were unbearable. With a sigh, he pulled his suitcase from the trunk. When he turned around, Eugenie was standing in front of the hotel, arms folded, still wearing the same outfit. She was pouting as she watched the cars battle it out on an avenue that rivaled the Champs-Élysées.

". . . spector?"

Lebrun was waiting, hand outstretched. Sharko regained his wits and shook it nervously. The embassy attaché quickly glanced toward the spot that the French cop had been staring at a few moments before. Nothing there.

"One final piece of advice. Noureddine is no softy. He's the kind of guy who thinks you're betraying Egypt the moment you disagree with him—you get my drift. So try not to offend him, and keep a low profile."

"Shouldn't be too hard to keep a low profile in the land of the hieroglyphs."

18

The central police station of the governorate of Qasr el-Nil looked like the poorly maintained palace of a deceased sheikh. Protected by tall black fences, its dark facade opened onto a garden containing a mix of palm trees and police vehicles, which seemed more like grocers' delivery vans. Only the large blue two-note revolving lights showed the difference. In front of a long staircase, six military guards—each with white short-sleeved shirt, kepi bearing the insignia of an eagle stamped with the national flag, Misr assault rifle across the shoulder—slapped the edge of their hands against their chests at the exit of a corpulent man endowed with three stars on his epaulettes.

Hassan Noureddine rested his sausagelike fingers on his hips and sniffed the gas-and-dust-laden air. Small black mustache, eyes dark as overripe dates beneath bushy eyebrows, pockmarked cheeks. He waited for Sharko and Nahed Sayyed to reach his level before greeting them. He politely shook the hand of his French counterpart, even gracing him with a languorous "Welcome." But he was more interested in the young lady, with whom he exchanged a few words in Arabic. The latter leaned forward with a smile, which was mostly forced. Then the man turned around, torso rigidly straight, and plunged back inside the building. Sharko and Nahed exchanged a look that needed no comment.

In the giant entrance foyer punctuated with functional offices, stairways guarded by police sunk toward the basement level. A tumult of voices rose, chants in Arabic, litanies repeated by a chorus of women. Sharko crushed a mosquito on his forearm—the fifth one, despite all the lotion he'd slathered on. Those critters dug in everywhere and seemed resistant to any form of protection.

"What are those women chanting?"

106

" 'Prison is powerless against ideas,' " Nahed murmured. "They're students. They're protesting the ban on allowing the Muslim Brotherhood to stand in the elections."

Sharko discovered a modern, well-equipped police force—computers, Internet, technical specialties like making composite sketches—but one that still seemed to work by ancient rules. Men and women, most of them veiled, waited in clusters in the foyer; office doors opened as if at the doctor's, and whoever was fastest got in first. The idea of waiting in line didn't seem to exist.

Sharko and his interpreter had to hand over their cell phones—to keep them from taking pictures or recording conversations—and were ushered into an office worthy of a gallery in the Palace of Versailles. Everything was outsized. Marble floors, Canopic and Minoan vases, figural tapestries, gilded bronzes. An immense fan spun on the ceiling, stirring the viscous air. Sharko smiled to himself. National heritage: everything here belonged to the state, and not to the conceited pig who sat heavily in his chair while sucking on a local cigar. While many Cairenes carried their excess weight gracefully, this fellow wasn't one of them.

The Egyptian tendered his open palms toward two chairs; in them sat Sharko and Nahed, who took out a small notebook and a pen. She was wearing a long khaki-colored dress and a matching tunic that slightly revealed her tanned neck. The police chief stared at her openly with his large, porcine eyes. Here, people liked to show that they appreciated women, unlike in the street, where a pejorative *tsss, tsss* hissed whenever some unveiled female crossed a Muslim's path. The chief rubbed his mustache, then lifted a sheet of paper in front of him. As he spoke, Nahed filled her notebook with stenographic symbols before translating:

"He says that you're a specialist in serial killers and complicated crimes. More than twenty years' service with the French police, in the Criminal Investigations Division. He says it's very impressive. He asks how things are in Paris."

"Paris is having trouble breathing. And how are things in Cairo?"

The chief of police crushed his Cleopatra between his teeth with a smile as he talked. Nahed picked up the conversation.

"Pasha Noureddine says that Cairo is trembling at the rate of killings that is shaking the Middle East. He says that Cairo is being strangled by Islamic networks, which are much more of a threat than the swine flu. He says they attacked the wrong target when they burned all those pigs in the municipal ditches."

Sharko recalled the distant black smoke that he'd glimpsed at the city outskirts: pigs being incinerated. He answered mechanically, but his words made him want to vomit:

"I agree with you."

Noureddine nodded, continued to blather on for a few minutes, then slid an old envelope toward the inspector.

"Concerning your case, he says everything is there, in front of you. The file from 1994. Nothing computerized; it's too old. He says you're lucky he was still able to find it."

"I suppose this is where I should thank him?"

Nahed translated that Sharko thanked him from the bottom of his heart.

"He says you can look at the file here and come back tomorrow if you wish. The doors are wide open to you."

Open, yes, but armored, with guards who'd be watching his slightest actions and movements. Sharko forced himself to thank the man with a movement of his chin, pulled off the rubber bands, and opened the file. Photos of the crime scene were crammed into a transparent envelope. There were also various reports and information sheets about several girls, including their identities—no doubt the victims. Dozens and dozens of pages written in Arabic.

"Please ask him to tell me about the case . . . Just the thought that you'll have to translate all this for me is making me feel queasy."

Nahed did so. Noureddine puffed languidly on his cigar and let out a cloud of smoke.

"He says it goes back a long way, and that he doesn't remember much about it. He's thinking."

Sharko felt like he was working his way through one of those old adventures of Tintin, *Cigars of the Pharaoh*, with fat Rastapopoulos sitting there before him. It bordered on the absurd.

"Still, young girls whose bodies have been thoroughly mutilated and their skulls sawed open tend to stick in the mind."

Nahed contented herself with making eyes at the inspector. The Egyptian officer began speaking slowly, leaving pauses for the young woman to translate.

"He remembers some of it now. He was already in charge of the brigade. He says they died one or two days apart. The first lived in the Shubra neighborhood, in the north part of the city. Another in a low-rent district near the Tora cement factories, next to the desert. And the third, near the 'trash cities' of Ezbet el-Nakhl, the quarter of the garbage collectors . . . He says the police were never able to establish a connection among the girls. They didn't know each other and attended different schools."

To Sharko, the names of these neighborhoods meant absolutely nothing. He shook his shirt up and down to dry it. Sweat was pouring down his back. The breeze felt good, but he was dying of thirst. Hospitality did not seem to be these policemen's strong suit.

"Any suspects? Any witnesses?"

The fat man shook his head and continued speaking. Nahed hesitated a moment before translating his words.

"Nothing very specific. We only know that the girls were killed in the evening, as they were returning home, and that they were found near where they were abducted. Several miles from their building each time. The banks of the Nile, the edge of the desert, the sugarcane fields. All these details are in the reports."

Not bad for a guy who could barely remember. Sharko thought for a moment. Isolated spots, where the killer could operate in peace. As for the MO, there were as many common points as there were differences with the bodies in Notre-Dame-de-Gravenchon.

"Could you give me a map of the city?"

"He says he'll get you one right away."

"Thank you. I'd like to study these reports this evening at my hotel. Would that be possible?"

"He says no. They must not leave the building. It's procedure. On the other hand, you can take notes, and they'll fax your office the documents that interest you—after being vetted, of course."

Sharko pushed the envelope a bit further. He wanted to test the limits of his investigative territory.

"Tomorrow I'd like to visit the places where the crimes and the abductions occurred. Can you assign someone to drive me to the spots?"

The man shrugged his fat, starred shoulders.

"He says his men are very busy. And that he doesn't quite understand why you want to go to places that certainly no longer exist. Cairo is expanding like . . . like a fungus."

"Fungus?"

"Those are his words. He's asking why you Westerners don't have any faith in them and feel the need to redo everything your way."

The Egyptian's voice remained casual, weighty, but was full of nuances. Those of domination, authority. Here they were at his place, on his turf.

"I'd just like to understand how these poor girls found themselves in the hands of the worst kind of killer. Feel how that predator managed to move around in this city. Every killer leaves a smell, even years later. The smell of vice and perversion. I want to get a whiff. I want to walk in the places where he killed."

Sharko's eyes bored darkly at Nahed, as if he were speaking directly to her. The young Egyptian translated his words. With a decisive gesture, Noureddine crushed his barely smoked cigar in an ashtray and stood up.

"He says he doesn't understand your job or your methods. The police in this country aren't here to sniff around like dogs, but to act, to eradicate vermin. He does not wish to revisit things buried in the past nor reopen wounds that Egypt would just as soon forget. Our country already has enough ills to face with terrorism, extremists, and drug traffic." She tilted her head toward the thin file. "Everything is in there; there's nothing more he can do for you. The case is way too old. There's an office next door. He says you're welcome to get up and go use it . . ."

Sharko did as told, but first he plunked the copy of the Interpol telegram in front of the police chief's nose. He spoke to Nahed, who repeated in Egyptian Arabic:

"A detective by the name of Mahmoud Abd el-Aal had sent this telegram. He's the one who was following the case at the time. Chief Inspector Sharko would like to speak with him."

Noureddine stiffened, pushed the paper out of his line of sight, and spat out a slew of indistinguishable words.

"I am translating word for word: 'That son of a dog Abd el-Aal is dead.'"

Sharko felt like he'd taken an uppercut in the belly.

"How?"

The Egyptian officer showed his teeth as he spoke. Above the tight collar of his shirt, the veins in his neck stood out.

"He says they found him burned to death at the end of a filthy alleyway in the Sayeda Zenab neighborhood, a few months after this affair. Some score settling among Islamic extremists. Pasha Noureddine says that when the police went to Abd el-Aal's apartment after the tragedy, they discovered the charter of the Islamic Action Party hidden among his papers, with certain passages circled in Abd el-Aal's own hand. He was a traitor. And in our country, traitors end up 'croaking' like dogs."

In the foyer, Noureddine firmly adjusted his beret. He leaned toward Nahed's ear, his hand on her shoulder. The young woman dropped her notebook. The police chief talked to her for a while, then headed off toward the stairs from which the chants could be heard.

"What did he say?" asked Sharko.

"That there's a map of the area in the office where we're going."

"He seemed to say much more than that."

She nervously brushed her hair behind her shoulders.

"That's just an impression."

She led him to a room containing the bare functional necessities. Desk, chairs, dry-erase board, basic office supplies. A closed window looked out on Qasr el-Nil Street. No computer. Sharko flipped a switch that was supposed to turn on the ceiling fan.

"It's not working. They palmed this office off on us on purpose."

"No, no, what are you imagining? It's just by chance."

"Sure, chance. There are no chances with these guys."

"Since you got here, I've felt you were a bit . . . distrustful of us, Inspector."

"That's just an impression."

The cop noticed the presence of a guard not far from the door. They were being watched. Clearly, orders had been circulated.

"Can I make copies?"

"No. Everything is password protected. Only the officers' computers have USB ports or CD drives. Nothing ever leaves here."

"Defense secrets, of course. Fine, we'll make do with what we've got."

Sharko opened the file. He plunged his hand into the sleeve of photos and hesitated before laying them out. He wasn't in top form, and Nahed seemed disturbed.

"Is everything okay?" he asked.

She nodded without answering. The inspector arranged the photos before him. The young woman forced herself to look and brought her hand to her mouth.

"This is monstrous."

"I wouldn't be here if it wasn't."

Dozens of photos depicted death in all its guises. Someone had surely photographed the bodies only a few hours after they'd been killed, but the heat had accelerated the damage. Sharko peeled away at the horror. The corpses had been dumped in the open, lacerated, mutilated with a knife, with no particular concern for staging the scene. The cop snatched up the identification sheets, studied the victims' photos that their families had supplied. Poor-quality photos, shot at school, in the street, at home. They showed the girls as lively, smiling, and young, with things in common—their age (fifteen or sixteen), eyes, and black hair. The inspector handed the sheets to Nahed and asked her to translate. At the same time, he contemplated the map of Cairo pinned to the wall, with all the street names in Arabic. The city was a monster of civilization, ripped open north to south by the Nile, bordered to the east and southeast by the Mokattam mountain range, gnawed to the south by a vast, sandy space littered with the ruins of the ancient city.

The cop planted further pushpins in the key spots the young woman indicated. The victims' bodies had been discovered roughly ten miles apart, on a circle peripheral to the city's main agglomeration. The garbage collectors' area to the northeast, riverbanks where the Nile widens to the northwest—just a few miles from the police station—and the white desert to the south. Schoolgirls from poor or modest families. Nahed knew Cairo like the back of her hand. She was able to pinpoint each girl's school and home neighborhood. Sharko was interested in the incredible amount of space occupied by the Tora cement factories, the largest in the world, near which one of the victims had lived.

"Earlier, you mentioned a makeshift neighborhood near the cement factories. What did you mean?"

"They're homestead communities made up of temporary shelters built by the poor, with little regard for city regulations and no access to public services. No drinkable water, no street cleaning, no trash collection. There are a lot of them in Egypt, and they're making the size of the city explode. The state provides about a hundred thousand lodgings a year, when they'd need seven times that much to absorb the population growth."

The cop took notes as she went on. Names of the girls, places where discovered, geographic locations . . .

"What are these, like slums?"

"Cairo's slums are worse. You have to see them to believe it. The second victim, Boussaina, lived near one of them."

The inspector looked closely again at the photos, their faces and distinguishing marks. He refused to believe it was just coincidence. The killer had intentionally moved from neighborhood to neighborhood. Poor girls, not especially pretty, who wouldn't draw attention. Why those three in particular? Was he used to being around poverty, perhaps for his work? Had he already met them? Something in common—they had to have something in common.

For the next hour, Nahed struggled to highlight the salient points of the autopsy report; it was technical and difficult work for a translator. She revealed that traces of ketamine, a powerful anesthetic, had been found in all three bodies. Estimated times of death showed that the attacks had taken place in the wee hours of the night. As for the actual cause of death, this was the most disturbing of all. The mutilations were due to knife wounds, but all were postmortem. It seemed the deaths themselves resulted from damage caused by the opening of the skulls and, apparently, from the removal of the brain and eyes.

In all likelihood, the skulls had been cut open while the girls were still alive, and the multiple stab wounds had been inflicted afterward.

Sharko mopped his brow with a handkerchief, while Nahed sank into silence, her eyes vacant. The policeman could easily imagine the scene. The killer had first kidnapped these girls after dark, anesthetized them, then taken them someplace out of the way to practice his horrors, armed with his instruments of mayhem: the medical saw, scalpels for enucleation, a broad-bladed knife for mutilation. He surely had a car; most likely he knew the city and had done some exploring. Why the posthumous mutilations? An irresistible need to dehumanize the bodies? To possess them? Could he be filled with such hatred that he could get it out only by an act of ultimate destruction?

In the heavy, stifling air of the office, the inspector labored to link the MO to the one used in France. Here, despite everything, there was a ritual, organization, and no particular effort to hide the bodies. In addition, the killer had opened his victims' skulls while they were alive. But in France, most of them had died of gunshot wounds, fired randomly, judging from the different impact sites of the projectiles. And they'd taken pains to render the corpses anonymous: hands severed, teeth extracted.

Was there really a link between them? What if he'd been mistaken all along? What if chance was finally having its say in all this? Sixteen years . . . sixteen long years . . .

And yet, Sharko still felt an impalpable connection, the same diabolical will to attain and harvest two of the human body's most precious organs: the brain and the eyes.

Why these three girls in Egypt?

Why the five men in France, including one Asian?

The cop guzzled down the glasses of water that Nahed regularly brought him and sank still deeper into the shadows, while Ra's emanations tortured his back. He was dripping with sweat. Outside was an inferno of sand, dust, and mosquitoes, and he already longed to be in his air-conditioned room, huddled under the netting.

Unfortunately, the rest of the paperwork was just fluff. None of it had been handled very thoroughly. A few scattered sheets, handwritten, stamped by the prosecutor, bearing the depositions of relatives or neighbors. Two of the girls were returning from work, and the third from a place where she often went to swap cloth for goat's milk. There was also the long list of seals—useless. In this country, they seemed to expedite murder cases the way they would the theft of a car radio in France.

And that was precisely what didn't ring true.

Sharko looked at Nahed.

"Tell me, have you seen the name Mahmoud Abd el-Aal anywhere in these reports? Have you noticed any notes signed by him, other than these few pages?"

Nahed quickly glanced through the handwritten pages and shook her head.

"No. But don't be too shocked by the flimsiness of these files. Here, they go for action over paperwork. Repression over reflection. Everything's biased, tainted by corruption. You can't imagine."

Sharko took out the copy of the Interpol telegram.

"See here, Interpol received this telegram more than three months after the bodies were discovered. Only a persistent and committed cop would have sent it. A cop with integrity, values, who wanted to see this thing through to the end."

Sharko picked up the pages and let them fall in front of him.

"And they want me to believe there's no more than this? Just formalities? Not a single personal note? Not even a copy of the telegram? Where did the rest go? Inquiries at pharmacies or hospitals about the ketamine, for instance?"

Nahed contented herself with shrugging her shoulders. Her face was serious. Sharko shook his head, one hand on his brow.

"And you know what's most disturbing of all? It's that, strangely enough, Mahmoud Abd el-Aal is dead."

The young woman turned away and walked toward the glass door. She glanced into the hall. The guard hadn't moved.

"I'm not sure what to tell you, Inspector. I'm here simply to translate, and—"

"I've noticed how much Noureddine was harassing you, and you were trying to avoid him every way possible without succeeding. What is it?

An exchange of services? Or is it a custom in your country that you have to agree to whatever that tub of lard says?"

"It's nothing like that."

"I saw you trembling several times when looking at those photos, or at the descriptions of the case. You were once the same age as those girls when they died. You were in school, just like them."

Nahed pursed her lips. Her hands squeezed each other tightly. With an evasive gaze, she glanced at her watch.

"It's nearly time for our meeting with Michael Lebrun, and—"

"And I'm not going. I can drink French wine any day of the week back in France."

"You might offend him."

He picked up a photo of one of the smiling girls and pushed it toward Nahed.

"I couldn't care less about diplomacy and canapés. You don't think these girls deserve our attention?"

A weighty silence. Nahed was supremely beautiful, and Sharko knew enough not to trust a woman solely because she was beautiful. But beyond this he sensed a hurt, an open wound that sometimes clouded her jade-colored eyes.

"Very well. What can I do for you, Inspector?"

Sharko approached the blinds in turn and lowered his voice.

"None of the cops in this station will talk to me. Lebrun's hands are tied by the embassy. Find me Abd el-Aal's address. He must have a widow, maybe children or brothers. I want to talk to them."

After a long silence, Nahed gave in.

"I'll try, but especially—"

"Mum's the word, you can count on me. When I get my phone back, I'll call Lebrun and tell him I'm very sorry but I'm not feeling well. The heat, jet lag . . . I'll tell him I'm coming back here tomorrow, just to wrap things up. Your job is to meet me at the hotel at eight, hopefully with the address."

She hesitated.

"No, not at the hotel. Take a taxi and"—she jotted a few words onto a slip of paper and handed it to him—"give him this paper. He'll know where to take you."

"Where is it?"

"In front of the Church of Saint Barbara."

"Saint Barbara? That's not a very Muslim name."

"The church is in the Coptic district of Old Cairo, in the southern part of the city. The name belonged to a young girl who was martyred for attempting to convert her father to Christianity."

19

Freyrat, in the heart of the Lille medical area, late afternoon. The crucible of psychiatry. A two-story concrete monster, the meeting place of every mental deviance: schizophrenia, paranoia, trauma, psychosis. Lucie entered the austere structure, asking at the reception for Ludovic Sénéchal's room. She wanted to be the one to tell him about the death of his old friend Claude Poignet. She was directed to the Denecker Wing on the second floor.

The diminutive room would have depressed a clown. The out-of-reach television was on. Ludovic was stretched out on his mattress, hands behind his head. He slowly turned his face toward his visitor and smiled.

"Lucie . . ."

Surprised, she came forward.

"You can see?"

"I can make out shapes and colors. People not wearing lab coats are most likely visitors. What other woman would come visit me?"

"I'm happy it's getting better."

"Dr. Martin says my sight will return gradually. At this point it's just a matter of two or three days."

"How did they do that?"

"Hypnosis. They understood what wasn't working. Or more to the point, they understood without understanding."

Lucie felt ill at ease. She hated playing the painful role of death's messenger. Meeting the eyes of a victim's loved ones was probably the hardest part of her job. She did everything she could to put off the announcement. Ludovic was a sensitive soul and not in the best shape right now.

"Tell me about it."

The man sat up. His pupils had regained a reassuring mobility.

"The psychiatrist explained it all to me. He put me under hypnosis, then asked me to tell him what had happened in the hours and minutes before I went blind. So I related how my day had been spent. What I bought from the old collector in Liège, the anonymous reel discovered in the attic. Being alone in my mini-cinema, watching movies all night long. Then the images from the anonymous short, as they appear. The slit eye, the shots of the little girl on the swing. And it was there, strangely, that I started telling him about my father, just out of the blue. The women he'd bring back to the house when I was a kid, a few years after my mother's death."

"You never breathed a word of this to me."

A small, dry laugh floated across the room.

"Look who's talking! We spent weeks chatting online, seven months flirting, and I know practically nothing about your private life. Sure, I know you're a cop and that you have two daughters who I got along with, but other than that, what is there?"

"That's not what we're talking about."

He sighed, looking sad.

"With you, it's never what we're talking about. Well, anyway . . . It came up suddenly, under hypnosis. The naked women I'd sometimes see coming out of my father's room. All that . . . breathing I'd hear through the walls. I wasn't even ten yet. The shrink understood that the block might have come from there. Something, probably some image, had brought those memories back up and triggered my hysterical blindness."

Lucie suspected it was related to the subliminal images. Without the censorship of the conscious mind, they had slammed against the deepest recesses of Ludovic's psyche and kicked up a mess.

"But that's not what drove me blind, because I could still describe what happened next in the film. Talk about the little girl. When she ate, or slept. When she brushed the camera away with her hand, as if she was annoyed. Then, suddenly, the psychiatrist told me I had screamed under hypnosis and he'd had to wake me. He managed to calm me down and asked what had happened. So then I started telling him about the episode with the rabbit."

Lucie immediately straightened up. The strange Quebecer, on the phone, had also mentioned rabbits. He had revealed that the whole thing started with children and rabbits.

"What rabbit?"

Ludovic tensed and pulled his knees against his chest.

"I must have been eight or nine. One day, my father brought me into his workshop, where he kept all his tools. There was a rabbit that had taken shelter in the back of an old U-bend conduit. A large wild rabbit. I was small enough to crawl through the conduit and catch it, but not my father. So he ordered me to do it. And I did. I crawled on all fours and forced the animal to leave its hiding place. My father grabbed it by the ears. The rabbit was bleeding from its hind paws—it was struggling to get free. I cried out for him to let it go, but my father was beside himself. He took an ax and . . ."

His two hands flew to his face, as if he'd just received a spurt of blood.

"That scene . . . Until the hypnosis, I'd forgotten it, Lucie. It had completely gone out of my mind."

"More like it had been buried way deep. So deep that nothing had been able to bring it back to the surface. In the anonymous film, did you see any rabbits?"

"No, no . . ."

The cop still didn't understand. Poignet had pored through every frame without noticing anything. So then what?

Clumsily, Ludovic picked up his bottle of water and took a few swallows.

"You saw the film. Tell me what you found. Were you able to show it to my friend the restorer?"

Lucie looked him in the eyes and blurted out, "Claude Poignet is dead."

Ludovic's fists clenched on the sheets. A long silence.

"How?"

"He was murdered. The ones who did it came looking for the film."

Ludovic straightened up and brushed his hair back, heavily. He was on the verge of tears.

"Not him. Not Claude. He was just an old man who didn't bother anybody."

Feeling his way, Ludovic walked toward the Plexiglas window, his eyes vacant. Lucie could see from the reflection that he was crying.

She needed to keep herself from pity, from feeling. "I promise you we'll find the people who did this. We're going to find out what happened."

She stayed with him for some time, explaining the early stages of their investigation. She even told him about the unknown person who had rifled through his film collection. Ludovic should know the whole truth.

"I feel so alone, Lucie . . ."

"The psychiatrists are here to help you."

"I don't give a damn about the psychiatrists."

He sighed.

"Why didn't it work out with us?"

"It wasn't your fault. It's never really worked out with anyone for me."

"Why not?"

"Because sooner or later, the person always starts asking me why."

She felt uneasy; the heat was getting on her nerves. And that chemical stench . . .

"The man I spend the rest of my life with will have to take me as I am, here and now. And not keep trying to bring up the past. Questioning me about this or that. I'm a cop because I'm a cop—that's the way it is, you just have to deal. The past is dead and buried, okay?"

Ludovic shrugged.

"Listen, I should let you go. I'm sure you've got things to do."

"I'll visit again."

"Sure, you'll visit again."

He leaned his forehead against the window. Sadly, Lucie went out and sucked in a large breath of fresh air. She was mad at herself for having been so short with him, with men in general. But those were the stigmata of her past sufferings. The first man she had truly loved had abandoned her all too abruptly, her and her girls.

In the parking lot, watching visitors come and go, she thought it might not be a bad idea to put a watch on Ludovic's room—and maybe Juliette's as well. She'd talk to her boss about it.

She returned to Criminal Investigations headquarters late that afternoon, on Boulevard de la Liberté, a hundred yards or so from the center of Lille. Up there, information was being exchanged at a healthy clip between the Violent Crimes unit in Paris, CID in Rouen, and the Lille teams.

For the moment, they were using e-mail and phones. The various data would soon be integrated into computer files that all the officers could access. Cross-references would be noted; the info would circulate at its best. It seemed that every chance was on the side of the law.

Lucie walked into her captain's office. Kashmareck was talking with Lieutenant Madelin. The young hotshot, no more than twenty-five, face like a class valedictorian, had just finished going over Claude Poignet's autopsy. The triple fracture of the hyoid bone suggested strangulation, and the presence of lividity—an accumulation of blood on the pressure points between body and floor—on the left deltoid and hip proved that Poignet had been murdered while on his side: the killers had left him lying that way at least a half hour before hanging him.

Kashmareck emptied his coffee cup. He ran on caffeine the way others did on water.

"A half hour . . . The time it took to rewind the film and poke around a bit to stage their scene. Killers who kept their cool, didn't panic."

Lucie barged into their ruminations:

"So Poignet didn't die by hanging but by strangulation."

The captain picked up a photo of the studio and pointed to the floor in one corner of the room.

"Yes, right there. We found drops of blood. Probably a nosebleed caused by asphyxiation. What else did the autopsy show?"

Madelin skimmed through his notes.

"Knife to open his chest—whatever the kind of blade, it was sharp, that's for certain. According to the ME, the removal of the eye was very . . . professional. I'll read what it says: 'Circular opening of the transparent membrane that covers the eye, slicing of the oculomotor muscles, then of the optic nerve, and finally removal of the eyeball. Much like a surgical procedure.'"

The captain nodded in agreement.

"That fits perfectly with the data I'm starting to get from Rouen. The skulls of the five bodies, sawed open with professional skill . . . which supports the theory that it's the same killers. Go on."

"For the rest . . . it's technical, but nothing very revealing. Samples were sent to toxicology, just in case. But I doubt Poignet was drugged."

"Fine. We'll all get to read the report. We're expecting the international warrant from the judge—the request has been sent to the Belgian authorities to search Szpilman's place. It won't be our show over there—they're in charge, we just watch, but it's better than nothing . . . What else? Uh . . . We're checking the Canadian phone numbers you gave us, Henebelle, just to make sure we can't reach your anonymous tipster from Montreal."

He put his hands to his face and heaved a sigh, gazing at his notes in dry-erase marker on a not very white board. A labyrinth of arrows.

"Madelin, go over the calls Poignet made or received in the twenty-four hours before his death. Henebelle, you go next door. The lab made blow-ups of the pieces of film the victim had instead of eyes. Bring the info back here and see what else they have to say. Fingerprints, other clues . . . I'm going to reach out to the guys canvassing the neighborhood to see if they've got anything new. Tonight we'll throw it all into the hat and cross our fingers. For now, I need something concrete, something solid, before we have to start thinking."

20

The image Sharko had formed of Cairo changed like the shimmering water on the surface of the Nile. The taxi driver, an *osta bil-fitra*, or "born cabbie," who spoke a little French, had taken him via the city's narrow roads. The Egyptian populace lived outdoors, in a state of excitement and nonchalance. Every one of life's scenes was an excuse for communication. Butchers cut their meat on the sidewalk, women peeled vegetables in front of their houses, bread was sold in the street, right from the ground. Sharko felt like he was moving through a living tableau when, in the midst of the chaotic traffic, he was dazzled by the perfect movement of a cotton galabia, swaying to its owner's regal gait. He felt the breath of Islam in the overheated streets; the mosques were ablaze with beauty, and in their excess they aimed an eye at their single god. There is no other god than God.

Then Coptic Cairo appeared around him. There, young people wearing plain leather sandals asked for neither money nor pens, but offered you images of the Virgin Mary. There, the walls were redolent of ancient Rome, and the Bible seemed to peel open its parchment writings. Peaceful, ocher-colored alleyways, with only the crunch of sand brought in by the hot winds of the *hamsin*. In the middle of the most populous city in Africa, Sharko finally felt at peace. Alone in the world. He tapped into the city's great ambiguity.

He paid the driver—an amazing guy, brimming with funny stories— and called Leclerc to keep him abreast of his inquiries. In exchange, he learned about the death of the old film restorer and the theft of the reel. Things were hopping in France, but not the way he would have wished. The investigation was taking on apocalyptic proportions, bodies were piling up, the mystery was deepening.

He joined Nahed, who was waiting for him in front of Saint Barbara's.

The young woman was elegantly dressed in fine pleated garments of pastel tones, apparently linen. Her eyes seemed heavily made up, and a touch of very lightweight fabric spilled over her shoulders like a cape. Sharko walked up, motioning to the church.

"Is this the heart of your city that you mentioned in Lebrun's car?"

"Do you like it?"

"I'm surprised by it."

Nahed unveiled her magnificently even teeth. Sharko had to admit that any man would have loved to get lost with her in the maze of the capital. And this evening, he was one of them.

"Every neighborhood of Cairo is a quiet little town. A space with its own codes and traditions. I wanted you to discover this."

She joined her hands in front of her, shyly.

"My car is a bit farther on. I have what you asked for."

"Abd el-Aal's address?"

"Mahmoud lived alone, right next door to his brother, at the other end of Talaat Harb Street. The brother's name is Atef Abd el-Aal and he still lives at the same address."

"Talaat Harb . . . Wasn't that where Lebrun said we should meet?"

"Indeed. Talaat Harb is a street from the Belle Époque, full of history and nostalgia. Your counterpart surely wanted to make an occasion of it. I ran into him, after our session at the police station. He took your declination rather well."

"All the better. Thank you again."

They talked while walking past the Coptic cemetery. Nahed explained that her father, a journalist for *Le Caire*, had been crippled in one leg following a clash between Copts and Muslims in 1981. Her mother, a French-woman, had lived in Paris before leaving everything behind to come on a mission for the city's Dominicans. Her parents met; Nahed was born in a modest quarter and had never been outside her homeland. She'd been in French immersion programs to study the language at the university, taught by incompetent professors who spoke it even less than she did. She'd ended up at the French embassy, with the support of the newspaper's owner, a powerful Egyptian. Good position but small salary; she wasn't complaining. Here, a job—an *honest* job, she specified, stressing the word—didn't allow you to escape the deep-seated, tenacious poverty of Egypt, but it attenuated it and gave you the illusion.

She invited him to sit in an authentic old Peugeot 504, parked at the edge of Coptic Cairo, near the Amr mosque. They drove up the right bank of the Nile along the Corniche. Daylight was dwindling. The minarets of the distant mosques, the houseboats and *awamas* lit up. People were walking in family groups and buying yellow beans with lemon. Sharko could feel the power of the river, and the people's need to honor it.

They talked some more. When Nahed asked him about his wife, Sharko leaned the arch of his eyebrow against the window, his gaze fixed on the peaceful currents, and confided simply that he missed his wife and daughter and that he'd never see them again, except in his dreams. He didn't open his mouth after that. What for? What could he tell her? That there wasn't a single night when their absence didn't grip him so hard it woke him from his sleep, barely able to breathe? That his job had destroyed the lives of those he held dearest and was dragging him slowly but surely toward the abyss of a joyless old age? No, he had nothing to tell. Not here, and not now. Not with her.

After about ten minutes, they reached Talaat Harb. Clothing stores as far as you could see, bars, movie houses with French names, old buildings with Haussmannian facades and columns, windows decorated with Grecian-style statues—a reminder that the Egyptian elite, at the turn of the twentieth century, wanted to make the center of Cairo a European district. It almost worked. Pedestrians strolled about in scattered hordes—Americans, French, Italians. Nahed found a parking spot in a neighboring street, and a moment later she was giving the building's concierge some baksheesh, just because he'd opened the door for her. The *baou ab* with the henna-dyed beard, miserable in his tattered espadrilles, acted as porter, car washer, and errand runner, in stark contrast with the classy interior of the place. A rich person's building, apparently, radiating grandeur.

Once alone with Sharko in the elevator, the young woman covered her head and veiled her face. She transformed herself: enigmatic and suddenly full of secrets. All he could see were her eyes, magnificent jewel cases, while her mouth, divined through the transparency of the fabric, said in a pure voice:

"It would be silly if Atef Abd el-Aal refused to talk because of some religious scruple."

Sharko was charmed, almost entranced.

"How do you know he's Muslim?"

"It's more likely he is than not."

"What do you know about him?"

"The embassy files didn't reveal much. He was a vendor, and today he owns two factories that make custom shirts, a successful business that started taking off one year after his brother's death. He sells the clothes wholesale to the shops in Alexandria. He and his late brother were originally from Upper Egypt. Poor family, from the country. They came to Cairo when they were teenagers, with their uncle."

She knocked on a door; another door opened onto the wizened face of an old woman. Nahed began talking with her before turning to the inspector.

"His neighbor says he's on the terrace; he always has tea up there at this hour, before evening prayer. We'll recognize him because he'll be reading *al-Ahram*, the independent newspaper."

When Sharko arrived on the terrace, he couldn't believe his eyes. People lived on the roof of the building, inside and out of minuscule tin bungalows. Multicolored lamps hanging from cables bobbed like felucca sails. People were sitting in armchairs or lying on mattresses, at sky level. Lit televisions pierced the falling night on all sides. It was like being in a kind of luminous anthill in open air, teeming and precarious. Nahed leaned in toward his ear.

"Before, the top echelons of society lived in these buildings—landowners, pashas, ministers. These bungalows were used for storing foodstuffs, doing laundry, or housing the dogs. After the revolution of 1952, everything changed. Today, the *sufragi*, the former domestics of that time, have taken over the lodgings in the main building and rent out these bungalows to the poor."

It was hard to believe, but these people really lived in sheds of less than five square yards, in the middle of the busiest shopping street in Cairo. Poverty wasn't in the gutter or the subway like in Paris, but up in the air, on the rooftops. Nahed pointed a finger toward the back of the terrace.

"There he is."

Suspicious gazes turned in their direction. Reclining men with blood-shot eyes prepared "coal," a pebble of opium that they heated before slipping it under their tongue, while others smoked their *mu'assel* mixed with hashish in old *chichas*. Children played dominos, others studied, women cooked. Sharko and Nahed approached Atef Abd el-Aal, who sat on a straw chair looking out over Talaat Harb. He was wearing a nicely cut suit and shined shoes. Slicked-down hair, about forty-five. His steaming cup of tea sat on the white stone parapet. He did not get up to greet them and uttered two abrupt words, which Sharko didn't understand. At that, Nahed replied with a long tirade in Arabic, explaining the situation. She said that the man with her was an inspector with the French police, who wanted to ask him questions regarding his brother and an old criminal case that had similarities with an ongoing investigation.

Ataf carefully folded his newspaper on his knees, looked Nahed over from head to foot, and slowly began picking at an amber rosary. Once more, the translator acted as intermediary between the two men.

"He doesn't wish to speak anymore about his brother."

"Tell him that just before he died, Mahmoud was working on a murder case. Three girls, killed four months before his own death. Ask him if he knew about it."

Atef kept silent a moment before speaking.

"He wants to see your police ID."

Sharko held it out. Atef stared at it carefully and ran his index finger over the colors of the French flag before handing it back to the inspector. Then he spoke again.

"He says his brother was very secretive. He never talked about his investigations. That's why Atef never suspected him of belonging to extremist networks."

Sharko let his eyes wander toward the city lights. The air was finally cleansed, the Egyptians returned to their streets, their roots, the calm of their mosques and churches.

"Did he sometimes take his case files with him? You lived right next door to each other—did he ever do any work at home?"

"He says no."

"Do you know Hassan Noureddine? Has he already been to see you?"

"No again . . . Given the way he's answering, I don't believe he knows anything."

Sharko took the photo of one of the victims from his pocket and put it down in front of the Egyptian. Nahed gave him an outraged glance, realizing he must have pocketed it at the station house while she was out getting him water.

"What about her?" said the cop. "She doesn't mean anything to you either? Don't tell me your brother never showed you her face."

Atef turned his honey-colored eyes aside, his lips tight. He leapt up and shoved the policeman in the chest.

"*Izhab mine houna! Izhab mine houna! Sawf attacilou bil chourta!*"

He glared at Nahed, brandishing his cell phone. Some residents of the terrace turned toward them.

"He's ordering us to leave or he'll call the police. Let it go—we won't get anything out of him."

The cop hesitated, not wanting to quit now. The Arab's violent reaction might mean he was hiding something. Atef came forward and shoved him again, just as aggressively.

"*Izhab mine houna!*"

Sharko felt like smashing his face in, but the men on the terrace had stood up and were coming menacingly close, fine-boned Kabyles with nervous features. Things were heating up. Sharko, who had turned toward his possible attackers, suddenly felt a hand in the back pocket of his trousers. His eyes met Atef's. In a fraction of a second, he understood that the man had shoved something into his pocket and was asking him to keep quiet about it.

Sharko took Nahed by the hand.

"Come on, let's get out of here."

They had trouble clearing a path. It was a tangle of elbows and shoulders, and darkening, opium-spiraled eyes. The sound of *tsss, tsss* hissed from all sides. They flew down the stairs. Nahed was furious.

"You shouldn't have stolen that photo! How many others do you have?"

"A few."

"You can be sure Noureddine will spot it and notify the embassy. What were you thinking?"

"Come on, let's move."

Nahed rushed ahead in front of him. Sharko dug into his pocket and found a scrap of paper. Still moving, he quietly unfolded the piece of newsprint and read a note scribbled in French:

Cairo Bar, Tewfikieh, one hour. Avoid being seen. She's watching you.

He immediately pocketed the note and looked at Nahed, full of regret. In her delicate garments, she swayed marvelously as she descended the stairs. And she was betraying him. When they reached the street and began walking, the young woman removed her veil, which she abandoned on her shoulders. Sharko stared at her.

"It's very strange. Without your veil, you have a completely different face. The mysterious, ambiguous creature suddenly regains the clear complexion of the modern woman. How many personalities are you hiding, Nahed?"

"Just one, Inspector."

She seemed to be blushing, struggled to find her words.

"And now what do we do?"

Sharko could now see her game more and more clearly. Since reading Atef's note, everything fell into place. The choice of Nahed as his helper despite the risks with her supervisor. The whereabouts and details about Mahmoud Abd el-Aal, which she'd managed to obtain. They were feeding him scraps while keeping an eye on him. For now, he decided to play it cool; he'd have plenty of time to question her later.

"I think I'm going to go back to the hotel, take a shower, and hit the hay. It's been a very long day since I woke up in France this morning."

"You haven't even eaten yet. Let me invite you to a charming little restaurant in Mohandessin, on the banks of the Nile. They serve excellent fish and Swiss wine—rather than French."

She wanted to keep him as long as possible. Sharko began thinking she'd probably mistranslated what was said on the terrace, or even at the station house. Like Hassan Noureddine, she controlled the territory, and there was absolutely nothing he could do. Who was behind all this? The police? The embassy? What kind of hornet's nest had he wandered into?

"I'd love to, but I'm really not hungry. Thank you all the same . . . Too hot, too exhausted, and too many mosquitoes."

He took out a map they'd given him at the hotel.

"I can find my way back; it's just over there. What do you say we meet tomorrow morning at ten in front of the station house? There's really no rush anymore. The doors are closing one after another, and I'm already getting used to the idea that I'll go back empty-handed. It's not my case, anyway."

She lowered her gaze, looking disappointed. Sharko had an urge to rip her tongue out. Quite the actress.

"All right," she conceded. "Until tomorrow, then."

Before he could leave, she added:

"That fat pig Noureddine never laid a hand on my body. And he never will."

They parted ways. Sharko let her take her distance, and saw her turn around several times. That confirmed his suspicions. Then he walked slowly toward Tharwat Street, which intersected with Mohamed Farid Street. But just after turning off, he disappeared at a run into a narrow alley chosen at random.

The good doggy had slipped his leash.

At this point, Cairo and its burning night belonged to him.

It filled him with limitless satisfaction.

21

In the tech department of the crime lab, a stone's throw from the squad house, Lucie held in her hands the enlargements of the film frames discovered in Claude Poignet's eye sockets. Two glazed, coarse-grained surfaces in black and white. The images were practically identical. You could see, in a slightly skewed position, as if the camera had been knocked over, the hem of a pair of jeans and the toe of a shoe that Lucie hadn't noticed the first time. The background was lost in shadow, but the feet of a table were visible, as was a wall. The ground was a floor.

"Are these shoes combat boots?"

Lucie was talking to the technician sitting next to her at his computer screen. Julien Marquant, forty-plus, was one of the crime scene photographers. At each homicide, he served up the worst on glossy paper. Some people photographed supermodels; for him, it was cadavers. The heads of suicides splattered open by a .22, drowning victims bloated with water, hangings . . . Julien was an excellent photographer whose talents would remain hidden in the police files. Given the late hour, he was the person most liable to inform his colleague on the subject.

"Looks like it."

He showed her the photos he'd taken at the victim's house. Notably the ones of blood found on the floor of the lab upstairs. Lucie made a connection that now struck her as self-evident:

"It's his place—Claude Poignet's. He had cameras, film stock—the movie was shot in his own house. Holy shit . . ."

"Yes. The two frames we found in his eyes were negatives, so they came from the original master, rather than from a positive print."

Lucie regretted not having reacted sooner. Poignet had explained all that business about positive and negative prints, originals and copies. Julien Marquant tapped his index finger on the photos.

"You want to know what I think? I think the killers operated the camera. They must have—I don't know—placed it right next to the victim's dying body. As if to capture the last images he saw before dying."

Lucie shivered as she stared at the photos. Poignet's final seconds of life were in front of her, before her eyes. The poor man had passed away with those very images—those of a stranger wearing combat boots who was watching him die, while the other one strangled him.

"As if . . . Claude Poignet himself were the camera. The bastards wanted to go inside him."

"Exactly. You said it yourself—the victim had a processing lab, an old 16 mm camera, and reels of raw stock. The killers used it all. They filmed, then went into the darkroom and soaked the images they wanted in a vat of developer. Then they cut them out and put them in the victim's eye sockets. The operation is rather technical and must have taken a good hour."

Lucie pressed her lips tight. These two sick twists weren't content with just stealing back the film; they'd devised a screenplay worthy of a horror movie, going so far as to leave the police something to go on. Thoughtful, organized individuals, so sure of themselves that they'd taken the chance of lingering at the crime scene to "play." Lucie laid out her thoughts:

"They've very kindly given us two elements. The exact position of the body before he was hanged, and the shoes. Combat boots—which confirms that the fellow who went to Szpilman's and the one who helped commit Poignet's murder are one and the same. A soldier, perhaps?"

"Or somebody trying to pass for one. Or neither: anybody can buy combat boots. Especially since they know their way around movies and props. One of them can use a 16 mil camera, take the film out in the darkroom, and develop it. Believe me, if you're a beginner, you wouldn't have the first clue how to operate one of those old gizmos."

"The fingerprint guys didn't come up with anything in the darkroom, apart from the victim's prints. We'll have to send some men back there, this time to look at the equipment, the cameras. The killers surely abandoned some DNA, especially if an eye came in contact with the viewfinder.

They must have made *some* mistakes. You don't just play around with death like that . . ."

She gathered up the photos and thanked him. Back in the street, she walked slowly, deep in thought. After the *how* came the *why*. Why had the killers left those frames in place of his eyes? What were those sadists trying to say?

Plunged into these psychological reflections, she thought of Sharko, the peculiar fellow she'd met on the sly at Gare du Nord. Would he be able to find the answer, with his experience and years in the trade? Would he do a better job than she with this tough and unusual crime? She was dying to talk to him about this new homicide, to see how he'd handle it from the height of his fifty-odd years.

Following her train of thought, Lucie tried to make links with the Gravenchon case. There, too, the victims had had their eyes removed. A doctor, a professional, according to Sharko. Now they could add the talents of a "filmmaker." The profile was becoming more refined, even if nothing specific was quite emerging yet. Why steal the eyes? What was their importance to the person taking them? What did he do with them afterward? Did he keep them as trophies? Lucie also remembered the obsession with the retina and the iris in the short film. The slice of the scalpel on the cornea, the blinks of the eyelids . . . And she recalled Poignet's remark: "The eye is just a common sponge that soaks up images."

A sponge . . .

Suddenly excited, Lucie took out her phone, peeled through her contact list, and dialed the number of the medical examiner.

"Doctor? Lucie Henebelle. Is this a bad time?"

"Hold on—let me ask the large black gentleman decomposing on my table . . . No, he's fine. What can I do for you, Lucie?"

Lucie smiled; the examiner knew her through and through. Truth to tell, she was a "preferred customer."

"This probably sounds stupid, but . . . it's about something I've heard people say, without ever getting a definitive answer: can the eye retain some sort of imprint of what it sees just before death?"

"Excuse me? In what sense?"

"A violent image, for instance. The very last image before the vital functions stop. A cluster of specs of light that could be reconstructed—I don't know—by analyzing stimulated photoreceptive cells, or parts of the brain that might have preserved the information somewhere?"

A pause. Lucie felt a bit embarrassed, expecting him to burst out laughing at any moment.

"The fantasy of the optogram."

"What?"

"You're asking me about the fantasy of the optogram. Toward the end of the nineteenth century, popular opinion decided that a murder, because of its violent and sudden nature, could leave an impression on the dead person's retina like sensitive film . . ."

Sensitive film, eye, image . . . words that had been circling around each other since the beginning of this whole affair.

"Doctors at the time began studying the subject. They thought you could extract a portrait of the criminal from the retina of a corpse. The fantasy of the optogram was that the crime would be directly recorded by the body as the victim was being murdered. In the medical community at the time, this meant taking the eyeball from its socket and removing its crystalline lens, then photographing it to extract tangible proof of the crime. Doctors actually used this method to help the police. And they really arrested people. No doubt innocent people."

"And . . . is such a thing as a retinal imprint plausible?"

"No, no, of course not. As the term suggests, it's remained just a fantasy."

Lucie asked one last question.

"And what about in 1955? Did they still believe in it?"

"No, they weren't as backward as all that in 1955, you know."

"Thanks, Doctor."

She said good-bye and hung up.

The fantasy of the optogram . . .

Fantasy or not, the killer or killers meant to draw attention to the image, its power and its relation to the eye. That particular sensory organ must have been important to the killer, symbolic. That incredible instrument was the well that carried light to the brain, the tunnel that conveyed knowledge of the physical world. It was also, aesthetically speaking, the place where cinema began. No eye, no image, and no cinema. The link was tenuous, but it did exist. Lucie now considered the killer a split personality, divided between the medical—the eye as an organ that can be dissected—and the artistic—the eye as medium and bearer of images. Since there were two killers, perhaps each had his own specialty. *A doctor and a filmmaker* . . .

Still deep in thought, Lucie stopped at a sandwich shop. Her phone was vibrating. It was Kashmareck. He dispensed with the preliminaries.

"How far have you gotten?"

"I'm just leaving forensics with some news. I'm on my way."

"Perfect timing. I know it's late, but we have to go to the Saint-Luc university clinic, near Brussels."

"Belgium again?"

"Yes. We went through the victim's phone calls. Among them, Poignet had reached someone named Georges Beckers, who specializes in images and the brain. You gave me his business card. He works in neuromarketing— I didn't even know there was such a field. Just after he scanned the film, Claude Poignet sent him the URL of the server where he'd stored the copy and asked him to analyze it. We've got the digitized film, Lucie. Our tech boys are downloading it. I'm putting a lip-reader on it right now, as well as image specialists. We're going through it with a fine-toothed comb."

Lucie gave a silent sigh. The killers had been outsmarted by technology. They had killed someone to preserve their secret, and this secret was now spreading throughout the entire police computer network.

"Did this Beckers discover anything?"

"According to him, old Vlad Szpilman had already been to their research center, with the very same movie, a little more than two years ago. Szpilman was a friend of the former director, who died of a heart attack a few months ago."

Lucie thought for a moment before answering.

"Vlad Szpilman must have had the same intuition as our restorer did. According to his son, he liked to watch the same film dozens of times over; he had an expert eye. He must have come to suspect that some strange things were hidden in this film. So he had it analyzed. Two years ago is quite a while back, all things considered."

"Let's get rolling. Beckers has been alerted, and he's waiting for us. Okay for you?"

She looked at her watch. A little after eight.

"Let me just run by the hospital. I want to see my daughter and tell her why I can't fall asleep with her this time."

22

Sharko wondered if he was really going to walk into the Cairo Bar, a crummy-looking place in a dank, unlit alley in the Tewfikieh district. Along the entire length of the alley rested carts, covered with simple sheets, and black cats scampered atop the chalk walls. Sharko walked down the few steps that led to the bar. You really, *really* had to enjoy strong sensations to venture into that place. A washed-out sign read COFFEE SHOP; the large windows were covered with sheets of newspaper layered over each other, preventing anyone from seeing what might be going on inside. The facade was as raunchy as the pathetic sex shops that sprouted in certain Paris neighborhoods.

The cop checked one more time that he was carrying his police ID, even though he sincerely doubted it would be of much use here, and plunged into the lion's den. He was immediately assailed by a heady odor of hashish, mixed with the smells of mint and *mu'assel* from the hookahs. The light was muted; the powerful air conditioner rumbled. The thick wooden tables, old Vienna-style lamps, bronze art objects hanging on the wall, and large steins of beer made the place look like an English pub. A waitress, Caucasian and scantily clad, threaded between the shapes, her tray loaded with glasses brimful of alcohol. Sharko had expected to find faces eaten away by syphilis, drugs, or drink. Instead, he was amazed at how attractive the clientele looked, mostly young and flamboyantly dressed.

Just his luck: in the middle of one of the oldest Muslim cities in the world, he'd stumbled into a gay bar.

All I needed!

Honeyed gazes followed him as he walked firmly to the bar, which was manned by a fellow with white skin, blue eyes, and blond hair. Sharko glanced at his watch—the taxi had dropped him off ten minutes early—and nodded toward an amber-colored bottle labeled OLD BRENT.

"Whiskey, please."

The bartender looked him over a bit too insistently before serving him his drink. Sharko was immediately approached on the right. *Here come the come-ons!* The guy was in his twenties, swarthy complexion, draftee's haircut. Around his neck he had tied a scarf tucked into a bright shirt. He whispered into Sharko's ear:

"*Koudiana* or *barghal*, 'please'?"

"Nothing at all. And fuck off, 'please.' "

The cop snatched up his glass—they served doses that could kill a horse here—and went off to sit in a corner. He looked over the customers, noted the behavior of the rich in their designer suits and imported shoes, on the make, and of the poor, much more effeminate, dazzlingly beautiful in their modest clothes. Sex and prostitution must have been, here as elsewhere, a means of wresting yourself from poverty, for the space of a night and a few exchanged bills. People greeted each other Egyptian style, four pecks on the cheek and taps on the back; they weren't yet kissing on the mouth, but the intent was clear. Sharko was bringing his glass to his lips with a sigh when a voice reached him from behind:

"I wouldn't drink that if I were you. They say a young painter went blind here after drinking that whiskey. The boss, the Englishman, makes his own liquor to double his profits. It's common practice in the old cafés of Cairo."

Atef Abd el-Aal sat down opposite him. He clapped his hands and indicated "two" to the waitress. Sharko set down his whiskey with a grimace, without having touched it.

"Your French is damn good."

"I've long frequented a friend of your country. And I work with a lot of your compatriots living in Alexandria. The French make excellent business partners."

He leaned over the table. He had lined his eyes with khol and combed his fine hair back. His pupils were subtly congested by the effects of hashish, probably taken before coming to the bar.

"No one followed you?"

"No."

"This is the only place we can be left alone. The police never come down here; certain people around us are powerful businessmen who control the district. Now that the police know we saw each other on the terrace, I'll be under surveillance. I traveled by rooftop after leaving my house."

"Why should they put you under surveillance? And why keep an eye on me?"

"To keep you from sticking your nose where you shouldn't. Give me back the note I wrote you on the terrace. I don't want to leave any trace of our meeting in this establishment."

Sharko complied and lifted his chin toward the faces buried in the shadows.

"And what about all these people around us? They've seen us together."

"Here, we're outside the law and social regulations. We know each other by female names; we have our own codes and our own language. The only goal of our meetings is *wasla*, the practice of homosexuality between *koudiana*, the submissives, and *barghal*, the dominants. We'll always deny having seen one of our own here, no matter what. We have rules as well."

Sharko felt as if he were diving into the unsuspected and secret entrails of the city, to the rhythm of the night.

"Explain to me more precisely why you came to Egypt," said Atef.

Sharko retraced the story in broad strokes, without giving away the confidential aspects of the case. He spoke without getting too detailed about the bodies discovered in France, the similarities in modus operandi with the young Egyptian victims, the telegram his brother had sent. Atef had the somber expression of a djinn. His eyes were veiled.

"Do you really think these two episodes are related, given how far apart they are in time and place? What proof do you have?"

"I can't tell you that. But I have the feeling they're hiding things from me, that documents are missing from the file. My hands and feet are tied."

"When are you going back?"

"Tomorrow evening. But I promise you that if I have to, I'll come back as a tourist. I'll find the families of those poor girls and interview them."

"You're a persistent one. Why should the fate of some miserable Egyptians who died so long ago interest you?"

"Because I'm a cop. Because the passage of time shouldn't make a crime any less hateful."

"An avenger's speech."

"I'm just a father and a husband. And I like seeing things through to the bitter end."

The waitress brought two imported beers and warm mezes. Atef invited Sharko to help himself and spoke in a low voice.

"Your hands and feet are tied because the entire Egyptian police system is corrupt. They fill their ranks with the poor and the ignorant, most of whom come from the country or Upper Egypt so that they won't oppose the system. They pay them barely enough to survive on so that they'll be forced to become corrupt themselves. They provide false papers for money, shake down taxi drivers and restaurant owners, threaten to have their licenses revoked. From Cairo to Aswan, police brutality is known far and wide. Just a few years ago, they were still arresting us for homosexuality—and believe me, being in those prisons was no joke. With less than thirty pounds a month to live on, thirty of your euros, people like that *become* the system. Half the police in this country have no idea what they're doing it for. They're told to repress, so they repress. But my brother wasn't of that stripe. He had the values of men from Port Said. Pride. And respect."

Atef took out a photo from his wallet and handed it to Sharko. It showed an upright man, young, solid in his uniform. He shone with the savage beauty of the desert dwellers.

"Mahmoud always dreamed of being a policeman. Before he was accepted, he had joined the youth center in Abdin to do bodybuilding; he wanted to be up to the level of the gymnastic tests at the police academy. He got ninety percent on his final exams. He was brilliant. He got by without money and without bribes. He was never an extremist; he had nothing to do with that gangrene. That was all a frame-up to make him disappear."

Sharko delicately set the photo on the table.

"A frame-up by the police, you mean?"

"Yes. By that son of a whore Noureddine."

"Why?"

"I could never find out why. Until today, when I finally learned from you that it was all related to that investigation. Those girls who were viciously murdered . . ."

Atef stared vacantly at his beer bottle. Made up that way, he gave off a wholly feminine sensuality.

"Mahmoud wouldn't let the case go. He always brought back his files, photos, and personal notes to the apartment. He told me the case had quickly been classified, and that his superiors had assigned him to another investigation. Here, spending your time on the murder of poor people doesn't bring in much money, you understand?"

"I think I'm beginning to."

"But Mahmoud kept right on with it, quietly. When the police came to search his place after his charred body was discovered, they took everything. And now, you tell me those documents no longer exist. Someone had an interest in making them disappear."

At the slightest noise, Atef looked around. The smoke emitted by the *chichas* blurred the faces, darkened the risqué gestures. Some men exited. In this place, one arrived alone but left in twos, for a busy night.

Sharko took a swallow of beer. The atmosphere was like the situation: tense.

"And your brother hadn't told you anything? Details? Any points in common among the murdered girls?"

The Arab shook his head.

"It goes back a long time, Inspector. And when you talk about this case in hints and whispers, you're not really helping me."

"In that case, let me refresh your memory."

Sharko spread the victims' photos on the table. This time, he recounted exactly what Nahed had translated for him in the un-air-conditioned office at the police station. The discovery of the bodies, the precise indications of the autopsy report. Atef listened carefully, touching neither his drink nor the mezes.

"Ezbet el-Nakhl, where the trash collectors live . . ." he repeated. "Now that you say it, yes, I do believe my brother went there for his investigation. Then Shubra . . . Shubra . . . the cement factories. It all vaguely rings a bell."

He closed his eyes for a moment, opened them again, picked up a photo, and stared at it attentively.

"I believe my brother was convinced that there did exist a link among these girls. The crimes were too close together in time, too similar for the killer to have acted randomly. The murderer must have had a plan, a path he was following."

Sharko's throat grew tighter by the minute. Mahmoud had sensed the killer, and he'd acted in all the right ways, starting from the principle that a killer rarely struck by chance. A true European-style detective—no doubt the only one in this vast city.

"What kind of plan?"

"I don't know. My brother didn't tell me a whole lot, because . . . I didn't like what he was doing. But I do know who he might have talked to more openly."

"Who?"

"My uncle. The one who got us out of poverty, so long ago. The two of them were very close and spoke about all sorts of things."

Behind them, bottles of alcohol circulated, the atmosphere began to churn. Hands moved closer, fingers caressed wrists in a sign of desire. Sharko leaned over the table.

"Let's go see your uncle."

Atef hesitated a long time.

"I'd really like to help you, in memory of my brother. But this I should do alone. I'd rather remain careful and not be seen with you. We'll meet again tomorrow, in front of the Saladin Citadel overlooking the Necropolis, an hour and a half after the call to prayer. Six a.m., at the foot of the left minaret. I'll be there with your information."

Atef downed half his beer.

"I'm going to stay a bit longer. You go now. And especially . . ."

Sharko finally picked up his glass of whiskey and emptied it in one gulp.

"I know, not a word. See you tomorrow."

Once outside, the cop intentionally lost himself in the streets of Cairo, carried along by the human flow, the colors and smells.

He might have a lead.

The temperature had dropped a good fifteen degrees, and the sweat from the club grew cool along his scalp and ears. The cop didn't feel like going back to his deathly little room and confronting what was inside his head. The city carried him, guided him in its whirlwinds of mystery. He discovered improbable cafés hidden between two buildings, and hookah joints lit by Chinese lanterns among which people glided, carrying reddened coals. He crossed paths with wandering vendors of vinyl wallets and paper handkerchiefs, dove into atmospheres whose very existence he would never have suspected. He smoked and drank without worrying about the water the tea was made from, without fearing the *tourista*. Somewhere back in the Muslim portion of the city, carried along by drunkenness, he watched the slaughter of three young bulls, their throats slit in the middle of the street, which butchers hacked into pieces before wrapping them in pouches ready for distribution. In the heart of the night, human waves unfurled: poor people, children with bare feet, women with black veils, while a well-dressed man in a suit handed out political pamphlets. Bags of meat were being tossed to the crowd along with the advertising; people elbowed each other and shouted. The whole city vibrated like a single being.

In the midst of his euphoria, Sharko suddenly felt a surge of nausea and squinted his eyes. Over there, standing apart from the crowd, was a man plunged in darkness, wearing a mustache and a hat that looked like a beret.

Hassan Noureddine.

The man stepped to the side and disappeared down a street.

The Frenchman tried to open a path toward him, but the human flow jostled him. He forced his way through the crowd, the tide of arms, and began running. When he arrived at the square, the police chief had vanished. Sharko moved forward into the deserted alleyways, turned in every direction, then finally stopped, alone in the middle of the silent houses.

They were following him. Even here. What did that mean?

And what if he'd just been dreaming? What if that silhouette had only been a vision, like Eugenie?

Sharko turned back. The air here seemed frozen. This silence, this darkness, the blackness of the building facades. He quickened his pace and finally rejoined the hubbub of the main street. Somewhere else, the buzzing was getting louder; the inimitable chants of the women filled the air, to the rhythm of clacking castanets and tabla drums. Sharko was in Egypt; he was discovering people so open that they drank from the same glass at the table, that they lived outside and cooked their bread on the sidewalk.

But in the midst of that jubilant crowd, a monster had struck.

A bloodthirsty ghoul, who had leapt from neighborhood to neighborhood to spread darkness.

That was more than fifteen years ago.

Alone in room 16, which overlooked Mohamed Farid Street, wrapped like an Egyptian in his sheets to ward off mosquitoes, Sharko crushed his hands against his ears. Eugenie was flinging cocktail sauce all over the walls and yelling at him. She didn't want any more corpses or horrors; she cried and pulled at her hair with shrill screams. And the moment Sharko dozed off, dying from exhaustion, she clapped her hands sharply and he jerked awake again.

"All those people are watching you. They're spying on us, dear Franck, through the window, through the keyhole. They're following us, sniffing out our scent. We have to go back home before they do us harm. You want them to torture me like Eloise and Suzanne? Remember Suzanne, naked, her rounded belly, tied up on a wooden table? Her screams? She was begging you, Franck. She was begging you. Why weren't you there to save her? Why, dear Franck?"

The Wernicke's area in Sharko's brain was throbbing. He got up and glanced into the street. He saw the tops of people's heads, white robes swaying in the thick air. Not a trace of the arrogant fat cop. Then he double-checked that the door and shutters were locked tight. The paranoia remained, swarming beneath his flesh, and Eugenie still refused to leave. At the end of his rope, the schizophrenic policeman rushed toward the small refrigerator, gathered up all the ice cubes, and threw them into the bathtub. Shut in the bathroom, he ran the cold water and sank below the surface, breath taken away, body freezing. The tall enameled edges threw up familiar ramparts, reassuring him. The world seemed to shrink onto his body and mash up everything around it.

He ended up falling asleep in the empty tub, curled up and trembling like an old dog, alone, so far from home, with his inner phantoms. Against his chest he held the little locomotive, O-gauge Ova Hornby, with its black car for wood and coal.

He never realized he was crying.

23

The chronically jammed Brussels ring road was dumping its last batch of workers into the city's outskirts. After the strong heat of the previous days, a yellowish haze tarnished the sky, despite various antipollution initiatives. Armed with a GPS, Lucie and her boss easily found their way to the University of Saint-Luc health services, located in a suburb of the Belgian capital. With their tree-lined surroundings and meticulous, linear architecture, the buildings gave off a sense of peace and strength. From what Kashmareck understood, the clinic, in addition to its role as a hospital, also performed specialized research, supported by an up-to-the-minute technological infrastructure. Among other things, it was involved in neuromarketing, the main point of which was to gain a better understanding of consumer behavior by identifying how the brain worked at the time of purchase.

Georges Beckers was waiting for the detectives in the medical imaging department, located on the basement level of the university hospital. Short and stout, the man wore a jovial face, with puffy jowls and a collar of white beard. There was nothing to suggest that he was at the forefront of neuroimaging research, assuming it was possible to have an archetypal researcher. He briefly explained that, between medical consults, his department leased out the scanners for advertising purposes—something that was strictly prohibited in France.

As they walked down the hallway, the police captain steered the conversation toward their case.

"When did you first meet Claude Poignet?"

Beckers answered in a thick Belgian accent:

"It was about ten years ago, at a conference in Brussels on the evolution of imagery since the Age of Enlightenment. Claude was very interested in the way images traveled from generation to generation. In illustrated books, films, photographs, and even collective memory. I'd gone there for science, and he for film. We hit it off immediately. It's really tragic, what happened to him."

"Did you get together often?"

"I'd say two or three times a year. But we were in constant touch by e-mail or telephone. He followed my work on the brain closely and he taught me a great deal about how movies work."

At the end of the corridor, they halted before some wide windows. On the other side lay a cylinder, located in the middle of a white room. Before the scanner stood a kind of table on tracks, fitted with a kind of hoop used to hold the head in place.

"This scanner is one of the most cutting-edge machines in existence. Three teslas of magnetic field, a picture of the brain every demi-second, powerful statistical analysis system . . . I hope you're not claustrophobic, Captain?"

"No, why?"

"In that case, you're the one who'll go in the scanner, if you wouldn't mind."

Kashmareck's face darkened.

"We came to see about the film. On the phone, it sounded like you'd discovered something."

"Indeed I did. But explanation works best with demonstration. The machine is free this evening, so we might as well take advantage of it. An MRI in a machine that costs millions of euros is not an opportunity that comes along every day."

The man was apparently obsessed with science and aching to use his little toys. Like it or not, Kashmareck was going to serve as guinea pig and no doubt feed the statistics that researchers delighted in. Lucie patted her boss's shoulder and gave him a smile.

"He's right. Nothing like a good shower of X-rays."

The captain grunted and gave in. Beckers provided the explanations:

"Have you seen the film?"

"Haven't had time yet—we've just downloaded it onto our servers. But my colleague here described it to me in the car."

"Perfect. This will give you a chance to see it. But you're going to do it from inside the scanner. My assistant is waiting. Do you have any dental fillings or body piercings?"

"Uh . . . yes . . ."

He looked at Lucie, hesitant.

"Here, on my navel . . ."

Lucie brought her hand to her mouth to keep from laughing. She turned around and pretended to be inspecting the machines, while the scientist pursued his explanations.

"Take it out. We'll get you settled and give you glasses that are actually two pixelated screens. During the viewing of the film, the apparatus will record your brain activity. Please . . ."

Kashmareck sighed. "Jesus, if my wife could only see this!"

The cop moved away and joined a man in a lab coat in the room below. Lucie and the scientist headed to a kind of control room loaded with screens, computers, and colored buttons. It looked like the main deck of the starship *Enterprise*. While they were settling Kashmareck in, Lucie voiced the question she'd been dying to ask:

"What happens now?"

"We're going to watch the movie at the same time as him, but directly, inside his brain."

Beckers took a moment to enjoy the astonishment on her face.

"Today, my dear lieutenant, we're going to explore important mysteries of the brain, especially with regard to images and sounds. The oldest card trick in the book—divination—is about to be relegated to the attic."

"How so?"

"If you show your colleague a playing card while he's in the scanner, I'd be able to guess which it is just by looking at his brain activity."

In the room below them, the captain lay stretched out on the table, not feeling very reassured. The assistant had just fitted him with strange glasses with square frames and opaque lenses.

"Are you telling me that you can read people's minds?"

"Let's say it's no longer a fantasy. Today, we're able to project simple visual thoughts onscreen. When you see a specific image, thousands of tiny areas of the visual cortex, which we call voxels, light up in an almost unique way and identify the relevant image. Thanks to complex mathematical treatments, we can then associate an image with a cerebral cartography, and we record all of it in a database. Thus, at any given moment, we could use the system in the opposite direction: to each group of voxels visualized by the MRI, there corresponds an image, at least in theory. If the image is in our database, we can reconstruct it, and thus display your thoughts."

"That's astounding."

"Isn't it? Unfortunately, the voxel, our smallest unit, measures fifty cubic millimeters and already contains around five million neurons. Despite the power of our scanner, it's like seeing the outline of a city from up in the sky, without being able to make out the pattern of the streets or the architecture of its buildings. But it's already a giant step. Ever since one brilliant scientist had the idea, a few years ago, to make people drink Coke and Pepsi in a scanner, the possibilities have become limitless. They were blindfolded and asked which soft drink they preferred before tasting it. Most answered Coke. But in the blind test, the same people said they preferred the taste of Pepsi. The scanner showed that an area in the brain, called putamen, reacted more strongly for Pepsi than for Coke. Putamen is the seat of immediate, instinctive pleasures."

"So the ad campaign for Coke claims that people prefer it, while in reality their bodies prefer Pepsi."

"Precisely. Today all the big advertising firms are clamoring for our scanners. Neuromarketing allows them to increase brand preference, maximize the impact of an advertising slogan, and optimize its memorization. We've been able to highlight areas of the brain involved in the purchasing process, like the insula, which is the site of pain and pricing, as well as the median prefrontal cortex, the putamen, and the cuneus. Soon all an ad will have to do is enter your visual or auditory field to have an impact. Even if your eyes and ears aren't paying attention, it will be studied so as to stimulate the memory circuits and the purchasing process."

"That's terrifying."

"It's the future. What do you do when you're tired, my dear lieutenant? Life is increasingly demanding and exhausting, so to relax you settle in at home, in front of your screens. You open your mind to images like a faucet, with your awareness lowered, almost asleep. And at that moment you become the perfect target, and they inject whatever they want into your head."

It was both staggering and horrible. A world governed by images and the control of the subconscious, in which the barriers of rationality were bypassed. Could one still speak of free will? Seeing all these perfected tools working on the brain, Lucie was reminded of the fantasy of the optogram: they were in the heart of the matter, and it wasn't so fantastic after all.

"So I'm not entirely off the mark if I say that an image can leave an imprint in the brain?"

"That's exactly right—you've understood the basis of our work. You study fingerprints; we study brain prints. Every action leaves a trace, whatever it might be. The whole trick lies in knowing how to detect it, and having the tools that let you exploit it."

Lucie thought of all the investigative techniques the crime lab used when dealing with a case. Here they did the same thing, but with gray matter.

"Obviously, we're still in the Middle Ages of technology, but in a few years we'll probably have machines that will allow you to visualize dreams. Do you know that in the United States they're already talking about installing scanners in courtrooms? Imagine those machines projecting a defendant's memories. No more lies; verdicts that are always reliable . . . And I'm not even talking about other fields, like medicine, psychiatry, or business. There's also neuropolitics, which offers the possibility of accessing voters' deep-seated feelings toward a given candidate."

Lucie recalled the film *Minority Report*. It was a dizzying prospect, but this was the reality of tomorrow. A rape of consciousness. The director from 1955, with his subliminal images, was already part of the process. Perhaps he had understood, well before his time, the function of certain areas of the brain.

On the other side of the glass, the poor captain disappeared into the magnetic tunnel. Lucie was pleased to have avoided that bit of pure anxiety. Watching the film was already trying enough.

"What do you think of the film from 1955?" she asked.

"Impressive, on all fronts. I don't know who the director was, but he was a genius, an innovator. With his use of subliminal imagery and multiple exposures, he was already acting on areas of the primitive brain. Pleasure, fear, the desire to confront taboos. In 1955, such a process was completely unheard of. Even advertisers came to it later on. And the man who can beat advertising to the punch is hands down a genius."

The same words had come out of Claude Poignet's mouth.

"And what about the mutilated woman and the bull? Special effects?"

"No idea. That's not really my specialty—I was more interested in how the film was put together, not its content . . . Excuse me a moment, my assistant is signaling that all's ready."

Beckers turned toward the monitors. On the screen Lucie saw what was supposed to be her boss's brain. A throbbing ball, the seat of emotions, memory, character, and lived experience. On another screen, Lucie could see the first image from the digitized film, set on PAUSE. The scientist made several adjustments.

"Let's get started . . . The principle is simple. Once activated, neurons consume oxygen. The MRI simply colors this consumption."

The film progressed. The captain's brain activity was haloed with colors; the organ seemed to be gliding over a rainbow that veered from blue to red. Certain areas lit up, faded, moved around like fluids in translucent tubes.

"Do you think Szpilman did the same thing with your former director two years ago?" Lucie asked. "Use the machines to dissect the film?"

"Most likely, yes. As I told your boss on the phone, the director had talked a little about the experiment at the time. And about a very strange film. But I really hadn't thought much more about it."

Beckers returned to his screen and began commenting in real time:

"Every image that enters your visual field is extremely complex. It's first treated by the retina, then transformed into a nerve impulse that the optic nerve carries to the back of your brain, to the visual cortex. At that stage, multiple specialized zones analyze the various properties of the image. Its colors, forms, movement, and also its nature: violent, comic, neutral, sad. What you see there certainly does not allow us to guess what image the witness is observing, but the data do allow us to identify some of the parameters I just mentioned. These days, experts in neuroimagery have fun guessing the nature of a film just by analyzing these masses of colors. Comedy, drama, suspense . . ."

"And how would you analyze this film?"

"Overall, extreme violence. Concentrate on those areas . . ."

He pointed his finger to certain places on the electronic depiction of the brain.

"They're lighting up on and off," Lucie noticed. "Is that the subliminal imagery?"

"Yes. I timed their appearances. A hidden image always corresponds to when those areas light up. For the moment, it's just the pleasure centers. You can easily guess why. The actress, nude, in risqué postures. Those gloved hands stroking her."

Lucie felt embarrassed at penetrating, to some degree, her hierarchical superior's deepest intimacy. The captain had no idea he was seeing, at that very moment, subliminal images of the actress in his simpler device. He had even less idea that his brain was getting off on them and risked setting off an embarrassing physical reaction.

The digitized film continued to advance. Lucie recalled what Claude Poignet had shown her on the viewer. They were getting close to the other kind of image: the actress's mangled body on the grass with the large eye sliced into her belly. Beckers moved his finger on the screen.

"This is it. Activation of the median prefrontal and orbitofrontal cortex, as well as of the temporoparietal junction. The really shocking images have just started occurring, hidden behind apparently tranquil scenes. Up until now, everything is coherent. But hang on a bit . . ."

The black-and-white film was three-quarters of the way through. The little girl was petting a cat, sitting in the grass, still framed by that strange, drooling fog and a black sky. A neutral scene, which in principle should elicit no emotion.

"Here we go . . . The signals in the brain get excited, even independent of the precise moments when the subliminal images occur. Same thing for the amygdala and parts of the anterior cingulate cortex. The organism is steeling itself for a violent reaction. You must have felt the same disturbance when you watched the film—a desire to run away, perhaps, or turn it off."

It was well before the scene with the bull that the colors exploded in Kashmareck's brain. They were lighting up on all sides. A few moments later, his brain activity returned to more normal levels. Beckers shook his notes.

"At precisely eleven minutes, three seconds you see the brain activity reacting to violent images, which lasts for a minute. But this part of the film contains none of the subliminal images that were inserted in the original. Not the naked woman, not the mutilations. Not a thing."

"So what is it, then?"

"A complicated process of hidden imagery, using superimposition, contrast, and light. I believe both the subliminal images and that white circle at the upper right are just red herrings. They're the visible element that allowed the film to mask the *real* hidden message. Unconsciously, the eye is constantly drawn by that distracting spot, which keeps you from concentrating too much on other parts of the image and noticing what's really going on. The filmmaker took care to thwart even the most observant viewers."

Lucie could no longer keep still. The film was drawing her in; it possessed her.

"Show me those hidden images."

"Let's first let your captain join us."

Lucie couldn't help watching the scene with the bull once again, while Beckers sat down at another computer. It gave her gooseflesh, especially when the camera zoomed in on the girl's eyes: cold and devoid of all feeling. The eyes of an ancient statue.

A few minutes later, Kashmareck returned. He was as white as the shell of the scanner.

"Weird goddamn movie" were his only words. He too had been turned inside out, manipulated, shocked, and was trying to figure out why he felt so strange. Beckers briefly recapped what he'd just said to Lucie, tapping on his keyboard. Video processing software came up. The scientist opened the digitized film and moved the progress bar to eleven minutes and three seconds. Nearly identical images appeared one behind the other, as if on a filmstrip viewed under a lightbulb. With his mouse, Beckers pointed out an area in the first image, at lower left.

"It's always in the low-contrast areas that this happens. In fog, the black sky, very dark zones, omnipresent at this point in the film. Visual tricks that allowed our filmmaker to express his secret language."

With his mouse, he rolled the cursor rapidly over the screen, using it to underscore his explanations.

"If you look at this image just as it is, what do you see? A girl sitting in the grass and petting a cat. Around her there's this fog, and these large dark flat areas, on the sides and in the sky. If you don't know there's anything to find, you'll pass right by it. That's what happened to Claude, who was concentrating entirely on the subliminal images, which were straightforward and clearly distinct from the rest of the film."

Lucie came closer, her brows knit.

"Now that I'm looking, I'd almost say there were . . . faces, lost in the fog. And . . . and in all those dark patches around the image."

"Faces, that's right. A crowd of children's faces."

The scene was odd; barely perceptible faces surrounded the little girl, like malevolent succubae. The more Lucie's eye became acclimated, the more details she made out. Small feet shoved into socks; matching outfits, like hospital pajamas; a uniform floor that looked like linoleum. A parallel, latent world slowly took shape. Lucie thought of optical illusions—the image of a vase, for instance, that turns into a couple making love after you've stared at it for a moment.

In the drop-down menu, Beckers selected the brightness and contrast option and opened a dialogue box on which he could play with the settings.

"Let's suppose it's 1955 and we're in a movie theater. And we add a filter over the lens of the projector. A filter that heightens contrast. Then we also increase the brightness. I'm re-creating these manipulations by applying different values, which I've already tested. Now watch . . ."

He hit APPLY, and something strange happened to the image. What was initially invisible came to the fore, while the more obvious scene bleached into white light.

"Because of the increased brightness, the main image—the girl petting the cat—becomes overexposed and fades out. But the image in the darker areas, which at first was underexposed, now emerges fully."

The two combined images produced a bizarre effect, but this time one could clearly make out a group of children, all standing, and rabbits huddled in a corner.

Lucie swallowed hard. This was it: the rabbits and the children. On the phone, the Canadian had said everything started from there.

Kashmareck mopped his brow.

"This is incredible. How did the filmmaker pull off something like that?"

"Hard for me to explain the precise technical procedure, but I think he mainly played with double exposures, using a series of adjustable masks over the camera lens. There's one basic characteristic of film—photo or movie—which is that it remains impressionable as long as you haven't run it through fixative in a darkroom. Basically, you could shoot several movies on the same roll of film; you just have to rewind without opening the magazine. If you do it randomly, it just becomes a jumble and you won't see a thing. But with a lot of technical know-how and a good knowledge of lighting, composition, and framing, you can get remarkable results. Claude Poignet admired Méliès. He once told me Méliès had used up to nine successive superimpositions to build certain special effects. The work of a magician and a fine jeweler all at once. I have no doubt this film here is of the same caliber, and that your director could easily rival Méliès."

Lucie cautiously analyzed the faces onscreen. Little girls of seven or eight, with severe expressions and pinched mouths. None of them was laughing—on the contrary, they seemed to be prey to sheer terror. What were they afraid of?

Her heart leaped. She pointed her finger at the screen.

"That one, a bit in front. She looks like the girl on the swing."

"That's right."

The room the girls were in appeared cramped, windowless. Beckers rubbed his thick lips with a sigh.

"Our filmmaker didn't simply want to hide weird images in his film, he wanted to conceal a whole other film, a parallel film, completely insane. A monstrosity."

"A film within a film that no eye could see?"

"Yes. Directly injected into the brain, without the slightest conscious censorship. Without the possibility of turning away. Look carefully."

He made the next fifty frames go by slowly, which in reality constituted only a second of film time.

"The superimposed images appear only every ten frames. Which means that for every second of projection time, you get five superimposed frames, each spaced two-tenths of a second apart. It's too little, in the midst of all those images, for the eye to notice anything, but almost enough to give the sense of movement. Movement that gets imprinted on the brain . . . It's your brain that sees the film, not your eyes."

Lucie struggled to understand. This was probably what had determined the choice of fifty images per second. He wanted to slip in the maximum number of hidden images without the viewer's eye noticing them.

"Now you're going to imagine something else," Beckers continued. "So here we have our movie projector, with its filter and strong light that lets the invisible images be seen."

With a click, he opened a window to adjust the settings for film projection.

"Now imagine that you regulated the projector's shutter at the rate of five frames a second, as most of those old machines could do, while your reel was still running at fifty frames a second. That means that the only images being projected onscreen are the ones we're interested in; the others are blocked by the baffle."

Beckers got up and turned off the lights. All that remained were the flickering screens on which danced various sectional views of the brain.

"The film we're about to see will be jumpy, since it's being shown at five frames a second, whereas the illusion of continuous movement doesn't really kick in until around ten or twelve. But it's still enough"—his voice was toneless—"to get the picture. I think your man understood things about the brain well before the rest of the world."

He halted his hand over the mouse and looked his visitors in the eye. His face was serious.

"Do me a favor, please. If someday you get to the bottom of all this, be sure to tell me. I wouldn't want these images rattling around in my head with no explanation for the rest of my life."

The film began.

Camera. Action.

24

S harko was climbing painfully out of the tub as one of Cairo's three thousand muezzins called the faithful to dawn prayer. The powerful, mysterious voice seemed to descend from the heavens like an oracle. The cop remembered the loudspeakers that were omnipresent in the streets. The sun hadn't yet risen, and already the entire city vibrated beneath the teachings of the Koran.

The inspector stretched backward, his spine stiff. A probable compression of vertebras L1 and L2, the doctor had once told him. He was getting older, for God's sake, and sleeping for several hours folded in two in a bathtub was not exactly age appropriate. As for the mosquito bites, they irritated his skin to the point where he wanted to peel it off with a knife. He slathered his entire body with a thick coating of lotion, heaving a sigh of relief.

He swallowed his Zyprexa tablet, which was spectacularly ineffective in such a hot and stressful climate, then packed his bags. The flight to Paris was scheduled for about 5:00 p.m. Not yet really here, already gone. And in a hell of a rush to get back to the "cool" of Paris, with its mere eighty-something degrees.

After buying some bean fritters on the street corner, Sharko hailed the first cab he saw and asked to be taken to the Saladin Citadel.

The Nasr dropped him off fifteen minutes later in front of the impressive fortification, perched above the city. The first rays of sunlight, off to the horizon, enflamed the plains around Heliopolis, and in the background stretched the slopes of the Mokattam Mountains, the mythic City of the Dead spread out at their feet. While crunching on his fritter, Sharko took in an eyeful. The tombs devoted to the three dynasties of caliphs and sultans who'd governed Egypt for over a thousand years were haloed in the colors of dawn. Reds, yellows, and blues paid homage to the vast necropolis, now inhabited by the wretched poor. Sitting on the base of one of the minarets as if he ruled the world, Sharko realized just how fractured Egypt was becoming with each passing year: on the one hand, the majestic, untouchable past, with its pharaohs, mosques, and madrassas; and on the other, the much less resplendent future, devoured by chaos and the poverty of a population growing out of bounds.

A car suddenly pulled up at the edge of the small road, about twenty yards away. Sharko walked toward it as Atef got out and opened the trunk of his well-manufactured 4x4. The two men shook hands.

"Nobody followed you?" asked the Arab.

"What do you think?"

Atef was wearing a khaki-colored outfit, like a safari suit. Loose-fitting shirt, trousers with wide side pockets, hiking boots. Sharko, for his part, had gone with the tourist option: Bermuda shorts, docksiders, and sand-colored shirt.

"I've got the info," said Atef. "We're going to where the garbage collectors live. There's a hospital there, the Salaam Center."

"A hospital?"

"If you're looking for a common thread among the victims, that's it. The girls had all gone into city hospitals, almost at the same time. That was in 1993, the year before they died. And one of them, Boussaina Abderrahmane, went to the Salaam Center."

"How come?"

"My uncle isn't sure. Mahmoud hadn't told him about it in too much detail. But we'll soon find out."

Sharko had sensed it: the killer had some connection with the world of medicine. The medical examiner's saw, the removal of the eyes, the ketamine. And now the hospitals. The path was coming into focus.

The Arab picked up the handle of the tire jack, which he wiped with a cloth.

"Bad luck. I just got a flat in the left front tire. It's supposed to never happen with these Japanese cars. Let me just fix this and we'll get going."

Sharko took a few steps back to gauge the extent of the damage.

His skull then seemed to shatter into pieces.

The blow had knocked him flat on the ground.

Dazed, he tried to stand up, but less than ten seconds later his hands were joined behind his back. The rasp of adhesive tape. Atef bound his wrists and stuffed a rag into his mouth, which he surrounded with several layers of tape. He snatched the policeman's cell phone.

Shoved into the trunk, Sharko heard, before the wall of steel cut him off definitively from the light:

"You're going to join my brother, you son of a dog."

The car sped off.

In an instant, Sharko understood that he was about to die.

25

Lucie hadn't gotten a wink of sleep. How could she even begin to forget the horrors viewed in the neuroimagery unit? How could she rest easily after such a burning flood of darkness? Huddled in a corner of the hospital room with her laptop, she replayed over and over the hidden film that Beckers had burned for her on a DVD.

The film within a film, adjusted to the right contrast, speed, and brightness settings.

The one about the rabbits and the children.

Children, for the love of God.

Once more she pressed PLAY, feeling the need to understand, beyond the images themselves, what could have happened in those distant, forgotten years.

The images succeeded one another at the rate of five frames per second. It made for a staccato viewing experience, with gaps in information between each scene. But the feeling of movement and continuity was almost there, filtering through at the edge of the senses. With repeated watchings, Lucie's eye had learned to focus on the scene that interested her, and to screen out the initial, superimposed, parasitic image. At this point, she saw only a single film: the hidden film.

Twelve children, girls, were standing, squeezed together, hands clutching their chests. They were all wearing pajamas that were surely white, a bit too large for their slight frames. Their eyes were rolling in their sockets, and almost every face was twisted in thick, tenacious fear. It was as if a heavy black storm full of monsters was thundering over them.

Almost every face . . . Because the one on the child from the swing was frozen in a cold expression, the same emptiness in her eyes as when staring down the immobilized bull. She stood in front of the group, at the head of the line, and didn't move.

Thirty or forty rabbits, little creatures not yet fully grown, were trembling in a corner. Ears flat back, fur raised, whiskers twitching. The cameraman was probably located in another corner, which allowed him to keep both the girls and the rabbits in his field of vision, at a distance of about five or six yards.

The child from the swing suddenly turned her gaze left. Quite clearly, she was looking at someone unseen by the viewer. The same mysterious presence that hovered over everything was lurking outside the camera's range and seemed to be coordinating the whole scene.

Who are you? Lucie thought. *Why are you hiding? You need to see without being seen, don't you?*

Suddenly, the girl's lips pulled back, uncovering her teeth. Her features creased. Lucie had the sudden impression of confronting an incarnation of absolute evil. Like a warrior, the child began running toward the rabbits, which hopped in every direction. With a rapid movement, she grabbed one by the scruff of its neck and, with a grimace that must have been accompanied by a shriek, ripped its head off.

Blood spattered over her face.

She dropped the tattered animal and attacked another, still yelling. Lucie clenched her fists. Even though the film was silent, one could gauge the power, the savageness of the child's scream.

In a cacophony that the cop could easily imagine, all the girls started panicking. They huddled tighter together, while the terrified rabbits ran between their legs. Their faces turned toward the corner where the girl from the swing had looked the first time. Lucie was certain that someone was standing there, talking. Someone the cameraman had taken care never to film. No doubt the organizer of these abominations. The guru. The monster god.

The children's features tensed further, their shoulders drooped, their terror burst forth. One of the girls rushed out from the group with a howl and leaped at the animal hopping in front of her. She grabbed it by the ears and slammed it against a wall.

The next pictures defied anything the human spirit could conceive.

Carnage, hecatomb, madness: this is what emerged from the horrifying sequence. One by one, the little girls set about slaughtering the animals. Spurts of silent shouts, blood, bodies flying, crashing against walls, or being trampled. No limit to the horror, the barbarity. The image wavered as the camera hesitated, not knowing where to turn next. The cameraman tried to catch the girls' faces and movements, zooming in and out to capture the dizzying quality of the scene.

In less than a minute, the forty or so rabbits had been massacred. Dark spots polluted faces and clothes. The children were panting, on their feet, on all fours, squatting, completely disunited from one another. Their faces had become haggard, their eyes staring at guts and blood.

The film ended. Black screen on the computer.

Lucie folded down her laptop with a long sigh. She opened her hands, palms stretched toward her face: her fingers were still shaking. Uncontrollable tremors that hadn't left her since the day before. Once again, she felt a physical need to hold her sick daughter. In pajamas, she rushed toward Juliette's bed and hugged the sleeping child in her arms. On the verge of tears, she caressed her hair tenderly. She rarely wept these past years. You can sob so much during a period of depression that it seems like you're all cried out. But here, she felt the faucets threatening to open again, that a rain of grief could submerge her. A cop's equilibrium is so fragile. It's like a nutshell that slowly cracks open, with every tap of a manhunt or crime scene.

Feeling an irrepressible need, Lucie got up suddenly, picked up her cell phone, and dialed Sharko's number, which she'd gotten from administrative services. She had to talk about this case with someone. Spew it all up into an understanding ear, someone who could listen, who was in tune with her. Or so she hoped. To her great dismay, she got his voice mail. She took a breath and blurted out:

"Henebelle here. We've got some news about the film—I'd like to talk to you about it. How's it going in Egypt? Call me when you can."

She hung up, stretched out on her back, and closed her eyes. The film was her obsession, its images seared into her brain. Kashmareck hadn't been very talkative on the way back either. Though they should have been going over the case in detail, each one preferred to concentrate on the strip of asphalt, lost in private thoughts. The captain had merely said, "We'll talk about this tomorrow, Lucie. Tomorrow, okay?"

Okay, tomorrow. It was already tomorrow. A sleepless night populated with monstrosities.

Juliette suddenly turned and nestled against her mother's chest.

"Mom . . ."

"It's okay, baby, it's all okay. Go back to sleep. It's still early."

Sleepy voice, full of love.

"Will you stay with me?"

"I'll stay with you. Forever."

"I'm hungry, Mom."

Lucie's face beamed.

"You're hungry? That's great! You want me to—?"

But the girl had already fallen back asleep. Lucie sank into a sigh of relief. Maybe the end of the tunnel. This particular one, at least.

Children, she thought, returning to her case. Hardly older than Juliette. What monster could have forced them to act that way? What mechanism could have triggered such violence in them? Lucie could still see the room, the outfits, the antiseptic environment. Was it a children's hospital, like this one? Were those girls patients suffering from some commonplace illness, or a serious mental disturbance? Was the man who always kept out of camera range a doctor? A scientist?

The doctor and the filmmaker. A cursed pair, who had worked together some fifty-five years ago. And whose ghosts had perhaps returned.

These unanswered questions circulated endlessly in her head. Flashes popped before her eyes, while dawn gradually spread its first colors over the steel and concrete of the medical center.

Who had created that sick film, and for what reason?

What had they put those poor girls through, lost in the thankless anonymity of concealed images?

If there had been a large cave nearby, Lucie would have taken refuge in the darkest corner, knees huddled against her chest, and thought, thought, and thought some more. She would have tried to give the killer a face, flesh out the silhouette. She liked to feel the killer she was tracking, smell the odor he left in his wake. And she was pretty good at that game; Kashmareck could attest to that. Beckers, with his scanners, would surely have seen in her brain an area that didn't light up in anyone else when confronted with a scene of violence: that of pleasure and reward. Not that she felt any pleasure; she pretty much felt like puking at each new investigation, vomiting to the death before the horrors that humans were

165

capable of inflicting. But an invisible lure snared her every time. A hook that ripped out her throat and destroyed her inside, but she couldn't get rid of.

This time, it wasn't a little fishing gear that had titillated her.

No, the line was much heavier than that.

Perfect for going after sharks.

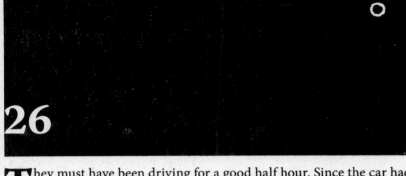

26

They must have been driving for a good half hour. Since the car had started jostling about, Sharko couldn't make out the sound of traffic. Just a sizzling noise beneath the tires. Then, more and more, it seemed that the end of the world was taking place, behind the metal of the trunk lid. A demonic wind howled, a spluttering rain crashed down from all sides with a sort of chiming sound.

A sandstorm.

Atef was bringing him into the desert.

He tried every way he could to free himself, to no avail. The layers of packing tape cut into his wrists. The filthy rag stuffed in the back of his throat had made him feel more than once like throwing up. Fuel shook around in a can, under his nose. Was he going to die like a dog? How? Were they going to pour gasoline over his head and incinerate him, just like Mahmoud? He was scared, with a stark fear of suffering before passing to the other side. He could stand a lot, and death came with the territory, but not suffering. Today, the great shadowy hand was going to close over him like a sarcophagus.

Join Suzanne and Eloise, but from the bad end of the road.

The 4x4 stopped. As a gray light filtered in, kilos of sand rushed into the recess and stung him in the face. The wind trembled. His nose covered with a cloth, Atef Abd el-Aal yanked him from the trunk and pulled him by the arms. It felt as if someone were whipping his cheeks, his forehead, his eyes. They walked for two minutes, straight ahead. In the haze of dust and sand, Sharko could make out a stone ruin with caved-in roof, buffeted by storms and wear. A long-abandoned shelter.

His tomb. The most miserable, anonymous place in the world.

Once inside, Atef released him. He collapsed, coughing into his gag.

A splash of water to the face. The sand dribbled down his collar. Atef swore in Arabic.

The Egyptian ripped open the inspector's shirt and wrapped several layers of tape around his chest, attaching him to a metal chair. Sharko breathed with difficulty through his nostrils. Thirst gripped his insides. Atef ripped off his gag. The cop coughed up repeatedly, before spitting out in a thread of bile:

"Why are you doing this?"

Atef gave him a shot in the nose with his fist. His features were twisted with hatred.

"Because they asked me to. And they're paying me like a sultan for it."

He waved Sharko's cell phone.

"You got a message."

He listened and snapped the phone shut.

"A woman from your country, nice voice . . . You getting it off with her? Is she good, you son of a dog?"

He let out a great burst of laughter and began scrolling through the call log.

"You haven't called anyone since yesterday—that's good. You're a man of your word, which is unusual for you Westerners. And for your information, my uncle's been dead for the past ten years."

The torturer disappeared into another room. Around the stone structure, the wind roared; the skin of the desert adhered to the exits and slid into the cracks. Windows were broken, loose tiles littered the floor, iron bars jutted from the walls like daggers. Sharko tried the tape around his wrists: it burned.

The Egyptian returned with a large battery, alligator clamps, knives with curved tips, and a jerry can of gasoline. At that moment, the cop knew he was done for. He struggled, receiving in exchange a punch in the stomach. He slowly lifted his chin. Blood was running from his nose.

"Your brother. It was you . . ."

"He could never accept my homosexuality. I owe him four days in the putrid jail at Qasr el-Nil. One thing they're especially fond of over there is hanging you on the *falaka,* whipping the soles of your feet, and shoving their nightsticks up your ass."

From a small bag he pulled a miniature tape recorder and a water gourd. He took a swallow.

"I took care of him myself. It was child's play. He had to be stopped from looking into that affair."

"Who's giving the orders?"

"You wouldn't believe me if I said I have no idea. But so what? Those people gave me a life, they allowed me to be a person of respect. And now, you're going to tell this tape recorder everything the French police know about the case. You will answer my questions. If you don't, I will cut you up piece by piece."

He rubbed his mouth, his eyes demented. The grains of sand whipped across the hovel, crackled on the walls. He barked something in Arabic, then turned on the battery. The clamps snickered in a bouquet of sparks; the air seemed to crackle. Suddenly, without warning, the Egyptian shoved them onto Sharko's chest.

His screams mixed with the wail of the desert.

Atef pushed a button on the recorder. The asswipe was getting off on this.

"Tell me about the unearthed bodies. Do you have any way of identifying them?"

Tears welled in the policeman's eyes.

"Go . . . fuck yourself. Snuff me if you want . . . I don't give a shit anymore."

Atef shook his jerry can.

"I'm going to burn you a little, play around with my knives, then leave you here in the desert—alive. The hyenas and vultures will make a meal of you within hours. Your body will never be found."

He smacked Sharko across the face with the gas can.

A crack, a spurt of blood.

"They want the recordings, do you understand? I have to prove I did my job, that they can trust in me. If you weren't so tenacious, this wouldn't be happening. But you—you're like my brother, you'd have taken this all the way to the end. By digging around, talking to the right people, you would have ended up coming across the trail of the hospitals on your own."

The voltage needle on the battery spun across the dial in a tenth of a second. Sharko contorted, teeth clenched. A fat vein swelled on his forehead, and his organs felt like they wanted to leave his body. When the electrical storm passed, he felt his head droop to one side. A violent slap made him come to.

"How much do you know about Syndrome E?"

The inspector raised his chin, at the limit of unconsciousness. His entire body tormented him.

"More than . . . you could ever imagine."

Another slap. His eyes shot toward the back of the room. Eugenie was sitting cross-legged in a corner, rubbing grains of sand between her fingers. She was giving him her harshest stare.

"Can you tell me what the hell we're doing here, my dear Franck?"

Sharko couldn't see clearly; he was blinded by tears. His lips opened in a sad smile. Blood began pouring from his nostrils and gums.

"You really think I had a choice?"

Atef knit his brow. He brandished his clamps again threateningly.

"What are you talking about?"

Eugenie stood up, eyes blazing.

"You always have a choice!"

"Not with my hands tied behind my back."

Sharko's eyes were rolling in their sockets, following the girl's movements around the room. Atef took a step back and turned around. Then the inspector leaped up and charged forward, headfirst, while still bound to his chair. He butted Atef in midabdomen with all his strength. The blow sent the Arab flying backward. There was a sharp intake of breath as he hit the wall. A steel spike jutted out of his left breast. His limbs went limp, but he wasn't dead. His face was contorted in pain and his mouth gave no sound. He raised his hands to the metal rod, but had no strength to do anything more. Blood began flowing from his lips. Surely a perforated lung.

Sharko let himself fall on his side, exhausted, his back aching horribly. Eugenie had moved closer to Abd el-Aal and looked at him with a grimace.

"That's your life all over. Corpses, fear, suffering . . . I'm not even ten yet, Franck, and just look at what you've made me witness in all these years. It's disgusting."

In his ungainly position, Sharko had dragged himself to the knives, clutching onto them with his fingers.

"I've never kept you here. I never forced you to come with me. Don't say it isn't true."

He managed without too much difficulty to undo his bonds. Standing up, he leaped at the fat water gourd and drank until his thirst was slaked. The liquid dribbled down his chin and chest, where the clumps of hair had been singed. He smelled of char, of cinder. With a piece of cloth, he wiped his nose and walked up to the still-breathing Atef. Sharko looked through his torturer's pockets: papers, wallet, a cigarette lighter. He took the keys to the car, reclaimed his cell phone, and poured gasoline over the Arab's head. The dying man's eyes still found the strength to open wide.

Sharko turned toward Eugenie, sitting in a corner.

"You don't have to watch this."

"I want to watch you. I want to see what horrors you feed on to keep living."

"He deserves it. Can you understand that?"

Sharko clenched his jaws, hesitating. Slowly, his furious eyes rose toward Atef's. He came within inches of his lips.

"I've hunted down garbage like you all my life. I would have killed every last one of you if I'd had the chance. I loathe people like you from the depths of my soul."

He flicked the lighter and smiled:

"Thanks for the clue about the hospitals. And this is for your brother, you son of a dog."

He stood there, not moving. He wanted the Arab to go to hell with the image of his face as the last thing he saw. He was still smiling when Atef contorted in a final breath, when his skin began to crackle. Then, with no longer a thought for Eugenie, he charged forward, head down. All around him was the apocalypse. The desert was churning; you couldn't see farther than ten yards. The black smoke mixed with the swirling sand. Sharko spotted the 4x4 and took shelter in it. He had to wait half an hour for the sandstorm to end, which headed off west like a giant steamroller. A search of the car hadn't yielded anything—not a cell phone, not a handwritten note. Just a pen and some Post-its. The caramelized pig had been careful. As for the message on his own phone, it was just Henebelle. Sharko would call her when he got back to Paris.

The vehicle contained a GPS that could be set to English. The policeman tried out "Cairo center." And crazy as it seemed, the machine calculated and indicated a direction—some ten miles away, six of them over the burning stones of the desert. They wouldn't find Abd el-Aal for quite some time.

He looked at his hands. They weren't trembling. Steady. He had burned a man alive in cold blood, without repulsion, driven by no more than a dangerous hatred. He hadn't thought he was still capable of it, but the shadows were still within him, alive as ever. You never got rid of things like that.

Before setting off, Sharko carefully noted the GPS coordinates of where he was, though he doubted he'd ever have to come back here.

Very soon, he recognized the first foothills of the Mokattam Mountains, as well as the Saladin Citadel. Once in the city, he tossed the GPS out the window and stashed the 4x4 in an abandoned corner near the Necropolis, leaving its doors unlocked. Given the area and the number of auto parts resellers per square yard, it would take less than an hour for the vehicle to be stripped.

He was lucky. In France, he would have had trouble getting away with such a crime, with the police force's technical know-how and its doggedness in uncovering the truth. But here, between the heat, the desert, the vultures, and above all the incompetent cops . . .

On foot, Sharko rejoined the wider streets on the other side of the citadel. For once, the rumble of traffic had a calming effect. A taxi honked, and Sharko raised his arm. The driver stared at him strangely when he climbed in back.

"That's okay?"

"That's okay."

Sharko asked for the Salaam Center, in Ezbet el-Nakhl.

"Are you sure?"

"Yes."

He rubbed a handkerchief over his face and it came away covered in sand and blood. Every time he moved he heard a whining sound, even down in his shoes.

Initially, he'd considered telling everything to Lebrun, then thought better of it. He couldn't quite picture himself confessing to the French embassy that he'd killed a man in self-defense on Egyptian soil. No one would believe his story; Noureddine had it in for him. He wouldn't get any special treatment. He'd be risking a diplomatic incident, prison time. Egyptian jail—no, thanks, he'd had enough torture. No choice in the matter: he had to keep his secret, act alone. And, consequently, forgo the chance to gain information by digging into Atef Abd el-Aal's past.

On the way, he tried to put some order into that convoluted story.

Fifteen years ago, a killer with medical training violently murdered three girls, leaving behind no visible traces. The case quiets down, but a scrupulous Egyptian policeman persists, picks up the trail, and fires off a telegram to Interpol. The killer, or people in contact with the killer, become aware of it. Are they cops? Politicians? Top-level executives with access to privileged information? Whatever the case, these people decide to make Mahmoud disappear along with most of his evidence. They employ his brother, who essentially becomes their lookout on Egyptian soil. Here, anything can be bought. The silent partners know what hatred lies between the brothers. Time goes by. The discovery at Gravenchon gives a new kick to the anthill. The link with Egypt, tenuous as it might be, is established. Sharko flies over; the Arab contacts his employers, probably after the meeting on the building rooftop. "They" ask him to dig a little deeper, try to find out what the French cop intends to do. And they probably give him final instructions: eliminate the policeman if he sticks his nose any deeper into the case. To capture Sharko and make him fall into the net, Abd el-Aal tells him about his uncle before trying to get rid of him the next day.

In his interrogation, the Arab had mentioned a Syndrome E. "How much do you know about Syndrome E?" What was lurking behind that chilling term? And what discovery was making the men behind this business so afraid?

With a sigh, Sharko felt his arms and cheeks. He was here, alive. Maybe his brain was on the tilt, but his carcass still had some gas in its tank. And despite the small rolls of flesh that had comfortably settled onto his midriff, his bones that often screamed in pain, he was proud of this body that had never let him down.

Today, he had once again become a street cop.

An outlaw.

27

Claude Poignet's killers hadn't escaped the Locard exchange principle, which states: "One cannot go to and return from a place, or enter and leave a room, without bringing in or leaving behind something of oneself, and without taking away something that was previously in the place or room." No one is infallible or invisible, not even the most thoroughgoing bastard. In the darkroom, the forensic technicians had found a minuscule blond eyebrow hair, as well as traces of sweat around the eyecup of one of the 16 mm cameras used to film the murder. Though evaporated, the sweat had left enough dried skin cells, picked up by the CrimeScope, to allow for DNA analysis. Not much chance of the killer's name popping up in the fingerprint database, but at least they'd now have a genetic profile, which they could use for comparison in a subsequent arrest.

The thing now was to make an arrest.

Criminal Investigations Division, Lille. Eyelids heavy, Lucie finished her third coffee of the morning, black, no sugar, sitting at a table with the main investigators involved in the case, which internally had been given the sober label "Deadly Reel." The film had just been shown in its two versions: first the "official" one, then the variant with the children and rabbits. Following this was a presentation of stills depicting the more evident subliminal images: the nude woman, then the same woman mutilated, fat black eye on her stomach.

The jokey atmosphere that normally characterized task forces, especially in the summer months, had quickly soured. Sighs, whispers, closed faces. Everyone gauged the complexity of the case, measured the killers' perversity, and provided his own commentary. Captain Kashmareck restored order:

"We have a digitized copy of the film, which is something the killers don't know. I am therefore requesting you not let that information get out. These people killed to get hold of this film, which means that its hidden content must lead somewhere. Any ideas about what you've just seen?"

A hullabaloo broke out. Among all the remarks offered, from the very constructive "It's disgusting!" to "Those children are completely nuts," there wasn't really anything worth the climax of a *Columbo* episode. Kashmareck cut short the chatter.

"Two things to note here. First, we're in touch with a historian specializing in films from the fifties, someone Claude Poignet had contacted. The man had set the old restorer's request aside, but when he learned of his death he immediately got back to work trying to identify the actress. We're keeping our fingers crossed. On our side, we're going to make prints of the actress, who I still want us to think of as an actress, and spread it around the film societies and revival houses—you never know. Second, in a minute I'm going to bring in a former expert in psychomorphology, who today specializes in lip-reading. She knows how to read silent films and will help us get down every last word that comes from the girl's mouth. Madelin, did you check with Kodak and the lab that manufactured the film stock?"

The young go-getter opened his notepad with a sigh.

"It no longer exists—these days it's a McDonald's. I was able to trace the former owners, but they're dead."

"Fine. Morel, you get hold of young Szpilman and issue a warrant to come here and try to establish a composite portrait of the fellow in combat boots. Crombez, you get on forensics to keep them moving with the DNA and the rest. We've got the warrant from the international court for a search of Szpilman's place with the Belgians at two o'clock. We need someone there. Henebelle, you on it?"

"Sure. Belgium seems to be my thing these days. Have they questioned the film archive to find out which donor had given them the deadly reel?"

"They're working on it."

Lucie spoke to Madelin: "And what about the phone numbers of our Canadian caller?"

"Once again, I reached out to Quebec Sûreté to get the info. For the two numbers you provided, the first one came from a phone booth in the center of town, and the other, the mobile, ended up at a fictitious name and address."

Lucie nodded. The informant had displayed exemplary distrust. The captain, who was nervously twiddling a cigarette, took the floor again:

"I've got a meeting in Paris with the top brass tomorrow morning. Péresse from Rouen, Leclerc from Violent Crimes, and Sharko, a behavioral analyst."

Sharko . . . Lucie squeezed her lips shut. He hadn't even bothered to call her back.

"Anything new from Egypt?" she asked.

"Not for the moment—this Sharko probably didn't get anything from his trip over there. In any case, I want to have something to tell them tomorrow. After we hear from Caroline Caffey, our lip-reading specialist, everyone gets to work."

Kashmareck went out, returning a few moments later with a woman who set all the men's eyes ablaze. About forty, she had long legs, blond hair, and the face of a Russian doll. She quickly scanned the group, settled into a chair that seemed to be reaching out for her, and opened a memo pad. With her firm, decisive movements, she must have been used to subduing the troops. She explained briefly, in discursive tones, that she worked for the military, customs, and the police, especially in antiterrorism and hostage negotiations. A heavyweight in her field. Lucie had never felt such attention around her. The testosterone level was rising. At least this bombshell had the power to capture their minds.

Caroline Caffey took control of the laptop, its contents displayed on a wide screen via a rear projector.

"Doing a lip-reading analysis of this film was not easy. In Canada as in France, there are various dialects, from street slang to formal discourse. The little girl is probably part of the country's French-speaking community, as she speaks Quebec French, or more precisely Joual, an urban working-class sociolect from the Montreal area. It's a way of speaking very similar to what you hear in the north of Bordeaux. Lots of long vowels, for instance."

Straight as a ruler in her Chanel suit, she used the mouse to advance the film to the adult actress from the beginning. It was just before she had her eye slit with a scalpel. Her lips began to move. Caffey let it run and translated simultaneously:

"She's speaking to the cameraman and saying, 'Open the door of secrets to me.'"

"Is that in French French or Quebec French?" asked Lucie.

Caffey accorded her a look heavy with indifference.

"Miss?"

"Henebelle. Lucie Henebelle."

She'd called her Miss. Damned observant.

"Hard to say, Miss Henebelle. Those are her only words. But I think French French. Especially because of the word 'secrets,' which she would have pronounced with her mouth open wider in Canadian French."

Lucie jotted in her Moleskin: "Adult actress: French" and "Little girl on swing: Montreal." Caffey forwarded the film a bit and came to the girl on the swing set. Explosion of joy on the child's face. Camera focused in tightly enough so that you couldn't see the surroundings. The filmmaker didn't want anyone to recognize the place. As soon as the little girl started talking, Caroline imitated her:

"Can we play on the swings again tomorrow? . . . Will you come see me again soon? . . . Lydia wants to play on the swings too . . . Why can't she go outside?"

The girl rose toward the sky, filled with joy. The camera lingered on her face and eyes, played with different shots, establishing a dynamic. There was an evident closeness between the cameraman and the little girl; they knew each other well. The more she watched these images, the more Lucie felt herself gripped in the gut by that innocent kid. An incomprehensible bond, a kind of maternal affection. She did her best to push away this kind of dangerous sentiment.

Next relevant scene. Close-up on the child's lips as she ate potatoes and ham at a long wooden table. Caffey began decoding:

". . . I heard them talking. A lot of people are saying mean things about you and the doctor . . . I know they're lying—they're just saying that to hurt us. I don't like them. I'll never like them."

Caroline Caffey's sentences rang out in the silence. The words and the tone she used gave the images a baleful character. You could feel the unease growing, the storm about to break. Lucie jotted down and circled the word "doctor."

Scene of the little girl and the kittens in the grass. She smiled widely, affectionately petting the two animals. Lucie thought of the other film, the hidden film, which at that very moment was nesting in the frames and had lodged in her brain.

". . . I'd like to keep them . . . Oh, too bad . . . Will you bring them back again? . . . Sister Marie du Calvaire hated kitties . . . I love them . . . Yes, bunnies too. I love bunnies . . . Hurt them? Why did you say that? . . . No, never."

Lucie took notes, picking up on the irony of the statements. Never hurt rabbits, when at that very moment, buried within those very images, she was slaughtering them with eleven other little girls. What could have precipitated such a drastic change? She underscored "Sister Marie du Calvaire" with three red lines. Was the girl in a convent in Montreal? A Catholic school? A place where medicine and religion might coexist?

Next scene, strange: the camera moves closer and farther from the little girl, taunting her. The girl is angry. Her eyes have changed.

". . . Leave me alone, I don't feel like it . . . I'm sad about Lydia, everybody is sad, and *you* think it's funny." She pushes the camera aside. "Go away!"

"What happened to Lydia?" Lucie noted, drawing a box around the name. The camera turned around the girl to create a dizzying effect. *Cut.* Following scene: the field.

Caroline Caffey stopped the projection. She swallowed before continuing:

"Nothing more after this, other than screams in the scene with the rabbits. There's one more thing that might interest you: if you look closely at certain sequences, there are details that I noticed on the little girl's face. It has changed. In some images she's missing a front tooth. And even if it doesn't show very clearly, she acquires red blotches on her skin. Her hair remains the same length. They must have cut it regularly."

"So she got older between the beginning of the film and the end," deduced Kashmareck.

"Indeed. This film was not made in a week, but certainly over a period of several months. As it progresses, you feel a growing tension in the girl's mouth, a tension that seems to correspond to her words. It's too short and probably too abbreviated to draw valid conclusions, but I get the feeling that her psychological state is deteriorating. No more smiles; her face becomes dull, angry. In certain scenes, even though they're in bright light, her pupils are dilated."

Lucie twirled her pen between her fingers. She remembered the absolute fury of the children in the room with the rabbits.

"Drugs . . . or some kind of medication?"

Caroline nodded.

"Quite likely."

She shut her memo pad and stood up.

"That's all I can tell you. I'll send you a document with my analysis as soon as I can type it up. Gentlemen, miss . . ."

An exchange of glances with Kashmareck, indicating that she'd wait for him outside. Not a single question about the ongoing case, not the slightest emotion regarding what she'd just seen. A pro. After she left the room, the captain clapped his hands together.

"Think carefully about what she's just told us. And I believe we can all thank Henebelle for this superb case in the middle of summer."

Every head turned toward her, and a few bad wisecracks blurted out. Lucie took it all in stride—what else could she do? Kashmareck restored order one last time:

"Okay, everyone clear on what to do?"

Silent nods.

"Get to it, then."

Lucie remained behind a few moments, alone in front of the computer, facing the little girl halted on her swing. She ran her fingers over the frozen smile. It was as if the child were smiling at her, radiating innocence.

Lost in thought, Lucie's mind returned to Sharko. She was even getting a bit worried. Why this silence? She looked at her phone. Who was he really, that behavioral analyst she couldn't stop thinking about? What was his past, his service record? What horrific cases had he dealt with when he was younger? She dialed up the national police administrative office.

Her rank granted her access to information on any police officer in France. Past cases, ongoing ones, even superior officers' comments . . . The entire CV. Once she had identified herself, she asked for the career highlights of Franck Sharko. Reason? She had to take over one of his cases. Her request would be logged, but too bad.

A few seconds later, she was politely informed that her request could not be granted, with no further explanation. Before hanging up, she asked whether anyone had requested her own file. They answered in the affirmative. The day before yesterday, to be precise, the head of Violent Crimes had: Martin Leclerc.

She hung up with an annoyed pout.

So Sharko and his boss had calmly rifled through her jacket. They knew about her past. And that bastard had made sure not to reveal his.

Go ahead, help yourself.

With a sigh, she raised her eyes back to the little girl on the screen. Someone's daughter. Montreal. Canada. Today, that unknown girl must have been twice her own age. And perhaps she was still alive, somewhere in the depths of that faraway country, carrying within her all the secrets of this horrendous episode.

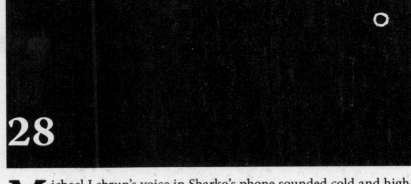

28

Michael Lebrun's voice in Sharko's phone sounded cold and high-handed.

"Where are you?"

"In a taxi. I'm going to buy some Egyptian whiskey for my boss and a few presents. Tell Nahed not to bother waiting for me at the hotel. I'll meet her at the police station early this afternoon."

"No, *I'll* meet you there. Noureddine called me. He's fit to be tied. You'd be well-advised to return the stolen photos to him as quickly as possible. And don't expect him to open any more doors for you—that's over."

"Not a problem. Nothing more to be gained from that file anyway."

"You can be certain I'll be informing your superior about this."

"Please do. He gets off on this kind of thing."

A pause. Sharko leaned his head against the window. Far to the north, the colors of Cairo grew duller as the taxi approached the trash collectors' quarter.

"Head feeling better?" asked Lebrun.

"What?"

"You had a headache yesterday."

"Much better, thanks."

"No more slipups before your flight this evening, Inspector."

Sharko thought about the charred face of Atef Abd el-Aal, who was rotting pathetically in the sun.

"There won't be any slipups. You can trust me."

"Trust you? I'd sooner trust a rattlesnake."

Lebrun hung up sharply. Those embassy guys were a sensitive bunch to say the least, attached to their protocols like good little do-bees. No relation to Sharko's concept of how a cop's job should be done.

The black taxicab halted in the middle of the road, simply because the road itself had stopped dead. No more pavement, just earth and loose rocks that only a pickup truck or *tok-tok* could make it through. The *osta bil-fitra* explained in approximate English that to get to the Salaam Center, you just had to hold your nose and walk straight ahead.

So Sharko started walking—and discovered the unimaginable. He plunged into the beating heart of Cairo's trash cities. Blue and black garbage bags, swollen with heat and rot, rose so far that they hid the sky. Flocks of kites with dirty feathers flew overhead in precise circles. Heaps of rusted tins and metal drums agglutinated into makeshift shelters. Pigs and goats roamed freely, the way cars might circulate elsewhere. His nose buried in his shirt, Sharko creased his eyes. At the top of the heap, the trash bags began shimmying.

People. People lived in those mountains of refuse.

As he advanced through these entrails of despair, Sharko discovered the garbage people, the ones who picked through all this trash to squeeze out the last droplets of juice, the bit of cloth or paper that might earn them the slightest piastre. How many were living in this slum alone? A thousand? Two? Sharko thought of carrion insects, which took turns on corpses during the decomposition phase. The city's trash arrived by the cartload; people ripped open the plastic bags like wild dogs, sorted out the paper, the metal, even the cotton from disposable diapers.

Swarms of children came running up to Sharko, clung to him, smiled at him despite everything, and made him understand, with hand gestures, that he should take their photo with his phone. They weren't even asking for money, just a little attention. Moved, Sharko joined in the game. With every shot, the sooty urchins came over to see, then burst out laughing. A little girl, dirty as charcoal, took the inspector's hand and stroked it gently. Even filth and poverty could not eliminate beauty. She wore clothes stitched together from old Portland cement sacks. Sharko knelt down and ran his hands through her greasy hair.

"You look like my daughter . . . You all look like her . . ."

He dug into his pockets, pulled out three-quarters of his change, and handed it out to the children. Hundreds of pounds—nothing for him, but masses and masses of sorted cloth for them. They disappeared down the variegated streets, fighting over the coïns.

The cop was suffocating. He took off at a run straight ahead. Egypt had him by the throat. He thought of Paris, of the hectic lives people led, with their phones, their cars, their Ray-Bans pushed up on their scalps. People who pissed and moaned when their train arrived five minutes late.

A semblance of humanity seemed to reappear past the last towers of refuse. Sharko discovered buildings that resembled bottom-rung housing projects. Farther on stretched little stalls, actual dwellings, if one could call them that, with laundry hanging from the windows like the multi-colored hordes of misery, and goats on the rooftops. Sharko even discovered a convent of nuns, the Coptic Orthodox Community of Sisters. Children clad in uniforms walked in groups through a courtyard, praying and singing. Here, too, despite everything, life asserted its right to exist.

He finally reached the Salaam Center hospital, a long, low grayish building that looked like a dispensary. Inside, one could feel the lack of resources, the struggle these shadow-people led against impossible odds. A cursory waiting room with basic furniture, secondhand chairs, small tables, and swinging doors with round portholes that looked like something out of Egyptian films from the forties. Boxes containing first aid kits, stenciled with the symbol of the French Red Cross, were stacked in the corners.

In English, Sharko spoke to a nun sitting in the waiting room. She was with a child, whose every breath produced a long wheeze. Going from person to person, the cop managed to reach the office of the hospital's director, Taha Abou Zeid. The man's features bespoke his Nubian ancestry: dark skin, thick lips, pencil mustache trimmed straight as a ruler, broad nose. He was typing on an old hand-me-down computer that wouldn't have fetched ten euros in France. Sharko knocked on the open door.

"Excuse me?"

The man raised his eyes and answered in English.

"Yes?"

Sharko introduced himself. Chief inspector with the French police, on an investigation in Cairo. The doctor explained his own role. A devout Christian, he and the sisters of the Coptic convent managed to support a day care center, a hospital, a rehab center, and a maternity ward. The hospital's main mission was to care for and teach hygiene to the Zabbaleen, the "garbage people," who crammed by more than fifteen thousand into the buildings around the site, plus five thousand who ate and slept directly in the piles of trash.

Five thousand . . . Sharko thought of the little girl who had hugged him. For a moment he forgot his case, and asked instead:

"I saw those poor people in the streets of Cairo. Kids not even ten years old, who were scavenging for trash and putting it on donkey carts . . . Garbage collectors?"

"Yes. There are more than ten thousand of them, spread over the capital's eight major slums. Early every morning, the men and the kids who are old enough head into Cairo in their carts to collect refuse. Their wives and the smaller children sort it out. Then the trash is sold to merchants, who themselves sell it to local recycling centers. Pigs eat the organic waste, and in this way ninety percent of the city's garbage is either recycled or reused . . . A very ecological model, if it weren't based on such poverty. Our mission, here at the center, is to remind these people that they're still human."

Sharko nodded toward a photo behind him.

"That looks like Sister Emmanuelle."

"It is. The Salaam Center was founded in the 1970s. *Salaam* means 'peace' in Arabic."

"Peace . . ."

Sharko finally took out a photo of one of the victims and showed it to the doctor.

"This photo is over fifteen years old. The girl, Boussaina Abderrahmane, came to this hospital."

The doctor took the photo; his face darkened.

"Boussaina Abderrahmane. I've never forgotten her. Her body was discovered about three miles from here, in some sugarcane fields to the north. It was in . . ."

"March 1994."

"March 1994 . . . I remember now. It was such a shock. Boussaina Abderrahmane lived with her parents on the outskirts of Ezbet el-Nakhl, near the subway stop, on the other side of the shantytown. She went to

Saint Mary's, the Christian school, during the day, and earned a little money at night working in a jeweler's studio. But tell me something—a policeman was already here, a long time ago. His name was . . ."

"Mahmoud Abd el-Aal."

"That's right. A policeman who was, how shall I put it . . . different from the others. How is he?"

"He died, also a long time ago. An accident."

Sharko let him absorb the news, then continued:

"Can you tell me about her? Why had she come to your hospital?"

The doctor ran a hand over his wizened face. Sharko saw in him a worn-out man who nonetheless gave off an indefinable aura, the aura of goodness and courage.

"I'm going to try to explain this, assuming one can comprehend the incomprehensible."

He stood up and began rummaging through thick files stacked up on old shelves.

"Nineteen ninety-three, ninety-four . . . Here, this is it."

Everything had its place in this chaos. The doctor looked through the sheets of paper and handed the inspector a newspaper clipping. Sharko handed it back.

"I'm sorry, but I—"

"Oh, of course. Stupid of me. It's an article from the newspaper *al-Ahaly*, dated April 1993. I'll summarize it for you."

Sharko's brain was already ticking. April 1993, one year before the murders. The article took up the entire page, dotted with school class photos.

"Starting on March 31, 1993, and lasting several days, our country experienced a very strange occurrence. Around five thousand people, mostly young girls, underwent a curious phenomenon. For most of them, it took the form of a fainting spell in class that lasted a minute or two, preceded by a severe headache that came on without warning. They were immediately brought to the nearest hospital and given a thorough checkup. But since the hospital couldn't find anything out of the ordinary, the girls were sent home."

The doctor indicated a map of Egypt behind him, pointing out different regions with his finger.

"Some of the girls in the same classroom did not faint, but instead started exhibiting aggressive behavior. Screams, banging on the wall, unprovoked violence toward their schoolmates. The phenomenon started in the Beheira governorate, then in the blink of an eye reached fifteen of the nineteen governorates in Egypt. It struck quickly in cities like Sharkia, Kafr el-Sheikh, and Cairo. You could compare it to an earthquake, with the epicenter in Beheira and shockwaves that reached all the way to the capital."

Sharko leaned both hands against the desk, his entire weight on his wrists.

"But what exactly are you talking about? Some kind of virus?"

"No, not a virus. Specialists tried to study the phenomenon. All sorts of rumors began circulating. Nationwide food poisoning, eating unripe beans, gas seepages from basements. A virus would have explained a lot, but the way it had spread didn't correspond, and again the medical tests turned up nothing. So they soon shifted to something else. They started suspecting the Israelis of poisoning the water in the schools or of secret biological warfare. They even considered 'aftereffects' of the Iran-Iraq War. Nothing was too irrational. And still the medical tests revealed absolutely nothing. And nothing could explain why the phenomenon mainly affected girls."

"So then what?"

"A group of psychiatrists suggested it was some kind of mass hysteria."

"Mass hysteria?"

The doctor pointed to a book with an English title.

"I had a bit of an interest in such phenomena. They've been around for a long time. In most cases, a few dozen people in the same place would suddenly come down with feelings of unease, pain, nausea, pruritus, or skin eruptions. Such things were already being recorded a thousand years ago. In 1999, in a school in Belgium—not that far from you—some forty students were hospitalized after drinking lemonade, though there was no evidence of intoxication. In 2006, a hundred students in the Vietnamese province of Tien Giang came down with digestive illnesses. I could cite tons of cases. Gulf War Syndrome, which affected American GIs in 1991. A few weeks after they returned home, these soldiers began experiencing memory lapses, nausea, and fatigue. At first they suspected contamination by neurotoxins, but in that case, why would their wives and children, who had remained on American soil, have come down with the same symptoms, at the same time, and throughout the country? It was a veritable collective hysteria that cut across the United States."

"Was Boussaina Abderrahmane affected by the thing that happened in Egypt?"

"Yes, along with six other girls in her class. In their case, it was the aggressive form of the hysteria that got them. Vulgar language, thrown chairs—according to their teacher, they had become like wild animals. They even attacked another girl, with whom they usually got along fine. Why should this hysteria sometimes unleash such violence? Unfortunately, we don't know. Could it have been stress caused by overly strict teachers? The students' poor living conditions? Their lack of education? Whatever the case, it happened. Truly happened."

Sharko was seething. What he was hearing went beyond all understanding. *Collective hysteria* . . . He showed the photos of the other victims.

"And what about them? Did you know them too? Did Mahmoud Abd el-Aal ever mention them?"

"No. Don't tell me that—"

"They were also killed, at the same time. Didn't you know?"

"No."

Sharko put the photos back in his pocket. It was likely the police had done everything possible to keep the news from getting into the press and causing widespread panic. For his part, Inspector Abd el-Aal had been professional and prudent, safeguarding his information and avoiding leaks. Taha Abou Zeid stared in front of him for a moment, then shook his head.

"The incident itself lasted only a short time, but Boussaina bore its traces forever. It was as if there had been a permanent change in her behavior. She experienced regular episodes of aggression. Her parents kept bringing her in, because she was pulling away from her schoolmates emotionally, growing more solitary, and clearly wasn't happy. They chalked it up to adolescence, or her difficult environment. But . . . it was something else."

"What?"

"Something psychological, which affected her deep down. But I didn't really have the psychiatric skills to get to the bottom of it, and then she was murdered."

"And what about her classmates?"

"The violent episodes stopped, and there were no particular problems afterward."

Sharko let out a prolonged sigh. The farther he went, the more walls he ran up against. Could the killer have specifically targeted those girls affected by that mass hysteria? Could he have concentrated on the most extreme cases, the ones who'd remained symptomatic? And if so, why?

"Was this incident generally known?"

"Of course. It was taken up by every scientific community that had anything to do with social or psychiatric phenomena. It would have been hard for the Egyptian government to keep a lid on something that huge. There were even articles in the *Washington Post* and *New York Times*. Look in any archive—you'll find them."

So the killer could have found out about this from anywhere in the world. And by digging a little, reaching out to the right people, he could easily have gotten the addresses of the affected schools. Here, in Ezbet el-Nakhl. Then in the Shubra quarter, and Tora.

Little by little, the puzzle was taking shape. The killer had struck in areas far enough apart so that no pattern would emerge, and yet patterns were exactly what he was looking for. Why wait a year? So that the episodes wouldn't be quite so present in people's minds, and neither the police nor anyone else would make the connection. He had been careful to separate his crimes from the wave of mass folly, and when Mahmoud Abd el-Aal had finally established the link, they'd done away with him.

This case defied all logic. Sharko thought of the film Henebelle had found in Belgium, and also of the mysterious Canadian contact. Ramifications extended around the world like the tentacles of an octopus. Had foreigners come here to learn about the phenomenon and find the girls touched by the wave? The inspector decided to try his luck.

"I suppose Abd el-Aal must have already asked you, but . . . do you recall anyone coming to ask you about the mass hysteria or about Boussaina before she was killed?"

"It's all so long ago."

"I saw boxes of medicine when I came in, stamped with the symbol of the French Red Cross. Do you work with them? Do you come into contact with a lot of foreigners? Have any Frenchmen been here?"

"It's funny . . . I can recall the Egyptian policeman so well now. I think he was like you. The same questions, the same persistence."

"Just someone trying to do his job."

The doctor gave a sad smile. He must not have smiled very often here.

"Those medicines come from all over, not just the French Red Cross. We're an Egyptian aid organization dedicated to promoting communities, personal wellness, social justice, and health. We get support from all over, including the Red Crescent, the Red Cross, and many other humanitarian agencies. Thousands of people have been through here—volunteers, visitors, politicians, and curiosity-seekers. And if I remember correctly, 1994 was also the year of a major conference of the SIGN alliance, the Safe Injection Global Network. Thousands of researchers and scientists were pouring through the streets of Cairo."

Sharko noted the information. Possibly the beginning of a lead. One could easily imagine a volunteer or humanitarian organization staff member on a trip to Cairo at the time of the murders. Easy for him to gain access to the hospitals and patients' addresses. It might turn up something, but going back fifteen years through the morass of administrative red tape promised to be no cakewalk.

Everything was starting to fall into place. Back then, an Egyptian cop had sensed the involvement of a foreign killer, who had come to Egypt under cover of an association or conference. That explained the telegram to Interpol—Abd el-Aal was trying to find out if the killer had struck somewhere else in the world. The telegram must have triggered his execution. Which suggested that someone on the inside with access to the information—a policeman, soldier, or upper-level functionary—had been involved.

"I have one last request, Doctor. I have the names of the two other girls. I'd be very grateful if you could look up the hospitals that serve their neighborhoods, call them, and let me know if those two had been affected by the hysteria as well."

"That will take all afternoon. I'm very busy, and—"

"Wouldn't you like to be able to give the parents of those children an answer someday?"

After a pause, the doctor agreed, lips pressed tight. Sharko gave him his cell number.

"Your book about collective hysteria—can I borrow it? I'll send it back from France very soon."

The Nubian nodded. Sharko thanked him warmly.

Then he left him there, in the middle of that poverty that no one gave a damn about.

29

The police academy in Liège—the administrative headquarters of the local police force—had requisitioned a locksmith, a sergeant, and two detective trainees to accompany Lucie to Szpilman's. In principle, the Frenchwoman didn't have the right to touch a thing. She was there solely to help advise the local police and take notes.

Lucie was not feeling particularly reassured by the closed door of the Liège residence. Since the previous day, Luc Szpilman had failed to answer the phone calls informing him of the impending search, nor had he answered the summons to the police station to help establish a composite sketch of the man in combat boots. The cops' insistent ringing of the doorbell didn't help matters. When the locksmith came forward with his tool kit to pick the lock, Lucie moved to block him, arms outstretched.

"It's no use."

She nodded toward the lock, which looked broken.

"Don't touch the doorknob. Did you bring gloves?"

Debroeck, leading the unit, took several pairs out of his uniform pocket. He distributed them to his colleagues and offered a pair to Lucie. No words were exchanged. The men unholstered their Glock 9s and entered the house, followed by Lucie brandishing her Sig Sauer. The locksmith remained outside.

Inside the house, flies were buzzing.

The coldness of the crime lay before them, suddenly and without warning. Lucie wrinkled her nose.

Luc Szpilman's body was splayed behind the sofa, and the body of his girlfriend on the steps leading to the kitchen. A trail of blood spread behind her.

Stabbed in the back, both of them, multiple times.

Ten, twenty, thirty stabs each, slicing through pajamas and nightgown, from calves to shoulder blades. Not easy to count.

Lucie ran her hand heavily over her face. Three days that she'd been groping her way through this macabre terrain, and it was beginning to affect her nerves. This gruesome spectacle was like a frozen tableau, as if the bodies might suddenly revive and continue trying to flee. Because that's what they were trying to do. It wasn't hard to imagine the scene. Night, probably. The killers force the lock, at the other end of the large house, and enter. It's maybe two, three o'clock in the morning; they think Luc Szpilman is alone and asleep. But—surprise—the kid is right in front of them, sitting on the couch with his girlfriend, rolling a joint, which was still there on the coffee table in the living room. Luc suddenly recognizes one of them, the guy in combat boots who'd come for the film. The kids panic, try to run away. The killers catch them and stab them in the back, once, twice.

And then that inexplicable frenzy.

Lucie and the police remained frozen in place, keeping their own thoughts. The youngest of them, a trainee barely twenty-five years old, excused himself to go outside, his face white. He worked for the local police, not the feds, and wasn't used to this kind of case. You come to search a house, easy peasy, and find yourself looking at two corpses riddled with stab wounds and already covered in flies.

Thinking quickly, Debroeck moved to protect the crime scene from contamination: the Belgian police force trains its officers well. Lucie, for her part, tried to look past the corpses and made a mental grid of the surroundings. Open drawers, furniture tipped over. She noted the presence of a smashed wall safe. The frame of the painting that had hidden it lay shattered on the floor.

"First, they keep Luc Szpilman from helping with the composite sketch, and second, they make off with anything that can compromise them."

"What could have compromised them?"

"The discoveries his father had surely made about the anonymous film. The documents he might have exchanged with the Canadian informant. They came to do some housecleaning. God dammit!"

Lucie turned around and went out, needing to breathe in some fresh air.

It was them. Claude Poignet's murderers had continued mopping things up. No ritual or theatrical display this time.

Just a senseless act committed by wild animals.

30

Leaning against Kashmareck's car, Lucie gave her boss the rundown. He had joined her at Szpilman's, shortly after the arrival of the CSI teams and two medical examiners. For several hours, people in uniform had been going in and out of the house.

Lucie nodded toward the open door.

"The MEs gave an estimated time of death. It happened the same night as Claude Poignet's murder. The killers knew the restorer's death and the theft of the film would send us running back here. So they eliminated the only person who could identify them. As for the girlfriend . . . she was just in the wrong place at the wrong time. They weren't being too particular."

She sighed.

"The computer's hard drive and all the books in his library have disappeared. There were volumes on history, espionage, genocide. Maybe Szpilman had written notes in the margins? Perhaps there was one book in particular that might have pointed us toward something? Damn, if I'd only known the first time I came here!"

"The thefts are what interest me. Old Szpilman was just a collector."

"He was more than that. He did serious research into this film, studied it inside and out, made contact with a guy in Canada who knows what he's talking about. Somehow or other, the killers found out."

Kashmareck pulled two small bottles of water from his climate-controlled glove compartment and tossed one to Lucie.

"You okay?"

"Absolutely."

"It's all right to say no."

"I'm fine."

"And your daughter, how's she doing?"

Another sigh. "Better. Big breakfast this morning, and she wolfed down her lunch. They've removed her IV. Now we're waiting for the famous verdict of the bowel movement. Just life."

Kashmareck flashed her a smile that lately had become a rare sight on his face.

"We all go through it. Kids exist to remind us that our priorities aren't always the ones we think. Even if it's hard sometimes, they put order in our lives."

"How many kids do you have?"

"More than I should." He looked at his watch. "Okay, I'm off to see the locals about getting real-time access to info from Lille. You head back. Go spend a few hours with your daughter while they wrap up here. You're not looking too hot, and the next few days threaten to be even worse."

"Got it."

She pressed her lips together, without moving.

"You know, Captain, there's something about this latest crime."

"What's that?"

"On site, the MEs counted thirty-seven stab wounds for the girl and forty-one for the kid . . . They had them all over their bodies, including the genitals. Deep wounds, several inches down. Sometimes the knife went to the hilt—they could see the marks the metal left around the slits. Given the characteristics, the similarities in the stabbing patterns, they think it's the work of a single attacker."

The commanding officer answered with silence. There was nothing to say. Lucie stared at him intently.

"There's pure madness in this, Captain. In their movements, their way of operating. Something not right in the way they've been proceeding. The same kind of irrationality we saw in those kids in the film, more than fifty years ago."

31

Eugenie was tickled pink to be leaving. She jumped up and down and squealed with delight in front of the hotel. Sharko, meanwhile, carried his suitcase to the taxi that was waiting for him at the foot of the building. No embassy Mercedes to bring him back this time. As agreed, he had returned the photos to Lebrun at the police station, at 2:00 p.m. on the dot. The embassy's inspector had come alone, and their brief conversation had not gone entirely well, especially when Lebrun had noticed the bruise near Sharko's nose. Sharko had said something about slipping in the bathtub. No further comment.

Alone on the sidewalk, the cop looked around him in the vain hope of seeing Nahed, telling her good-bye, wishing her good luck. She hadn't answered any of his calls, no doubt on embassy say-so. His throat tight, he got into the taxi and told the driver to take him to the airport.

Eugenie sat next to him for a while, then vanished during the trip. Sharko could finally enjoy the landscape without the shouting in his head. His only real moment of respite since arriving in Egypt.

Earlier that day, Taha Abou Zeid, the Nubian doctor at the Salaam Center, had called him to confirm his suppositions: the two other victims had also suffered the effects of the mass hysteria, in its most aggressive form. And according to the recollections of several doctors, who of course had not kept any records, the girls had remained symptomatic until their cruel deaths.

That was the point in common.

The collective hysteria.

The same link that might have united the five anonymous bodies in Gravenchon.

The taxi left the city center and took the Salah-Salem expressway. The breath of Cairo was slowly absorbed into the cloud of exhaust.

His forehead flattened against the window, alone with his dark thoughts, Sharko saw a train in the distance. Outside the car, near the smokestacks, four men clung on as best they could, gaining footholds on pipes or stepladders. Whatever their religions or beliefs, they huddled close together to avoid falling. And they fled into the wind, into the sun, toward the burning dust of Cairo. These men were risking their lives to get out of paying a three-pound fare, but they were smiling and seemed happy, because their poverty reminded them, better than anyone, how much life was worth living.

Then Sharko saw the ones at the airport, who crowded at the discount windows for flights to Libya, a large canvas bag their only luggage. These people, on the contrary, were fleeing Egypt to try to wrest themselves from poverty. They were heading for a country where oil decided everyone's fate. Someday they'd be sent back home, or perhaps they'd end up in some rickety skiff off the Italian coast.

Sharko had never seen the beauty of the great pyramids, but he did see that of a people whose only luxury was their dignity. As his plane rose into the air, he recalled the joke the Coptic taxi driver had told him while bringing him to the church of Saint Barbara, the night of his meeting with Nahed:

"Someone asks three people, a German, a Frenchman, and an Egyptian, what Adam and Eve's nationality was. The German answers, 'Adam and Eve exude good health and vital hygiene: they must be German!' The Frenchman declares, 'Adam and Eve have sublime, erotic bodies: they can only be French!' But the Egyptian concludes, 'Adam and Eve are naked as jaybirds, they don't have enough to buy shoes, and yet they're convinced they live in Paradise: what else could they be but Egyptians?'"

After fifteen minutes in the air, Sharko started leafing through the book on mass hysteria. As Dr. Taha Abou Zeid had briefly explained, this phenomenon had cut across time periods, nationalities, and religions. The author based his thesis on photos, eyewitness accounts, and interviews with specialists. In France, for instance, witch hunts in the Middle Ages had provoked an inordinate fear of the devil and mass acts of insanity:

screaming crowds hungry for blood, mothers and children who cheered to see "witches" burning alive.

The cases in the book were astounding. India, 2001: hundreds of individuals from different parts of New Delhi swear they were attacked by a fictional being, half man, half monkey, "with metal claws and red eyes." Certain "victims" even leap from the window to flee this creature, who'd surged right out of the collective imagination. Belgium, 1990: the Belgian Society for the Study of Space Phenomena suddenly receives several thousand sightings of UFOs. The most likely cause was held to be sociopsychological. A sudden mania for looking for flying objects, exacerbated by the media: when you want to see something, you end up seeing it. Dakar: ninety high school students go into a trance and are brought to the hospital. Some speak of a curse; there are purification rituals and sacrifices to remedy the situation.

Sharko turned the pages—it went on forever. Sects committing group suicide, panicked crowds, haunted house syndrome like the Amityville Horror, collective fainting spells at concerts . . . There was even a chapter on genocides, a "criminal mass hysteria," according to the terms of certain psychiatrists: organizers who plan coldly, calculatingly, while those who execute sink into a frenzy of wholesale destruction and butchery.

At bottom, there was no real explanation for these outbreaks, which were given various names: mass psychogenic phenomenon, mass or collective hysteria, epidemic hysteria, mass syndrome of psychogenic origin . . . It didn't appear in the psychiatric bible, the *DSM-IV*, but its existence could not be denied. Scientists spoke mainly of psychological root causes, but could not explain what triggered the phenomena—the seismic epicenter—or their very real physical manifestations: vomiting, nausea, joint and muscle pain . . .

Shortly before landing, Sharko shut the book and gazed out the window, at nothing. A bloodthirsty, sadistic individual might be seeking something in hysterical phenomena, and mutilating, killing, and stealing eyes and brains to get at it. Why? What ends could possibly justify such barbaric means? Was there even an end?

The lights of Paris finally appeared three thousand feet below. Thousands of people, huddled in front of their computers and television screens or glued to their cell phones. In a way, this was the most modern and dangerous form of mass hysteria: a vast group of humans, their minds linked by the world of images. A modern madness from which no one could escape.

Not even Sharko.

32

Under the kiss of dusk, Sharko finally reached his building in L'Haÿles-Roses. Compared with the Egyptian capital, Paris and its outskirts, with their purified subway lines, the calm faces plunged into a book or staring out the window, had become almost reassuring. Once he'd set down his bags, the cop switched on his railroad trains and let himself be carried away by the gentle rattling of the connecting rods and wheels and the whistling of steam. The sounds, smells, and little habits that went with them brought him a measure of comfort.

But the spell of Cairo remained in the pit of his stomach.

As did the delicate prickle of the alligator clamps planted on his skin.

With a sigh, Sharko went back to his living room. He set on the table the jar of cocktail sauce, glazed chestnuts, and his presents, which he'd bought at the duty-free before departure: the bottle of whiskey and carton of Marlboros for Martin Leclerc, the perfume burner for Martin's wife, Kathia.

Despite the late hour, fatigue, and aching joints from all the transportation, Sharko dragged himself to Roseraie Park, just opposite his building. A tradition, a habit, a need. Marc, the guard, was as usual watching one of his countless police shows. He opened the gate with the friendly smile you give to those you're used to seeing without really knowing them.

At the far end of the park, his usual bench awaited—an old half cylinder cut from a tree trunk, languishing under the oak where he and Suzanne had carved their initials so long ago: *F & S*. Facing the tree, eyes vacant, he ran his fingers over his chest. Once again he saw the flame of the cigarette lighter waver before the Arab's twisted mouth; he remembered the peculiar smoke of burning flesh. His jaws clenched, he used a penknife to carve a small vertical line in the bark, next to seven others.

Eight scumbags who would never harm anyone again.

He folded his blade, then sat on the bench, leaning forward, hands joined between his slightly parted knees. Seeing himself like this, he thought that he really had aged prematurely. Not physically, but emotionally. The warm air brushed over his neck like a child's caress. Shadows were settling on the capital, a large sleeping cat that you saw from below. And with them, their nauseating cloud of crimes and assaults.

He stared sadly at a patch of grass. It was precisely here that he'd first met Eugenie. At the time, sitting cross-legged, she was reading *The Adventures of Fantômette*, his daughter's favorite book, and she'd smiled at him. A poisoned smile, the initial signs of paranoid schizophrenia. The beginning of his torture, as if the deaths of Suzanne and Eloise hadn't been enough.

Even in the worst moments of his illness, Sharko had always enjoyed the support of Kathia and Martin, the man who, despite administrative and personal difficulties, had managed to keep him afloat. In 2006, Leclerc had become head of a new department, the Bureau of Violent Crimes, and offered him a job as behavioral analyst—a relatively recent position in the police force that consisted of investigating unsolved violent crimes without leaving one's desk, at least in theory. Cross-referencing information, establishing a psychological profile, and using computer and informational tools as a way of determining the killer's motives—tools such as ViCLAS (Violent Crime Linkage Analysis System), Interpol, or STIC (Information and Communications Technology Resource). On the strength of his degree in psychocriminology and his twenty years on the job, Sharko, a paranoid schizophrenic cop, had conducted a different sort of manhunt, outside the mainstream.

He sighed when his cell phone vibrated in his pocket. The screen read "Lucie Henebelle." It was almost midnight. Sharko answered with a tempered smile. The woman should have been asleep like everyone else. But no, there she was, on her phone.

"It's a bit late to be calling, Lieutenant Henebelle."

"But never too late to answer . . . I knew your plane landed at Orly at 9:30. I figured you wouldn't be asleep yet."

"That's quite a gift for divination. Do you also know what they served on board?"

Lucie was getting some fresh air outside the children's hospital.

"I left you a message yesterday. You didn't call back."

"Sorry, but someone was serving grilled fish on my chest."

A silence. Lucie took back the reins of the conversation.

"I have new information for you. They've—"

"I'm already up to speed. I called my boss when I got in. The murder of Szpilman Junior and his girlfriend, the theft of the film, and the hidden film they found inside the original. I haven't yet downloaded it from the server. At the moment, I'm on something else."

"On what else?"

"A bench. I've just covered two thousand miles, my body looks like a calculator because of the mosquitoes, and I'm trying not to think about the case for a little while, if it's all right with you."

Sharko lodged the phone between his ear and shoulder, then wiped off the toe of his shoes with a paper napkin. He looked under his sole and discovered that there were still grains of sand encrusted in the grooves. He dug a few out with his fingers and studied them attentively.

"Why are you calling?"

"I told you, I—"

"You what? You need to talk about corpses even at night? You want to know what I found out over there to feed your own obsessions? Is this what you run on, what keeps you moving forward day after day? I'd be curious to know what you dream about, Henebelle."

Lucie had stopped in the middle of the ambulance lane. White and blue lights danced on the low northern sky.

"Leave my dreams out of this, Inspector, if you don't mind, and you can also take your two-cent psychologizing and shove it. I was going to suggest a quick round-trip to Marseille regarding our case, but apparently that doesn't turn you on. After all, I'm just a lieutenant, and you're a chief inspector."

"You're right, it doesn't turn me on. Good night, Henebelle."

He snapped the phone shut. Lucie stared at hers for several seconds, livid. The guy was a flaming asshole. And that was the last time she'd be calling him—he could go fuck himself! Seething with rage, she bought a chocolate bar at the vending machine and downed it in two bites.

"Thanks for the extra calories, you goddamn effing shark!"

Then she headed for the stairs. A wide smile stretched across her lips when her phone started ringing and she read the name: "Sharko." She waited until the last ring before taking the call.

"So? You want to know after all?"

"What's in Marseille, Lieutenant Henebelle?"

Lucie waited a moment before answering.

"A specialist in fifties-era films called a little while ago. He managed to identify the actress in the short. Her name is Judith Sagnol. She's still alive, Inspector."

Sharko stood up from his bench with a grimace. He sighed.

"All right . . . I'm going to download the film tonight. Finally see what all this is about. What time can you be in Paris tomorrow?"

"Arrival Gare du Nord at 10:52. Departure Gare de Lyon at 11:36, to get to Marseille at 2:57. Sagnol has been contacted—she'll be waiting for us at her hotel. I told her we were reporters doing a story on vintage porno films."

"Great topic. But change the time of your departure. I'm going to arrange for you to attend the morning meeting in Nanterre, with your boss. We'll leave together from there."

"Fine. And now tell me what you discovered in Egypt."

"Three beautiful pyramids called Cheops, Khafre, and Menkaure. See you tomorrow, Henebelle."

Before leaving the park, he ran his fingers one last time over the eight vertical bars etched in the trunk.

And there, alone in the dark, he gritted his teeth.

33

Lucie and her captain arrived together at the Criminal Investigations Division's central headquarters in Nanterre. In preparation for the full day Lucie had opted for a rather masculine outfit: tight jeans, gray short-sleeved sweatshirt, and work boots with reinforced toes. She liked to dress like a guy, blend into the crowd. It wasn't yet ten o'clock, but the sun was already baking the asphalt. Slowly, the cloud of smog rose over the capital and its outskirts.

The air was cooler inside the building. In the conference room, Sharko and Martin Leclerc were having a heated argument over the strongly worded letter that the head of Violent Crimes had just been faxed by the French embassy in Egypt.

"Lebrun cc'd Josselin. This whole business is going to blow up in your face."

Sharko shrugged.

"The big boss has had it in for me since the beginning. One more fuckup won't make a difference."

"Yes, that's the point—one more fuckup will make all the difference! You're handing him the ammunition he's been waiting for. Do you see what a spot you've put me in? As if I didn't have enough shit to deal with right now."

His cell phone rang. When he looked at the display, his face fell. He answered and moved away.

"Kathia . . ."

Sharko watched him pace back and forth. His boss and friend didn't seem to be his usual self. Too nervous, too removed from the case. His thoughts were interrupted by Lucie and Kashmareck, who had just entered the room. Martin Leclerc quickly hung up, his lips pinched. The four cops shook hands and exchanged pleasantries. Lucie gave the inspector a tight smile, while Kashmareck and Leclerc went off to confer over coffee.

"Egypt doesn't seem to have agreed with you," she said quietly. "Your nose . . . What happened?"

"A really big mosquito. Happy to be here among us?"

Lucie looked around her, eyes sparkling.

"The heart of the French criminal police. The place that all the major cases pass through. Just a few years ago, I knew it only through the novels I read between typing reports for my bosses."

"Nanterre is okay, but back in the days of Number 36 . . ."

"Oh, Number 36—that's legendary!"

"One day, I left the north to come work at Criminal Division HQ, the famous 36 Quai des Orfèvres. Imagine my pride, the first time I walked up those creaking old stairs, just like Inspector Maigret. I had access to the darkest, most twisted, most intriguing cases. I was happy as a clam. Except that I'd lost everything around me. Hometown, quality of life, human relations with my neighbors, friends . . . Number 36 stinks of murder and sweat in crappy offices—if you really want to know."

Lucie sighed.

"Is it just me, or do you have a special gift for being a wet blanket?"

A few minutes later, they sat down at a round table, everyone taking out sheets of paper and pens. Péresse arrived late, waylaid by the Paris traffic.

Leclerc gave a brief summary: the purpose here was to set out all their findings and pull together the threads of the investigation, so that everyone would be on the same page. To get everyone in the swing, he played the 1955 film in the original and hidden versions. Once again, all faces wrinkled with curiosity and disgust.

Péresse, the chief inspector from Rouen, then got things rolling with several pieces of bad news. Inquiries at hospitals, detox centers, and prisons in Normandy had yielded zip about the five unearthed bodies. Since the missing persons reports had turned up nothing either, the trail of illegal immigrants or undocumented aliens in France remained the most promising avenue, especially since there'd been an Asian in the batch. For now, the Rouen criminal police were collaborating with the other branches of law enforcement to try to infiltrate human trafficking networks. It might be a dead end, admitted Péresse, but given how few leads his teams had to work with, for the moment he couldn't see any other possibilities. He hoped something would come of the DNA lifted from the bodies, for which they would have the results in the next day or two.

Kashmareck had more to offer, describing in detail the vicious killings of Claude Poignet, Luc Szpilman, and the girlfriend. Initial findings suggested they were the work of the same killers and that they'd occurred the same night. An individual of about thirty, solidly built, wearing combat boots, and another who remained completely invisible. Two cold-hearted, organized, sadistic murderers, one of whom knew about film and the other about medicine. Executioners who would stop at nothing to shut down any and all leads to the deadly reel.

The captain from Lille then detailed what Belgian investigators had unearthed about Vlad Szpilman's past:

"We got some very interesting information yesterday about the old man and where the film came from. The Belgians confirmed that Szpilman borrowed the reel from the International Federation of Film Archives in Brussels—and by 'borrowed,' I mean swiped. Szpilman was a bit of a kleptomaniac. FIAF said that about two years ago, some guy showed up to see the film, which was supposed to be on their shelves, at which point the curator discovered it was missing. Naturally, he had no idea Szpilman was the one who had it."

"Two years? So the killers were already looking for the reel?"

"So it seems. Whether he intended to or not, Szpilman pulled the rug out from under them."

"And where did the film come from, exactly? Before ending up at FIAF."

"It was in a batch of short features acquired from the National Film Board of Canada when it unloaded part of its archives. According to the old Canadian files, the film arrived there in 1956 as an anonymous gift."

Sharko leaned back in his chair.

"An anonymous gift," he repeated. "Barely made, and already someone ships it off to the archives. How did the guy looking for the reel find out it had ended up at FIAF?"

Kashmareck leafed through his notes, wetting his index finger.

"That's in here . . . here it is. Most of the films are referenced by title and year, as well as country of origin, serial number of the film stock, and place of manufacture. It's all in a central database that can be accessed from the FIAF Web site. You can find out what films have gone to which archive. Then you just have to filter with the available data—year, manufacture, country—to refine your search. You can even receive alerts when a film moves to another archive. That's evidently what happened in this case."

"Can we trace the users who logged on to the FIAF site?" asked Henebelle.

"Unfortunately not—the requests aren't stored."

Sharko looked at Henebelle out of the corner of his eye, just to his left. The light struck her face in a peculiar way, as if it darkened on contact with her skin. The cop could see her doggedness, her concentration, the dangerous flames burning in the depths of her blue irises. He knew that look only too well.

Leclerc took note of Kashmareck's findings and continued:

"And Vlad Szpilman? Who was he, apart from a collector and occasional klepto?"

"The Belgians had something to say about that too. According to friends, Vlad Szpilman seemed to be pursuing his own investigation, also during the past two years. He had begun stealing, or in any case acquiring, every film and documentary he could lay his hands on concerning the American, English, and even French secret services. CIA, MI5, documentaries on the Cold War, the arms race, and that's not the half of it."

"These last two years," repeated Sharko. "And by coincidence, the Canadian informant said on the phone that *he'd* been looking into this matter for two years as well. Everything seems to have started the moment Szpilman got hold of the film."

"That's also around the time when Szpilman went to the neuromarketing center to have the film analyzed," Lucie completed.

Kashmareck nodded in agreement. "But that's not all. Szpilman also spent a good deal of time at the public library in Liège. One time, he left a document in the photocopier that the librarian kept meaning to give back. According to her, Szpilman spent all his time in the twentieth-century history section."

He took a sheet from his leather shoulder bag and passed it around. Lucie grabbed it up first. It was a black-and-white photo that appeared to have been copied from a book. In the middle of a field, German soldiers pointed their rifles at women and the children they held tightly against them. The caption read GERMAN SOLDIERS EXECUTING JEWISH MOTHERS AND THEIR CHILDREN FOR A PHOTOGRAPHER, DURING THE HOLOCAUST BY BULLETS AT IVANGOROD, UKRAINE, 1942. Lucie stared at the look on the face of the German soldier in the foreground, with his rifle raised. The glazed expression in his eyes, the twist of his lip were unspeakably evil. How could someone kill for the benefit of the camera? How could someone ignore a presence that immortalized on film a face confronting death?

Lucie passed the photo to Péresse. Kashmareck laid a book on the table.

"Here's the book the photo came from. It's about the Ukrainian Holocaust. I found the image on page 47. On the next page, all the bodies of the Jewish women and their children are lying on the ground, each killed by a bullet to the head."

Sharko leafed through the book and studied the pictures.

"The genocide of Jews," he said.

He thought of the book he'd read on the plane. A "criminal collective hysteria." It couldn't be a simple coincidence. Szpilman was on to something that related to the murdered Egyptian girls.

Kashmareck nervously fingered a cigarette, which he would gladly have smoked then and there. He continued:

"It's clear that for some reason Vlad Szpilman started spending a lot more time at the library in the last couple of years. He never borrowed any books, so left no traces in the library's records. The same for his Internet searches. A total ghost."

Lucie broke in:

"I saw books in his private library, books that the killers made away with. They all dealt with the major historical conflicts. Wars, genocides . . . and a number on espionage as well. I . . ."

Lucie tried to remember. She hadn't paid special attention to the crowded bookshelves.

"I remember names like . . . I think it was 'artichoke'?"

"Artichoke," confirmed Leclerc. "A CIA program to study interrogation techniques. In the 1950s, there were a fair number of experiments, some of them rather unsavory, using hypnosis and various drugs, such as LSD, to induce amnesia or other altered states."

"The fifties," Lucie repeated. "And the film dates from 1955. Another coincidence? I have several images from that film stuck in my head, especially the ones of the little girl's dilated pupils, as if they'd given her drugs. And also the one of the bull stopping dead in front of her. You talked about LSD and hypnosis—could that be it? And besides . . ."

She undid the elastics on her folder and took out a photo, which she pushed toward Leclerc.

"Here's a shot of the little girl, taken from the film, before the attack on the rabbits. Compare it with the photo of the German soldier. Look at the expression on their faces, just before they kill."

Leclerc put the two side by side.

"The same cold-blooded expression."

"Same look, same hatred, same desire to kill. One about thirty years old, the other barely seven or eight. How could a kid that young have eyes like that?"

Silence. Wearing a somber expression, the head of Violent Crimes passed the pictures around, then walked to the water cooler at the other end of the room to refill his glass and check his cell phone. He returned, trying to look composed, but Sharko could see that all wasn't well. Something was going on with Kathia.

"Anything else, Captain Kashmareck?"

The cop from Lille shook his head.

"Szpilman's call record over the past months didn't give us anything. We think he mainly communicated with the Canadian online. But for the moment, our teams have hit a dead end. The Belgian used a ton of systems that made his communications completely untraceable. And none of his e-mails have yielded anything that seems relevant to this case."

Leclerc gave a brief nod to thank him, then turned to his chief inspector.

"Your turn. Egypt . . ."

Sharko cleared his throat and began narrating his adventure abroad. He intentionally neglected to mention the episode with Atef Abd el-Aal in the desert, and instead claimed to have found the lead to the hospitals by questioning someone close to one of the victims. He realized that he was still an amazingly gifted liar.

During his monologue, Lucie watched him carefully. A real mug, this guy, an old-fashioned sort of body, with hands full of little scars, ancient razor nicks around his cheeks and chin, strong temples, and a nose that must have been broken more than once. If he hadn't been a policeman, he might have been a boxer, a middleweight. Not exactly a perfect specimen, but Lucie thought he had charm, and an inner strength that emanated from his powerful build.

"Those girls had been afflicted with some kind of collective hysteria," the cop concluded. "And if you look carefully at the film, it's exactly what happened with the little girls and the rabbits."

"True enough," admitted Leclerc. "And what do you make of it?"

All eyes turned to Sharko.

"Let's recap. Nineteen fifty-four or fifty-five, probably near Montreal, in what looks like a hospital room. Little girls on one side, rabbits on the other. A camera to film the whole business. The phenomenon occurs. The girls start slaughtering the animals in a frenzy. Nineteen ninety-three, Cairo. An inexplicable wave of hysteria strikes all of Egypt, north to south. The information circulates in scientific communities throughout the world. One year later, a killer attacks young girls who'd been affected by the wave in its most aggressive form. Three murders, three brains removed."

"Not to mention their eyes," said Lucie.

"Not to mention their eyes . . . Finally, 2009, or sixteen years later. We unearth five bodies buried about six months or a year earlier. All killed or wounded by gunfire. Bullets in the chest, the head, entry wounds front and back. What does this latter scene suggest?"

Lucie spoke up:

"People trying to flee in all directions? Who were also afflicted with a kind of madness?"

"Or people trying to attack, exactly like the little girls. A quick, sudden attack, with no warning. No choice but to slaughter them and hide the bodies."

He stood up and leaned against the table, palms perfectly flat.

"Imagine a group of five men. In their twenties, well built, in good physical shape. Mainly former junkies, but they've stopped using. They were forced to by circumstance—prison, confinement, disciplinary training. These individuals do not come from easy backgrounds and they all have multiple old fractures, the kind you get in fights. Not to mention their tattoos, which indicate a need to create an identity for yourself, to look tough or like you're part of a clan. The presence of an Asian underscores the diversity of the group, and suggests that they don't really know each other. These men are brought together somewhere. They're watched over by at least two other men, armed with pistols or rifles."

"Why two?" Péresse interrupted.

"Because of the bullets' angles of entry and the disparity of the impacts. Front, back . . . Then there's a glitch of some kind, something goes wrong. The young guys blow a fuse and start acting violent, out of control. Like the little girls with the rabbits. Like the young Egyptian murder victims. They fall into a collective hysteria."

Leclerc took a deep breath. "A kind of aggression that puts them in a blind fury. They see red, like . . . like a raging bull."

"Yes, that's exactly right, a raging bull. And yet, if we're to believe the film, they think they've managed to tame the bull. But these men can't be tamed. They shout at them to stop, but nothing works. So, at a loss, they open fire. The guards have no choice. They kill or wound them. One way or another, our killers—the movie guy, the medical guy—are immediately aware that a kind of hysteria has manifested again. So they show up and, as before, remove the eyes and brains. Then, burial six feet underground."

"So in your view, the same perps who killed the girls in Egypt also killed the five men here?"

"I believe so, even though there's a huge difference with the MO used in Egypt. There, the victims were still alive when the heinous acts were committed—there was torture and postmortem mutilation. Here, they were killed much faster."

Kashmareck had snapped his cigarette in half from too much fidgeting. "What are these killers really after?"

"I'm not sure yet, but I think it's linked to these outbreaks of mass hysteria. In any case, I get the sense we're not dealing with isolated individuals working on their own. People paid Atef Abd el-Aal to kill his brother, and the bodies in Gravenchon bear the mark of a real professional."

Sharko looked at his boss.

"By the way, if you could also get someone to look into the term 'Syndrome E' . . . It was the doctor at the Salaam Center who mentioned it, along with the collective hysterias. Just a term he remembered, without knowing what it meant."

Leclerc jotted down some quick notes.

"Very well. Right, then . . . I'll write up the minutes of this meeting. Our priorities are: get the list of humanitarian aid workers present in Cairo in March 1994. I can take care of that. Inspector Péresse, you pursue the lead of human trafficking—you never know."

"Fine."

"You, Captain Kashmareck . . ."

"I'll keep working with the Belgians. And I have a serious murder case on my hands as well, with Claude Poignet. My teams are working full tilt. And vacations aren't helping."

"Understood." He turned to Sharko. "And you . . ."

The inspector looked at his watch, then nodded toward Lucie.

"We're heading off to Marseille. The actress in the film has been identified. Her name is Judith Sagnol and she'll certainly have something to say. Henebelle? Anything to wrap it up?"

Lucie leafed through her memo book.

"She's now seventy-seven. She lives in Paris, but these days she spends a lot of her time at the Sofitel in the Old Port. She's the widow and heiress of a former corporate attorney who became her husband in 1956, a year or two after the film was made. She appeared in a few pornos from the fifties and posed for nudie photos, calendars, and some 8 mm 'home movies.' According to the historian who identified her, she was no angel; she performed rather explicit sex acts in closed circles."

"Did this historian have any ideas about who owned the film?"

"None. He doesn't know where our reel came from or who made it. For the moment, that remains a mystery."

Sharko stood up, picking up his folder and his shoulder bag.

"In that case, let's hope Sagnol still has her faculties intact."

34

Later that afternoon, the mistral was blowing hard over Marseille, a hot slap that deposited the Mediterranean ocean spray onto tanned faces. Sharko and Lucie walked down the Canebière, patched sunglasses and shoulder bag for him, small backpack for her. At that time of day and year, it was impossible to approach the Old Port in a car because of the mass of tourists. The sidewalk cafés were overflowing, faces and yachts paraded by, the atmosphere was festive.

Or almost. Not for a second, during their trip down from Paris, had the two cops talked about anything but the case. The deadly reel, Szpilman's paranoid behavior, the mysterious Canadian informant . . . An inextricable tangle of knots, where the leads and their conclusions never quite seemed to match up.

Their hopes of unraveling the mess were now pinned on Judith Sagnol.

She was living at the Sofitel, a four-star hotel that offered a fabulous view of the entrance to the Old Port and the magnificent minor Catholic basilica called Bonne Mère. In front of the establishment were palm trees, porters, and luxury cars. At the reception desk, the hostess informed the two "reporters" that Judith Sagnol had gone for a walk but had asked them to wait for her in the hotel bar. Lucie glanced anxiously at her watch.

"Less than two hours before we have to head back . . . The last train to Lille leaves Paris at eleven. If we miss the 6:28 at Saint-Charles, I won't be able to get home."

Sharko headed toward the bar.

"These people like to make you wait. Come on, we can at least enjoy the view."

The receptionist came to find them around 5:30 at the poolside terrace to let them know Mme. Sagnol was expecting them in her room. Lucie was boiling mad. She went off to get some privacy, cell phone at her ear. The conversation with her mother was less difficult than she'd feared: Juliette had eaten well and her digestive system was more or less back to normal. If everything kept on like this, she'd be out the day after tomorrow. Finally, the end of the tunnel.

"Will you manage by yourself until tomorrow?" Marie Henebelle asked her daughter.

That was just like her mother. Lucie looked around toward Sharko, who was sitting alone at their table.

"I'll be fine."

"Where will you sleep?"

"I'll figure it out. Can I talk to Juliette?"

She exchanged a few affectionate words with her daughter. A smile now on her lips, Lucie returned to Sharko just as he was taking out his wallet.

"Leave it," she said. "This is on me."

"Suit yourself. I had just enough to cover it."

She paid for the beer and mint soda with a grimace: twenty-six euros and fifty cents. No standing on ceremony in this joint! They headed for the elevator.

"How's the kid?"

"She should be out soon."

The inspector nodded slowly; he almost managed to smile.

"That's good."

"Do you have children?"

"Nice elevator, this . . ."

They did not exchange a look or another word on the way up. Sharko stared at the buttons as they progressively lit, and seemed relieved when the door finally slid open. They walked down a long, muffled hallway, still silent.

Lucie felt a shock when Judith appeared in the doorway. At almost eighty, the 1950s pinup had kept that dark, penetrating gaze she displayed in the film. Her irises were deep black, and her wavy, steel-colored hair fell onto bare, tanned shoulders. Plastic surgery had wreaked havoc, but couldn't hide the fact that this woman had once been beautiful.

Dressed lightly—plain blue silk dress, bare feet with nails polished cherry red—she invited them onto the balcony and ordered up a bottle of Veuve Clicquot. The bedsheets were unmade, and Lucie noted the presence of a man's underwear at the foot of a sink. No doubt a gigolo whose services she paid for.

Once seated, Judith crossed her legs in the manner of a bored starlet. She did not apologize for keeping them waiting. Sharko didn't beat around the bush and showed his official ID.

"We're not reporters but police. We've come to ask you about an old film you appeared in."

Lucie sighed discreetly, while Judith gave a mocking smile.

"I figured as much. The reporter interested in my career hasn't been born . . ."

She looked at her manicured nails for a few seconds.

"I quit acting in 1955. That goes back quite a way for stirring up old memories."

Sharko took a DVD out of his bag and put it on the table.

"Nineteen fifty-five is perfect. It's about the film burned onto this DVD. My colleague got the original from a collector named Vlad Szpilman. Does the name mean anything to you?"

"Not a thing."

"I noticed a DVD player and TV in your living room. May we show you the film?"

She gave Sharko the once-over, with the same arrogant expression she'd used on the cameraman at the beginning of the famous short.

"You're not really leaving me a choice, are you?"

Judith slid the disk into the drive. Seconds later, the film began. Close-up of the actress, twentysomething years old, dark lipstick, Chanel suit, looking straight at the camera. Clearly, seeing this was not to the septuagenarian's liking. Her features tightened in an anxious expression. After the scene of the slit eyeball, she grabbed up the remote and hit STOP. She stood up sharply and went outside to pour herself some more champagne. Sharko and Lucie glanced at each other, then joined her on the balcony.

The old voice was harsh, dry:

"What do you want?"

Sharko leaned against the railing, his back to the port and the amateur sailors polishing their craft down below. A hellish sun beat against his neck.

"So was *that* your last film?"

She nodded, her lips still pressed together.

"We've come for information. Anything you can tell us about making the film. Its intent. About the little girl, the children, and the rabbits."

"What are you talking about? What children?"

Lucie took out a photo of the girl on the swing and handed it to her.

"This one. You've never seen her?"

"No, no, never . . . Was she in the film too?"

Lucie pocketed the photo with an aftertaste of disappointment. The part involving Sagnol must have been shot separately. Judith brought the flute to her lips, took a small sip, then put her glass back down, eyes empty.

"I didn't know, and still don't know, what kind of film Jacques asked me to be in. I was to shoot some sex scenes, and he paid me handsomely for it. I needed money. Any part was good enough for me. What they did with the images afterward wasn't my business. When you're in a trade like mine, you don't ask questions."

She pointed to the champagne.

"Help yourselves. It won't stay chilled very long in this heat. There was a time when I'd have to work a month to afford a bottle of that stuff."

Sharko didn't have to be asked twice. He refilled two glasses and handed one to Lucie, who thanked him with a movement of her chin. All things considered, a little alcohol wouldn't hurt, after the ups and downs of the past few days. Judith let the memories seep in slowly.

"I *never* thought I'd see those images again . . ."

"Who made the film?"

"Jacques Lacombe."

Lucie quickly jotted down the name in her memo book. They finally had a name: that, in itself, made their trip to Marseille worthwhile.

"I met him in 1948. He was barely eighteen and he had a headful of big ideas. At the time, he was filming magic shows at a Paris music hall, the Trois Sous. He had an ETM P16 camera. I dressed and made up the dancers for the show."

She acted out the movements.

"Bright red lipstick, blond wigs, see-through black lace dresses, not to mention the long Vogue cigarette . . . That was my idea, the cigarette—did you know that? It was all the rage at the time."

Her eyes wandered for a few seconds.

"Jacques and I had a beautiful affair that lasted a year. I discovered a brilliant man, far ahead of his time. Tall, dark, eyes like the ocean. Very Delon."

She took a swallow of champagne without seeming to notice.

"Jacques was a real cinematic innovator; he thought outside the box. For him, there were two ways to see a film: through the plot and the screenplay, or else, and more importantly, by the medium itself, which other filmmakers underused or didn't know a thing about. *He* worked on the film itself. He'd scratch it, or poke holes in it, or streak it, or mark it up, or even burn it. For him, film wasn't so much a surface to record images on but a virgin territory that he could inscribe to convey art. You should have seen him with a piece of celluloid. It was like he was holding a woman."

She smiled to herself.

"Jacques was influenced by the early techniques of European avant-garde cinema, like double exposure, which was used by surrealist filmmakers like Luis Buñuel and Germaine Dulac. The slit eyeball at the beginning is taken directly from Dalí and Buñuel's *Un Chien Andalou* . . . It was a little tip of the cap to his influences."

Lucie was trying to write down as much as possible, but the old woman was speaking too fast.

"He also hung out with magicians and became part of their inner circle. Houdini fascinated him, even though he was long dead. I remember how Jacques used the camera in fast motion to break down the movements of the magicians, pierce their secrets. He spent hours, days poring through the rushes, shut up in his little studio in Bagnolet. Pornography was another big interest of his; he dissected every shot, the mechanics of how images inspired pleasure. He had a phenomenal knowledge of montage, at a time when the available materials were pretty rudimentary, and he'd also invented a system of masks he attached to the lens. He made countless experimental mini-films, no more than a few minutes long, in which he managed to capture the viewer's attention and unmask our relation to violence and art. Every time, I was captivated, shocked, amazed. But the public and the film world didn't care for his genius or his work. Jacques really suffered from that lack of recognition."

Lucie cut in, taking advantage of this rush of memories.

"Did he ever describe his techniques? Did he talk to you about subliminal imagery?"

"No, he kept all his experiments secret. It was his private preserve. Still today, in the films of his that have been rediscovered, he did things even contemporary experimental filmmakers can't figure out."

"So then what happened?"

"Jacques wasn't doing so well; he couldn't catch a break. Producers gave him the cold shoulder. I watched him down gallons of vodka and live on hard drugs to keep going, working day and night. He lost interest in me, and we split up . . . It broke my heart."

She turned her eyes to the horizon, watched a cruise liner leaving the port, then returned to the conversation.

"In the time we were together, he had introduced me to the mysteries of the cinema, but also to some rather disreputable characters. I was pretty well-endowed, with a slightly concave bust, like Garbo—people loved that at the time. So I started acting in erotic films to make a living."

She sighed. Sharko, wanting to take maximum advantage of the champagne, poured himself another flute. He calculated that each glassful was worth about thirty euros, which made it taste all the sweeter.

"A year later, in 1950, Jacques went to Colombia to make *The Eyes of the Forest*, his one and only full-length feature. He'd managed to raise some paltry amount that barely covered his equipment and a small Colombian crew. The film ruined him for good. Because of it, Jacques got into all sorts of trouble with the French authorities and almost landed in jail."

"I've never heard of it. *The Eyes of the Forest*, you said?"

"Yes. It was never officially released. Banned from the start. Today, you can't find it; the existing copies were either destroyed or disappeared into the woodwork. Jacques had shown it to me once the editing was completed . . ." She grimaced. "It was a film about cannibals, one of the first of its kind, and he was very proud of it. But how could he be proud of such a horror? I had never seen such a vile, repulsive film in all my life."

Judith's voice had become throaty. Sharko went to sit at the table, next to Lucie.

"Why did he have troubles with the law?"

"*The Eyes of the Forest* required weeks of shooting in the middle of the jungle, with the rain, the heat, and swarms of insects. The crews were completely cut off from the world. Filming conditions weren't as comfortable back then as they are now. You went off with your camera equipment and a few tents over your shoulder. Some of the crew came down with various illnesses, from what Jacques told me. Malaria, leish-maniasis . . ."

"But what did the law have to do with it?"

She screwed up her face, uncovering teeth that were as perfect as they were false.

"In the last third of the film, you saw a woman impaled on a spike, through her mouth and anus. It was a . . . an abomination, and so realistic! Jacques had to prove in court that the Colombian actress was still alive, and show how he'd created the illusion."

She poured herself some more champagne, evidently disturbed. To Sharko she looked like a rumpled bird, just an old woman trying to stop time in its tracks.

"He didn't come back the same from that miserable place; he had changed. As if the jungle and its shadows had kept their hold on him. Jacques had shot with natives, tribes who were seeing civilized people for the first time ever. I've never been able to forget one of the more shocking scenes in the film: heads lined up along the river, planted on pikes. God only knows what really happened there, in the dark reaches of that land of savages . . ."

She rubbed her arms, as if she'd gotten a sudden chill.

"When that film failed, it was yet another major blow for Jacques. Overnight, he vanished from the French film scene. He and I stayed in touch; we'd remained friends and I still had hopes of winning him back. But after a few months, I stopped hearing from him. One day I went to his studio. Jacques had packed up all his equipment and his films. His former assistant told me he'd left for the United States, just like that, with no warning."

"Do you know why?"

"It was unclear. The assistant was sure he had a huge project there. Someone had seen his films and wanted to work with him. But we never learned anything more. No one ever heard what had really happened to him."

"No one . . . except you."

She nodded, her eyes vacant.

"It was 1954. Not a word for three years, then out of the blue I got a call. Jacques wanted me to come to Montreal. He had several days' work for me, and he said he could pay me a fortune. I was busting my ass at the time, taking off my clothes for the camera more often than for a lover, just to earn peanuts. Filming in the nude never bothered me—I figured it was a good way to become a star. But you know how it is—lost illusions . . . I was experiencing the same setbacks as Jacques, getting parts in only the most pathetic films, for a bunch of real sleazeballs. So I agreed without thinking twice. I needed the cash. And besides, it was a chance to see him again—who knows, maybe even get back together. I asked him to send me the script, but he said I wouldn't need one. So I took the plunge, sight unseen. He sent me half the fee, a plane ticket, and there I was, in Canada . . ."

Anxiety had settled into her face. The two cops were hanging on every word. Lucie had stopped taking notes. Judith let herself be carried away by the champagne; her expression veered from anger to tenderness to fear. Everything was resurfacing, after fifty years buried deep.

"The moment I landed in Canada, I knew I'd made a mistake. Jacques wore a look I'd never seen on a man. Lecherous, cold, indifferent. His head was almost shaved, and he looked unhealthy. He didn't even give me a hug hello, after all the nights we'd spent together. He brought me to the place where they were shooting, without a word of explanation about his long years of absence, what he'd been doing. We came to some abandoned clothing factories just outside Montreal, I don't know exactly where. There was only him, his camera equipment, and some people wearing gloves, dressed in black. I couldn't see their faces—they were wearing ski masks. There were also mattresses, and several days' worth of food. A room had been fitted up at the back of the warehouse . . . I understood that I was going to spend my days and nights in that dreadful place. And then I heard his voice. 'Strip down, Judith, dance, and go with whatever happens.' It was fall, I was cold and afraid, but I obeyed. I was being paid to. It lasted three days. Three days of hell. I suppose you've seen the sex scenes in the film, so you know what happened next . . ."

"We haven't seen them in their entirety," Sharko replied. "Just still images, hidden. Subliminal images."

The old woman swallowed hard.

"More of his tricks."

The inspector leaned forward.

"Tell us about the other scenes. You lying nude in the field, as if you were dead."

Judith stiffened.

"That was the second half of the shoot: I had to lie there, naked and motionless, in a field near the factories. It was barely forty degrees out. Two of the men who'd had sex with me painted my stomach like a disgusting wound. But when I was lying in the grass, I was shivering. It was cold and my teeth were chattering. Jacques was furious that I couldn't keep still enough. He took a syringe from his pocket and told me to hold out my arm. He—" She brought a hand to her mouth. "He told me it would keep me from feeling the cold and from moving too much . . . And also that it would dilate my pupils, like a real corpse."

"Did you do it?"

"Yes. I wanted the rest of the fee; I'd come all that way. And I wanted to make Jacques happy. We had lived together! I thought I knew him. When he gave me the shot, I started to feel disconnected from the world. I wasn't cold anymore but I was practically unable to move. They laid me back down in the grass."

"Do you know what he injected you with?"

"I think it was LSD. Strangely, those three letters, which didn't mean anything to me at the time, came into my head whenever I thought about that scene later on. He must have said them while I was drugged."

The cops' eyes met. LSD—the experimental drug used during the Artichoke program, the subject of one of the books stolen from Szpilman's.

"Jacques always liked realism; he was a perfectionist. The makeup wasn't good enough for him, so . . ."

Judith stood up and lifted the hem of her dress, unveiling her nudity without shame. Her tanned stomach was covered with white scars, which looked like little bloodsuckers beneath her skin. Sharko fell back in his chair ever so slightly, while Lucie remained frozen, her mouth tense. There was something sinister about seeing this body, so worn down and steeped in past sufferings, under the cheery sunlight of Marseille.

Judith let go of the fabric, which fell back to her knees.

"I didn't feel any pain while he was cutting me . . . I couldn't even understand what was happening. It was like I was having hallucinations. Jacques continued to film for hours on end, constantly making more cuts. They were only skin deep and didn't draw much blood, so he accentuated them with makeup. There was something terrifying in his eyes while he was slashing me. And at that moment, I realized . . ."

The two police kept silent, encouraging her to continue.

"I realized that he had actually killed that Colombian actress. He had gone all the way—it was obvious."

Sharko and Lucie looked briefly at each other. Judith was on the verge of tears.

"I don't know how he got it past the French authorities. He must have shown them the poor woman's twin and they were taken in by it. But with me, he didn't lie. And he was true to his word about the fee."

Lucie squeezed her pencil harder. Apparently Jacques Lacombe was well off, since he'd paid Judith good money. If he'd managed to get his films known in the States, make a name for himself, what was he doing in some moth-eaten warehouse in Quebec shooting those scenes from hell?

"When I got back to France, I was disfigured, but I had enough to live on decently and keep my head above water. I was lucky enough after that to meet a good man, who had seen my films and loved me regardless."

Lucie spoke in a gentle voice. The woman, despite all her wealth, filled her with pity.

"And you never reported any of this to the police? You never brought charges?"

"What was the point? My body was ruined, and I wouldn't even have gotten the second half of the money. I would have lost everything."

The inspector looked Judith straight in the eye.

"Do you know why he shot those scenes, Madame Sagnol?"

"No. I told you, I didn't know what the content of—"

"I'm not talking about the content of the film. I'm talking about Jacques Lacombe. Jacques Lacombe, who called you—you specifically—after several years of total silence. Who leaned in close to mutilate you. Who filmed you in the most provocative postures . . . Why make a film with scenes like that? What was the point, do you think?"

She thought for a moment. Her fingers squeezed the large sapphire on her ring finger.

"To feed perverse minds, Inspector."

She sank into a long silence before continuing.

"To offer them power, sex, and death through film. Jacques didn't want to just provoke or shock with images. He wanted the image to alter human behavior. That was the point of his entire body of work. It's probably why he was so interested in pornography. When a man watches a porno film, what does he do?"

She made an unambiguous hand gesture.

"The image acts directly on his impulses, his libido; the image penetrates him and dictates his actions. That, ultimately, is what Jacques was looking for. Over there, he kept mentioning this weird thing when he talked about the power of the image."

"What weird thing?"

"Syndrome E. Yes, that's right—Syndrome E."

Sharko felt his chest tighten. It was the second time the expression had come up, and always in sinister circumstances.

"What does that mean?"

"I have absolutely no idea. He kept repeating it. Syndrome E, Syndrome E, as if it were an obsession. An unattainable quest."

Lucie jotted down the phrase and circled it, before asking Judith:

"Did it seem that Lacombe was working with a partner? A doctor, maybe, or a scientist?"

She nodded.

"A man also came to see me, a doctor—there's no doubt about it. He supplied the shots of LSD. The two of them clearly knew each other well; they were complicit."

The filmmaker and the doctor. It corresponded to the profile of the Cairo murders, to the killing of Claude Poignet as well. Luc Szpilman had mentioned a man in his early thirties: that couldn't possibly be Lacombe, who would have been too old by now. So who, then? Someone obsessed with his work? An heir to his insanity?

"But all that was a long time ago, too long for me to tell you anymore. Half a century ago, and whatever happened over there is just vague fragments in my head. Now that we know what harm that horrible LSD has caused, I suppose I'm lucky to be alive."

Sharko emptied his flute and stood up.

"We'd still like you to watch the entire film, in case certain details come back to you."

She nodded limply. The cops could tell she was overcome with emotion.

"What did Jacques do for you to be so interested in him after fifty years?"

"We're not sure yet, unfortunately, but there's an ongoing investigation that has to do with this film."

Once the viewing was over, Judith sighed deeply. She lit a long cigarette at the end of a holder and blew out a curlicue of smoke.

"That's just like him, that way of filming—the obsession with the senses, his use of masks, the lighting, and that viscous atmosphere. Try to see his short films, the 'crash movies,' and you'll understand."

"We will. The film doesn't remind you of anything else? The settings, the faces of those children?"

"No, sorry."

She seemed sincere. Sharko took a blank calling card from his wallet, on which he wrote his name and number.

"In case you think of anything else."

Lucie also handed her a card.

"Please don't hesitate."

"Is Jacques still alive?"

Sharko answered without a moment's hesitation.

"Finding that out and locating him are our top priorities."

35

Leaping from the taxi, they sprinted for the train station. The traffic and the heat were as infernal as ever. Lucie ran ahead; Sharko followed behind, his steps heavier but keeping up all the same. No hot pursuit of a killer, no criminal to arrest or bomb to defuse, just the 7:32 express to catch.

They dashed onto the train at 7:31. Ten seconds later, the conductor blew his whistle. The air-conditioning in the cars finally gave the two detectives some oxygen. Panting, they headed for the bar car and ordered cold drinks while mopping their faces with paper napkins. Sharko could barely catch his breath.

"One week . . . with you, Henebelle, and I'll . . . lose ten pounds . . ."

Lucie downed her orange juice with noisy swallows. She finally took a minute to breathe, running a hand over her soaked neck.

"Especially if . . . you come running with me at . . . the Citadelle in Lille . . . Six miles, Tuesdays and Fridays . . ."

"I used to run too, back when. And I guarantee you . . . that I would have kept up . . ."

"You didn't do so bad this evening . . ."

Their hearts resumed their normal rhythms. Sharko clanked his empty Coke can on the bar.

"Let's go sit down."

They found their seats. After a few minutes, Lucie made a brief recap, eyes glued to her notes. In her mind, the sea and sun of Marseille were already far behind.

"So this one expression kept coming up: Syndrome E. You have no idea what that could mean?"

"None."

"In any case, we now have a name, an important one: Jacques La-combe."

"A doctor, a filmmaker . . . Science and art . . ."

"The eye and the brain . . . The film, Syndrome E."

Sharko rubbed his chin for a long time, lost in thought.

"We should get in touch with the Sûreté in Quebec. We need to know who this Jacques Lacombe really was, what he went over there to do, in the States and Montreal. We need to trace this back to those children. They're the key to this, and my sense is they should still be alive. There have to be traces of them somewhere. People who can tell us. Help us understand . . . understand . . ."

The words were like a dark warning in the back of his throat. His fingers scratched at the seat in front of him. He stopped when he noticed Lucie looking at him curiously.

"This stuff really seems to have a hold on you," she said.

Sharko clenched his jaws, then turned his face toward the center aisle. Lucie sensed that he didn't want to look back on his life, so she fell silent and thought about the case. Judith Sagnol's hoarse voice echoed in her head. Jacques Lacombe had made this film to feed perverse minds, she'd confided. A way for the director to express and immortalize his madness. What kind of monster had Lacombe been? What sort of animal had he become in the jungles of Colombia? What had he carried along in his wake, so that even today people were willing to kill to get their hands on his "oeuvre"? Had he really killed and decapitated people in the Amazon just to make a movie? How deep had he gone into horror and insanity?

The landscape sped by, mountainous when the train left the Alpine foothills to its right, then flat and unvarying once past Lyon. Lucie was half dozing off, lulled by the slow rocking of the steel mastodon slicing through the countryside. Several times, coming out of her daze, she noticed Sharko staring at the empty seats in the other row and muttering things she couldn't understand. He was sweating excessively. He got up at least five or six times during the trip, heading for the toilets or the bar car, to come back about ten minutes later looking either angry or appeased, mopping his forehead and neck with a paper napkin. Lucie pretended to be asleep.

They arrived at Gare de Lyon at 11:03. Night had fallen, faces were sallow with fatigue, and sticky air flowed into the station, carrying the effluvia of the city. The first train to Lille departed the next morning at 6:58. Eight hours is a long time when you have nothing to do and nowhere to go. Lucie's thoughts drifted. No way she was going to wander around Paris at night. On the other hand, she felt funny about going to a hotel, with her ridiculous backpack and no change of clothes. Still, some cheap hotel was certainly the best solution. She turned to Sharko to say good-bye, but he was no longer there. He had stopped about ten yards behind and his hands were spread in front of him; his brow was furrowed and he was looking toward the ground, throwing glances Lucie's way, making her feel like the topic of a heated argument. Finally he smiled, brushing the air with his fingers as if he were high-fiving someone. Lucie went toward him.

"Whatever are you doing?"

He shoved his hands in his pockets.

"I was negotiating . . ." His face beamed. "Listen, you don't have any-where to go. I can put you up for the night. I have a big couch, which is certainly more comfortable than an Egyptian bed."

"I don't know anything about Egyptian beds, and I wouldn't want—"

"It's no bother at all. Yes or no."

"In that case, yes."

"Great. Now let's try to catch the commuter rail before it stops running."

And he started walking toward the turnstiles. Before heading after him, Lucie turned one last time toward the place where he'd been stand-ing alone several seconds earlier. Sharko, noting this, took his hands from his pockets and showed her his cell phone with a smile.

"What, you didn't think I was talking to myself, did you?"

36

After the telephone call in the train station, Lucie expected to find Sharko's wife when they entered the apartment. The entire way there, she had tried to imagine what kind of woman could stick to a man of his breadth. Did she have the bearing and disposition of a lion tamer staring down a wild beast, or on the contrary was she docile and sweet, prepared every evening to take the full brunt of the tensions cops built up over the course of their endless days?

As soon as the inspector opened the door, Lucie realized that there was no one to greet them. Not a soul. Sharko removed his shoes before going in, an oddly dignified gesture. Lucie started to do the same.

"No, no, keep your shoes on. It's just a habit of mine. I have a lot of habits I can't manage to break, which is sort of a pain in the ass, but what can you do?"

He closed the door and turned all the locks. At a glance, Lucie noted that it wasn't really the apartment of a single man. Several feminine touches—thick plants all around, a pair of rather retro high heels in a corner. But there was only one place setting on the table in the dining area, already set for a meal, facing the wall. She thought of Luc Besson's film *The Professional*. In some ways, Sharko gave off the same sadness as Léon, the contract killer, but also an incomprehensible sympathy that made you want to learn more about him.

Photos of a beautiful woman, old yellowing pictures stuck in frames, confirmed that the cop was probably a widower. What divorced man would keep wearing his wedding band? Farther back in the living room, other photos hung on the wall: dozens of glossy paper rectangles arranged haphazardly, showing a little girl from infancy to the age of five or six. In some pictures, there were three of them: him, the woman, the kid. The mother was smiling, but Lucie—she couldn't explain why—sensed a kind of absence in her gaze. Everywhere, Sharko seemed to be squeezing his two loved ones against him, so strongly that their cheeks were pressed tightly together. Lucie felt a shiver as the truth suddenly dawned on her: something must have happened to Sharko's family. A horrible, unspeakable tragedy.

"Please, have a seat," said the inspector. "I'm dying of thirst . . . How does a nice cold beer sound?"

He was talking from the kitchen. A bit troubled, Lucie set her bag down on the carpet and walked into the room. A large living room, almost too spacious. She noticed cocktail sauce and candied chestnuts on a low coffee table, then the computer in a corner.

"Anything cold is fine for me, thank you . . . Hey, can I use your Internet? I'd like to do a search for Jacques Lacombe and Syndrome E."

Sharko returned with two bottles and handed her one. He put his down on the coffee table, then shot an odd glance off to the side.

"Excuse me a moment."

He disappeared down the hallway. Ten seconds later, Lucie heard whistling, then a rattling sound, just like what she'd been hearing in the express for three and a half hours. Miniature trains—she could have sworn it . . .

Sharko returned and sat in a chair, Lucie following suit. He emptied half his beer in one gulp, as if it were nothing.

"It's after midnight. My boss has already got someone working on Syndrome E. You can do your search tomorrow."

"Why waste time?"

"You're not wasting time. On the contrary, you're saving it. You're giving yourself time to sleep, think of your loved ones, and remember that there's more to life than work. Seems so simple, doesn't it? But by the time you realize it, all you have left are old photos."

Lucie was silent a moment.

"I take a lot of photos too, trying to preserve traces of time . . . We keep coming back to images, no matter what. Images, as a way of conveying emotion, penetrating everyone's most intimate thoughts." She tipped her chin toward the haphazard arrangement. "I understand you better now. I think I get why you're like this."

Sharko was already finishing his beer. He wanted to let himself go, float on a cloud and forget the hardships of the past several days. The charred face of Atef Abd el-Aal, the slums of Cairo, the abominable eye-shaped scars on Judith Sagnol's wrinkled flesh . . . Too many shadows—way too many.

"What do you mean, 'like this'?"

"Cold. Distant at first. The kind of guy people think they should avoid. It's only when you dig a little deeper that you realize there's a heart beneath the tough outer shell."

Sharko squeezed the empty beer bottle.

"And those photos—what do they tell you?"

"A lot."

"Such as?"

"Are you sure you want to hear this?"

"Show me what you've got, Lieutenant Henebelle."

Lucie accepted the challenge with a look. She raised her bottle in front of her and waved her arm at the door.

"The first thing that's interesting is their location. They're on full display in your living room, turned toward the entrance. Why not the bedroom, or somewhere more private?"

She nodded toward a garbage can in the kitchen, where two boxes and the remains of a pizza were in plain sight.

"When a deliveryman or a stranger comes to the door, you open slightly, with exact change in hand. You never let them past the threshold; there's no rug for wiping your feet, outside or inside. The photos are in their line of sight; a visitor can see them without seeing the rest. You, your family, the impression of happiness and normalcy. Do you turn on your toy trains to make it seem a child is playing in the other room?"

Sharko's eyes narrowed.

"You've got my interest. Keep going . . ."

"Your past is something you don't like to talk about outside of your apartment. But when someone is here, on this chair, those photos shout out loud that something tragic happened to your family. There are no new photos of your wife or child. You're several years younger on the most recent ones, and you look a lot happier. At the time your daughter was five or six. It's the age of the first big change, the first separation. School, playdates, kids going off in the morning and not coming back till evening. So we try to compensate, take pictures—lots of pictures—to slow their departure, to keep them at home and make up for their absence by artificial means. But you— No more memories, as if . . . life had suddenly stopped dead. Theirs, and then yours. That's why you quit working the streets and took a desk job. The streets stole your family from you."

Sharko now looked like he was elsewhere. His eyes were glued to the floor and he was leaning forward, hands hanging between his thighs.

"Keep going, Henebelle, keep going. Go on, let it all out."

"I'm thinking maybe a case that went bad, that involved your family, put them face-to-face with the things you'd always tried to protect them from. What? A case that encroached on your personal life? A suspect who went after them?"

A wounding silence. Sharko encouraged Lucie to continue.

"With those photos, you expose your inner self to the outer world. Here, in your apartment, you manage to open up, to be the man you used to be, the father and husband, but the moment you cross that threshold, the moment you close your door, you lock yourself up. Two dead bolts on the door . . . Isn't that just another way of armoring yourself still further? I suspect very few people enter in here, Inspector, and the ones who spend the night are fewer still. Earlier, you could very easily have pointed me toward a hotel and taken off, the way you did the first time, when we met at Gare du Nord. So here's my question: what the hell am I doing here?"

Sharko raised dull eyes toward her. He stood up, poured himself a tumbler of whiskey, and retook his seat.

"I can talk about my past, despite what you seem to think. If I never do, it's because I have no one to tell it to."

"I'm here."

He smiled at his glass.

"You, the little lady cop from up north who I've known for a few days at most?"

"People tell their life stories to a shrink who they know even less."

Sharko knit his brow, then got up to put away his bottle of whiskey.

He took the opportunity to make sure there weren't any medications lying around. How had she guessed about the shrink? He sat back down, trying to keep his cool.

"Well, why shouldn't I tell you, after all? You seem to need it."

"Is that what you learned from my personnel file?"

She gave Sharko a defiant look. The cop accepted the challenge.

"The photos speak for themselves. It was more than five years ago. We were driving on the highway, me, Suzanne, and Eloise . . . And one of my tires blew out on a curve."

He stared lengthily at the floor, swirling the liquor in his glass.

"I could tell you the date, the exact time, and what the sky looked like that day. It's etched in here, for the rest of my life . . . The three of us were coming back from a weekend away in the north. It had been a long time since we'd just gotten away like that, far from this stinking city. But right after the blowout, I got distracted for a moment. I forgot to lock the car doors. And while I was checking the tire, my wife went running across the road like a madwoman, with my daughter. A car came speeding around the bend . . ."

His fingers clenched.

"I can still hear the screech of brakes. Over and over . . . Only the sound of trains on their tracks can make it stop. That incessant rattling sound you hear as we speak—it's with me day and night . . ."

A bitter swallow of whiskey. Lucie retreated into herself—what else could she do at such a moment? The man sitting near her was far more damaged than she could have imagined. Sharko continued:

"You worked a case involving child kidnappings. You tracked down a man who carried within himself the purest expression of perversion. It was the same for me, Henebelle. My wife, my own wife, had been kidnapped by the same type of killer, six months before she gave birth to Eloise. I hunted him down day and night; nothing else existed. During that investigation, I lost my friends, I saw people I loved disappear before my eyes, carried away by the madness of a single individual."

He nodded toward a wall of his apartment.

"My neighbor, an old Guianese woman, was killed because of me. When I finally found Suzanne, tied up on a table, I could barely recognize her. She had been subjected to things that even you couldn't imagine. Things . . . that no human being should ever suffer."

Lucie could feel him on the tightrope, ready to fall at any moment. But he hung in there. He was made of a different fiber, a material that no projectile could penetrate.

"She was never the same after that, and the birth of our daughter couldn't change it. Her eyes remained empty most of the time, even if, once in a while, between two doses of medicine, the sparkle returned."

A leaden silence. Lucie could not imagine the pain this man carried inside him. The solitude, the gaping fracture of his soul, the tragic open wound that bled nonstop. For perhaps the first time in all those years, Lucie told herself, he didn't want to feel alone anymore, if only for a single night. And despite the blackness of the world around her, she was glad to be sharing this moment with him.

Sharko downed his glass in one swallow and stood up.

"I'm the walking caricature of the worst a cop can withstand. I'm bloated with pills and torment, I've killed and been wounded as much as one person can, but I'm still standing. Here, on my own two feet, in front of you."

"I . . . I don't know what to say. I'm so sorry."

"Don't be. I've had it up to here with sorry."

Lucie gave him a limp smile.

"I'll try to remember that."

"Okay. I think it's time for bed now. We have a big day ahead of us tomorrow."

"Yes, it's time . . ."

Sharko made as if to leave the room, then came back toward his colleague.

"I have a favor to ask you, Henebelle. Something I could only ask a woman."

"And after that, I have one final question. But tell me."

"Tomorrow morning, at seven sharp, could you turn on the shower in the bathroom? You don't have to take one—or, of course you can if you want, but what I mean is, I just need to hear the sound of the shower running."

Lucie hesitated for a moment before she understood. Her gaze drifted toward a photo of Suzanne, and she nodded.

"I'll do that."

Sharko gave her a thin smile.

"Your turn. Ask your question."

"Who did you call earlier, in the train station? Who did you supposedly 'negotiate' with so that I could sleep in your apartment?"

Sharko took a few seconds before answering:

"The computer, over there . . . You can use it for your search. You just have to push the ON button. No password required. Why would I need one?"

37

The films of a madman . . .

Lucie had spent a good part of the night rummaging around on the Internet, and this was the only impression it left her of the work of Jacques Lacombe, a man with a steely gaze and a mouth as thin and straight as a razor blade. The digitized photo, posted on a fanatic's blog, dated from 1950. It was taken at a party the last time the director had been seen in public. Squeezed into a shiny dinner jacket, wineglass in hand and hair slicked back, Lacombe stared at the camera so intensely that it gave Lucie chills. She couldn't look directly at his eyes.

Certain amateurs had tried to draw up a biography of the filmmaker, but they always dead-ended at the same place: in 1951, after the turbulent shoot in Colombia and his run-in with the law, Lacombe had simply disappeared. Only a part of his work—they estimated that a good 50 percent of his films had been lost—continued to circulate among a small circle of devotees. All that remained of this dark character were a handful of short features, most of them running less than ten minutes, which film buffs called the "crash films."

Crash films . . . shot between 1948 and 1950, before Colombia. As the Web authors explained, this was a series of nineteen films whose sole aim was to display things never before attempted in the medium, a kind of artistic exploit on celluloid. Lacombe didn't care about the point of a film, only about the public's reactions: its passivity toward images, its relationship to plot and story line, its voyeuristic tendencies, its fascination with intimacy, and also its tolerance for conceptual cinema. He challenged people's watching habits and turned filmmaking conventions on their heads. Always a need to innovate, disturb, shock . . .

And then there was that small white circle in the upper right, on each of his nineteen mini-films. Lucie understood that this was probably

Lacombe's maker's mark, his signature. Digging further, she found a description of some of his techniques, his experimentations with masks, mirrors, and multiple exposures. Some people advanced a hypothesis about the presence of the white circle at the top of each film. They called it the "blind spot," which from a psychological viewpoint corresponded to a small part of the retina that was lacking photoreceptors. Some of the sites even suggested an exercise:

■   ○

If you closed your left eye and looked only at the square from a distance of about six inches, the circle disappeared from sight. Lucie was amazed by this flaw in human optics. Ultimately, wasn't Jacques Lacombe trying to say, with his signature, that the eye was an imperfect instrument that could be fooled by any number of means? Wasn't he clearly stating that these flaws were the engine driving his films? At bottom, these short features surely hid the first burblings of a sick and perverse mind. A mind obsessed by the impact of images on human beings—their veracity, their strength, and also their destructive power. He was a visionary ahead of his time.

Stretched out on the couch, her eyes half shut, Lucie understood better why Lacombe had never made it. His "crash films" turned out to be weird and boring beyond belief. Who would go see an hour-long movie called *The Sleeper*, which simply showed a man sleeping? Or the movement of an eyelid opening and shutting in slow motion, at a thousand frames a second, projected for more than three minutes? There was also crash film number 12: counting and showing each second of the twelve minutes the film lasted, which, by induced effect, was reduced to a simple display of numbers . . . These films were as distant and inscrutable as the mind of their maker.

When the alarm on her watch sounded, Lucie was lying with her hands behind her head, staring at the ceiling. Six fifty-five. She had barely slept an hour or two. A cop's night. She got up, head full of cotton wadding, and felt her way to the bathroom. A wide, silent yawn: this wouldn't be an easy day.

In the bath, everything was incredibly orderly: a new toothbrush in a glass, blue towels hanging from the rack, their folded edges perfectly symmetrical, a razor with gleaming blade, a clean bathtub with a shower head above it. There was also a medicine cabinet—the kind of small furnishing that says more about someone's life than lengthy explanations. Lucie looked at her reflection in the cabinet mirror. She could open it, have a look at the medications, rummage even deeper into Sharko's privacy . . . What was there to find behind that door? Antidepressants? Stimulants? Anxiolytics? Or just vitamins and aspirin tablets?

She took a breath and turned on the taps in the shower. The water splashed against the tiles in a cold, intense downpour. Lucie had understood Sharko's request: he wanted, in those first moments when dreams still have hold over the senses, to relive his wife's presence. To believe in it just once more, if only for a fraction of a second.

Lucie returned silently to the living room, leaving the water running. A few moments later, she heard a door close . . . the water stop . . . the little trains start up, for the twenty minutes that followed.

Later, Sharko appeared, elegantly dressed. White shirt with thin blue stripes, tie, gray twill slacks. As he moved toward the kitchen, he left in his wake a scent of cologne that Lucie identified as Fahrenheit. The man gave off an aura of reassuring strength, a presence that Lucie had been missing for a long time. She rubbed her hands over her face and yawned discreetly.

Sharko turned on the radio. A lively tune filled the room. Dire Straits. Things were starting to move.

"I won't ask if you slept well. Coffee?"

"Please—black, no sugar."

He gave her a sidelong glance as he placed a packet in the coffee machine and turned it on. When their eyes met, he turned away toward the cabinet and took out a teaspoon.

"Nothing that remarkable about Lacombe, I suppose? Otherwise you wouldn't have hesitated to wake me up in the middle of the night."

Lucie came closer with a smile.

"Not much beyond what Judith Sagnol already told us. The enigmatic type, vanished into the woodwork in 1951, never heard from again. I also searched around for Syndrome E, including on medical and scientific sites—nothing, no matches found. If the Internet doesn't know about it, it must be pretty secret."

Sharko handed her her coffee and went to water his plants, near the kitchen window.

"You should go freshen up a bit. It's been a long time since I've seen a woman first thing in the morning, but you definitely look like you got up on the wrong side of the bed."

"I've been up all night thinking."

"Naturally."

"We have to go to Canada, Inspector."

Sharko paused a moment before setting down his watering can. His jaw tightened.

"Listen, I can't get those children's faces out of my head either. I saw their fear, then that frenzy in their eyes, their movements. I know that the people hiding behind that camera must have done monstrous things. But our job is in the present, Lucie, the present. It's already shitty enough as it is. And besides, for the moment, we don't have anything concrete to help us learn what happened to those kids."

"Yes, we do. I did some research on the Web. In the 1950s, Montreal was heavily Catholic and had loads of orphanages run by nuns. Every child who passed through those institutions has a file that can be consulted at the city's national archives. They have a Web site, which says you can come in without an appointment and examine the files on site. Everything is classified, organized, listed . . ."

"But none of that means we should be looking in Montreal."

"The film comes from Montreal. So does the informant's call. So does the little girl, according to the lip-reader. And don't forget what Judith Sagnol told us about the old Montreal warehouses where she spent her stay. In the archives, it would be best to have an actual name, but a search year will do. The files contain photos. We could—"

"All we have is the date of an old film and a few prints of the kid taken from screen shots, in black and white and of poor quality."

"And a first name she said in the film: Lydia . . . One of her playmates, I assume. Maybe a roommate? A year, one name, and a photo might be enough."

"Yeah, maybe . . ."

"We're moving forward inch by inch, but we are moving forward. We can print photos of some of the other girls from the film. In some shots, you can see the refectory, the swing set, bits of the yard, which might help us identify the institution. It's not a lot, but it's something. If we can find out who the girl was, or the other girls, we might have a chance of understanding all this."

Sharko picked up his coffee cup and brought it to his lips. He took a large swallow.

"Canada is far away and we've got a lot to do here . . . I'll have to think about it."

The inspector's telephone rang. It was Leclerc. His tone was smooth and direct.

"I've got good news and bad news."

Sharko put his phone on speaker.

"I'm with Lieutenant Henebelle right now."

"What? At your place?"

"She spent the night at a hotel, and now she's here listening. Go ahead—what's the bad news?"

Lucie preferred not to call Sharko on his lie: it was fair enough. The voice boomed in the speaker, serious:

"Good morning, Lieutenant Henebelle."

"Sir."

Leclerc cleared his throat.

"I got an answer from the Sûreté in Quebec about Jacques Lacombe. He died in 1956. His charred body was found at his home. It was ruled a household accident. He lived in Montreal."

Sharko pressed his lips together.

"A household accident . . . What had he been doing before?"

"The Canadians filled me in on that too. He moved to Washington in 1951, where he worked as a projectionist at a little neighborhood movie theater for two years. In 1953, he went to live in Montreal, where he again worked as a projectionist."

Sharko thought for a moment.

"None of that jibes with his sudden departure from France, his will to succeed as a filmmaker, or his genius . . . Especially since in 1955 he made that awful film with the children. There's more to this. I don't believe his death was accidental. Nineteen fifty-six was just after he'd shot that film—that's too much of a coincidence. Who can dig deeper into his past? Who can find out about the circumstances surrounding the fire?"

"Nobody. Who'd want to handle it? The Americans? The Canadians? Us? We'd have to open a new case about something that took place more than fifty years ago, and for there to be an investigation, it'd have to be ruled a homicide. Not to mention all the administrative clearances. No, nothing we can do there."

Sharko sighed, leaning on the table.

"Fine . . . so what's the good news?"

"We just got back the DNA results, and we've identified one of the five bodies. The one who was shot in the shoulder and tore his skin off."

Lucie noticed how brightly the inspector's eyes shone.

"Who was it?"

"Mohamed Abane, twenty-six. Rap sheet as long as my arm. A real model childhood, with brawls, drugs, theft, racketeering. Finally did ten years for aggravated rape and mutilation."

"More."

"His victim, a twenty-year-old woman, almost didn't make it out alive. His way of thanking her was to cauterize her genitals. Abane was barely sixteen at the time."

"A real charmer."

"He was given time off for good behavior. Released from Fresnes eleven months ago."

Sharko's fist tightened on the phone. For the first time since the case had begun, they finally had a concrete lead.

"Last known address?"

"He was staying with his brother Akim, in Asnières."

"Give me the exact address."

"Péresse already has a team on the way—they'll be there any minute. Did you think they were going to wait for you? It's their job, not yours. Get yourself here to the office—I've got the beginnings of a list for you: humanitarian organizations present in Cairo in 1994, at the time the girls were murdered."

"That can wait."

Sharko hung up. Lucie paced back and forth, hand under her chin.

"What are you churning over, Henebelle?"

"Lacombe died in a fire, one year after making the film. That same year, a copy arrives at the Canadian archives as an anonymous gift. What if Lacombe sensed his life was in danger? What if he'd made several copies of the film and sent them to various archives to preserve his secret, but also to make it go viral? We've seen how quickly the film went from hand to hand, collection to collection."

Sharko nodded. The woman had the knack.

"In his way, Lacombe knew how to safeguard his treasure. By sending it off, simply making sure it existed and could one day be deciphered and understood. Yes, that could be."

Lucie agreed. One by one, the pieces of the puzzle were falling into place, even if they couldn't yet make out the final design. Sharko quickly dialed another number.

"Who are you calling?"

"A former colleague at Number 36 for Abane's address. Don't be long in the bathroom. I'll drop you at the subway in ten minutes and you can get back home."

Lucie smoothed out her wrinkled sweatshirt.

"The hell you will. I'm coming with you."

38

Asnières-sur-Seine. A tidy little town in the outskirts of Paris, with a pretty center and pleasant shops. All around them and to the north, things weren't so nice. Blacktop replaced nature, the sky was crisscrossed by fat ivory-colored birds taking off from Charles de Gaulle, interminable bars of mouse-gray buildings closed off the horizon. The *banlieue* in all its splendor. And through the middle of it ran a river.

Sharko and Lucie got off at the Gabriel Péri subway stop and quickly walked westward. Akim Abane, the brother of one of the five corpses from Gravenchon, had no criminal record and worked as a night watchman in a large department store. An upstanding guy, apparently, who lived on the fourth floor of a dark, uninviting apartment complex. At the bottom of the high-rise, Lucie was treated to a few relatively inoffensive whistles from some teenagers perched on a square of grass.

The man who opened up for them had the sharp, dry features of a Mediterranean. A flinty face on a vigorous, muscular body. Someone familiar with weightlifting and bench presses. Sharko made the first move:

"Akim Abane?"

"Who are you?"

To Sharko's relief, Péresse's men hadn't arrived yet. He congratulated himself on his speed and showed his ID. Abane was lounging at home in shorts and a white T-shirt, which bore the legend FONTENAY MARATHON.

"I'd like to ask you some questions about your brother, Mohamed."

The Arab didn't budge from the doorway.

"What's he done now?"

"He's dead."

Akim Abane hesitated a moment before balling up his fist and punching the door frame.

"How?"

Sharko kept it brief, sparing him the worst.

"Apparently killed by a gunshot. They found his body buried near a construction site in Seine-Maritime. Can we come in?"

Abane moved aside.

"Seine-Maritime . . . What the hell was he doing there?"

The man didn't shed a tear, but the news had shaken him, so much so that he had to sit down on the sofa. The cops invited themselves inside.

"I knew it would end like this someday . . . Who could have done such a thing?"

"We don't know yet. Do you have any ideas?"

"I don't know. He had so many enemies. Here in the housing development, and outside."

Lucie cast a quick glance around the room. Flat-screen TV, gaming console, running shoes everywhere: too much stuff in too little space. She noticed some photos in a frame. She moved closer, her brows knit.

"Were you twins?"

"No, Mohamed was a year younger than me, and an inch or two taller. But we were just like each other. I mean physically. Otherwise I was nothing like him. Mohamed had a screw loose."

"When did you see him last?"

Akim Abane stared at the floor, eyes vacant.

"Two or three months after he got out, around New Year's. Mohamed had come crying to me saying he wanted to change his life, make up for what he'd done. I never believed him. It wasn't possible."

New Year's . . . So that brought the dating of the skeletons to less than seven months. Sharko already knew the answer to his next question, but he let the brother give it:

"Why's that?"

"Because guys like him never stop. They showed me photos of that girl he'd burned between the legs, ages ago. The image is stuck here, in my brain. It wasn't human . . ." He sighed. "Mohamed stayed with me a week or so. Let's see—it must have been around mid-January when he left with just some personal stuff in a bag."

He fell silent for a few moments.

"I never believed for an instant that he'd do it . . . and I was right."

"Do what?"

With a sigh, Akim Abane stood up, opened a drawer, and riffled through some papers. He handed Sharko a slightly crumpled brochure.

The inspector's heart leaped.

In that fraction of a second, everything became clear.

The brochure vaunted the merits of the Foreign Legion.

He raised his eyes to Lucie, who was also taken aback.

Akim took his seat again, hands joined between his powerful legs.

"One day, Mohamed found that in a magazine, in jail. To hear him tell it, you'd have thought it was a revelation. The military—that's what he wanted to join. Wipe the slate clean. Change his identity, start from scratch. Yeah, sure . . ."

He picked up the framed picture, showing him standing next to his brother, and stared at it a long time.

"You stupid shit, what'd you have to go die for?"

Deep inside, Sharko was rejoicing. The Foreign Legion . . . It fit so perfectly with what they'd discovered in the past few days. Lucie picked up the questioning.

"Do you have any proof that he joined the Legion? Letters, phone calls, anything? Had he bought a train ticket for . . . the south?"

"Aubagne?" Sharko specified.

The Arab shook his head.

"No, I'm telling you, he never joined. I knew him—he wasn't capable. Too unstable, and he had a real problem with authority. Can you imagine him over there? I came home from work one day and he'd cleared out. Hadn't even taken his brochure. Not a good-bye, nothing . . . I knew someday the cops would come knocking on my door."

The inspector tightened his jaws, eyes staring at the illustrated ad of a soldier in white kepi, posing proudly with all his medals. It was clear to him that Mohamed Abane had joined the Legion after all, but there wasn't any direct proof. Even his brother didn't believe it.

"Do you have any family, a relative or friend your brother might have gone to stay with after he left here?"

"Apart from some real creeps, I can't think of anyone."

Sharko continued to think. While everything seemed to be falling in place, there was still a huge piece that didn't fit: why sever the hands, pull the teeth, and scrape off the tattoos of someone who could simply be identified through DNA? In the Legion, they must have known that Mohamed Abane had a long rap sheet. They might erase the past of their recruits, but they were scrupulous about verifying it first. They clearly would have known the Arab was registered on the national DNA database and would be well aware of the extent of his crimes.

Unless . . .

Sharko raised his dark eyes toward the photo of the two brothers.

"I have a question that might seem strange . . . Your identity card didn't go missing around that time, did it?"

Akim nodded.

"Actually, it did. I must have lost it at work or in the street. How did you guess?"

Sharko didn't respond. Lucie was just as confused as the bodybuilder. The cop had all the answers he needed, and his conviction had been reinforced. He held his hand out to the Arab and Lucie did the same.

"Some cops from Rouen will be here very soon. They'll ask a lot of questions and take notes. Don't be alarmed—it's just routine."

Before leaving, with Lucie ahead of him, Sharko turned back toward Akim, who hadn't moved from his sofa.

"By the way . . . your brother had a tiny particle of plastic sheathing under his skin, near his neck. Do you know if he'd had an operation?"

"No, no . . ."

"Any stays in the hospital?"

"I don't think so. But the truth is, I have no idea."

"Thank you. I promise that you'll have answers. The people responsible for this are going to pay. I'm going to see to it personally."

And he gently closed the door behind him.

39

Lucie and Sharko were sitting at the kitchen table in the apartment in L'Haÿ-les-Roses. They had bought some pastries on the way. She was biting into a croissant, while he had gone for a pain au chocolat, which he dunked meticulously in his coffee. For the first time in several days, clouds of a perfect white fluffed in the sky outside the window. Sharko spoke between two mouthfuls:

"It all fits. Bodies no one can identify—probably foreigners who came to France by whatever means available. That's often how it works with the Legion."

Lucie picked up the thread: "The professional way they went about hiding the corpses and removing any identifying marks. The description we got from Luc Szpilman, the combat boots . . . Soldiers . . ."

"Not to mention the hair analysis, showing that three of them had quit taking drugs in the weeks before death. It fits perfectly with guys who want to start their lives over, guys you take charge of with an iron hand. Young legionnaires in training. Cadets."

Sharko shoved in a mouthful of pastry. He seemed in good spirits, almost happy.

"What was that business about the missing ID card?" asked Lucie.

"Simple logic. Mohamed Abane was the classic deviant personality. With a background like his, he could never have gotten into the Legion. Recruiters in Aubagne will overlook practically any crime, except the really serious ones—murder, rape, sex crimes . . . Abane faked his identity so he could join."

"By stealing his brother's card?"

"Sure. All you need to show at the Foreign Legion recruiting station is a valid ID. That's all. It's the only link between your past and your future.

Mohamed Abane just showed them his brother's card. The two men looked a lot alike, so the recruiters were fooled and thought they were dealing with a clean record."

Sharko was beaming. Lucie suddenly saw him as sure of himself, overflowing with vitality. A man who was regaining a taste for the hunt and the field. He drank his coffee, lost in thought.

"It almost all fits . . ."

"Almost?"

"Almost, yes. I was thinking about the five murdered cadets. There's nothing worse than the selection process, and especially the ten weeks of drills that come after. Hell on earth. They put you through every kind of physical and psychological torture, until you're ready to off yourself. It's easy to imagine one or several recruits fighting back or popping a cork. If we push it a bit further, let's suppose they run into a serious hitch. An instructor who has no choice but to shoot, because they've given these guys real guns. But then, why would they have removed the brains and eyes before burying them?"

He was moving so fast that Lucie had to think for a few moments before answering:

"Because they're trying to hide much more than just a hitch? Because, behind all this, there's that diabolical film and those children locked in a room, slaughtering animals?"

"And the girls who were brutally murdered in Africa. Egypt, France, Canada. It's all related without being related. The real problem is that the Foreign Legion hasn't set foot in Egypt for more than fifty years. Apart from a similarity in MO, apart from that hysterical phenomenon we suspect, we don't have any link between the two series of crimes. As for the film, we're still not sure what it has to do with all this."

Lucie ran a hand over her face. Nervous exhaustion was weighing more and more heavily on her. Sharko continued to think aloud.

"They really are good. Notre-Dame-de-Gravenchon—there's nothing there. Not even a military training camp. We should make sure, but I'm convinced the Legion has never set foot there. Maybe if we'd found the bodies around Aubagne, but there . . . they completely covered themselves."

"So what are you saying, that we have no way of getting at the Legion?"

"Accusations are serious business, and you know how it works. Even if our reasoning holds water, we need actual proof. Witnesses, paperwork, traces of some kind. But all we've got is our conviction. Neither my department nor Criminal will launch an investigation based on simple deductions. Stolen ID or no, Mohamed Abane's past works against us. The Legion will deny categorically that they'd ever recruit someone like that. No violent crimes with them—that's a golden rule."

A silence. Lucie wiped her hands on a napkin.

"And if someone decided to bring charges against the Legion even so, what would that be like?"

Sharko let his arm fall in front of him, in a sign of despair.

"We'd have to present our findings to the minister of defense. On the off chance it worked, we'd need a court order and a mountain of paperwork just to be allowed to question a few handpicked individuals. The whole thing would eat up a lot of time and come to the attention of the Legion top brass, who could easily spin it however they wished. Assuming it still went forward, we'd still run up against the Military Secrets Act. We'd certainly have to deal with some bigwig, a colonel or general, probably with top secret clearance or higher. I've run up against that kind of joker before, a few years back. You might as well be talking to an anchor at the bottom of the sea. The Legion is body, the Legion is mind. Even if some of them saw things, and even assuming they're still on French soil, they won't say a word."

Lucie slowly slid her finger around her coffee cup.

"And what if we got around procedure?"

Sharko looked at her coolly.

"Out of the question."

"Don't tell me you haven't thought of it."

Sharko shrugged.

"You're too young to go off the rails. You want some friendly advice? Stop inviting trouble. Your kids will never forgive you."

"Can it with the sermons. We go in aboveboard. We show up and ask to talk to the commanding officer about a suspect we're looking for, for instance. If he agrees to see us, we guide him toward our case nice and easy. If he's really involved, he's almost sure to react."

"React how? You think he's going to shout the truth from the roof-tops?"

"No, but maybe he'll get nervous, or make some phone calls. We can trace his line . . . or stake out his place. I don't know . . . long-range mics, maybe?"

Sharko let out an unpleasant snicker.

"You've been watching too much *Mission: Impossible*. His house must be stuffed to the gills with high-frequency detectors. Little army toys, capable of picking up any wave emission for dozens of yards around. And you can bet his phone is on a dedicated encrypted line. Most of those guys are total paranoiacs—that's why they get chosen for the job. What say we get real?"

"So just like that, we let them get away with it and keep our traps shut?"

Sharko didn't answer; he stared at his open hands on the table. Lucie squeezed her napkin between her fingers.

"Well, *I'm* not going to keep my mouth shut. If you don't feel like coming, I'll go alone. When you step in it, you have to see it through to the bitter end."

She disappeared quickly into the bathroom. Sharko sighed. She was capable of doing it—a real hothead. After thinking it over a while, he got up, walked down the hall, and stopped in front of the locked bathroom door.

"Do you need a visa or something like that to go to Canada?" he called in a loud voice.

Water from the shower splattered against the tiles.

"What?"

"Let's explore the Canada lead first. The more I think about it, the more I believe we might pick up the trail of those little girls in the archives. And if nothing pans out, we'll try going after the Legion. So—do you need a visa?"

"I have a passport. That's usually enough, but sometimes not, from what I could make out online. But it would make things easier if we had an international letter rogatory."

Sharko's mouth was pressed against the locked door. From the other side, he could hear Lucie soaping herself up. He couldn't stop himself from picturing her naked. It gave him an odd feeling in the pit of his stomach.

"Fine . . . We have good relations with the Canadians; they train our behavioral analysts. We also have all the contacts we need over there. I'll take care of that for you at Violent Crimes. Do you know if there are any direct flights from Lille to Montreal?"

"Yes, but— Ow! I got soap in my eye. Wait a minute!"

Sharko smiled. Rustle of the shower curtain. Then the woman's voice once again:

"Aren't you coming with me?"

"No. You get the next TGV. I'll take care of sending the info to your boss—don't worry about that. We'll get you e-tickets for Quebec."

"What about you?"

"I'm going to see Leclerc about the list of humanitarian groups in Cairo at the time of the murders. It's possible the killer is on that list of names."

Suddenly the door opened. Lucie was wrapped in a large towel, her hair and ears covered in foam. She smelled of vanilla and coconut. Sharko jumped back a step; he felt strange.

"Why are you trying to keep me at a distance?" she asked in a hard voice.

Sharko clenched his jaws. He gently wiped away some foam from Lucie's temples and abruptly turned around.

"Why, Inspector!"

He disappeared down the hall, without looking back.

40

Everything had sped up for Lucie since leaving L'Haÿ-les-Roses. She had only a few hours to do what would normally have taken someone two days. Her plane was scheduled to leave at 7:10 that evening from Lille-Lesquin airport. The administrative services where Sharko worked had taken care of her arrangements as if by magic: paperwork, travel authorization from the higher-ups, e-tickets sent to her in-box. The Boeing would land at 8:45 p.m. Quebec time. A room was reserved for her at the Delta Montreal, a three-star hotel located between Mount Royal and the Old Port, a short walk from the archives. She had just printed out the international letter rogatory, which had arrived only moments before via e-mail. Strictly within the confines of the investigation, they were allowing her four full days on site. Four days was a lot of time to look through old documents. They'd been liberal.

As Lucie was returning home, she thought of Sharko's last words to her on the train platform at Bourg-la-Reine: "Take care of yourself, kid." The words had echoed in the hollow of his throat like pebbles rattling against each other. They had shaken hands—thumb above for him, smiles exchanged, 2–0—then, like the first time, Sharko had walked away, shoulders hunched, without turning around. With a pinch in her heart, Lucie had stared for a long time after his broad silhouette as it disappeared anonymously into the stairway.

After a stop in the bathroom, she packed her bag with the bare minimum, stuffed it in the trunk of her car, took out the trash, and headed for the Oscar Lambret Medical Building. She was more excited than ever. Canada, an international case . . . for *her*, the "little lady cop" who just a few years before was filling out forms in police headquarters at Dunkirk. Somewhere in there, she felt proud of her rise in the world.

Lucie entered the hospital room with two black coffees bought from the vending machine. Her mother was still there, faithful at her post. She and Juliette were playing with the gaming console. Coloring books lay open on the bed. The little girl gave her a wry smile. She was beaming, and her skin had finally regained the honey color children of her age should have. The doctor had officially announced that she'd be discharged the next morning. Lucie hugged her child in her arms.

"Tomorrow morning? That's wonderful, darling!"

After a ton of kisses, Juliette went back to her game, all cheerful. Lucie and Marie stood at the doorway to the room, coffees in hand. Lucie took a deep breath and blurted out:

"Mom, I'm afraid I have to ask you to watch Juliette for at least four more days—four days and nights, I mean. I'm really sorry. This has been a really difficult case and—"

"Where are you off to now?"

"Montreal."

Marie Henebelle had a gift for making you feel guilty with a look.

"Going abroad now? Nothing dangerous, I hope."

"No, no. I just have to search through some old archives. Nothing very exciting, but somebody has to do it."

"And of course that somebody is you."

"You might say that."

Marie knew her daughter too well; she knew that even if Lucie were going off to face the devil himself, she'd claim she was just out to pick mushrooms. She jerked her chin interrogatively at a gray stuffed animal, a hippopotamus.

"Your ex came by."

"My ex . . . You mean Ludovic?"

"Have there been others?"

Lucie remained silent. Marie looked sadly at Juliette.

"You should have seen how much fun those two had together. Ludovic spent two hours here with her. He was going home, and he said that if you want to call him, you can. You should."

"Mom . . ."

Marie seized upon Lucie's gaze and didn't let go.

"You need a man, Lucie. Someone to get you settled down, who can bring you back to reality when you need it. Ludovic is a good boy."

"Yeah, the only problem is I don't love him."

"You never gave yourself time to love him! Your twins spend more time with their grandmother than with their mother. I'm the one watching and raising them. Does that seem normal to you?"

Ultimately, Marie was right. Lucie thought again about Sharko's view of the job: a devouring monster that ultimately spat out ruined or damaged families.

"After this case, Mom. I promise I'll slow down and think about it."

"Think about it—*right* . . . Like after the last case. And the one before that, and before that . . ."

Her eyes were filled with reproach, along with a kind of pity.

"It's too late for me to remake my daughter. You're set in stone, missy, and it takes a pickax to change anything in that hard head of yours."

"At least I know where I got it from."

Lucie managed to wrest a half smile from her mother, who caressed her cheek with her hand.

"Don't worry about it. Let me just make a quick stop at the house. What time do you have to leave here?"

"Five at the latest. Just enough time to get to the airport and check in."

"That leaves you three short hours to spend with your daughter. Good lord, you'd think we were in the visiting area of a prison!"

41

After dropping Lucie off, Sharko had sped to Nanterre. The young female detective had left a burning trace in his mind, an indelible presence that he found he couldn't erase. He could still see her, wrapped in a towel, covered in foam, in *his* bathroom. Who would ever have thought that someday a woman would shower where Suzanne had once showered? Who would have thought that the sight of a semi-undressed body could once again make his heart race in his chest?

For now, he paced back and forth in his boss's office. Lucie was far away, and his mind was on other matters. He was yelling at Leclerc, who was seated at his desk.

"We can't just keep our mouths shut like this. Others have gone after the Foreign Legion before us."

"And they all got shot down. Péresse and the boss feel the same way. You need to forget about your shortcut and get me something concrete. Josselin is willing to assign two investigators from Criminal to retrace Mohamed Abane's steps from the moment he left his brother's. That's the only legal recourse we've got."

"It's going to take forever and it'll get us nowhere. You know it as well as I do."

Leclerc stretched his chin toward an express pouch lying in front of him.

"As I said on the phone, before you make the shit hit the fan bypassing Péresse, I got hold of the list of humanitarian groups who were in the Cairo area. We've got a few names, especially the mission leaders. But the thing that's really interesting is the SIGN conference itself. Have a look . . ."

Martin Leclerc's face was somber, closed off. He shuffled some papers needlessly and took care not to meet Sharko's gaze. The chief inspector picked up the file and started reading:

"A Smile for the World's Orphans, around thirty people. Planet Emergency, more than forty. SOS Africa, sixty . . . I'll spare you the best ones . . ." He squinted. "March 1994, annual meeting of the Safe Injection Global Network. More than— More than three thousand persons from all over the world! WHO, UNICEF, UNAIDS, a ton of NGOs, universities, doctors, scientists, health professionals, people from industry . . . More than fifteen countries. But—what the hell am I supposed to do with this?"

"March 1994 was the month and year of the murders, wasn't it? We're waiting for a detailed list of SIGN participants, which we should have later today. At first glance, it looks like between a hundred fifty and two hundred Frenchmen."

"Two hundred . . ."

"As you see, we're a long way from combat boots and flak jackets here. So let the Legion go for now—we've got enough on our plates as it is, with Canada, these lists, and the Abane investigation."

Sharko leaned on the desk.

"What's with you, Martin? We used to go at these things like bloodhounds, and today you're burying it all under lists of names. Once upon a time, you would have been all over this."

"Once upon a time . . ." Martin Leclerc sighed. His fingers clutched a sheet of paper, which he crumpled and tossed into the wastebasket. "It's Kathia, Shark. I'm losing her."

Sharko absorbed the blow, but deep down he'd been expecting it for several days now. Kathia and Martin Leclerc had always symbolized the very image of a stable couple, who had weathered so many storms that nothing could split them apart.

"It started with the Huriez case, didn't it? Why didn't you say something?"

"Because it is what it is . . ."

Sharko recalled every detail. One year earlier, cocaine smuggling near Fontainebleau. One of the small fry in the network gets pinched, Olivier Hussard, twenty years old. Kathia's godson . . . She asked her husband to intervene, use his influence to get a lighter sentence. But Martin Leclerc was inflexible, faithful to the standard of his office.

Sharko had blamed himself. Carried away by his own demons, he hadn't noticed anything wrong with his chief. *He* was the analyst who was supposed to recognize behavior patterns.

"I had a right to know, Martin."

"You had a right to know? And what piece of shit rule gave you the right to know?"

"Our friendship, that's all."

A heavy silence fell over the room. In the distance they heard the roar of a motorcycle.

"I went to see the boss, Shark. Day before yesterday."

"What? Don't tell me you—"

"Yes. After this case, I'm resigning. I can't hold on for eight more years, waiting for retirement with my guts in a knot. Not without her. She's been staying at her sister's for the last few days, and it's driving me insane. And besides, can you see me growing old alone, like—"

He stopped short. Sharko stared at him.

"Like me, you mean?"

Leclerc took refuge in his stacks of papers, which he piled up, moved around, piled up again.

"You're being a pain in my ass, Shark. Get out!"

The inspector detached himself from the desk, dazed. His eyes were slightly teary. Leclerc couldn't imagine how badly his words had stung. Sharko clenched his fists.

"Do you know what your leaving means for me? For the few years I still have to go?"

Leclerc banged on the desk with his fist.

"Yes! Yes, of course I know! What do you think?"

This time, Leclerc stared his subordinate right in the eyes.

"Listen, I'll do everything I can so that—"

"You'll do nothing. If you leave, I'm gone, and you know that perfectly well. No one's going to want an old, damaged cop. Not even in a closet somewhere. It's as simple as that."

Leclerc looked at his friend and shook his head.

"Please don't hold a knife to my throat. It's hard enough as it is."

Shoulders stooped, Sharko finally headed for the door. He turned around when his hand was on the knob.

"When I lost my wife and daughter, you and Kathia were there for me. Whatever happens and whatever you decide, I'll accept it. And now, you should go tell Josselin that I'm going home early to get some rest, because I'm hearing voices on all sides."

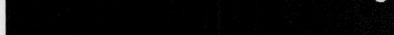

42

The highway rolled by. Long, monotonous, endless. Sharko had just passed Lyon, heading due south toward Marseille. Windows open, radio blasting. His cell phone was sitting in front of him, next to the steering wheel.

"The worst part is that I have no idea how to help him. Go see Kathia? That's not the answer. I feel like I'm swimming through molasses."

"What's that mean, 'swimming through molasses'?"

Sharko glanced over at the passenger seat.

"It means straining, working hard for nothing, turning around in circles. Exactly like what I'm doing now."

Eugenie was playing with a lock of her hair, twisting it around her fingers. She put on her most vixenish look.

"By the way, did you notice how much Lucie looks like Suzanne?"

The inspector almost choked. That kid certainly had some unpredictable reactions. He shrugged.

"She looks about as much like Suzanne as your jar of sauce looks like a locomotive."

"To you, I mean. She looks like Suzanne to you . . . And to your heart of stone as well. I know. It's getting all warm in there."

"You're raving."

"That's right, *I'm* the one who's raving . . . Lucie has gotten to you— that's why you want to protect her. Canada is far away."

The inspector's cell phone started vibrating.

"I like Lucie. I hope things work out for the two of you."

"You're out of your mind, kiddo."

He answered the call. It was one of his contacts at Central Intelligence.

"Have you got the info?"

"What do you think? The current commander of the Legion is a colonel by the name of Bertrand Chastel. Guy's got quite a pedigree."

"Let's hear it."

"Career legionnaire, belonged to the most prestigious combat units. Commander of the Second Parachute Regiment in Lebanon, then Afghanistan. Then he changes hats, becomes head instructor in Guiana, develops some new kind of training program and forms a super-elite squad. The guy seems to get off from living on the edge. The kids sweat blood under him, and most of them come out of it with their heads rewired for battle, if you get what I mean. Back in France, he spends three years at DGSE before returning to his first love and taking over the First Foreign Regiment, then the Fourth, then the Recruitment Corps two years ago."

The acronym immediately set off an alarm in Sharko's head. DGSE: General Directorate for External Security.

"A stint in secret service in the middle of his career as a legionnaire? What was he doing there?"

"You think it's spelled out in black and white? All this stuff is top-priority defense secret. He knows some real movers and shakers, including most members of the Consulting Committee for Defense Secrets. We're in the upper echelons here, Shark, and in the upper echelons there are a lot of locked boxes. When you open them, you get Pandora's boogie jumping in your face. I'm not sure what it is you're looking for, but I can tell you right now this guy is untouchable."

"That's my business. Is he in Aubagne these days?"

"Yes. I called with some bogus excuse to check."

"Terrific. Thanks, Pops."

"Meanwhile, we never had this conversation and I don't want to know what you're up to. But watch your back all the same."

Sharko hung up. He threw a vindictive glance to his right. Eugenie had finally beat it.

He turned down the volume of the car radio, which was jangling his nerves. After the flatness of the countryside came valleys, mountains, and rivers. Valence, Montélimar, Avignon. The foothills of Provence. The temperature rose, and sun cooked his flesh through the windshield. Sharko's throat was dry, not because of lack of water but because of Henebelle.

Eugenie was right. That diminutive blonde had given his fossilized innards a real shake-up. Something was heating up in his chest, his belly, and his loins. Everything felt tangled in knots, and it hurt. It hurt because there shouldn't have been anyone other than Suzanne. Because he was fifteen years older than Lucie, and through her eyes he could see all the flaws that had destroyed him and his family. The relentlessness, the absences, and that need to track down Evil, true Evil, until you found yourself with your back to the wall, shattered and exhausted. There was no way out of that pursuit. No closure or satisfaction.

The day was already coming to an end. Eight hours of driving behind him . . . eight hours to think, in part, about his plan of attack.

It was pure suicide, and he knew it.

No matter, he'd already been dead for quite a while. He'd already died so many times.

He left the Autoroute du Soleil—the Sunshine Highway—and continued another thirty miles or so on Highway A52, exiting at Aubagne. He briefly spotted the buildings of the Foreign Legion recruitment center along Highway A501. Long white containers, with perfect lines and a rigor that was purely military. A few minutes later, he turned onto Route D2, then onto a road that led him to a sentry box manned by a corporal on guard duty. White kepi, red chevrons, spotless uniform. Sharko presented his police ID.

"I'm Chief Inspector Sharko, from the Central Bureau for the Suppression of Violent Crimes. I'd like to speak to Colonel Bertrand Chastel."

Giving the full name of his department always made an impression. Sharko explained that he was looking for a repeat offender, who had most likely joined their ranks not long ago under an assumed identity. To make more of an impact, he had piled some charges onto the so-called criminal's record: rape, torture . . . The soldier asked him to wait a moment and disappeared inside his cabin. Sharko knew his ploy had worked when the man reappeared and pointed him toward the parking lot.

"You can park in a visitor space, there behind you. The colonel will see you. A second lieutenant will come get you. I just need to ask for your service revolver."

The inspector handed it over.

His folder under his arm, he silently followed the officer who had come to fetch him. On the immaculate walls of the enclosure, the famous motto *Legio patria nostra* was inscribed in gilded letters. Columns of men of all nationalities—Poles, Colombians, Russians—marched in formation around the parade ground to the rhythm of military chants. Others, farther back, wearing blue sweatpants and white T-shirts, were running down the stairs at breakneck speed, urgency and fear in their eyes. Plebes . . .

Their extremism was frightening: these brothers in arms with their shorn heads and steely eyes were not yet thirty years old, and they were ready to die at a moment's notice for the French flag.

Sharko's attention was suddenly drawn by a one-story building, in front of which was a sign that read DCILE: COMMUNICATION AND INFORMATION DIVISION. He quickened his step to catch up to his guide.

"Tell me . . . what exactly do they do at DCILE?"

"It's a public relations office that processes requests for information and coordinates with the news media. The production office handles promotion for the Foreign Legion throughout France and abroad."

"Do you also have a video department? Shooting and postproduction of films for the army?"

"Yes, sir. Documentaries, promotional and commemorative films."

"And it's legionnaires themselves who handle this?"

"Senior military staff. Officers and noncommissioned officers from the land army, mostly. Any other questions, sir?"

"No, that's it. Thanks."

Sharko thought of the men who had killed the film restorer, Claude Poignet. One of them was a filmmaker attached to the military, and he was surely hidden here, safe and sound in his combat boots, in one of those huge barracks . . . It fit together more and more.

They arrived at the buildings for the 1st Foreign Regiment, seat of the high command, where the CO resided, the absolute authority. Sharko's throat was dry, his hands moist, and he would have felt much less apprehensive facing a bloodthirsty killer than a decorated colonel, who had presumably devoted part of his life to serving his country. As a professional, the cop had deep respect for these soldiers and their sacrifice.

They walked down muffled hallways; the soldier knocked three times and stood at attention in front of the closed doorway.

"At ease! Come in!"

After introducing Sharko and executing his regulation about-face, the second lieutenant left the cop alone with the colonel, who was busy signing papers. The policeman estimated that the commanding officer must have been about his age and build, minus the pudginess and taller by an inch or two. His faultless gray crew cut further amplified the Euclidean geometry of his face. On his dark uniform, a small badge read COLONEL CHASTEL in red letters.

"I'll ask you to wait a few more seconds."

The superior officer raised his ice-blue eyes, then went back to his chore without exhibiting any particular emotion. If the colonel was involved in the affair, Sharko thought, if he had kept up with the news following the discovery of the bodies in Gravenchon, he would certainly know Sharko's face, who he was. If so, had he been steeling himself for this visit since the corporal on guard had called ahead? Or had he simply not recognized him?

While Chastel signed papers, Sharko took the opportunity to check out the office. The seven articles of the legionnaire's code of honor dominated a bay window that looked out on the parade ground. The walls were covered with countless commemorative plaques and photos, in which the colonel, at various ages, posed alone or with his regiment. The ocher soil and dust of Afghanistan, the shattered structures of Beirut, the exuberance of the Amazonian jungle . . . A muffled violence radiated from those faces with their sharply etched features, from those fingers clutching their assault rifles. At bottom, these pictures showed nothing other than war, conflict, death, and in the middle of it all, men who felt at home there.

The colonel finally stacked up his papers and pushed them to the edge of his impeccably neat desk. There was no other chair. Here, one tended to remain standing, at attention.

"I still envy those years when no one had heard of paperwork. May I see your ID?"

"Of course."

Sharko handed it over. The officer looked at it scrupulously before giving it back. His fingers were thick, his nails well manicured. Like Sharko, he had left the field some time ago.

"You are looking for someone in our ranks who committed murder, if I've understood correctly. And you've come to arrest him on your own?"

His voice was deep, monolithic, rough. If he was dissimulating, he was good at it.

"For now, we're only at the investigation stage. A surveillance camera proved that his vehicle was present about ten miles from Aubagne, at the A52 tollbooth. But there's no trace of the same vehicle when you get to the A50. Therefore, he has to have stopped between the two."

"Have you found the vehicle?"

"Not yet, but we're working on it."

Colonel Chastel shook the mouse of his computer, then typed what was no doubt a password on the keyboard.

"You are surely aware that the Legion does not recruit men who have committed rape or murder?"

"He probably used a false identity."

"Not very likely. Give me his name."

Sharko looked him in the eye, as deeply as he could. It was there, soon, in the flash of an instant, that he had to catch the tiny sparkle that could turn everything around. He undid the elastics holding his folder shut and took out an enlarged photo. He placed it on the desk, facedown on the wood.

"It's all on there."

Bertrand Chastel pulled the sheet toward him and turned it over.

The photo showed Mohamed Abane when he was alive. A close-up of his face.

Chastel should have reacted. Nothing—not the slightest emotion on his closed features.

Sharko clenched his jaws. It couldn't be. The inspector felt destabilized, but tried not to show it and to stay on point.

"As it says under the photo, he must have presented himself here under the name Akim Abane."

The legionnaire pushed the sheet back toward Sharko.

"Sorry, but I've never seen him."

Not a tremble in his voice, lips, or fingers. Sharko took back the picture, his brows knit.

"I imagine you can't see every new face that joins your ranks. In fact, I was rather expecting you to type his name into the computer, as you were getting ready to do before I showed you his portrait."

A short pause. Too long, deemed Sharko. Nonetheless, Chastel lost none of his composure or self-possession. Thick-skinned, this one.

"Nothing happens here without my knowing or seeing it. But if it will reassure you."

He typed the information into the computer and turned the screen toward Sharko.

"Nothing."

"You didn't need to show me the screen—I would have taken you at your word."

With a firm motion, Chastel pulled the monitor back toward himself.

"I'm quite busy. Second Lieutenant Brachet will see you to the exit gate. Good luck with your fugitive."

Sharko hesitated. He couldn't leave like this, with all these doubts. Just as Chastel moved to pick up his phone, Sharko leaned toward him and pressed on his hand, forcing him to put the receiver back in the cradle. This time, he knew he was crossing the line, and that it could all come tumbling down.

"I don't know how you knew I'd show up here, but don't try to fuck with me."

"Remove your hand at once."

Sharko pushed his face to within four inches of the officer's. He went straight to the point, all or nothing.

"Syndrome E. I know all about it. For God's sake, why the fuck else do you think I'd be here?"

This time Chastel registered the blow and couldn't entirely hide his astonishment: eyes wandering, temporal bones rolling beneath the skin. A bead of sweat pearled on his forehead, despite the air-conditioning. He kept his hand on the phone.

"I have no idea what you're talking about."

"Oh, yes, you do! You know exactly! What I don't get is how you managed to keep so cool when you saw Abane's portrait. Even someone like you can't have that much self-control. How did you know? How did you—?"

Sharko squinted.

"Microphones."

He straightened up, hands pressed against his temples.

"Good God almighty. You went to my place and planted bugs."

Chastel bolted to his feet, fists planted on his desk like a gorilla.

"I promise you're going to regret coming here and threatening me. You can expect your career to come to a very sudden end."

Sharko gave him a vicious smile. He went back on the attack.

"I'm here on my own. Nobody's aware of my trip to Aubagne, as you already know. And if it eases your mind any, we won't be launching any investigations against the Legion. Everyone is in agreement: Mohamed Abane, or rather Akim Abane—call him what you want—was never here."

"You are completely insane. What you're saying makes no sense."

"So insane that I'm going to ask you for money, Colonel Chastel. A lot of money. Let's say a tidy sum, enough to let me resign and afford a nice, comfortable retirement. But a mere drop in the bucket for the DGSE slush fund. You think I want to keep shoveling shit for the rest of my life?"

Sharko didn't give him time to answer; he had to move fast. He pulled a sheet of paper from his folder and slapped it down in front of the legionnaire.

"The proof of my good faith."

Chastel deigned to lower his eyes.

"What's this, GPS coordinates? What does this mean?"

"If you or your friends ever take a little jaunt to Egypt—you never know—this is where you'll find the body of a certain Atef Abd el-Aal, a Cairene sentinel. Unless you already knew about this too? Give this paper to the French or Egyptian authorities and I'll spend the rest of my days in prison."

The officer's frozen features looked like poured concrete. Sharko leaned forward, his face smug.

"I'll also forget about that business with the mics. You see, we have to trust each other, you and I."

He headed toward the door.

"No need to see me out—I know the way. I'll contact you in a few days. Oh, and one more thing: should I meet with any unfortunate accidents, I've taken precautions."

He jerked his chin toward the Legion's code of honor.

"Maybe you should reread that."

He then turned around and left.

No one saw him out.

As he walked past those soldiers, trained and prepared to kill, knives in their belts, he wondered if he hadn't just signed his death warrant. He now had the Foreign Legion and probably the secret service on his back. He had suspected there was considerable weight behind this affair, and he'd been right. Some very high brass . . .

He drove pedal to the metal down the long, straight lines of Highway A6. With the back of his hand, he wiped away the small tears that were leaking from the corners of his eyes. He had confided his weaknesses, his deepest wounds, to Henebelle, because he knew she was like him, and a kind of trust had spontaneously grown up between them. He had shown her his psychological scars.

But other ears had been listening. Chastel and his fucking henchmen . . .

Now he felt exposed, betrayed, almost ashamed.

Seven hours later, he walked through his door. He set about searching his apartment top to bottom and found four listening devices. One hidden in the base of the halogen lamp, and the other three in the radiator thermostats. Standard miniature equipment, available to any police department. He knew he wouldn't find any prints, and that there would be nothing to learn from them.

In a rage, he threw them onto the floor.

And it was Eugenie who crushed them under her heel.

At that moment, the Sig Sauer resting in his holster and the three dead bolts on the door to his apartment seemed terribly insubstantial.

43

Lucie had taken an airplane only once before, on a holiday in the Baleares when she was about nine, and she'd loved it. She remembered her father and mother holding her close and petting her hair when the turbulence frightened her. It was one of her last memories of the three of them together, and it was all so far away now.

Lost in thought, she sat with her forehead pressed against the window of the Boeing 747 as it hovered above Quebec. The flight attendant had just woken her and asked her to fasten her seat belt: they were beginning their descent. Lucie had slept most of the way, heavily and, unusually, without waking. Now, in the pale light of the setting sun, she admired the stretches of lakes and forest, rivers and swamps that civilization had still spared. A vast, wild terrain, miraculously preserved. Then the mouth of the Saint Lawrence appeared, with the first major signs of human presence, before the jet flew over the famous lozenge-shaped island.

Montreal: a flare of modernism amid the waters.

The flight attendant verified one more time that everyone's seat belt was fastened. The passenger seated next to Lucie, a big blond fellow, had practically dug his fingers into the armrests. He stared at her with cocker spaniel eyes.

"Here it comes again—I'm starting to feel like I'm dying. I really envy people like you who can sleep anywhere."

Lucie gave him a polite smile. Her mouth was pasty and she didn't feel like making chitchat. The landing at Montreal-Trudeau airport was soft as could be. The ground temperature was about the same as a classic summer in the north of France. No real sense of disorientation, particularly since much of the population was French-speaking. Once the usual business was behind her—customs, verification of the letter rogatory, the wait at baggage claim, currency exchange—Lucie hailed a cab and let herself collapse onto the backseat. Evening was just beginning here, but across the Atlantic night was well under way.

Her first impression of Montreal, in the gathering darkness, was of a modern and incredibly luminous city. The skyscrapers launched their beams of light toward the stars; the many cathedrals and churches played on tones of red, blue, and green projected by spotlights. In the center of town, Lucie was surprised by how wide the avenues were, and the rigorous geometry of the streets. Despite the subway entrances with their very Parisian look and the effervescence of the small cafés and restaurants nearby, you didn't have the impression of closeness and warmth that animated the French capital on mild evenings.

By the time she arrived at the Delta Montreal, an imposing high-rise with a summit bathed in blue light, Lucie no longer had the energy to go out and see the city—including the famous underground Montreal. Claiming her key, she settled into her room on the fifth floor, put on her bathrobe, and lay down on the bed with a long sigh. She didn't feel at home in this anonymous place, with its succession of strangers, traveling businesspeople, and vacationing couples. Nothing more depressing than to be alone at night, without a sound outside. Where were her daughters' laughter and tears, the light daily hubbub of her apartment that had been with her for all those years? How could she let herself go so far away from her ailing little girl? What was Clara doing at camp? Questions that a mother, a good mother, should never have to wonder about.

Despite her worries, she gradually began to doze off. Her eyes fluttered open when the hotel phone rang. She stretched out her hand and brought the receiver to her ear.

"Yes?"

"All settled in, Henebelle?"

A pause.

"Inspector Sharko? Uh . . . yes, I just got in. But . . . why didn't you call on my cell?"

"I tried. No go."

Lucie picked up the mobile phone that was lying next to her. The battery was charged. The screen showed no calls. She tried to get a dial tone.

"Damn, it must be out of range. Speaking of distance, it must be four or five in the morning for you. You're already up?"

Sharko was sitting at his kitchen table, in front of an empty cup of coffee and his loaded Sig Sauer. His cheek was in one hand, his elbow resting on the tablecloth, his eye turned toward the entry door in the living room. His telephone was sitting on the table, with the speaker on. On the chair opposite him, Eugenie was humming the latest song by Coeur de Pirate. She was munching on candied chestnuts and sipping a mint soda. Sharko turned his face away.

"How was the trip?"

"In a word, exhausting. Crammed full of vacationers."

"And how about the hotel—is it nice? You do have a bathtub, at least?"

"A bathtub? Uh . . . yes. And how about you—what's new?"

"Here's a thrill: I'm about to inherit a list of two hundred people who attended a scientific conference in Cairo at the time of the murders. We've decided to focus on just the French for now."

"Two hundred? That's a lot. How many are working on it?"

"Just one—me. For starters, we should be able to eliminate a good number with the killer's profile we have from 1993. Pare it down as much as possible, before delving into everyone's past. You can imagine what a chore it is."

The sound of an engine rose from the street. Out of reflex, Sharko snatched up his gun and rushed to the window. After shutting off the light, he slightly raised the shade, his throat tight. A truck, topped with an orange revolving light, slowly advanced along the sidewalk. It was just the street sweepers emptying the trash cans, as they did every week, in the early morning torpor. The cop sat back down, half reassured. His temples were beating hard; hypervigilance and paranoia, amplified by his illness, kept him both awake and exhausted.

"Is something wrong, Inspector?"

"No, everything's fine. Tell me, did you notice anything suspicious at your place in Lille?"

"Such as?"

"Such as hidden microphones. I found four of them here."

Sitting cross-legged in the middle of the bed, Lucie felt her blood go cold.

"The knob to my outside door grated a bit a few days ago. They must have broken into my apartment too—I'm sure of it."

Lucie felt the blow. The feeling of violation. They had penetrated into her space, her cocoon. They might have gone into her room, into her girls' room.

"Who did it?"

"I don't know. What's certain is that the colonel in charge of the Foreign Legion is involved."

"How do you know that?"

"I just do. Don't tell anyone about the mics, okay? We'll take care of it when you get back."

"How come?"

"Quit asking questions! Keep me posted. Talk to you soon."

"Inspector! Wait!"

The air-conditioning rumbled hypnotically. And it felt so good to hear Sharko's voice.

"What, Henebelle?"

"There's something I need to ask you . . ."

"What's that?"

"Have you saved a lot of lives in your career?"

"Some, yes. But unfortunately not always the ones I would have liked."

"In our profession, we comfort the families by finding the people who killed their loved ones. We probably give a handful of people a reason to go on living, because we give them an answer. But, Inspector, haven't you ever felt like just quitting the whole thing? Don't you ever tell yourself the world would be no better or worse off without you?"

Sharko spun his weapon on the table, flicking the grip with his finger. He thought of Atef Abd el-Aal. Of those eight marks on the tree trunk. Of all those he'd been able to take care of, with the certainty that they'd never do it again.

"I felt like quitting every time I saw a smile on the faces of the bastards I put in jail. Because that smile was something that no bars and no prison could contain. And later, you start seeing that smile in shopping malls, playgrounds, schools, wherever you go. That smile makes me retch."

He slammed his palm down on his gun, stopping its movement. His fingers closed over the barrel.

"I wish only one thing for you, Henebelle: that you never come across that miserable smile. Because once it gets into you, it never comes out."

Lucie clenched her jaws. She stared at the ceiling with a sigh. The shadows were coming back fast and furious.

"Thank you, Inspector. I'll keep you posted on what happens. Good night."

"Good night, Henebelle. Take good care of yourself."

Lucie hung up, sadness pressing down on her.

At that moment, she understood that to go back, to return to the life of a woman and a mother, would not be easy. Because that smile he was talking about, she had already come across, way too early in her young career.

It had been gnawing at her insides for a long time.

44

Lucie spent an agitated night filled with bad dreams. Images had seized on the quiet hours to harass her: the little girl on the swing, the bull, the rabbits, Judith Sagnol with her pupil slit, her belly mutilated with a large, black eye.

Twisting and turning in bed, watching the digital clock on the television dilute the time minute by minute, Lucie was waiting for only one thing: the sun to finally rise.

And rise it did. At nine o'clock, she was walking in the streets of the Canadian city, taking advantage of the morning freshness to clear away the fatigue in her muscles.

The central archives of Montreal were located about a hundred yards from the Old Port, in the heart of a thickly tree-lined neighborhood. They were housed in a Beaux Arts–style government building, with large blocks of white stone and massive colonnades, that had once been the university's business school.

When Lucie entered, her backpack stuffed with fruit from the hotel, a bottle of water, her memo book, and a pen, she felt like a ridiculous ant lost in a desert of paper. According to the first archivist she talked to, these walls, beneath the high, sculpted ceilings and magnificent chandeliers, contained more than twelve miles of data, split between private, governmental, and civic records. One could delve into the lives of the great families of Montreal and Quebec, the Papineaus, Lacostes, and Merciers, as well as find information about immigration, education, energy, tourism, and legal affairs, not to mention some nine million photos and two hundred thousand drawings, maps, and plans. A citadel of paper within a city of steel and concrete.

To give herself the best chance, Lucie had prepared a brief summary of what she hoped to find. The archivist who had greeted her referred her to someone else, who should know more about Quebec's history in the 1950s. The badge on the second archivist's white blouse read PATRICIA RICHAUD.

"I'm looking for a little girl who almost certainly was in a convent or orphanage in the fifties," Lucie explained. "To be more precise, around 1954 or '55. The institution was probably located in or around Montreal. I also have the name of a nun she would have known: Sister Marie du Calvaire."

The archivist looked at the picture of the girl on the swing, then beckoned Lucie to follow her.

"Do you know how many Sister Marie du Calvaires there were at the time? Unfortunately that bit of information won't help you much."

Patricia Richaud was about fifty, with blond hair fastened in a ponytail and small round glasses. The two women walked down endless corridors, which didn't at all match the fusty image one might have of such a place. Clean, pure lines, futuristic design. There were even guided tours—people were already moving around in groups in the vast library. Lucie was sure they had walked a good five minutes, going up and down various stairways, before they reached a small, circular, windowless room with fluorescent lights. The files were lined up in hundreds of cabinets that rose many feet in the air and could be reached with rolling ladders. Among other things, the cop could read JUVENILE DELINQUENCY CASES (1912–1958), SOCIAL WELFARE CASES (1950–1974), and so on. The archivist halted in the middle of the room.

"Here you are. If you ask me, this is where you have the best chance of finding what you're looking for. Most of these files concern orphans under the age of sixteen. The juvenile delinquency cases, for instance, concern children abandoned by their parents in circumstances that made it likely they'd turn to crime."

Taking advantage of a break in the conversation, Lucie pointed to another part of the alcove, which particularly caught her attention: RELIGIOUS COMMUNITIES (1925–1961).

"And what about those?"

Richaud instinctively touched the pendant she was wearing, which hung from a gold chain.

276

"You're in luck—we received those files only a few weeks ago. Normally they would have been restricted because they belonged to religious institutions. But now Quebec is turning away from its religion. We are now a world besotted with modernism, and one by one those institutions are being forced to close due to a cruel lack of funding. And so their records have come to us, because they have nowhere else to store them."

She sighed.

"As you can see, there are quite a number of these files, since they also include orphanages from neighboring towns and regions. These religious communities were quite active at the time, especially in taking in illegitimate orphans."

"Illegitimate? Can you be more specific?"

As if she hadn't heard, the specialist headed toward a group of metal file cabinets. She opened one, containing a seemingly infinite number of index cards.

"Here are the indexes. If you had the child's name, you could locate the relevant file in just a few minutes. But since you don't have much information, you should consult the card for the year she was placed or that of the institution, in those other drawers over there. They contain the lists of children admitted. It's likely you'll find the same names in several institutions at different times, as back then it was common practice to transfer the children, and orphans never stayed in the same place for more than a few years at a time. Once you have the card of a particular individual, you should refer to her file to compare it with your photos. I'll leave you to it. Don't hesitate to call me on that telephone over there if you have any questions."

"Can you also make outside calls on that phone? My cell doesn't seem to be working."

"Yes, but we'll have to charge you. And be sure to call the reception desk when you wish to leave, or you'll never find your way."

Lucie summoned her back just before she could leave the room.

"You never answered my question. What illegitimate children?"

Patricia Richaud removed her small round glasses and rubbed them fastidiously with a chamois.

"As the name suggests, they are children born out of wedlock. You said you're with the police? What is it you're looking for, exactly?"

"I have to admit I'm not quite sure myself."

"If you're delving into Quebec's past, I would ask you not to treat it lightly. The period was dark enough as it is, and everyone here would rather forget it."

"Dark? What are you talking about?"

The woman left quickly, shutting the door sharply behind her. Lucie put down her backpack on a round table. What had she meant by that? *A dark period . . .* Did it have anything to do with her investigation?

She looked around her.

"Okay . . . not out of the woods yet."

She bucked herself up and, not knowing the family name, delved into the file cards that grouped the children by year. She thought it out: the film had been developed in 1955; the girl was about eight years old. Not likely she would have been admitted that same year, as she seemed to be familiar with the surroundings and personnel. And the lip-reading specialist had noticed a slight evolution in her growth. So Lucie started with 1954.

"Good God in heaven . . ."

For the year 1954 alone, they registered 3,712 admissions in the area's various religious institutions. A veritable exodus of children.

Lucie set to work. She had first and foremost a precious first name. A few syllables deciphered on the lips of a child filmed on an old black-and-white short. She opened her memo book and reviewed what she'd written the other day during the meeting: "What happened to Lydia?"

Lydia . . .

Lucie took out the thirty-odd lists from the year 1954 and began reading through the names, arranged in alphabetical order. Girls and boys were mixed. All that was written, by hand, was their last name, first name, and age, as well as the number of the corresponding file.

The first time Lucie came across the name Lydia—Lydia Marchand, seven years old—she was sure she'd found the right one. Armed with her file number, she rushed to the wall of papers and dug out the correct file. The ID photo did not correspond to the ones of the other little girls that she'd printed off the film. But perhaps Lydia hadn't been present for the rabbit massacre?

Lucie didn't give up. The important thing here was the institution where Lydia was living: Convent of the Sisters of the Good Shepherd, Quebec. The cop went back to the file drawers, found the card corresponding to that establishment, and took out the cards relating to the boarders, of whom there were 347.

Three hundred forty-seven boarders. And those were only the girls.

To find the girl on the swing, the one who'd been Lydia's friend, she had no choice but to go through the 347 files one by one and compare the ID photos of each with her own photos.

She spent the entire morning at it, without result. So that wasn't the right Lydia . . . First discouragement. Realizing the scope of her undertaking, Lucie took an apple from her bag and cracked her neck. Her eyes were already getting red. The harsh fluorescent lights and those names, written in such a small hand one after the other, were hardly ideal. Was she even in the right city?

She reassured herself she was. Everything led here, to Montreal.

At 1:15, she attacked the year 1953. At around 5:00, after two bananas and a visit to the bathroom, she dove into 1952. This time as well, there was an nth Lydia who led her to another religious institution, La Charité Hospital in Montreal.

Mechanically, Lucie pulled out the tall stack of files relating to that establishment and began her last search of the day. The archives closed at 7:00, and in any case her head was about to explode. Names, names, and more names.

When she opened a folder located about three-quarters of the way down the stack and saw the photo attached to it, her throat tightened.

It was the girl, the one on the swing.

Alice Tonquin.

Three years separated the file photo from the one Lucie had printed off the film, but there could be no doubt. The deep-set eyes, direct gaze, oval face . . .

Her heart pounding, the young cop read through the scant information in the file. Alice Tonquin, born at the Convent of the Sisters of Mercy in Montreal in 1948 . . . Lived there until the age of three . . . Then transferred two years in a row to live with the Franciscans of Mary in

Baie-Saint-Paul . . . Then to La Charité Hospital in Montreal in 1952 . . . End of her journey—or, rather, the rest must have been hidden in another file, since the one she was holding corresponded only to the girl's admission to La Charité.

The few details were purely administrative, but no matter: Lucie finally had the identity she'd been searching for. She took notes, circled "La Charité Hospital, Montreal," and picked up the phone in the room.

She made a call to her captain, Kashmareck, who since the beginning of the investigation had been in touch with the Sûreté in Quebec. She asked him to call them again and request an identity search for Alice Tonquin and Lydia Hocquart.

While waiting for him to call back, she called Patricia Richaud to tell her that she could come get her in a half hour, which would leave her time to put away the files.

In the quiet of the alcove, Lucie let herself fall into her chair and threw her head back. Then she drank the water in her bottle to the last drop.

She had done it. A photo, one simple photo, had brought her back through time and closer to her goal. She thought of Alice, that once nameless girl who now had a name. The little orphan with no father or mother, tossed about from hospital to convent, without bonds, points of reference, anything. Raised in the coldness of a religious institution: prayer at mealtimes, household chores, nights in the dormitory, an austere existence geared toward order and obedience to God. What future could she have had after such disastrous beginnings? How had she grown up? What had happened in that room with the rabbits? From the bottom of her heart, Lucie hoped she would soon have the answers to these questions. All those thoughts, all those faces that tormented her day and night, had to stop. Alice had to reveal her secrets.

The telephone in the room rang twenty-five minutes later, as she was putting away the last files. It was Kashmareck. Lucie picked up and didn't give him time to speak:

"Tell me you've got something!"

From the way he cleared his throat, she immediately understood that it had led to another dead end.

"Yeah, I've got something, but it isn't great. First of all, there's not a trace of an Alice Tonquin. Neither in Canada nor in France. Oh, the cops at Sûreté have her birth certificate all right, from the hospital in Trois-Rivières where she was born, but not much more than that. They told me it wasn't uncommon to lose sight of someone back then. With all the moving about between institutions, it was hard to keep track, and files got lost. After 1955, she was probably adopted by a family under another name, like a lot of those kids at the time. If she's still alive, it's under an unknown identity."

"Good lord, everyone seems to know about these mass adoptions except us. And what about her friend, Lydia Hocquart?"

"She died in 1985 in a mental hospital, from a heart attack. She suffered from severe behavioral disorders and her heart just couldn't take the meds she'd been swallowing all those years."

"Ask them to send you all the info, and e-mail it to me. What was the name of Lydia's hospital?"

"Hold on . . . here it is. Saint Julien Hospital in Saint-Ferdinand d'Halifax."

"And how long was she there?"

"That, I have no idea. It's all confidential medical information. You do realize that I'm normally the one who asks the questions?"

Behind Lucie, the door opened. Patricia Richaud silently inspected the environs, making sure everything was in its proper place.

"I'll call you back," said Lucie.

She hung up, jaws clenched. Severe behavioral disorders . . . mental hospital . . .

The archivist's throaty voice pulled her from her thoughts.

"Did you find everything you wanted?"

Lucie jumped.

"Uh . . . yes, yes. I did. I found the name I was looking for, and her last known home, La Charité Hospital in Montreal."

"The order of the Gray Sisters . . ."

"I'm sorry?"

"I was just saying that that establishment houses a Roman Catholic religious congregation, whom they still call the Gray Sisters. Their hospital was bought by the University of Montreal—the papers have been full of it these past weeks. By 2011, the sisters will be relocated to Saint Bernard Island, but for now most of them are still living in Ward B of the hospital, refusing to leave the premises. Their archives have already been transported here, which is why you were able to find what you were looking for."

The Gray Sisters . . . Just the name gave Lucie gooseflesh. She imagined stony faces, eyes like dull mercury.

"Would it be possible to get the list of the sisters who are still living there?"

Lucie was thinking of Sister Marie du Calvaire. Richaud knit her brow.

"That should be feasible, yes."

"And can you also tell me what this dark period of your country is about? I'd like to know what happened, exactly."

The employee remained frozen for a few seconds. She set down a heavy ring of keys on the table and swept her gaze over the piles of papers.

"It all has to do with those thousands of children, miss. An entire generation of little ones sacrificed and tortured. The only trace of it is what remains here, in this room. They called them the Duplessis Orphans."

She headed for the door.

"I'll be back with your list."

45

One o'clock in the morning, French time. Earlier that evening, Sharko had received in his in-box the list of attendees at the SIGN conference in 1994.

The inspector had printed out the document and gone back to his kitchen table, discreetly lit by a small lamp. From the outside, it had to look like he was asleep.

According to the information supplied by the ministry of health, the conference had lasted from March 7 to 14. The select participants had arrived and returned on an airplane specially chartered by the Egyptian government. It wasn't exactly the VIP tour, but it wasn't far off.

By a disturbing coincidence, the murders had all taken place between March 10 and 12, in the midst of the conference. According to the profile drawn up early in the investigation, one of the killers had a knowledge of medicine. The use of ketamine, the slicing of the skulls, the enucleation . . . The problem with this list was that the 217 French men and women in Egypt at that moment—not counting those from the humanitarian aid organizations, a whole other story—all had some notion of medicine, and the term "notion" was putting it mildly. Neurosurgeons, professors of psychiatry, medical students, researchers and department heads, biologists, most of whom had lived at the time in Paris or its environs. The cream of the French research community, individuals who seemed above reproach.

Two hundred seventeen lives—one hundred sixteen men and one hundred and one women—that he had to dissect in detail, on the basis of fifteen-year-old suppositions.

From the moment he held the sheets in his hand, Sharko felt increasingly certain that one of these individuals, aware of the phenomenon of mass hysteria that had afflicted Egypt in 1993, had made the trip a year later, using the conference as a pretext, with the sole aim of slaughtering three innocent girls in order to steal their brains and eyes.

The name of the killer or killers must have been hiding in these papers.

The questions that tormented him, the late hour, Eugenie's constant visits, and the palpable tension in the apartment prevented him from really concentrating on the list. His head was full of shadows.

Sharko sighed. He finished his mint tea, staring into space. The military, medicine, filmmaking, this business about Syndrome E . . . The cop knew he was involved in a case that went far beyond the standard manhunt. Something monstrous, the likes of which he'd never seen. And yet he'd confronted his share of monstrosities, more than he could count on both hands.

In the dead of night, his keen senses suddenly focused on the entry door.

An infinitesimal sound of metal pierced the silence in the hallway.

Immediately, Sharko turned off the light and grabbed up his Sig.

Here they were.

Beneath his door, he saw, very briefly, the beam of a flashlight, before everything went black again.

His jaw set, he slowly got up from his chair and crept toward the living room.

On the other side, the linoleum floor creaked slightly. Sharko felt the edge of his sofa and crouched down, his gun aimed blindly in front of him. He could have attacked from the front, by surprise, but he didn't know how many there were. One thing was for sure: they rarely went out alone.

The creaking in the hall stopped. The cop's palms were moist on the grip of his gun. He suddenly thought of the photos of the film restorer's body: hanging from the ceiling, disemboweled and stuffed with film. Not an enviable fate.

The door handle turned, very slowly, before returning to its initial position. In the following seconds, Sharko expected them to go for the lock, then burst in armed with knives or silencers.

Time stretched out forever.

Suddenly he heard a rustle under the door.

The creaking started up again, then decreased in a regular rhythm.

Sharko rushed to the door and gave the dead bolt a precise twist. The next second, he was in the hallway, barrel pointed forward. With his fist, he banged on the light switch and flew into the stairwell. Downstairs, the main door slammed shut. Sharko took the stairs two at a time, almost unable to breathe. The foyer, then the street. A long line of pallid streetlamps ran down the asphalt. Left, right—not a soul. Just the murmur of a slight breeze and the slow breath of night.

Behind him, the building's entry door flapped shut but didn't close completely. Sharko noted a small square of cardboard taped to the plate, preventing the bolt from going in. Whoever it was must have put it there earlier in the evening after a resident had gone through, and could therefore come back at any time without having to buzz in. Basic, but smart.

The detective ran back upstairs to his apartment. He switched on the lights, turned the locks, and, with his foot, pushed the white envelope that had been slid under the door into his living room. He did not pick it up until he'd put on a pair of latex gloves, which he kept in boxes of one hundred under the sink—can't be too careful.

The envelope looked elegant, lightweight, the kind used for correspondence. With a tightness in his throat, Sharko looked it over completely, then opened it with a knife blade.

He had a very bad intuition.

Inside, he found only a photo.

It showed Lucie Henebelle and himself coming out of his apartment. The morning after the night they'd spent here.

Lucie's head was circled in red marker.

Sharko leaped onto his cell phone and punched in the woman's number.

Still no ring, as if the number simply didn't exist.

It was them. Sharko was certain of it. Somehow or other, they had neutralized the SIM card of her cell phone.

The next moment, with trembling fingers, he dialed the number of the Delta Montreal. The hotel staff informed him that there was no one in Mme. Henebelle's room; the key was still at reception. Sharko told the operator that he had an urgent message for Lucie Henebelle, that she absolutely had to call him the moment she returned.

He'd thought he was putting her out of harm's way by sending her across the ocean.

But he had completely isolated her.

Thrown her into the lion's den.

Half an hour later, not knowing what else to do, he knocked at Martin Leclerc's door in the twelfth arrondissement, near the Bastille.

It was not quite two in the morning.

46

At a little after six in the evening, Lucie was sitting across from the archivist, in the alcove that smelled of old papers and distant history. Patricia Richaud nervously fingered her pendant of the Virgin Mary, while Lucie skimmed down the list of nuns still present at La Charité Hospital. A peculiar atmosphere reigned in that forgotten lair, at once heavy and tense.

Lucie stabbed her finger at the list.

"She's still there. Sister Marie du Calvaire. Eighty-five years old. She's still alive."

She sat back in her chair with a sigh of relief. This aged woman had lived with Alice Tonquin. She must know at least part of the truth.

Satisfied, Lucie focused her attention. Patricia had begun speaking.

"In the years you're asking about, they did not forgive a woman for giving birth out of wedlock. Mothers who did not observe that norm were treated as pariahs, sinners. Their own parents rejected them. Because of this, pregnant young women tried every means to hide their sin, often leaving their home for several months so they could give birth in secret behind the walls of the convent."

Lucie unconsciously circled the name "Alice Tonquin" in her small memo book. She couldn't get the little girl's face out of her mind; she knew that the old film she'd watched that first day, in her ex-boyfriend Ludovic's private cinema, would continue to haunt her for a long time.

"They abandoned their children there," she murmured.

Richaud nodded.

"Yes, the baby was then taken in by the nuns. The idea was that the orphan would later be raised by a good family, that it would have every chance in life. But starting with the economic crash of the thirties, the adoption rate plunged. Most of those children grew up and remained in the institutions. So they had to build more day cares, convents, orphanages, and hospitals. The Church began to carry more and more weight in the government. Gradually, it increased its influence over institutions such as health services, education, public welfare . . . The Church was everywhere."

Lucie had barely seen any of Montreal, but she'd noticed the countless religious monuments next to the offices of IBM and major financial corporations. A city marked by a weighty Catholic past, which neither modernism nor capitalism managed to obscure.

"When Maurice Duplessis came to power in 1944, it was the start of a critical period in Quebec's political history. People would later call that period the 'Great Darkness.' The Duplessis administration was first and foremost about anticommunism, the use of strong-arm tactics against trade unions, and an invincible political machine. His party often enjoyed the very active support of the Roman Catholic Church in electoral campaigns. And you know how powerful the Church is, miss . . ."

Lucie pushed Alice's photo toward the librarian.

"And what does this have to do with these orphans? How is this little eight-year-old girl involved in all this?"

"I'm getting to that. Between 1940 and 1950, the children placed in orphanages came, for the most part, from broken families that couldn't afford to keep them. The families paid fees to the orphanages to raise their progeny, fees that were much higher than the state allocations. Up to that point, the system worked reasonably well; the Church took in the money and used it to develop its charitable activities. But the mass arrival of illegitimate orphans posed a serious problem: first of all, they filled the institutions beyond capacity, but worse than that, no one was paying for them, other than the federal government, which offered an absurd daily allowance of seventy cents per child. Understand that these illegitimate children had to be housed, fed, and given the education that every human being has a right to. With such limited financial resources, and despite everything, the nuns still tried to raise and educate these orphans in hardship and poverty. Whatever eventually happened, no one can blame them for their courage. They weren't responsible . . ."

She paused a moment, her eyes staring into space, before resuming her explanation.

"Alongside that, in 1950, the Church built Mont Providence Hospital, a school that specialized in the education of orphans with slight intellectual deficiencies. The aim of the institution was to educate those children and help foster their integration into society. But in 1953, the hospital was on the verge of bankruptcy. The religious communities had gone more than six million dollars into debt to the federal government, and the government was demanding repayment. The nuns found themselves at an impasse, so they called on the provincial government. And it was at that point that everything changed, that the hell began, and Quebec would know what is certainly the darkest period in its history."

Lucie listened carefully. Once again they were smack in the period of her search, the early fifties. Despite the dampness of her skin, she couldn't repress a shiver. Patricia Richaud was now talking in a cold, almost didactic voice.

"Maurice Duplessis authorized a maneuver allowing that hospital, which was only for the slightly retarded, to be turned into an actual insane asylum. Why? Because in an asylum, the daily allowance paid by the federal government goes from zero to two dollars and twenty-five cents per person. Because in an asylum, there's no obligation to hold classes, and so they could do away with spending money on education. Because having the status of psychiatric hospital allowed them to use those children as free labor, without regard for human rights. The healthy children took care of the sick ones, bathed them, cooked their meals, assisted the nuns, nurses, and doctors. And so, overnight, the boarders at the special school of Mont Providence suddenly became inmates in a hospital for the insane."

Insanity . . . madness . . . The wave of children who suddenly started massacring animals, their eyes filled with incomprehensible hatred. Lucie felt her muscles stiffen.

"At that point, a whole monstrous system was set in place. The government promoted the construction of new psychiatric hospitals or transformed existing establishments into asylums. Saint-Charles-de-Joliette, Saint-Jean-de-Dieu in Montreal, Saint-Michel-Archange in Quebec, Sainte-Anne in Baie-Saint-Paul, Saint-Julien in Saint-Ferdinand d'Halifax . . . and that's not all of them. Those illegitimate orphans, whom no one knew what to do with, became the unfortunate victims of the Duplessis government. The nuns in those places were powerless. They had no choice but to bow to the regulations dictated by their mothers superior."

She sighed again. Her words grew heavier and heavier. Lucie noted and circled "Saint-Julien, Saint-Ferdinand d'Halifax," where Lydia had died. Was it possible that Lydia had never left that institution since childhood? Had the rabbit slaughter taken place there, years earlier?

"From the 1940s to the '60s, under government auspices, Quebec doctors employed by the religious communities falsified the medical records of the illegitimate orphans. They pronounced them 'mentally unfit' and 'mentally retarded.' In the blink of an eye, thousands of perfectly healthy children found themselves interned in asylums, mixed in with actual mental patients, for years on end. Simply because they had had the misfortune of being born illegitimate. Those children are now adults, and they're still known as the Duplessis Orphans."

What Lucie was hearing surpassed all understanding. A mass derangement, with the aid of bogus medical records and money under the table.

"You mean these Duplessis Orphans have been identified? They're still alive?"

"Some are, yes, of course, even though many of them have since passed away or eventually developed mental conditions for real, because of the treatments, the punishments, and the beatings they suffered during all those years. A hundred or so individuals have formed an association. For years they've been asking for restitution from the state and the Church. But it's a long, long struggle."

Lucie felt nauseated. She thought of the images from the film, of what Judith Sagnol had told them, of that antiseptic white room where the massacre had taken place, of the mysterious doctor who had been there beside the filmmaker . . . There was no doubt that Alice Tonquin and Lydia Hocquart had been Duplessis Orphans. Perfectly normal little girls declared insane by the system.

Lucie looked the librarian in the eyes.

"And . . . have you heard about the experiments in those asylums? Does the term 'Syndrome E' mean anything to you?"

Patricia pressed her lips tightly. She had discreetly slipped her pendant and its chain under her blouse.

"I've never heard of a Syndrome E. But there are two more things you should know. Since we have delved into these shadows, we might as well go all the way. At the beginning of the 1940s, and up until the 1960s, a law adopted by the legislative assembly of Quebec allowed the Roman Catholic Church to sell the remains of orphans who had died within their walls to the medical schools."

"That's horrible."

"Money encourages the worst monstrosities. But that's not all. You asked about experiments, miss, so I'll tell you. Adult patients—living patients—were sacrificed for experimental purposes in the depths of these insane asylums. I'm talking about the involvement of the American government in Quebec's dark period."

Lucie swallowed hard, her eyes glued to Alice's photo. She thought of Clara and Juliette, felt a sudden, overpowering urge to hear their voices, to touch them, hug them tight against her breast. She nervously fingered her useless cell phone.

"What sort of experiments? Medical things like . . . like what the Nazis did to deportees?"

A bell rang briefly in the room. Lucie jumped. It was almost seven o'clock, and the archives were about to close.

Patricia Richaud stood up, picked up her key ring, and looked Lucie in the eyes.

"The CIA, miss. We're talking about the CIA."

47

Reeling from these revelations, Lucie sat on a bench in a tree-lined park across from the archives. In the early evening, the place was empty, and it exuded an Olympian calm despite the big city surrounding it. She rested her backpack on her knees and massaged her face.

The Central Intelligence Agency, involved in this business. What could that mean? What did the American government have to do with patients interned in Canadian hospitals?

Through his own research, Vlad Szpilman had stumbled onto something—Lucie was sure of it.

She tried to draw the connection with her investigation, to add pieces to the puzzle. Naturally, she thought of the filmmaker Jacques Lacombe, who went to Washington in 1951 under peculiar circumstances. The starlet Judith Sagnol had mentioned a contact abroad, someone who'd wanted to work with Lacombe. Who? Then Jacques Lacombe arrives in Montreal in 1954.

And what if Lacombe were involved with the CIA? What if his modest job as a projectionist had only been a cover?

So many questions, turning over and over and over in her head . . .

Impatient, Lucie looked at her watch: 7:10. Patricia Richaud was supposed to meet her there in the park in twenty minutes, once she'd closed the office and seen to some routine duties. She was going to give her at least the start of an explanation of her claims about the involvement of American intelligence in experiments on human beings.

Too absorbed in her thoughts, Lucie didn't hear the man walking up behind her. He quickly sat down next to her and pulled a revolver from his jacket.

"You will stand up and follow me without making any trouble."

Lucie went pale. The blood seemed to drain from her body.

"Who are you? What—?"

He jabbed the gun barrel deeper into her side. His forehead was sweating. One wrong move and he'd shoot, Lucie was sure of it.

"I won't say it again."

American accent. Broad shoulders, at least fifty years old. He was wearing generic sunglasses and a cap that read NASHVILLE PREDATORS. His lips were thin, sharp like a palm leaf.

Lucie stood up; the man took up position behind her. The cop looked around for pedestrians, witnesses, but no luck. Alone and unarmed, she was helpless. They walked about a hundred yards without encountering a soul. A Datsun 240Z was waiting under the maples.

"You drive."

He pushed her roughly into the car. Lucie's throat was knotted and she was finding it hard to stay calm. The faces of her twins swam before her eyes.

Not like this, she kept thinking. *Not like this . . .*

The man took a seat next to her. Like a pro, he quickly patted her pockets, thighs, and hips. He took out her wallet, removed her police ID—which he looked at carefully—then turned off her cell phone. Lucie spoke in a slightly shaky voice:

"No need—it isn't working."

"Drive."

"What is it you want? I—"

"Drive, I said."

She started the car. They headed out of Montreal due north, via the Charles de Gaulle Bridge.

And left the lights of the city far behind.

48

Looking disheveled, Martin Leclerc paced nervously across his living room. He held the photo of Lucie with the tips of his fingers.

"God dammit, Shark! What the hell possessed you to go messing with the Legion?"

Sharko was seated on the couch, his head in his hands. The world was coming down around him and his chest felt like it was being crushed. He was suffering for the woman he'd sent straight into the danger zone.

"I don't know. I wanted—I wanted to draw them out. Stir things up a bit."

"Well, you succeeded."

Leclerc also put his hands to his head, his eyes looking at the ceiling. He sighed loudly.

"You know you never get anywhere with just a hunch, especially against guys like that! Proof! We needed proof!"

"What proof? You tell me!"

Desperate, angry, Sharko jumped up and stood in front of his boss.

"You know as well as I do that Colonel Chastel is mixed up in this affair. Begin legal proceedings against him. Mohamed Abane wanted to join the Legion; we find him buried with four other unidentified bodies. It could stick with a judge if you put your weight behind it. A cop's life is at stake!"

"Why Henebelle? What do they have against her?"

Sharko clenched his jaws. Every second of every minute, he had not stopped thinking of that blonde with her delicate build. And perhaps because of him, she was now going to suffer the torments he himself had known in the Egyptian desert. The torture . . .

"They want to use her as a bargaining chip. In exchange for information about Syndrome E that I don't even have. I was bluffing."

Leclerc shook his head, jaw tight.

"And you're telling me this Chastel was stupid enough to openly come after you and give himself away so easily? Wasn't he afraid we'd have a team waiting if he sent people to your place?"

Sharko looked his boss and friend deep in the eyes.

"I killed a man in Egypt, Martin. It was self-defense, but I couldn't tell anyone. They had me in the crosshairs, and that Noureddine wouldn't have missed. I gave Chastel the coordinates of where to find his body. He's got me the same way I've got him. It's our balance of terror."

Martin Leclerc stood there a moment with his mouth open. Then he turned toward the bar to pour himself a whiskey, half of which he emptied in one gulp.

"Fuck me . . ."

A long silence.

"Who was it? Who did you kill?"

Sharko's eyes fogged up. In nearly thirty years, Leclerc had never seen him like this. A guy who had hit the wall, completely drained.

"The brother of the cop who was looking into the murdered girls. He was one of their sentinels. He'd cut his own brother's throat, and he was this close to finishing me off. I killed him by—by accident."

Leclerc's face was a mix of disgust and anger.

"Can the Egyptians trace it to you?"

"First they'd have to find him. And even if they did, nothing connects me to Abd el-Aal."

The head of Violent Crimes emptied his glass. He grimaced and rubbed his mouth with the palm of his hand. Sharko stood behind him, his shoulders drooping under his rumpled jacket.

"I'm ready to come clean and pay for all my fuckups. But before that, Martin, help me. You're my friend. I'm begging you."

Sharko was lost, in a daze. Leclerc walked up to a framed photo sitting on a table in the living room: he and his wife, on a seawall overlooking the ocean. He picked it up and stared at it for a long time.

"I'm about to lose her because I tried to do the right thing, come what may. I thought my job was the most important thing in my life, but I was wrong. What's that cop done to you to get you so worked up about her?"

"Are you going to help me?"

295

Leclerc sighed, then took a brown envelope from a drawer. He handed it to Sharko. On the paper was written "Attention: Director, Criminal Investigations Division."

"You hold on to my resignation for now. I'll take it back when this is all over. And you take back your photo and everything you've said. You were never here tonight. You never told me anything."

Sharko took the envelope and gripped his friend's hand with his heavy mitt.

49

The stranger sitting next to Lucie finally removed his shades and stashed them in the glove compartment, along with the revolver.

"I don't mean you any harm. Please forgive my rather rude manners, but I needed you to come quietly."

Keeping her eyes on the road, she managed a glance at her companion. His eyes were a deep blue, protected by bushy gray eyebrows.

"Who are you?"

"Keep driving. We'll talk later."

The names of towns paraded by: Terrebonne, Mascouche, Rawdon. The areas they traveled through became less and less populated. They followed an interminably straight road, thickly surrounded by maples and conifers as far as the eye could see. Only rarely did their path cross a truck or car. Night was falling. Now and again they saw points of light in the distance, boats that must have been navigating the rivers and lakes. They had driven about sixty miles when the man told her to turn onto a path. The headlights lit the massive bases of tree trunks. Lucie felt she was on the edge of the abyss; she had seen only two or three houses in the past half hour.

A cabin emerged from the darkness. When the cop stepped onto the ground, feeling feverish, she heard the furious roar of a waterfall. The cool wind lifted her hair. The man waited a few moments, his eyes staring toward the shadows—shadows that were deeper here than anywhere else. He unlocked the cabin door. Lucie went in. The inside of the house smelled like cooked game. A woodstove with two burners squatted at the back of the room before a large bay window that looked out on the lilting sparkles the moon made on the surface of the great lake. In a corner were fishing rods, an old archery bow, woodsman's saws, as well as wooden molds next to little maple sugar figurines.

Puffing a bit, the man laid his gun on the table and removed his cap, revealing a sparse shock of salt-and-pepper hair. He looked even older and thinner with his jacket off. Just a tired, worn-out man.

"This is the only place where we can talk freely and safely."

He had abandoned his American accent and now spoke like a Quebecer. Lucie suddenly realized she knew that voice.

"You're the man I spoke to on the phone when I called from Vlad Szpilman's cell."

"Yes. My name's Philip Rotenberg."

American accent once more. A true sonic chameleon.

"How—?"

"Did I find you? I have a highly placed and extremely reliable source at the Sûreté. He got in touch the moment he got wind of your request for a letter rogatory. A young French cop who wants to poke around the national archives in Montreal—I immediately made the link with the phone call from a few days ago. I knew when you were coming in and where you'd be staying. I've been following you since yesterday. I now believe I can trust you."

Rotenberg noticed that Lucie looked like she was feeling faint. He moved toward her and helped her to a sofa.

"May I have some water, please," she said. "I haven't had anything to drink or much to eat. And it hasn't exactly been a restful day."

"Oh, of course. My apologies."

He walked swiftly to the kitchen and came back with some sausage, bread, water, and two beers. Lucie downed several glasses of water and some sausage slices before feeling a bit more like herself. Rotenberg had uncapped a beer, which he looked at intently, his hands around the small bottle.

"First of all, you need to know who I am. For a long time I worked in a law firm specializing in the defense of civil liberties in Washington, with the great lawyer Joseph Rauth. Does that name mean anything to you?"

Washington . . . Where Jacques Lacombe had lived.

"Not a thing."

"Then you know even less than I thought."

"I'm here in Canada to get answers. To try to . . . figure out why some-one would kill to get their hands on a fifty-year-old movie."

He took a deep breath.

"You want to know why? Because everything is contained in that film, Lucie Henebelle. Because within it is hidden the proof of the existence of a covert CIA program, which used unfortunate guinea pigs to pursue its experiments. This phantom program, the very existence of which remains unknown even to this day, was developed alongside Project MK-Ultra."

Lucie ran a hand through her hair, brushing it back. *MK-Ultra* . . . She had glimpsed that word in Szpilman's library, amid his books on espi-onage.

"I'm sorry, but . . . I'm completely lost."

"If that's true, there's a lot I have to tell you."

Philip Rotenberg walked toward the stove and shoved in a few more logs.

"Even in July, the nights are cool in the northern forests."

He snapped some branches, threw in a log, and lit it with a match. He watched the fire catch for a few moments. Lucie felt abnormally cold and rubbed her forearms.

"In 1977, I was barely twenty-five. The law office of Joseph Rauth, Washington, D.C. Two men, a father and son, arrived in Joseph's office. The son, David Lavoix, was holding an article from the *New York Times*, and the father seemed . . . troubled, absent. David Lavoix held out the clipping, which talked about Project MK-Ultra. Just so you know, the *Times* had sent the first shot across the bow two years earlier, in 1975, by revealing that in the fifties and sixties the CIA had conducted mind-control experiments on American citizens, mostly without their knowl-edge or consent. Investigative hearings were held and the American people were officially informed about the existence of this top secret project."

He nodded toward a large library.

"It's all in there. Thousands and thousands of pages in the archives, available to any citizen. The whole thing has long been a matter of public record—there's nothing secret about what I'm telling you."

Philip Rotenberg went to leaf through his documents. He quickly pulled out a copy of the *New York Times* from back then and handed it to Lucie.

Lucie opened the newspaper. A very long piece took up much of the front page. Certain words were underlined in ink: *Dr. D. Ewen Sanders . . . Society for the Investigation of Human Ecology . . . MK-Ultra Project . . .*

"That day, Joseph Rauth asked the humble Mr. Lavoix how his office could be of assistance. And young Mr. Lavoix answered, casual as you please, that he wanted to sue the CIA. The CIA! 'Why?' asked Joseph. Mr. Lavoix pointed to his father and said plainly, 'For the mental destruction and brainwashing of a hundred adult patients in the 1950s at Allan Memorial Institute, McGill University, Montreal.'"

Behind him, the fire was spreading through the logs and the kindling crackled noisily. In the middle of nowhere, in the heart of this wild, unknown province of Quebec, Lucie felt uneasy. She finally picked up her beer and uncapped it. She absolutely had to loosen the knot in her stomach.

"Montreal, once again," she said.

"Yes, Montreal. Still, the *Times* article didn't mention Montreal, or Canada. It simply said that in the fifties the CIA had established a number of covert organizations to develop its research into brainwashing, such as SIHE, the Society for the Investigation of Human Ecology. Nothing very remarkable in that, just one more revelation about Project MK-Ultra, as we'd been used to seeing in the *Times* for months by then. But look here, this underlined name . . ."

"Dr. D. Ewen Sanders. Head of research at SIHE."

"Ewen Sanders, that's right. Now, according to Mr. Lavoix, a certain Ewen Sanders had been, some years earlier, the chief psychiatrist and director of the Allan Memorial Institute. The place where David Lavoix's father, the rather passive individual there before us in the office, had gone to treat a case of simple depression and from where, long years later, he emerged with his mind entirely shot. For the rest of my life I will remember the sentence he managed to utter that day: 'Sanders killed us inside.'"

Sanders killed us inside. Lucie set the paper down on the table. She thought of what the archivist had given her to understand: experiments on human beings, conducted by Canadian psychiatric institutions.

"So this Project MK-Ultra had covert branches in Canada?"

"Precisely. Despite the 1975 hearings, no one knew that the American invasion of the mind had reached Canada. With his *Times* article, and by sheer chance, David Lavoix had touched on a major element that incriminated the CIA still further, and to the highest degree."

"So did you do it? Did you sue the CIA?"

With a gesture, Rotenberg invited Lucie to join him at his computer, on a desk near the library. He clicked through several password screens and then skimmed through his computer files. One bore the name "Szpilman's Discoveries." He clicked on another folder, titled "McGill Brainwashing," and moused onto a PowerPoint file. Underneath it was an AVI video file called "Brainwash01.avi."

"Nine of Sanders's patients, with their families' support, brought suit following Lavoix's example. The other McGill patients were either dead, too traumatized, or incapable of remembering the treatments they'd been subjected to. Now listen carefully to what I'm going to tell you—it's essential for what follows. In 1973, the CIA, informed that reporters were sniffing around their affairs, had destroyed all the files concerning Project MK-Ultra. But the CIA is, above all, an enormous bureaucracy. Joseph Rauth was convinced that some traces had to remain of such an important project, which had extended over twenty-five years and involved dozens of directors and a staff of thousands. Under the auspices of the Rockefeller Commission, we were authorized access to documents or other materials relating to research into mind control. We hired an ex-CIA operative named Frank Macley to look into it. After several weeks of investigation, he confirmed that most of the files had been destroyed by two high-ranking officials: CIA Director Samuel Neels and one of his close associates, Michael Brown. But through his persistence, Macley unearthed seven huge crates of documents relating to MK-Ultra at the Agency's records storage facility. Crates that had gotten lost in the administrative labyrinth. More than sixteen thousand pages on which the names had been redacted, but that related in detail how some ten million dollars had been spent for MK-Ultra via a hundred and forty-four universities in the United States and Canada, twelve hospitals, fifteen private companies—including Sanders's—and three corrections facilities."

He clicked on the PowerPoint file.

"From those archives, we recovered photos and a film, which I digitized and put in this folder. Here are some of the photos, taken by Sanders himself during his experiments, presumably at McGill."

Images scrolled by. There were patients in pajamas, strapped onto gurneys, lined up behind one another in endless corridors; then the same patients with earphones padlocked to their heads, sitting at tables in front of enormous tape recorders. Their faces were numb, passive; black rings sagged beneath their haggard eyes. Lucie had no trouble imagining the atmosphere of terror that must have reigned over the psychiatric hospital at McGill.

"Here are Sanders's tragic victims. He was a very brilliant psychiatrist whose great ambition was to cure mental illness, without ever managing to. It drove him crazy. One day he realized, completely by chance, that the intensive repetition of a tape that forced patients to listen to their own therapy sessions seemed to have a beneficial effect on their state of mind. But from there, it would escalate into horror. At first, Sanders forced his patients to put on headphones for three or four hours at a stretch, seven days a week. When they started to get exasperated and rebel, he created lockable headsets that couldn't be removed. So then the patients broke the tape recorders, and in response he put the machines behind cages. The patients ripped out the wires, so they were put in restraints. Sanders ended up giving them LSD, a devastating new drug that hadn't existed a few years earlier. For the psychiatrist, LSD was a miracle: not only did the patients remain tractable, but their conscious minds no longer blocked the way—so that words transmitted over and over through headphones would lodge directly in their brains."

LSD . . . Judith Sagnol . . . the presence of a doctor in the old warehouse . . . Could it have been Sanders? Had the doctor known Lacombe? Had the two men worked together on MK-Ultra? The questions piled up. And Lucie knew Rotenberg would have the answers.

Onscreen, the images passed in slow succession. The headphones on the patients' ears became more refined, the waiting lines on gurneys grew longer, the faces wilted.

"As you can see, Sanders equipped the rooms with loudspeakers that broadcast the same sentences over and over. He called them 'sleep rooms.'

Those lines of gurneys represent the wait for electroshock. Patients were subjected to treatments three times a day, for periods of up to eight weeks. Three times a day, miss. Thousands of volts coursing through your body. Can you imagine the damage something like that could do to your nerves, heart, and brain?"

"I can imagine perfectly well."

"Sanders literally wanted to cleanse the brain of its illness. No one on his devoted staff dared question his orders, for fear of losing their job. Sanders was a cold man, authoritarian and devoid of compassion."

"Are you telling me that no one, in his entire department, ever spoke out? They just let him do what he wanted?"

"Not only let him do it, but assisted. They obeyed, pure and simple."

Lucie felt her blood boil. It had happened: dozens of doctors, nurses, and psychiatrists who had blindly followed the orders of a madman, even though it flew in the face of their oaths and beliefs. Fear, pressure, and the vile orders of a superior authority in a white lab coat had muzzled them. Lucie couldn't help making a connection with the famous Milgram experiment, a tape of which she had seen once on the Web. Submission to an absolute authority, which let a human being abandon himself to his basest instincts.

"Sanders truly believed in these barbaric techniques. He held conferences, and even wrote a book called *Psychic Driving*—you can still find a copy now and then. The most illustrious doctors came to hear him lecture. It was at that point, at the beginning of the 1950s, that the CIA got in touch with him. The agency was strongly interested in his techniques and his writings. It secretly integrated him into Project MK-Ultra, and for years provided the funding for him to pursue his brainwashing experiments at the hospital. And that's how MK-Ultra entered Canadian territory."

"Is Sanders still alive?"

"No, he died of a heart attack in 1967."

"And what about the lawsuit?"

"Despite countless motions to dismiss by the CIA, threats, influence peddling, and claims that this was all protected under the military secrets restrictions, we did prevail. The CIA admitted its involvement in the experiments conducted in Canada and at Allan Memorial. The victims received financial compensation, but much more important than that, they had gotten justice and recognition. For Joseph Rauth and myself, the matter was finally over. We had gotten to the bottom of MK-Ultra and the CIA had admitted its mistakes. Case closed. And what a case . . ."

Rotenberg remained frozen in place, his eyes on the floor. On the computer screen, the old black-and-white photos continued to parade by. The hospital rooms at McGill were now equipped with televisions hanging nine feet from the patients' impassive gazes. The retired attorney pressed PAUSE.

"I pursued a brilliant career with Joseph, who died in the late nineties. I handled some terrific little cases, but nothing that ever matched the scope of that one."

"Forgive me, but . . . I still don't see how this relates to the film, or to Lacombe or the Duplessis Orphans."

Rotenberg nodded.

"I was just getting to that. Some thirty years after the Sanders case, I received a phone call from Belgium. This was about two years ago."

"Vlad Szpilman?"

"Yes. The man knew my career and everything related to the American intelligence agency, government affairs, and so on. He was a real history and geopolitics buff. He claimed to have revelations about experiments conducted in Canada on children in the fifties. Based on everything he'd read about MK-Ultra, he suspected the CIA was involved. At first I didn't believe it. I figured he was either some kook or another conspiracy theorist—those nuts had been coming out of the woodwork ever since the 1977 case. To get rid of him, I told him he was on the wrong track, that all the agency's misdeeds had been brought to light, and that children had never been involved in their brainwashing program. So he e-mailed me a black-and-white photo taken from a film, asking me to call back if I was interested."

Lucie clenched her fists.

"The photo of the children and the rabbits, is that right? 'The start of the whole thing'—wasn't that what you said on the phone?"

"Exactly. I can still see that room spattered with blood, those little girls in hospital pajamas, standing passively in the midst of all that carnage. An extremely disturbing picture. So I called him back, my curiosity aroused. He didn't want to send me the reel, but asked me to go over there, to see it at his house. I knew I was dealing with someone extremely suspicious, even paranoid, and remarkably intelligent. Two days later, I was at his place in Liège. He brought me into his projection room, and that's when I saw the film. The original and the one hidden inside it, which the old man had been able to reconstruct thanks to some contacts he had in neuromarketing."

Lucie listened attentively. The contact was probably the former boss of Georges Beckers, the jowly little Belgian who had persuaded Kashmareck to watch the film in an MRI scanner.

"From the very first image, I knew it was all true. It was like a certainty for me."

"Why such a certainty?"

He nodded toward the computer screen.

"It's all there in front of you. The relation between Szpilman's film and what happened in the hospital rooms at McGill. The undeniable link, the connection between the Duplessis Orphans and the CIA."

He closed PowerPoint and glided his mouse onto the AVI file.

"I'm going to show you the kind of video the CIA manufactured, which Sanders played in a continuous loop for his patients to wash their brains. But first I have to finish telling you what happened with Szpilman in Belgium. After that disturbing show, he started talking to me about mass hysteria . . ."

Lucie's chest grew tighter and tighter. She was hanging on Rotenberg's every word.

"The man was a veritable walking encyclopedia. He thought he'd found a connection among . . . several major outbreaks of violence that had helped shape the last century. According to him, the doctor behind the rabbit experiment was not Sanders, and the program wasn't MK-Ultra, but a parallel program, something even more covert, whose goal had nothing to do with brainwashing."

"So what was this program about, then?"

"Hold on—it gets better. At that point, Vlad ran to his library and brought out a batch of unpublished photos of the Rwandan genocide, which he'd gotten directly from a photojournalist he'd managed to contact. And he told me about something utterly staggering: mental contamination."

"Mental contamination?"

"Yes, that's right. Something that can be transmitted through the eye, and that is so violent that it actually alters the structure of the brain."

Lucie reacted right off the bat.

"A friend of mine, Ludovic Sénéchal, completely lost his sight after watching that film. It's called hysterical blindness. The images made his brain malfunction. Is that the kind of thing you're talking about?"

"It's much worse than that. Hysterical blindness is a purely psychological phenomenon. In the case of mental contamination, not only is the brain structure modified—I mean physically modified—but, worse, a chain reaction spreads from person to person, like a virus. You'll see what I mean. Just give me a second . . ."

He suddenly interrupted himself and turned toward the bay window.

"Did you hear that?"

"What?"

He ran to the table to grab up his weapon.

"A cracking sound."

Lucie remained calm. The beer had steadied her nerves.

"Isn't it just the fire?"

"No, no. It came from outside."

He turned off the lights and inched toward the window. The stove gave his face a red glow. Lucie came closer. He stretched his hand toward her.

"Stay away from the window!"

Lucie froze. Outside, everything was perfectly still. The black tree trunks rose like malevolent totems.

"Who are you afraid of?" whispered Lucie. "You can see there's no one around. And no one followed us—I'd never seen such long, straight roads in my life."

"Only a few months ago I still lived in the center of Montreal. Then someone tried to kill me."

He moved aside and lifted the tail of his shirt. Lucie saw wide scars.

"Two stabs with a knife. Another quarter inch and that would have been it."

"The CIA?"

He tightened his lip and shook his head.

"That's not how they operate. The recent discovery of the bodies in Normandy makes me think now that the guy was French."

"Secret service?"

"Perhaps."

"If I said Foreign Legion, would that sound right?"

"I couldn't say. I vaguely remember what the guy looked like . . . Square jaw, well built, military bearing."

The guy in combat boots, thought Lucie.

"What *is* for sure is that the attempt on my life was clearly connected with Szpilman's film and what we'd discovered. Even so, he and I were working in strict secret, trying to find the trail, marshal our facts, as you're trying to do now. He was a lot more careful than I was. I still don't know how the people following me found out. The leak could have come from anywhere. While I was investigating, I made a lot of phone calls and met a lot of people. In mental hospitals, archives, religious institutions. Those killers must have contacts, lookouts. Since then, I've been hiding out here, protected by reliable sources, in the middle of nowhere."

Squatting, gun in hand, he ventured another quick look through the bay window. He sighed heavily, and after thirty long seconds stood up again.

"Maybe an animal after all. There's no shortage of elks and beavers around here."

He regained his calm. In his younger years, this man must have stared down a fair number of dangerous and influential people, faced the darkness and managed to keep his wits about him, and yet he was ending his days as a full-blown paranoiac.

"I suppose you didn't turn up much in the archives?" he asked. "I went there myself, about a year ago. It's clear that the names corresponding to little girls' faces can be found in the religious communities. But as I'm sure you've discovered, they're inaccessible. It's the only thing I'm still missing: the names of those young patients, to help us find our way back to the mental ward with the children and the rabbits, to those girls, get their testimony, living proof that—"

"I have the names."

"You what?"

"Many religious institutions are closing for lack of funds. Their archives have been relocated to the center in Montreal. Didn't you know?"

He shook his head.

"Since I've been in hiding, it's harder for me to keep current."

"The little girl on the swing is named Alice Tonquin."

"Alice . . ." He sighed, as if the name had remained caught at the back of his throat for years.

"The Sûreté lost track of her, but her last known address was the convent of the Gray Sisters. I have the name of the nun who took care of her. Sister Marie du Calvaire. That's where I was headed before you . . . kidnapped me."

"How did you manage that?"

"We mined the film for everything in it."

He smiled imperceptibly.

"I think it's time I told you about the rest of our findings, Vlad's and mine. And that we were making progress thanks to your information. Let's go back to the computer . . ."

When he returned to the table, his eyes fell on Lucie's cell phone. He picked it up.

"Your phone . . ."

"What about it?"

"You said it wasn't working. Since when?"

"Um . . . I tried to use it when I landed in Canada and—"

Lucie didn't finish her sentence, having just understood. Rotenberg turned the device over and opened the cover in back, his hands trembling. He tore what looked like a small electronic chip from its compartment.

"That's got to be a tracking device."

His blue eyes widened in panic. Lucie's hands flew to her head.

"The guy sitting next to me, on the plane . . . I was asleep for almost the entire trip."

"Drugged, most likely. They must have been watching you for a while. And they used you to find me. They—they're here . . ."

Lucie thought of the hidden microphones in her apartment and Sharko's. It was easy for the killers to shadow her.

Rotenberg immediately pulled out his own cell phone and dialed 911.

"Philip Rotenberg. Send someone right away to Matawinie, right next to the lake, where it meets the Matawin River. I'll give you the exact GPS coordinates—please take them down quickly!"

"What is the nature of your emergency?"

"They're here to kill me!"

He gave the memorized coordinates and hung up, again urging them to hurry. Then, hunched over, he crept back toward the stove. Lucie imitated him. The fire made the inside of the house dangerously bright, and there was glass on all sides. Just as he approached the stove, the bay window exploded.

Philip Rotenberg was thrown backward, his body landing heavily on the floor. A red bloom began spreading on his white shirt. His chest was still heaving. From outside, flames suddenly surged. Large moving curtains, coming from the woods. In front and behind. A violent red dance suddenly enveloped the outer walls of the cabin.

Fire, which had cost Lacombe his life so long ago, was seeking new victims . . .

Lucie rushed to Rotenberg, who was wheezing through a hole in his throat. She pressed her two palms over the wound. Her fingers instantly turned purple.

"Hang on, Philip!"

The man gripped Lucie's wrists tightly. His eyes seemed to be preparing for death. Thick black smoke was pouring under the door.

"On my neck . . . The key . . . Pull . . ."

Lucie hesitated a split second, then did as told. She yanked on the thin chain at the end of which hung a small bit of metal. Blood had begun to foam from Rotenberg's mouth.

"What is this a key to?"

The lawyer murmured something inaudible.

A teardrop, then no more.

Lucie stuffed the key into her pocket and stood up partway, in a panic. She grabbed up the gun, looked quickly around her. There was only one place the fire hadn't attacked yet: the shattered bay window.

She tried to think fast. The sniper could have taken her out at the same time as Rotenberg, yet he hadn't. He wanted to force her outside like a rabbit from its warren.

Lucie had no doubt: the killer wanted her alive.

If she set foot outside, she was done for.

She began to cough. The temperature was rising, the wood starting to crack. She had to hold out.

Behind her, outside, the flames were rising greedily. It wouldn't be long before they engulfed everything. From her hiding place behind the stove, Lucie dragged herself to the coffee table, pulled off her sweatshirt, rolled it into a ball, and doused it with water. She stuffed it against her nose.

Wait, just wait . . . The attacker would surely start wondering, having second thoughts, thinking she might have gotten away. He'd have to give in.

A window shattered into pieces behind her. Lucie jumped in fright.

The flames began to invade the house, raging farther inward; the wood began to twist. The cop's mind grew cloudy, her eyes were stinging, the heat was growing unbearable. She dug her nails into her thighs. *Just hold on.*

One minute . . . Two minutes . . .

Just then, a silhouette appeared in the swirls of smoke next to the bay window. The shadow entered cautiously, pistol facing front. A gray head glanced around the room. Lucie suddenly jumped up with a shout and emptied her chamber, firing blindly.

The shape collapsed.

Lucie held her breath and rushed across the smoke-filled room. As she stepped over the body, she briefly recognized the face of her neighbor from the plane. On his feet were combat boots.

She threw herself outside, ran about a dozen yards, and collapsed on the ground.

She coughed for a long time before finally sucking in a huge gulp of air.

When she turned around, the house was nothing but a giant ball of fire.

Lucie had become a nameless person, without her bag, without papers, without ID.

And she had killed a man in a country that wasn't her own.

50

The blue halo of the police cruisers' revolving lights mixed with those of the two fire trucks parked next to the cabin. The firefighters had arrived with dizzying speed, and their powerful hoses had managed to contain the blaze before it could spread to the surrounding woods. But Philip Rotenberg's home was no more than a heap of rubble and smoke.

The tense silhouettes of the Royal Canadian Mounted Police moved cautiously around the two charred bodies, taking numerous photos and fingerprints. All sorts of uniforms were present: red jackets, black-and-yellow trousers, felt hats, and Strathcona boots for the Mounties; white lab coats for the CSI teams; black slickers and canvas pants for the firefighters. The emergency teams worked together perfectly, giving the impression of a synchronized ballet.

Lucie was handcuffed. No brutality or animosity, just a respect for procedure. Her papers, notes, and backpack had vanished in the fire, and she had killed a man with multiple gunshots. The weapon found at her feet had just been taken away in a transparent baggie for fingerprint and ballistic analysis.

Lucie had been placed under arrest at 11:05 p.m. Quebec time by a detective named Pierre Monette, who brought her to the precinct at Trois-Rivières.

In the ultramodern quarters of the local police, they emptied her pockets—the key Rotenberg had entrusted to her ended up at the bottom of another baggie—and two men, not exactly altar-boy types, interrogated her without giving her time to catch her breath. Lucie explained the situation as best she could. She told them about the murders in France, the experiments in the 1950s, her findings at the archives, and her fake kidnapping by Philip Rotenberg. In a calm, self-assured voice, she invited her interrogators, who were exchanging skeptical glances, to get in touch with Quebec Sûreté and the French police for further information about the case. She scrupulously jotted down all the contact information and telephone numbers she could remember.

Her letter rogatory would no doubt save her neck, even though, in such situations, foreign police didn't have the right to intervene directly, especially when it came to using a firearm.

Her cooperative attitude and clear explanations did not save her from spending the night in a cell. Once more, Lucie did not protest. She knew how investigations worked, and what a complicated situation the Canadian police had to deal with. Two charred corpses found in the depths of a forest, a Frenchwoman with no ID, some wild tale about the CIA and secret services—this was no small matter. Verifying her statements would take time.

The important thing was that she was alive. She'd see her daughters again.

Alone in the small rectangular room, she collapsed onto the bench, her nerves shot. The man she had killed that evening was only the second in her career. To snuff out a life, no matter whose, always leaves a deep, black fissure in your soul. Something indelible that can haunt you for a long time.

She thought about Rotenberg, who had just been about to reveal the whole truth. As with the film restorer, she had handed him to his killers on a platter. Hidden in the deepest reaches of the forest, the man had paid the price for her negligence.

Those bastards had used her once again, and Lucie hated herself for it.

Detective Monette came by at regular intervals to see how she was doing, to bring her water or coffee; he even offered her a cigarette, which she declined. Later that night, he told her that everything was coming along smoothly and that she'd probably be out before noon.

The hours that followed stretched interminably. No more visits, no one to talk with. Just the leaden morning sun assaulting the northern sky through the Plexiglas windows of the sinister gray cell. Lucie thought incessantly of her girls. Last night, she had almost bought it. What would have become of her daughters without her? Another two orphans in the

313

world. Lucie sighed deeply. As soon as this business was over, she was going to take some serious time to think about her future. About the future of all three of them . . .

At 10:10 that morning, a silhouette appeared in the frame of the peephole.

Lucie would have recognized it anywhere.

Franck Sharko.

When Detective Monette unlocked the door, Lucie rushed out and, without thinking, threw herself into the arms of the big cop. The inspector hesitated for a fraction of a second, then clamped his two large hands against her back.

"You're going to make my old ticker give out if you keep this up. Is it always like this with you?"

Lucie's eyes clouded up. She leaned back, smiling sadly.

"Let's say these are special circumstances. Hadn't you noticed?"

For a few seconds, Lucie forgot the dark hours she'd just been through, reassured by Sharko's solid presence. He nodded his chin toward the bars, with a becoming smile.

"I'll be back in a moment, just have to finish up the paperwork. Think you can hang out a bit longer?"

"I'd like to make a phone call first. I want to call my girls. Just to hear their voices."

"In a moment, Henebelle, in a moment."

Lucie went back and sat on her bench.

Once alone, she let out a long breath and put her hand to her chest.

51

L ucie returned, holding Sharko's cell phone. She sat at the table and handed it back to him. On the road from Trois-Rivières to Montreal, they had stopped at a Kentucky Fried Chicken.

"So?" asked the inspector.

"They're both fine. Juliette doesn't have any trouble eating anymore and is staying with her grandmother. She's feeling much better, thank God. And as for Clara, I could only reach the counselors at her camp—the kids are out at a campfire. I forgot it's already dinnertime over there!"

During the drive, Lucie had time to relate everything that had happened since her arrival in Canada. The Duplessis Orphans, Sanders's treatments, the CIA's involvement in experiments on human beings starting in the fifties. Sharko had swallowed, storing away the information without saying a word.

For now, the inspector was hungrily munching on his fried chicken leg, while Lucie nibbled at her coleslaw and sucked down great gulps of Coca-Cola, which helped settle her stomach.

"The sniper at the cabin wasn't trying to kill me, I'm certain of it. He wanted to smoke me out and take me alive. There was something else."

Sharko stopped eating. He put down his chicken, wiped his hands, and looked at Lucie.

"This is all my fault."

And he told her: his visit to Legion HQ, Colonel Chastel, his bluff, the photo of the young woman with her face circled in red. That same young woman sucked noisily on her straw as she took in the news.

"So that's why you finally agreed to let me come here—for four days, no less. You wanted to go it alone."

"I just wanted to keep you from doing something foolish."

"You shouldn't have. Those soldiers could have killed you. They could have—"

"Let it go. What's done is done."

Lucie nodded limply.

"What happens now? For me here in Canada, I mean?"

"The RCMP will take care of the paperwork to allow you to return to France. For the police, the case is just about establishing what went down at the cabin. Our department and the Sûreté in Montreal will handle the rest—meaning the huge shithole we're in up to our necks. They're also trying to find out the identity of your seatmate on the plane, Rotenberg's killer."

"Blond, crew cut, solid build, combat boots. Under thirty. It's one of the two guys we've been looking for since the beginning."

"Probably so."

"Definitely so. And what about the key the lawyer gave me before he died? Any news?"

"They're checking to see what it belongs to. It's got a number, so they're thinking a locker somewhere. Maybe the post office or a train station. In any case, they'll keep us posted. And . . . nice work at the archives, Henebelle."

"Deep down, you didn't believe in it. Am I right?"

"In the lead? Not really. But in you, yes. I believed in you the minute I saw you get off the train, that first time at Gare du Nord."

Lucie took in the compliment. She gave him a smile and couldn't repress a yawn.

"Oops, excuse me."

"Let's hit the road and get you back to the hotel. How long has it been since you slept?"

"A long time. But we have to try to find Sister Marie du Calvaire. We have to—"

"Tomorrow. I don't feel like having to scrape you up off the ground."

For once, Lucie gave in without even trying to argue. The fact was, she was worn out.

"Let me just make a pit stop and we'll get going."

Sharko watched her walk away. He would have liked to hold her in his arms, reassure her, tell her everything would be all right. But for now, his jaws remained far too paralyzed to form tender words. He finished his beer and went to wait outside. He made a quick call to Leclerc to let him know everything was okay. The head of Violent Crimes told him he'd be seeing judges and senior officials at the ministry of defense within the day, to start legal proceedings that would allow them to investigate the Foreign Legion and determine whether Mohamed Abane had actually joined.

When he hung up, the chief inspector felt as if things were finally taking huge steps forward.

52

"I thought I'd find you here."

Sharko let himself be surprised by the lilting female voice behind him. Sitting in an armchair in the hotel bar, he was quietly sipping a whiskey in the dim light while reading over his list of SIGN participants. The place was elegant without going overboard: light-colored carpet, thick red cushions on the seats, walls lined in black velvet. As she came up, Lucie noticed the glass of mint soda sitting on the table.

"Oh, are you waiting for someone?"

"No, no one. The glass was there already."

He didn't say any more. Lucie remained standing and spread her arms in a sign of resignation.

"Apologies for the outfit. Jeans aren't very dressy, but I really hadn't been planning to go out at night."

Sharko gave her a weary smile.

"I thought you were going to get some sleep."

"I thought so too."

Lucie walked over to one of the empty chairs facing him and moved to sit down.

"No, not that one!"

She straightened up, startled.

"You liar—you *are* waiting for someone! I'll get out of your hair."

"Don't be silly. That chair wobbles. What can I get you?"

"A screwdriver. Heavy on the vodka, light on the OJ. I could stand to decompress."

Sharko emptied his glass and headed to the bar. Lucie watched him go. He'd changed his clothes, rubbed a dab of gel in his salt-and-pepper brush cut, and put on aftershave. He walked with style. Lucie looked over the papers he'd left in his chair. Last names, first names, birth dates, job titles. Some had been crossed out. With his devil-may-care facade, Sharko gave an impression of indifference, but in fact he never quit.

The inspector returned with two glasses and handed one to Lucie, who had slid her chair closer to his. She nodded toward the lists.

"Those are the scientists who were in Cairo at the time of the murders, right?"

"Two hundred and seventeen of them, to be precise. Between the ages of twenty-two and seventy-three at the time. If the killers in Cairo are the same as in Gravenchon, we have to add sixteen years. That eliminates a number of them right off the bat."

He stacked up the sheets, folded them, and slid them in his pocket.

"I've got some fresh bad news, which in fact is good news. Shall we get it over with?"

"Yes, please. You once told me there was a time for everything. And right now, I really, really need to relax."

"Here it is. Colonel Bernard Chastel was found at his home today. He ate his service revolver this morning."

Lucie took a moment to absorb the development.

"Are they certain it's suicide?"

"The ME and the detectives had no doubts. I'll spare you the details. And another bit of news: according to the airline, the guy sitting next to you was named Julien Manoeuvre. Career military, assigned to DCILE, the communication and information branch of the Foreign Legion. The department that makes films for the army."

"Our filmmaking killer . . . The man with the combat boots . . ."

"The same. As if by chance, Manoeuvre happened to be on leave at the start of our case. Leave personally authorized by Chastel. Later, when Chastel saw that things were starting to go south, especially with my visit to his office and what happened here, he killed himself. No doubt he took precautions and got rid of anything that could compromise him."

"So he was involved up to his neck. He knew about the murders."

"Most likely. And one more thing—hold on tight for this one."

"I'll do my best."

"A search of Manoeuvre's place turned up a number of lists of films being transferred among the world's major cinema archives. You remember the FIAF Web site your chief told us about? That's how he found out about the reel two years ago. He must have gone immediately to FIAF to ask for films from 1955, except that someone had already stolen the one he was looking for. A collector we know well."

"Szpilman."

"That's right, Szpilman. So Manoeuvre, after getting *this* close, lost the scent, but he didn't give up. He must have continued asking around, keeping an eye on film exchanges and want ads, especially from Belgium. And that's how he finally ended up at Szpilman Junior's house after the old man died."

"But it's crazy—all this effort just to get hold of a film."

"As long as copies existed, Chastel and the others behind this whole mess were fucked. Manoeuvre was just a pawn, an operative. So was Chastel, probably, but at a higher level."

"This time, tell me there's going to be an official investigation into the Legion."

"Yes. And with luck, it will loosen some tongues, and all those warrants will lead somewhere. Let's not forget that there are probably two killers. Manoeuvre was one, but the other one, the one who removes the brains, is probably here on this list. And he probably acted alone in Egypt, since Manoeuvre was much too young."

At these last words from the inspector, Lucie sipped her drink, eyes shining with fatigue. In the subdued light, Sharko's features softened. The sound of music, low and simple, faded into the background. Everything in this place fostered a sense of calm and seduction. Lucie took a photo from her wallet and laid it on the table.

"I haven't introduced you to my two little treasures. Who I miss terribly. Today more than ever, I realize I'm just not ready to be so far away from them."

Sharko picked up the photo with a tenderness Lucie had never seen in him before.

"Juliette on the right and Clara on the left?"

"Other way around. If you look closely, you'll see that Clara has a slight defect in her iris, a black spot that looks like a tiny vase."

The inspector handed back the picture.

"What about their father?"

"He ran out a long time ago."

Lucie sighed, her hands around her glass.

"This case is very hard, Inspector, because it's not Clara or Juliette I see when I look at this photo, but Alice Tonquin, Lydia Hocquart, and all those other frightened little girls. I can see their faces, their terror. I hear their screams when they attacked those poor animals."

"We all have our ghosts. They'll go away when we crack this case. When all the doors have finally closed, they'll leave you in peace."

A silence. Lucie nodded, staring into space.

"And how about you, Inspector? Have you left any doors open in your life?"

Sharko twisted his wedding ring.

"Yes . . . There's a very, very big door I'd like to close. But I can't seem to do it. Maybe because deep down, I don't really want to."

Lucie put down her glass and leaned forward. Her lips were just inches away from those of the man she was dying to kiss.

"I know what door you mean. And I might be able to help you close it."

Sharko didn't answer immediately. Part of him felt like pulling back, getting up, disappearing, but the other part struggled to keep him there.

"You really think so?"

She leaned farther forward and kissed him on the mouth. Sharko's eyelids had lowered; his senses went numb, as if everything inside him had suddenly shut down.

He opened his eyes.

"You do know there's probably no future in what's maybe about to happen?"

"Personally, I think there is. But for now, let's at least give the present a chance."

He hadn't seen a woman naked since the death of Suzanne, and it almost made him feel ashamed. The slim, scented body glided through the shadows and came to press against his. The greedy, delicate hands finished unbuttoning his shirt, while fire roiled deep in his belly. He let her take the lead, but Lucie could feel a tension, an impalpable hold that prevented the man in front of her from letting go completely.

"Is something wrong?" she whispered into his ear.

"It's just that . . ."

Sharko pulled out of her embrace and slipped nimbly toward the center of the room. He turned over the chair near the bed and put away the O-gauge Ova Hornby locomotive, with its black car for wood and coal, in the drawer of the bedside table. He also put away the box of candied chestnuts. Then he went back to his partner and kissed her passionately. A bit too roughly, he pushed her back onto the bed. Lucie let out a little laugh.

"That train was too much. You really are an odd—"

Their mouths found each other again, their moist bodies slammed together. Sharko deftly turned off the lights as their hips rolled in the sheets. Despite the drawn curtains, light from outside spread over the bed, suggesting the forms that pleasure combined. A landscape of flesh, hollows, valleys, gave the impression of sinking beneath the fury of an earthquake. Lucie bit the pillow, in the grip of her orgasm; Sharko turned her over, with the tender violence of a she-wolf lifting her young, and plunged onto her, breathing hard. The tears, the screams, the faces of the dead, the Lydias and Alices became blurred, submerged by their sensuality. The seconds pulsed like electrical charges on the skin. In the tension of his burning muscles, Sharko stiffened, the veins in his neck bulging. And as his teeth clenched, as his movements took fire, he stared at the center of the room.

She was still standing there, feet together, hands hanging down at her sides.

And for the first time in his life, Sharko saw Eugenie cry.

The instant seemed an eternity. The inspector's eyes clouded up as well, while the woman beneath him moaned.

And in the magic of his senses in ecstasy, the little girl smiled at him. She raised her small hand and gave him a friendly wave.

On the verge of tears, Sharko answered with the same gesture.

The next moment, Eugenie walked out without looking back. The door closed silently behind her.

And Sharko finally let himself feel pleasure.

53

Sharko awoke with a start: his telephone was vibrating on the nightstand.

He detached himself from the warm body he held tightly against him and rolled onto his side.

At the other end of the line was Pierre Monette. He'd found the origin of the key Philip Rotenberg had entrusted to Lucie: it opened a locker in Montreal's main train station. The Canadian policeman arranged to meet him there at noon, after he attended to some other business.

The inspector hung up and turned back to the woman sharing his bed. With the tips of his fingers, he caressed her back. Her skin was so soft, so young, compared with the thick shell that had turned him into a street cop. So many roads separated the two of them . . . Delicately, he buried his face in her blond hair and became intoxicated one last time with the blend of perfume and perspiration.

He couldn't lie to himself anymore: he wanted her. Since they'd first met, he had never really been able to banish her from his mind. Quietly, he got up and went off to shower. While he ran the water, while he looked at himself in the mirror as he dressed, he searched for Eugenie. He remembered with surgical precision the small hand movement she had addressed to him the night before. And those tears running down her childish face. Could it be that Eugenie was happy? And that she would finally leave him alone?

No, no, he couldn't believe it. He was ill, suffering from paranoid schizophrenia, which required him to take medicine until the day he died. Things just didn't happen like that. Not in real life.

After swallowing his morning pill, he returned to the bedroom. Lucie was sitting at the far end of the bed, gazing at him steadily.

"Someday, will you tell me what those pills are for?"

As if he hadn't heard, he walked up and kissed her.

"We've got work to do. Breakfast, a visit to the nuns, then the train station. Sound good to you?"

He briefed her about the locker key. Lucie stretched, got up, and suddenly threw herself against him.

"I felt happy last night, and that's something that hasn't happened to me in a long time." She smiled. "I don't want it to end."

Sharko put his hands on her back, which he massaged with a tenderness that surprised even him. He spoke into the hollow of her ear, also in a half sigh.

"We should think all this through. Agreed?"

Lucie sank into his eyes and nodded.

"Someday I want to come back here and experience this country other than through a waking nightmare. I'd like it if it could be with you."

Regretfully, she gently detached herself from him. She wished that instant could last an eternity. She knew how fragile their relationship was, and she'd already begun thinking of the return to France. The business of life threatened to separate them without their even realizing it.

"I'm going back to my room to get my things. I could give the room up—what do you say?"

"You know the administration and how people gossip. Better we have separate bills. Don't you think so?"

"Yeah, I suppose you're right."

They had just left the Delta hotel. Like two perfect tourists, they walked slowly, side by side, heading toward the convent of the Gray Sisters, which, according to the map they'd been handed at reception, was less than a mile away. Without talking about what had happened the night before, they turned onto Rue René-Lévesque and moved forward among the awe-inspiring towers of corporate headquarters. They finally arrived at a wide path protected by a locked gate.

After they had identified themselves on the intercom, the gate opened to let them in. The noise of traffic soon faded into silence, the crests of the skyscrapers disappeared, yielding to a graveled path bordered by gardens.

At the far end stood the convent, once the general hospital of Montreal. It was shaped like an H, and in the middle of it rose the Roman chapel, the cross at its summit gleaming in the sun. Two long gray wings spread out on either side. The Guy Wing housed the community and the Saint Matthew Wing welcomed the elderly, the infirm, and the orphaned. Four floors, hundreds of identical windows, an icy architectural rigor . . . Lucie could easily imagine the ambiance that must have reigned in such a place in the fifties. Discipline, poverty, self-sacrifice.

They silently skirted the dark brick building. In front of an entrance to the Guy Wing, they ran into the mother superior of the Gray Sisters. Framed in black and white, her face was harsh, leathery like a host. She made an attempt to smile at them, but a Christlike dolor drew her features taut.

"The French police, you said? What can I do for you?"

"We'd like to speak with Sister Marie du Calvaire."

The mother superior's features tightened further.

"Sister Marie du Calvaire is more than eighty-five years old. She's suffering from arthritis and spends most of her time alone, in bed. What is it you want with her?"

"To ask some questions about her past. About the 1950s, to be exact."

The nun kept an impassive face. She hesitated.

"This is not about trouble with the Church, I trust?"

"Absolutely not."

"You're in luck. Sister Marie du Calvaire has an excellent memory. There are certain things you never forget."

She invited them inside. They walked down cold, dark corridors, with high ceilings and closed doors along the side. There were whispers; a couple of distant shadows vanished like fluttering handkerchiefs. A muffled noise vibrated from somewhere. Christian chants.

"Has Sister Marie du Calvaire always lived with you, Mother?" asked Sharko, almost in a whisper.

"No. First she left us in the early fifties, under strict orders. She joined the congregation of the Sisters of Charity at Mont Providence for several years, before coming back here."

Mont Providence . . . Lucie had already seen that name in the archives. She reacted immediately.

"So she worked at the school that was turned into a psychiatric hospital by order of the Duplessis government."

"Indeed. A hospital that ended up taking in as many lunatics as those of sound mind. Sister Marie du Calvaire worked there for several long years. At the expense of her own health."

"And why did she return here to you?"

The mother superior turned around. Her eyes shone like flames from a candle.

"She disobeyed orders and fled Mont Providence, my daughter. For more than fifty years, Sister Marie du Calvaire has been a fugitive."

54

The nun's room was unadorned to the point of destitution: gray stone walls, a bed, a chair, a prayer bench with a Bible resting on it. The sole decorations were limited to a pewter crucifix on the wall above the bed, an armoire stuffed with books, and a clock. A small, high oval window filtered a wan light. The old woman was sitting on top of the bedsheets, feet together, hands folded on her chest, and eyes to the ceiling.

The mother superior leaned toward her and whispered something in her ear, then returned to the two detectives. Sister Marie du Calvaire slowly pivoted her head toward them. Her eyes were veiled: a fine white film, through which one could still make out the color of the ocean.

"I'll leave you alone," said the mother superior. "You'll find your way out easily."

She disappeared without another word, shutting the door behind her. Sister Marie du Calvaire stood up with a grimace and walked like an old turtle toward a glass of water, which she drank calmly. Her black robe fell to the ground, making it look as if she were floating. Then she returned to her bed and sat down, propping her pillow against the wall.

"It will soon be time for prayers. Whatever it is you want, I would ask you to be brief."

Her hoarse voice sounded like paper being crumpled. Lucie came forward.

"In that case, we'll come straight to the point. We'd like to ask you about the little girls you took care of in the early fifties. Alice Tonquin and Lydia Hocquart, among others. And also about Jacques Lacombe and the doctor who came with him."

It was as if the sister had stopped breathing. She brought her callused hands to her chest. Behind her cataracts, her irises appeared to dilate.

"But . . . why?"

"Because even today, people are committing murder to protect what your eyes have seen," Sharko picked up, leaning on the prayer bench.

In the ensuing silence, they could hear the voices of nuns singing in the distance.

"How did you find me? No one has ever come to talk about that ancient history. I am no one. Hidden from the world. I haven't been outside these walls in more than fifty years."

"Even so, your name is on the roster of your community. It was never supposed to leave here, but since your convent is scheduled to close, the records were transferred to the national archives."

The old woman's mouth opened slightly; she caught her breath after inhaling several times. Lucie had the sensation her pupils were dilating still further, summoning the lights of a banished time.

"Please don't worry. We're not here to denounce anything or put your former actions on trial. We're simply trying to understand what happened to those girls at Mont Providence Hospital."

The sister lowered her head. Swaths of white cloth concealed her face, leaving visible only a shadowy presence.

"I remember Alice and Lydia very well. How could I ever forget them? I took care of them, in the orphans' ward of this convent, before moving to Mont Providence because of 'staffing needs.' I thought I'd never see my little girls again, but two years later they showed up there, at Mont Providence, along with ten other girls from La Charité . . . The poor lambs thought they were simply changing institutions, as so often happened at the time. They were used to it. They had come by train, all smiles, happy and carefree, the way you can be at that age."

She punctuated her monologue with long, heavy silences. The memories slowly rose to the surface.

"But once inside Mont Providence, they soon realized what was in store for them. The cries and screams of the insane mixed in with the religious chants. The bright faces of the newcomers mingled with the ravaged features of the mentally retarded. At that point, those girls understood they would be staying in that place for good. With a stroke of the pen, some doctor working for the state had turned them overnight from perfectly normal orphans into mental defectives. And all for financial reasons, because mental patients made the government more money than illegitimate children. And we, the nuns, were required to treat them as such. We had to . . . do our duty."

Her voice caught. Sharko's fingers clutched the old wood. Around them hung the odor of crumbling walls and worn flooring.

"Meaning?"

"Discipline, bullying, punishments, treatments . . . The poor girls who rebelled went from one room to the next; the severity increased, and each time the doors of freedom closed a bit more. The Nuns' Room, the Trades Room, the Gray Room . . . Girls from one room were not allowed to communicate with the girls from other rooms, under pain of severe punishments. It was as if they were being compartmentalized, as if they were being removed from reality in order to bring them closer to madness. Madness, my children . . . Madness—do you know what it smells like? It smells like putrefaction and death."

The sister was having trouble breathing. A long, long inhalation.

"The last room, where they assigned me when I arrived at Mont Providence, was the Martyrs' Room, a horrible place where they kept more than sixty of the most acute cases, of all ages. Hysterics, schizophrenics, the severely retarded. That's where they kept the stocks of medication, surgical instruments, and also the Vaseline . . ."

"Vaseline?"

"To grease the patients' temples before electroshock."

Her fingers with their yellow nails squeezed together. Lucie could easily imagine the horror of spending your days in such a place. The screams, the claustrophobia, the suffering, the mental and physical tortures. Inmates and supervisors were in the same hell.

"We were in charge of the patients, with the healthy girls as our aides. Cleaning their cells, feeding them, helping the nurses on rounds. Brawls and injuries were daily occurrences. There were all sorts of lunatics in there, from the harmless ones to the most dangerous. Of all ages, mixed in together. Sometimes the orphans who resisted or misbehaved spent a week in solitary confinement, tied to a mattress and treated with Largactil, the doctors' favorite drug."

She raised her arm. With every movement, the black fabric of her garment crinkled like crepe paper. A kind of madness seemed to have taken hold of her too. She had not emerged from Mont Providence unscathed.

"The girls who ended up in that room—the most headstrong ones, the most rebellious, and surely the most intelligent—had no hope of getting out. The nurses treated them exactly the same as the mental patients, without any distinction. And even though we took care of them every day, what we said carried no weight. We had to be submissive and obey orders—do you understand?"

"What orders?"

"Orders from the mother superior, from the Church."

"Had Alice and Lydia landed in the Martyrs' Room?"

"Yes—like all the girls who came from La Charité. Such an influx in the Martyrs' Room was unheard of. We couldn't understand it."

"Why not?"

"Normally, the newcomers were put in the other rooms. Only a few of them ended up in Martyrs', sometimes after years, because they were constantly acting unruly or defiant. Or because they finally went mad themselves."

"What happened to those orphans, Alice and the others?"

The nun's fingers clutched her cross.

"Very quickly, they were taken in hand by the doctor in charge of the Martyrs' Room. We called him the 'Superintendent.' He was barely thirty years old, thin blond mustache, and eyes that could freeze your blood. He was the one who regularly brought certain children into other rooms to which no one had access. But the girls used to tell me about it. They would put them in groups and make them wait there, on their feet, for hours on end. There were televisions and loudspeakers that broadcast sudden claps or loud noises to startle them. Then there was a man who would film them, always with the doctor present . . . Alice liked the filmmaker—she used to call him Jacques. They got along well, and sometimes she got to go outside with him. He took her to the swings in the park next to the convent; he played with her, showed her animals, and made movies of her. I think he became her little glimmer of hope."

Sharko's jaws tensed. He could easily imagine what a glimmer of hope might become in the hands of someone like Lacombe.

"In those rooms, the girls must have done more than just wait, watch films, and get startled?" he asked. "Were there other experiments . . . more violent ones?"

"No. But you mustn't think their passivity was harmless. The orphans returned from there anxious and hostile. Which only increased the punishments they were subjected to in the Martyrs' Room. A vicious circle. There is no escape from madness; it's everywhere. Without and within."

"Did they talk to you about the experiment with the rabbits?"

"There were in fact rabbits in the room sometimes, gathered in a corner, from what they told me. But . . . that's all . . . I never really understood what it was about."

"How did it all end?"

The sister shook her head, a grimace on her lips.

"I don't know. I couldn't take it anymore. I had devoted my entire life to the service of God and His creatures, and I found myself in a hell on earth, letting myself be enveloped by insanity. I claimed some sort of health problem and ran away from Mont Providence. I abandoned them. Those little girls that I had raised here myself—I abandoned them."

She made a sign of the cross and compulsively kissed her crucifix. The silence that followed was awful. Lucie suddenly felt very cold.

"I returned to my old orders, the Gray Sisters. Mother Sainte Marguerite had the infinite goodness to hide and protect me. They looked for me, as you can imagine, and I don't know what would have happened if they'd found me. But the fact is that my ancient bones have endured through the century, and my memory has never forgotten the horrors that took place there, in the depths of the asylum. Who could ever forget so much darkness?"

Lucie looked the nun deep in her cloudy eyes. No one could forget such darkness. No one.

The truth was about to pour out, here, right now, from her old lips. Her pulse pounding, Lucie nonetheless retained her cop's reflexes.

"This superintendent. We need to know who he was."

"Of course. His name was James Peterson. Or at least, that's the name we overheard. Because he always signed Dr. Peter Jameson. James Peterson, Peter Jameson . . . I still don't know which was his real identity. But one thing for certain, he lived in Montreal."

Sharko and Lucie exchanged a brief glance. They had their final link in the chain. The nun stood up, shuffled toward her library, and knelt, tears in her eyes.

"I pray to God every day for those poor children that I left back there. They were my little girls. I had watched them grow, inside these walls, before we all found ourselves in that place of depravity."

Lucie felt a kind of compassion for the poor woman, who was dying alone and in pain.

"There was nothing you could have done for them. You were a prisoner of the system and your beliefs. God has nothing to do with this."

With trembling hands, Sister Marie du Calvaire lifted her Bible and began reading in a murmur. Lucie and Sharko knew there was no further reason to remain in the room.

They left without a sound.

55

The two cops went on foot from the convent to Montreal's central train station, which wasn't far. They walked without speaking, plunged into their darkest thoughts. They could see those closed-off rooms in the hospital, echoing with the moans of the insane, the frightened little girls intermingled with the most dangerous cases. They could hear the crackle of electroshock treatments in padded chambers. How had something like this been allowed to go on? Isn't a democracy supposed to protect its citizens from such barbarity? On the verge of nausea, Lucie felt a need to break the silence. She pressed against Sharko, slipped her arm around his waist.

"You don't talk a lot. I'd like to know what you're feeling."

Sharko shook his head and pursed his lips.

"Disgust. Just deep, deep disgust. There really aren't any words to describe things like that."

Lucie leaned her head against his solid shoulder, and in that way they continued on to the station. Once at the entrance, letting go of their embrace, they headed toward one of the foyers of the vast edifice, which in the middle of summer was thronged with travelers. Carefree people, happy, or in a rush . . .

Detective Pierre Monette and a colleague were waiting at the coffee bar. The policemen greeted each other respectfully and exchanged pleasantries.

The lockers stretched in two long rows opposite a cash machine, under the red maple leaf of the Canadian flag. Lucie was surprised that someone of Rotenberg's caliber should have picked such an open, heavily trafficked spot, but she figured he must have hidden copies of the information in various places, as Lacombe had evidently done with his film before burning to death.

Detective Monette pointed to locker number 201, at the far left.

"We already opened it. This is what we found."

He took a small object from his pocket.

"A flash drive."

He handed it to Sharko, who brought it up to eye level.

"Can you copy the files for me?"

"Already done. Keep it."

"What did you think?"

"We couldn't make heads or tails of it. I'm hoping you can figure it out. Your case has got me curious."

Sharko nodded.

"You can count on me. We're going to have to ask you for a bit more help. We need you to do a top-priority check on a man named James Peterson, or Peter Jameson. He was a doctor at Mont Providence Hospital in the fifties and lived in Montreal. He'd be about eighty by now."

Monette took down the information.

"Got it. I'll try to call you later this afternoon."

As Lucie and Sharko headed back to the hotel, the inspector shot circumspect glances at the crowd, searching for Eugenie. He craned his neck, leaned over to check behind a nearby couple.

She was still nowhere to be found.

56

Sharko's hotel room had already been made up. Clean sheets on the bed, toiletries replenished. The cop pulled his old suitcase from under the bed, opened it, and took out his laptop.

Lucie gave a curious glance, then knitted her brow.

"Is that a jar of cocktail sauce in your luggage?"

Sharko closed the lid quickly, pulled the zipper, and turned on his computer.

"I've always had trouble with diets."

"Between that and the glazed chestnuts . . . Judging by its color, I'd say it didn't weather the trip too well."

Leaving the remark unanswered, Sharko slid the drive into the USB port of his PC, and a window appeared with two folders. They were labeled "Szpilman's Discoveries" and "McGill Brainwashing."

"It's the same directory as on Rotenberg's computer. He must have backed up his files."

"McGill or Szpilman first?"

"McGill. The lawyer showed me photos of the patients being conditioned, but there was also a film. A film that Sanders showed his patients as part of his brainwashing technique."

Sharko clicked on the file marked "Brainwash01.avi."

"Oh-one . . . That could mean there were dozens of others."

From the very first image, the two cops immediately understood. Sharko pressed PAUSE and pointed a finger to the upper right of the frame. He turned to Lucie, his face serious.

"The white circle . . . The same as on the deadly reel."

"And on the crash films. Jacques Lacombe's maker's mark."

A heavy silence, then Lucie's voice, crystal clear:

"He was working for the CIA. Jacques Lacombe worked for the CIA."
Lucie felt the new piece fit, undeniably.

"That explains his relocation to Washington in 1951, near agency head-quarters. Then his move to Canada, where MK-Ultra was still under way. They recruited him the same way they recruited Sanders. First they saw the potential in his films, the way he manipulated the unconscious. Then they contacted him and, as with the psychiatrist, gave him a cover—the job as a projectionist—and probably a healthy bank account to boot."

Sharko agreed.

"They enlisted the best talents they could find. Scientists, doctors, engineers, and even a filmmaker. They needed someone to make the movies they showed the patients."

Lucie nodded. In the heat of the investigation, she was no longer next to the man she'd recently slept with, but with a colleague who felt the same pain as she: that of a dangerous, impossible manhunt.

"Rotenberg told me the program involving the children and rabbits wasn't MK-Ultra, and that the doctor you never saw on film wasn't Sand-ers. Which means . . ."

"Jacques Lacombe worked on both projects. On MK-Ultra, with Sand-ers at McGill, and on the one that used the children, with that Peterson or Jameson at Mont Providence. The CIA knew it could trust him. No doubt it needed someone reliable to film what took place in those white rooms."

Lucie got up to pour herself some water. The night of giddiness and pleasure was already a distant memory. The demons had come charging back. Sharko waited for her to return and slid a tender hand over the back of her neck.

"You doing okay?"

"Let's keep going . . ."

He hit PLAY. Brainwash01.avi . . .

Lacombe's film, which had been shown to Sanders's patients, was mind-bogglingly bizarre. It was a mix of black-and-white squares, lines, and curves oscillating like waves. It gave the feeling of sailing in a psy-chedelic or Zen-like world, in which the mind no longer knew exactly what to latch onto. On the screen, the squares moved around, slowly, quickly; the waves swelled and vanished. Sharko replayed the video frame by frame, and that's when the hidden frames appeared.

Lucie wrinkled her features. They saw clawlike fingers gripping skulls on a table. Spiders filmed close up, mummifying insects in their gossamer threads. A fat black cloud in a perfectly clear sky. A large dark clot in a pool of blood. Horrors, aberrations—all the things Jacques Lacombe prized.

Sharko rubbed his temples, shaken.

"They must have shown it to the patients in a continuous loop. Combined with the sounds from the loudspeakers, it would have been a veritable brainwashing machine. That Lacombe was as crazy as Sanders."

"That's probably the image he had of mental illness: scenes of capture and imprisonment, the invasion of the body by foreign organisms. All that to create a shock to the brain. Just like Sanders, he wanted to eradicate illness by tapping directly into the unconscious. Bombard it, the way they bombard cancer cells with radiation today."

Sharko let go of his mouse and ran a hand through his hair.

"Barbarians . . . We're back in the days of the Cold War, the battle between East and West, when people were prepared to make any sacrifice to reach their goals."

Lucie sighed and looked the inspector in the eye.

"When I think it was these horrors that brought us together, you and I . . . Without these monstrosities, we would never have met."

"Only a relationship born in suffering could bring together two cops like us. Don't you think?"

Lucie pinched her lips. The harshness and madness of the world saddened her more than anything.

"Where's the rhyme and reason in all this?"

"There is none. There never was."

She nodded her chin toward the screen.

"The other folder. We should get onto Szpilman's findings—hopefully to find out his secrets and be done with this once and for all."

Sharko nodded gravely. Around them, the atmosphere in the room had become thick and viscous. The cop clicked on the "Szpilman's Discoveries" folder. Inside was a single PowerPoint file, labeled "Mental_contamination.ppt." Lucie's throat tightened.

"Wait a minute. Just before they shot him, Rotenberg was telling me about mental contamination. With everything that happened afterward, it had slipped my mind. Open the file."

"A batch of photos, it looks like."

The slide show began, delivering its pixelated poison. They saw the pictures of the German soldier aiming at the Jewish women, which the police had already seen at the meeting in Nanterre. The eyes of the soldier in the foreground had been circled in marker.

"His eyes . . . That's what Szpilman wanted to call attention to."

The following series of photos: mass graves.

The bodies of Africans in heaps, tangled together, gathered up by the army. The inhuman expression of a vile massacre.

"Rwanda," the inspector murmured with difficulty. "Nineteen ninety-four. The genocide."

A particularly horrible image showed the Hutus in action, armed with their machetes. The faces of the aggressors were contorted in hatred, their lips frothing with saliva, the veins on their necks and arms bulging beneath the skin.

Once again, the killers' eyes were circled. Lucie moved her face closer to the screen.

"Always the same look in the eye, always . . . The German, the Hutu, the little girl with the rabbits. It's like . . . a common feature of madness, transcending cultures and time periods."

"Different forms of mass hysteria. We're in the thick of it."

The war correspondent had then ventured among the bodies, lingering over the corpses, not shying away from the most horrific close-ups.

The following image froze Lucie and Sharko in complete stupor.

It showed a Tutsi, his eyes missing, his skull cut in half.

The photo bore the caption BEYOND MASSACRE: AN EXPRESSION OF HUTU MADNESS.

Lucie burrowed into her seat, a hand on her forehead. The photographer had thought this was a barbaric act by the Hutus themselves, but the truth lay elsewhere.

"I can't believe it . . ."

Sharko pulled on the flesh of his cheeks until his eyes slanted.

"He was there too. The sicko who steals the brains. Egypt, Rwanda, Gravenchon—and how many other places besides?"

Other documents followed: archival photos, scans of articles, or pages from history books.

Each concerned a genocide or a massacre. Burma, 1988. Sudan, 1989. Bosnia-Herzegovina, 1992. Horrible photos, taken in the frenzy of the moment. The very worst that history had to offer was on display before them. And always, eyes circled. Sharko looked for sliced skulls among the mountains of corpses, without finding any more. But they were surely there, somewhere among the dead. They simply hadn't been photographed.

The cop firmly hit PAUSE.

"Enough!"

He stood up, put his hands to his head, and paced the room. Lucie still couldn't get over it.

"Mental contamination," she kept repeating mechanically.

She filed through the last images; then the slide show ended.

Quiet in the room. Discreet rumble of the air conditioner. Lucie rushed to the window and threw it open.

Air. She needed some air.

57

Sharko squeezed his skull between his hands.

"The killer must have been there . . . present after every massacre, to steal the brains."

Pale, Lucie had come back to sit on the bed. She stared blankly at the screen.

"Szpilman didn't care about the political, ethnic, or existential reasons for the genocides. He was tracking something in those massacres, in which perfectly normal fathers and children suddenly went into a killing frenzy. Just before he died, Philip Rotenberg had talked to me about research that led the Belgian to that business of mental contamination. He'd said there might exist a phenomenon so violent that it could modify the structure of the brain."

"Like a virus, you mean?"

"Yes, except that there isn't anything really physical or organic. Just . . . something that passes through the eye and directly modifies human behavior, that liberates the impulse toward violence."

"A kind of criminal mass hysteria."

"In a way. Ever since I saw the film with the girls in the white room, I've had an image in mind: they're like a squadron of warplanes. The lead plane, the one that guides the rest, veers downward, and the other planes follow in formation, one by one, as if they were held together by an invisible thread. What if *that's* what this Syndrome E is all about? One highly violent individual sets things off, acts as a catalyst; then the mental contamination of violence spreads almost immediately from person to person? What if that was the goal of the experiments hidden in Lacombe's film? Trying to re-create the phenomenon for the camera? Establish concrete proof of its existence?"

Sharko walked almost mechanically around the room. Nothing existed around him. The case had absorbed him, and what Henebelle was saying struck him as at once far-fetched and frighteningly on target. Szpilman, through his own research and persistence, had stumbled onto the truth. He had spent years rummaging through books, contacting war zone photographers, collecting images, tracking down a horrifying discovery. Ultimately, the film that had no doubt come to him by arranged accident had been the cornerstone of his research, the missing piece that allowed him to grasp the very essence of his quest.

"There are people on this planet," he said, "who are trying to understand, medically—I would almost say surgically—the workings of this phenomenon, which Jacques Lacombe recorded more than fifty years ago for the purposes of secret experiments. Violent mental contamination starting from a catalyst. *That's* what Syndrome E is."

"Violent mental contamination starting from a catalyst," Lucie repeated. "A rare, random phenomenon that can strike anywhere, at any time. You can't study it in a laboratory, so you go looking out in the field. At the site of massacres, the places where outbreaks of mass hysteria occur. You look in the heads of corpses for a trace, a clue."

Sharko pursued her line of thinking, his hand on his chin.

"Chastel knew of the existence of Syndrome E, and that means two things. First, that the file, which in the fifties was in the hands of the CIA, has now been acquired by the French secret service. And second, that it's . . . intrinsic to the Legion itself. It's about a place where men, especially during the selection phase, are pushed to their physical and psychological limits. Where the slightest detail could suddenly set one of them off."

"The Legion is the perfect breeding ground for mental contamination. Is that what you're saying?"

"Exactly. Think of the photo of those soldiers facing the Jewish mothers, or the Hutus brandishing their machetes, the inherent violence of those scenes, their context. No doubt there are triggers that help bring about the syndrome, like stress, fear, external conditioning . . ."

"War, confinement . . . anything that involves some form of authority. Sister Marie talked about the anxiety the little girls exhibited after they'd been locked in those rooms and shouted at."

Sharko nodded emphatically.

"Absolutely. Before taking over as top commander, Chastel led the survival training in Guiana, a hellhole that could drive even legionnaires insane. There might have been an outbreak of the syndrome there. From that, Chastel might have caught the eye of our brain thief. He then did a stint with the secret service before ending up in Aubagne. I believe he was appointed top commander specifically to try to trigger Syndrome E among his own men, so that they could study the phenomenon on living beings."

"A kind of incubator. The equivalent of the 1955 experiments, but outdoors."

"Yes. But he got caught in his own trap. Mohamed Abane, a particularly violent individual, went out of control and dragged four other men down with him. They were probably massacred before Chastel could even intervene. At that point, the colonel immediately took charge of the situation. He, his henchman Manoeuvre, and our brain thief got to work: opening the skulls, removing the eyes, disposing of the remains."

Sharko stood up and waved the list of SIGN attendees. He was on the brink of nausea.

"Manoeuvre and Chastel were only second-stringers. We need the real killer. The one who mutilated the Egyptian girls. The one who, for all these years, has probably been traveling from country to country sawing open skulls. The architect. He's here, right in front of us, on this list of names. Burma dates back twenty-five years. If he went there after the massacre, our killer must be at least forty-five today."

Sharko closed up like an oyster, delved into his list, and began crossing out names. Still shaken, Lucie took the opportunity to log on to the hotel's Wi-Fi. She googled the name "Peter Jameson," which didn't yield anything relevant. She then entered "James Peterson." A number of results came up.

"Franck? You should come see this . . . A James Peterson matches our criteria."

As Sharko didn't hear her, she had to say it again. He raised his eyes toward her and waved his list.

"I should be able to eliminate about half."

He came toward her. Lucie pointed to the screen. She had clicked on a Wikipedia article about the man. The photo showed a thin, slight fellow, with angular features and intransigent eyes.

The two cops read silently. James Peterson . . . Parents emigrated from New York to France. Born in Paris in 1923. A remarkably gifted child who started university studies at age fifteen. Associate professor of physiology, before concentrating on the study of the nervous system when he wasn't yet twenty. Then moved to the United States, to Yale, where he specialized in research into direct stimulation of the brain using electrical and chemical techniques. This was the subject of his only book, *Brain Conditioning and Freedom of Mind*, published in 1952. In 1953, Peterson inexplicably abandoned the scientific field and was never heard from again.

Lucie tried other searches, but they didn't tell her anything further. Peterson had simply vanished. But the cops now knew where he'd gone after 1953: Mont Providence, under the hybrid identity of Peter Jameson. He had been recruited by the CIA, like the others, to perform experiments on children. For now, the trail dead-ended there. The cops awaited a call from Pierre Monette for more detailed information.

Lucie clicked on the link for the book James Peterson had written. The cover image appeared, and the two cops stared at it in amazement.

It showed an enormous bull, nose to nose with a small man wearing a blond mustache; his hands were behind his back and he was smiling. James Peterson himself.

"The bull facing off against the human, like in Lacombe's film," said Sharko. "What is this goddamn book about, anyway?"

With a few clicks, Lucie found a descriptive blurb of the work. She read aloud:

"Progress in physiology is such that, today, it is possible to explore the brain, to inhibit or excite aggression, and to modify maternal or sexual behavior. The tyrannical chief of a monkey colony yields to its subordinates, if one manages to stimulate a particular area of its encephalon. This direct access to the brain, through the miracle of astounding physical techniques, constitutes a more decisive phase in the history of man than the conquest of the atom."

Sharko sat up. He realized that the solution to their puzzle was buried in the pages of that book. He put on his jacket, which he'd left at the foot of the bed, and headed for the door.

"Come on. While waiting for the cop to call, we're going to see what horrors that book really contains."

58

James Peterson's book was still available online, but it wasn't in stock at the bookstores Sharko and Lucie tried. Given the title and description, a slightly savvier bookseller recommended asking at the University of Montreal Medical School—the third largest in North America—and more specifically, the Center for Neurological Sciences. Standing behind his advice, he managed to reach a professor named Jean Basso. He handed the receiver to Sharko, and the two men set an appointment for a short while later, enough time for Basso to refresh his memory of the book that he indeed owned.

In the taxi, Lucie and Sharko didn't talk much, so close did they feel to the unspeakable mire. They were brushing up against a darkness that had engulfed politics, religion, and science, and that had insinuated itself into the recesses of sick minds. Lucie thought of her family, her daughters, whom she tried to raise in a state of innocence in a world she still wanted to believe existed. The faces of Clara and Juliette again floated above those of Alice and Lydia, little girls who hadn't asked for anything and who had been given no chance. Today more than ever, Lucie felt powerless and terribly fallible.

They arrived at their destination.

The university rose like a monster of concrete and glass, between the western slope of Mount Royal and the infinite rows of student housing. But more impressive still was the great emptiness that reigned in midsummer. More than fifty thousand students absent, streets deserted, dining halls, gyms, libraries, and shops closed. It was like a ghost town, where all that remained were a few researchers and some maintenance and facilities staff.

Lucie and Sharko stopped in front of the beautifully designed science complex and began questioning the first people they saw. Eventually they obtained the name of a building: Paul Desmarais.

The structure was located at the other end of campus. More than half a mile away, after following the underground passageways that linked the various centers, they were ushered into an office and introduced to Professor Jean Basso, the head of what was now called the Central Nervous System Research Group. The man was a good fifty years old and affected an Einstein-like air.

Sharko explained their interest in Peterson's book, *Brain Conditioning and Freedom of Mind*.

"I know it well," Basso replied. "Who could not know his work on the brain? A remarkable scientist, who interrupted his research much too soon."

"Would you know why?"

"No."

Sharko was almost tempted to say, *We do. He conducted experiments not very far from here, on children used as guinea pigs for a secret CIA program, along with an insane filmmaker named Jacques Lacombe.*

"And do you have any idea what became of him?"

"None at all. Only the man's scientific life interested me. As for his private life . . ."

He waved a green-and-black book of about four hundred pages, its cover showing a man staring down a bull. The copy had been well used, its pages yellowed and dog-eared.

"I'll try to be brief and explain this in layman's terms. You have to realize that for scientists of the time, what happened inside our heads was, for all intents and purposes, like a big black box. Peterson, with true genius, focused on something fundamental to the neurosciences: What took place between sensory intake—the eye seeing a red light—and its behavioral outcome—the foot stepping on the brake? What were the mechanisms that clicked into place inside that black box, so that on the basis of a sound or a smell, a movement or behavior should result? The fundamental principle that guided Peterson's work was the tabula rasa, which posits that the mind of a newborn is a blank slate, on which experience writes its messages and thereby develops the various areas of the brain, which are related to certain senses. Basically, the origin of memories, emotional reactions, physical aptitude, of the words and ideas that constitute an individual are initially found *outside* that individual. Peterson conducted a slew of edifying experiments on animals to support his theories. For example, monkeys, which he deprived of several of their senses from birth. Cats, which he stimulated visually without respite. In the case of deprivation, the brain didn't grow, and in that of sensory overload, it reached a weight higher than the norm. Which proved that the structure of the brain developed according to sensory experience. In this book, we can sense Peterson's fascination with how the senses interact with the brain."

"Does the term 'Syndrome E' mean anything to you?"

"Mmm. No, nothing."

"And what about 'mental contamination'?"

"What do you mean by that?"

"The propagation of violence and aggressive behavior through the senses. Images and sounds so violent that they can modify the brain structure of a given individual, who through his actions then brings about a similar modification in the behavior of the group around him?"

Lucie surprised herself with the sentence she'd just uttered. But ultimately, wasn't *this* the heart of all their research?

The professor rubbed his chin.

"Like a viral phenomenon? With a Patient Zero, and the propagation of an illness through the intermediary of neighboring individuals? Your theory is interesting, but . . ."

The professor paused a moment before continuing:

"I'll have to look into it further. Peterson ultimately might have had a hidden agenda. Especially since he was in fact interested in areas of the brain conducive to violence, notably in monkey colonies."

Sharko and Lucie exchanged a look.

"How so?"

"He demonstrated that monkeys who suffer injuries to Broca's area and the amygdala develop abnormal social behavior patterns, an inability to control frustration or anger. Peterson went so far as to get them to attack tigers. In the same way, he had noted an abnormally reduced amygdala region in animals who became naturally aggressive. As if that part of the brain had atrophied. He never found an explanation for that atrophy."

Little by little, the cops understood the path Peterson had followed and the significance of his discoveries. With each passing second, they grasped still further the essence of Syndrome E. Lucie leafed slowly through the book. Old black-and-white photos jumped out at her. Cats, their skulls attached to dozens of electrodes. Monkeys with large boxes of wires clamped to their heads. Then Peterson himself, facing the bull: the same photo as on the book jacket.

Lucie showed it to the professor.

"What does this image mean?"

"Impressive, isn't it? Peterson was also a precursor of deep brain stimulation—using electrical impulses to provoke individual behavior."

Sharko suddenly felt a wave of fire in his belly. *Deep brain stimulation . . .* The term he'd come across in the ME's report, concerning the gruesome discovery in Gravenchon. Mohamed Abane had had a small particle of green sheathing under his skin, near the clavicle, and the ME had mentioned deep brain stimulation as a possible explanation for its presence.

"Explain that to us," he said in a neutral voice.

"Galvani, 1791: a frog's muscle contracts under electrical stimulation. The experiment was repeated by Volta in 1800, then by Du Bois-Reymond in 1848. Two decades later, in 1870, Fritsch and Hitzig notice that electrical stimulation to the brain of an anesthetized dog provokes localized movements in the body and limbs. Then we jump to 1932, and an experiment that strongly influenced Peterson: stimulating the brain of a nonanesthetized cat causes well-organized motor reflexes and emotional reactions: meowing, purring, hissing . . ."

It was terrifying. Lucie easily imagined Peterson, deep in his laboratory, opening skulls to gain access to the brains of animals while they were still alive and wide awake.

"Working with nonanesthetized animals was a huge step forward, for we then realized that electricity was the basis not only of movement, but also of emotion. It was in the hands of Peterson that deep brain stimulation would be born, in other words implanting electrodes in the brain through which one could transmit electrical impulses. Those large boxes you see, miss, clamped to the heads of those monkeys, are nothing more or less than the equivalent of circuit panels. By moving a small knob, you stimulate different areas of the brain, and thus provoke different reactions. Of course, the system was extremely crude and limited, but it worked."

This was all highly enlightening. Sharko imagined a series of switches that could be turned on and off, acting upon things like sleep, anger, or motor function. What happened if you flipped several switches at the same time? What did cats feel when they heard themselves meowing without really wanting to? Those experiments must have been limitless, in both horror and cruelty.

The professor continued talking, revealing a chilling and very real truth.

"Peterson was a bit of a showman—he liked to produce an effect. For the bull, he simply implanted electrodes in the motor areas of the animal's brain. The control box was outside the photographer's range, and Peterson was hiding a remote control in his hand. When he pressed a button, an electrical current inhibited the motor areas and prevented the beast from moving. It's instantaneous, like a freeze-frame."

Sharko put his hand to his forehead. With his schizophrenia and his treatments at La Salpêtrière, he had seen what scientists were capable of. But to such a degree . . .

Jean Basso noticed his disturbance and smiled.

"Hard to believe, isn't it? And yet it was fifty years ago. Today, DBS has become a relatively common and widespread technique. And the equipment is much more compact. These days, the electrical stimulator is implanted beneath the skin, attached to electrodes embedded in the skull. The patient himself has a remote control that lets him start or stop the stimulation at will. With it, we're able to help treat certain illnesses, such as Parkinson's or obsessive-compulsive disorder, and soon maybe even depression or chronic insomnia. Its uses are still being developed."

Sharko tried to repress the monstrous idea that had gradually been taking shape in his head. It was beyond comprehension. He nonetheless ventured the question:

"Do you think someone could do the same thing with violent behavior? Trigger or inhibit it at will, with a simple remote control?"

He was clearly thinking of Patient Zero—of the catalyzing element in a massacre, whom one could control scientifically, rather than waiting for it to occur randomly.

"Anything's possible. It's an awful thing to say, but electricity always trumps will or mind. With deep brain stimulation, you can stop someone's heart, put him to sleep, keep him awake, or erase his memory. The possibilities are endless. The difficulty lies in reaching the right area with the electrodes, and sending the impulse to exactly the right place. Long electrodes have to pass physically through the brain, and therefore cross through the areas governing motor function, language, and memory. It's no simple task and it creates problems we haven't yet figured out how to solve. But the biggest problem is the area itself. When it comes to violence, the amygdala is very small, it controls multiple functions, and it's in contact with some very sensitive parts of the brain. Being off by even a fraction of a millimeter can make the patient lose his memory, start raving uncontrollably, or become paralyzed for life. That's why we need time and money to establish sufficient guidelines to justify the use of implants. There's no room for error in neurosurgery. The technique is very promising, but once you delve into the reaches of the brain it can be either heaven or hell . . ."

Sharko shut the book and set it on the table. Having no more questions, the two cops said good-bye and went out, feeling as if their own brains were close to giving out.

59

The two French cops were sitting on a bench in the middle of the deserted campus. Calm reigned over the ghostly space. Sharko had taken out his list of 217 persons and was running his pencil down every name that hadn't been crossed out.

"Did you get what I got out of that, Lucie?"

"We're not just looking for someone with medical training, but someone capable of performing an operation as delicate as deep brain stimulation, a scientist interested in the structure of the brain . . . I imagine James Peterson isn't on the list. How old would he be today?"

"Too old. Even if he'd used another identity, there's only one person on this list born in 1923, the same year as Peterson, and she's a woman."

"Don't forget, the list is only of the French."

Sharko crossed out more names.

"I know . . . but the legionnaire Manoeuvre was French. It's unfortunately very likely our brain thief is too."

"Could Peterson have had children? Maybe a son who took up his work?"

"Monette should be calling at any moment. We'll know soon enough."

Lucie had leaned forward, her hands squeezed together between her thighs.

"We're almost there." She sighed. "The killer has to be hiding there, right before our eyes, and I think that— I think we're coming to the end of what we came to find here. Do you realize how far this stretches? If Syndrome E really exists, it calls so many things into question. Individual freedom, our ability to choose, responsibility for our actions. I can't believe everything that governs what we do is merely chemical or electrical. Where is God in all this? Feelings, the soul—these aren't just artificial constructs."

351

The number of suspects on the list was shrinking but still remained significant—about forty names.

"And yet . . . well, take a schizophrenic, for instance. He might see an imaginary person as clearly as you see that lab tech in his white coat over there. All because a few millimeters of his brain are on the fritz. It has nothing to do with God or witchcraft. It's chemistry. Just some shitty chemistry."

His phone rang. He looked at the caller ID.

"It's Monette."

He answered and put the phone on speaker.

"I have some info about your Peter Jameson," said the policeman.

Peter Jameson . . . So James Peterson had indeed come to Canada under an assumed name—though he hadn't exactly strained his brain to find one.

"He moved to Montreal in 1953 and worked at Mont Providence as a medical researcher in the ward for acute mental retardation. In 1955, he married a woman named Hélène Riffaux, a math teacher and Canadian national. Together they adopted a little girl, and Jameson dropped out of sight a few weeks later, taking his daughter and abandoning his wife. As far as we can tell, he left no traces or forwarding address. No one ever saw him again. The marriage was just a pretext for the adoption, which he couldn't have done otherwise. It's a bit short, but that's roughly all there is to know. Oh, one last thing, which might be important. The little girl was one of the orphans from Mont Providence."

Those words set off an earthquake inside Lucie and Sharko. They stared at each other, flabbergasted, and seemed to come to the same realization simultaneously.

"The girl! Tell us her name!"

"Coline Quinat."

Sharko's finger ran down the Cairo list. He had seen a Coline in there. Letter Q. Quinat. There she was. Sharko thanked him in a blank voice and hung up. Lucie had pressed against him, her eyes fixed on the printed line.

"Coline Quinat, born October 15,1948, researcher in neurobiology at the research center of the Army Health Services, Grenoble."

"The Army Health Services," murmured Sharko.

"Good God . . . Born in 1948, like Alice. It's her! Coline Quinat, Alice Tonquin. It's a perfect anagram. It was right there all along!"

Lucie covered her face in her hands.

"Not her . . . not Alice."

Sharko sighed, shaken by these revelations.

"Researcher in neurobiology . . . no doubt a bogus position to cover her real work for the army. It all fits together so well now. The tortured little girl herself becomes a torturer. The brain thief—she's the one. She's the one behind all these horrors. She's the one who killed and mutilated the young Egyptians. And she's the one who went to Rwanda, and wherever there had been massacres . . ."

Silence weighed on them for a few moments. Lucie was in shock. The person she'd wanted to avenge since the beginning was the very person she was hunting: the murderer, the one who removed the victims' eyes and brains. The architect. The mastermind. The sickest of the killers.

Sharko couldn't sit still; he was like a lion in a cage.

"Imagine this: after lots of trial and error, research, relentless pursuit, Peterson and Lacombe manage to film a major breakthrough—proof of the existence of mental contamination, which Peterson had always believed possible, and for which he'd managed to obtain CIA funding. But after their phenomenal results with the rabbits, the scientist convinces Lacombe not to tell the CIA about it. He knows how momentous this discovery is. Maybe he's thinking of selling his findings to some other country, which is ready to pay a fortune for the knowledge. Especially France, the country of his birth."

Lucie nodded, pursuing Sharko's line of thinking:

"Lacombe lets himself be swayed by Peterson and agrees. To protect their secret from the CIA, they hide the film about the rabbits in another weird short, Lacombe's specialty. Even if the CIA watched the film, since they owned the original and all the prints, they wouldn't see a thing. At most, they'd have picked up on a few subliminal images of Judith Sagnol. Lacombe, with his genius and latent insanity, bested the American intelligence community at its own game."

"Right. And Peterson, for his part, is already thinking of getting out, fleeing Canada, and he wants to take Alice with him, the one who allowed him to reproduce Syndrome E. Had she become an object of study for him? Had he developed some kind of affection for her? Did he see her as the living proof of his success? A trophy? A curiosity? Whatever the case, he gets married, adopts Alice, and kills Lacombe by setting the fire. Then, probably with help from the French, he vanishes back into his native country, taking Alice and Lacombe's original print with him."

"Except that Lacombe had taken precautions and made copies, hiding them in different places. The two men must have lived in constant fear and paranoia, not only of the CIA but of each other."

"Exactly. But all Lacombe's precautions couldn't save him. Protected and hidden, Peterson settles in France and probably pursues his experiments. His discoveries about Syndrome E fall into French hands, right under the CIA's nose. Alice pays the price for Peterson's fanaticism and madness. She's already suffered all those tortures at Mont Providence, and she was the first one to start slaughtering the rabbits. She's Patient Zero of Syndrome E—she triggered the wave of madness that affected all those other girls. The experiment inevitably left her with severe psychological scars—a violence and aggression deeply ingrained in the very structure of her psyche. But she was also brilliant, and probably picked up where her father left off."

"I remember Luc Szpilman's body, and his girlfriend's . . . All those knife wounds. There was a kind of frenzy, a blind, incomprehensible rage."

"The same as with the Egyptian girls, and the film restorer, and the rabbits. Alice is now sixty-two, and still hasn't stopped killing. Madness and violence have spread deep inside her, the way they've spread inside everyone involved in this business."

Lucie clenched her fists and shook her head, eyes fixed on the ground. "There's still something I don't understand. Why did they use deep brain stimulation on Mohamed Abane?"

"It's simple. There was a sudden, uncontrolled outbreak of Syndrome E at the Legion. Something went wrong, the glitch that led to the murder of five young recruits. Except that Abane, who'd only been wounded in the shoulder, was still alive. No way were they going to let him live because of what had happened, but on the other hand Abane was, like Alice, a Patient Zero. I think that before she had him killed, Alice Tonquin, or

Coline Quinat, wanted to experiment on him. She had a living, breathing guinea pig at her disposal, which must not have happened too often. She had her hands on someone who basically was just like her, and who must have made her relive the most painful times of her life. God only knows what tortures she put him through."

Lucie's face darkened.

"It's not only God who knows. We're going to know soon enough as well."

She stood up and watched an airplane slicing through the sky. Then she turned back to Sharko, who was nervously fumbling with his cell phone.

"You're dying to call your chief, aren't you?"

"I should, yes."

She gripped his wrists.

"There's just one thing I'm asking—let me see Alice face-to-face. I need to talk to her, look her in the eye, so that I can get her out of my head. I don't want to keep thinking of her as a poor innocent, but as the worst sort of killer."

Sharko recalled his own face-to-face with the dangling body of Atef Abd el-Aal, the morbid sensation of pleasure he'd felt when he'd flicked the lighter and watched the man's face go up in flames. He leaned closer to Lucie and whispered in her ear:

"This business has been going on for more than half a century. A few more hours won't make any difference. I'll call him before we take off. I want to be in the front row and not miss anything either. What did you think?"

60

They had caught the last flight out that evening, destination: Paris. Since the plane wasn't entirely full, they could sit next to each other. Her forehead flattened against the window, Lucie watched Montreal turn into a great luminous vessel that gradually let itself be swallowed by the shadows of night. A city that she'd only come to know by its darkest side.

Then came the endless black of the ocean, that unknowable mass that quivers with life and holds our fate in its undulating belly.

Next to her, Sharko had put on his sleeping mask and curled up in his seat. His head was nodding, and he could finally let himself go. They might have taken the eight hours of travel to talk, tell each other about their lives, their pasts, get to know each other better, but they both knew that they understood each other best in silence.

Lucie looked with sorrow and desire at that square jaw, that face that had lived through so much. With the back of her hand she lightly brushed the stubble on his cheek and remembered that their relationship was born in the very heart of their own sufferings. There was hope. Deep down, she wanted to convince herself there was hope, that all scorched earth eventually started yielding grain again, one summer or other. The man must have been through the worst life had to offer; day after day, he must have tried to roll a ball of life that eroded more and more with each new incursion into Evil. But Lucie wanted to try. Try to give him back a tenth, a hundredth of what he had lost; she wanted to be there when things weren't going well, and also when they were. She wanted him to hug her twins to his heart and, when he buried his face in their hair, perhaps think of his own child. She wanted to be with him, period.

She pulled back her hand, parted her lips just slightly to whisper all that to him, even though he was sleeping, because she now knew that a part of his brain would hear it, and that her words would register somewhere in the back of his mind. But no sound emerged from her mouth.

And so she leaned over and simply planted a kiss on his cheek.

Maybe that was how love began.

61

The minute they landed at Orly, everything accelerated. As soon as he'd heard, Martin Leclerc alerted Criminal Division headquarters in Grenoble. Without checking in at Number 36, Sharko had claimed his car at airport parking; he and Lucie headed south, their bags in the trunk.

Their final straight line . . . The last euphoric, destructive line of coke . . . It would be soon. At six in the morning, the Grenoble police would enter the home of Coline Quinat, age sixty-two, who lived on Voie de Corato, overlooking the Isère River.

Sharko and Lucie would be first in line.

The landscapes flew by, valleys following fields, the mountains growing taller, breaking through the dry earth. Lucie dozed off and started awake by turns, her clothes rumpled, her hair tangled and unwashed. It didn't matter—they had to see this through to the end. Like this—in one shot, without stopping, without catching their breath, without thinking twice. They had to get it all out. Have done with it once and for all.

Grenoble was a city with rough associations for the inspector. He remembered the shadows that had cast him to the bottom of the abyss only a few years before. Back then, Eugenie had appeared behind him in the car, sleeping soundly on the rear seat. Sharko didn't dare believe things could be so much better now, that the little phantom had disappeared from his head for good since his night with Lucie. Had he finally managed to close that door, which for so long had been open onto the faces of Eloise and Suzanne? Had he succeeded in wiping from his lips the honey of his unending grief? For the first time in years, he let himself hope so.

To become like everyone else again. At least, sort of.

They joined their Grenoble colleagues at about four in the morning. Introductions, coffee, bringing up to speed.

At 5:30, a dozen officers headed for the home of Coline Quinat. A bloodred sun had barely detached itself from the horizon. The Isère slowly became haloed in silver reflections. Lucie smelled the odor of a manhunt's end. The best moment for a cop, the final reward. Everything would soon be over.

They arrived at their destination. The facade of the house was large and impressive. The cops were surprised to spot light coming through the slats of the upstairs shutters: Quinat was already awake. Cautiously, the teams got into position. Bodies tense, glances rapid, prickling in the chest. At 6:00 a.m. sharp, five blows of the police battering ram overcame the lock on the heavy front door.

In a flash, the men flew inside like hornets. Lucie and Sharko immediately fell in with the ones dashing up the stairs. The beams from their flashlights danced on the steps, crossing over each other, as heavy boots clattered in sync.

There was no battle, no explosions or gunfire. Nothing to match the incredible surge of horror and violence of the previous days. Just the queasy sensation of invading a lone woman's privacy.

Coline Quinat had just stood up from her desk, her face pale and calm. She slowly put down her fountain pen and latched her eyes onto Lucie's, while the men rushed forward to cuff her. She stood quietly as they read her her rights, without resistance or protest. As if this were all following an implacable logic.

Lucie stepped forward, almost hypnotized, so shocked to finally see in the flesh a person lost in the black and white of a fifty-year-old film. Quinat was a head taller than she. She was wearing a blue silk dressing gown. Her short, graying blond hair framed a hard face, perfectly preserved, with a prominent jawline. *Her gaze* . . . Lucie became lost in that dark gaze, which had traveled the years without losing any of its severity, its terrifying emptiness. The gaze of that sick little girl that had so upset her. The woman's lips parted; she spoke:

"I figured you'd come sooner or later. After Manoeuvre's death and Chastel's suicide, the dominos were falling one by one."

She tilted her head, as if trying to read into Lucie's thoughts.

"Don't judge me too harshly, young lady, as if I were the worst sort of criminal. I only hope that in coming here, you've understood what my father and I were seeking to accomplish."

Behind her, Sharko whispered into the squad leader's ear. The next moment, he and his men retreated from the room, leaving Sharko alone with Quinat and Lucie. Sharko closed the door and stepped forward. Lucie couldn't contain her rage:

"Accomplish? You slaughtered a defenseless old man, you . . . hanged him and disemboweled him! You riddled the bodies of a woman and her boyfriend with stab wounds, who weren't even thirty years old! You *are* the worst sort of criminal!"

Coline Quinat sat on her bed, resigned.

"What can I say? I'm a Patient Zero and I'll be one all my life. Syndrome E emerged from my head that summer day in 1954. The violence became . . . embedded . . . inside me, and its ways of expressing itself are not always the most . . . rational. Please believe that if I could have dissected my own brain, I would have. I swear to you I would have."

"You are insane."

Quinat shook her head and pinched her lips.

"Inspector. None of this was supposed to happen. None of it. We just wanted to get back the copies of the film that Lacombe had strewn about. And we'd succeeded, for most of them. We had even gone to the United States. But . . . there was that cursed reel, which had traveled from Canada to Belgium. And then Szpilman. People like him exist, paranoiacs who dwell on conspiracies and the secret service, and they're the ones who frighten us most. Because they react the minute there's a malfunction—it's like they have a . . . sixth sense."

Sharko was standing next to Lucie.

"You said 'we.' 'We'd succeeded,' 'we wanted to get the copies' . . . Who is this 'we'? The French secret service? The army?"

She hesitated, then finally nodded.

"People. A lot of people who labor every day to safeguard this country. Inspector Sharko, don't confuse us with the riffraff you meet in the streets. We're scientists, thinkers, decision makers; we make the world go forward. But every advance demands sacrifices, whatever they may be. It's always been like that. Why should it change now?"

Lucie could no longer sit still. This calm and levelheaded discourse, coming from the mouth of a lunatic, was making her seethe.

"Sacrifices like those poor Egyptian girls? They were only children! Little girls, like you were! Why?"

Coline Quinat tightened her jaw. She was trying not to talk, but the need to justify herself was too powerful.

"My father passed away two years before the Burma genocides. He spent his entire life looking for manifestations of Syndrome E. The proof of its existence. He never went into the field, because he knew perfectly well that one could re-create it and study it in the laboratory. He used me, then dragged me in his wake, trained me, conditioned me to pursue his quest. Science studies, medical school, specialization in neurobiology. I had no say in the matter, I was . . . enlisted."

"Did they send you there? To the places where these genocides had occurred?"

"They did—with legionnaires, humanitarian aid groups, Red Cross doctors. We collected corpses and stacked them up by the dozens before they could start to rot. I took advantage of the occasion to study their brains. I had official accreditation."

"And what about Egypt—did you have official accreditation there as well?"

"Mass hysteria phenomena with violent manifestations occur so seldom and randomly that it was . . . almost impossible to do any serious studies. Naturally I went to Cairo."

"And you killed those girls. Mutilated them. Working alone, this time, without any orders. Or accreditation."

She answered evenly.

"There was only one way to verify that it was Syndrome E, and that was to open their skulls and look inside their brains, at the amygdala, to see if it had atrophied. At the time, we didn't have the kinds of scanners we have today. As for the mutilations"—she clenched her teeth—"that's just how it was. No doubt you'll call it uncontrollable impulses, or sadism, and you'd probably be right. Our minds have not begun to reveal all their secrets. Your old historian unfortunately had to bear the brunt of it. I wanted to show you that you weren't dealing with . . . one of those common criminals that are your daily bread. This case went far, far beyond that. I hope it had the desired effect."

A heavy silence, then she continued:

"My methodology in Cairo did not entirely please the powers that be, to say the least. But when they got wind of a telegram that some Egyptian cop had sent, they had no choice: they had to cover me, and themselves as well. Everything else was just collateral damage."

Lucie felt it all, every murderous impulse. The confirmation that the upper echelons of power had protected a woman who was dangerously insane, a murderer who would stop at nothing in the name of scientific progress, made her shake with rage.

"Once back in France, I studied those brains, and I noticed that the amygdala of those Egyptian girls had indeed atrophied. Do you realize what that means, Inspectors? We weren't talking about some genocide. The phenomenon had no particular origin, it had occurred with no real explanation, and it was capable, in certain cases, of propagating violence, sealing it once and for all into our head. I had concrete, definitive proof that Syndrome E truly existed and could strike anywhere. At anyone! You, Detective. Me, anybody. It crossed over years, peoples, and religions. I verified it again that same year in Rwanda. A very . . . fruitful time, if I may say so. I went into the mass graves, walked through the bodies, and once again I opened skulls. Imagine my amazement. One person's violence spreads to the brain of another, atrophying his amygdala and making him violent in turn. And so on, one after the other. A veritable contagion of violence. This was a major discovery, which challenged so many fundamental concepts of how we understood massacres . . ."

"An understanding that you and your collaborators kept to yourselves, naturally."

"The stakes were so high—not just militarily, but geopolitical and financial. Secrets had to be preserved. Mastering the emergence of Syndrome E and learning how to trigger it became my obsession. The last random manifestation to date is the one that happened at the Foreign Legion post. No matter where or how hard I looked, for years on end, the 'creation' of another Patient Zero was impossible. It required too much waiting and observation. It also needed test subjects. At the time, in 1954, scientists had a lot more leeway; they could profit from the excesses of the superpowers and their secret services. They had 'raw material' at their disposal, as in the back wing of Mont Providence Hospital. I was that raw material."

It was monstrous. The woman had become a block of cold meat, without emotion, without remorse. The purest, most extreme example of the relentless scientist.

Quinat sighed.

"But today, as we speak, there is a much quicker solution, which my father had already pointed out. A solution that technological progress has finally given us. Electrodes planted in the amygdala, which trigger extreme aggressive behavior with the simple push of a button, then spread the phenomenon to those nearby. You just have to place them in conditions of stress and fear, and get them used to authority so that Syndrome E will take root more easily."

Tirelessly she continued, evidently needing to justify her actions while detailing her most heinous crimes.

"Just imagine soldiers who no longer experience fear, who can kill without remorse, without hesitation, like a single, powerful arm. Obviously, many parameters are still beyond us, especially regarding the most favorable conditions for propagating the impulse from Patient Zero. How much stress should we apply to the others? And what's the best way to do it? But this will all eventually be figured out, mastered, and described in the protocols. With or without me."

Sharko, impatient, kept his eyes riveted on Quinat. His fists clenched compulsively.

"We found a piece of electrode sheath in Mohamed Abane's neck. What did you do to him?"

"Abane had survived Chastel's 'glitch,' and he was a Patient Zero. Before studying his brain, I conducted deep brain stimulation experiments on him. We especially stimulated the pain centers, in order to trace curves and fill out our statistical tables. We had to eliminate him in any case, so let's just say we got the most out of him first."

Lucie sensed that Sharko was on the point of bursting.

"Why did you steal their eyes?" she asked in a harsh voice.

Coline Quinat stood up.

"Come with me."

At his wits' end, Sharko shouldered a path through the group of policemen waiting outside the room. Quinat led them to a large, clean basement. She nodded toward an old gray rug. Lucie understood; she rolled up the rug, revealing a small trapdoor, which she opened. She wrinkled her features: beneath her was pure horror.

In a minuscule crawl space rested dozens of jars in which pairs of eyeballs floated. Blue, black, and green irises bobbed slowly in formaldehyde. In disgust, Lucie held out a jar to the inspector. Coline Quinat looked carefully at the container. Something baleful shone in her own pupils.

"Eyes . . . Light, then the image, then the eye, then the brain, then Syndrome E . . . It's all connected—now do you understand? One cannot exist without the other. These eyes are the ones through which Syndrome E was able to spread. They've always fascinated me, just as they fascinated Jacques Lacombe and my father. They are such perfect, precious organs. The ones you're holding belonged to Mohamed Abane. You have in your hands a Patient Zero, miss. Eyes that absorbed the syndrome spontaneously, in a way we might never be able to explain, and that guided it straight to the brain, thereby modifying the brain's structure. Aren't eyes like that worth preserving?"

There was now a kind of madness shining from Quinat's own eyes that Lucie had trouble defining. A madness born of the dogged determination of people who were willing to do anything in the service of their beliefs. Lucie turned toward Sharko, who was half hidden in the shadows, then grabbed Coline Quinat by the elbow and pulled her toward the men waiting at the top of the steps. Before putting her in the hands of the police, she asked:

"You're going to spend the rest of your life in prison. Was all this really worth it?"

"Of course! You can't imagine how much it was worth it!"

She smiled. And at that moment, Lucie understood that no bars could ever contain that kind of smile.

"Images, young lady. Increasingly violent images are everywhere. Think of your own children, numbed out in front of their computers and video games. Think of all those malleable brains, which the preponderance of images is modifying even in early childhood. None of that existed twenty years ago. If you ever have the chance, read the autopsy reports for Eric Harris, Dylan Klebold, and Charles Whitman, young men who walked into their schools with shotguns and fired on anything that moved. Go have a look at their amygdala, and you'll see it's atrophied. You'll understand that now it's the entire planet that's rushing toward its own genocide."

She pressed her lips together, then opened them again:

"Anyone. Syndrome E can strike anyone, in any home. Tomorrow, it might be you or your children. Who's to say?"

She added nothing more. The police led her away.

Chilled to the heart, Lucie went back downstairs alone, without making any noise, as if devoid of energy, exhausted, and with only one wish: to return home, curl up in her daughters' arms, and get into bed. Sharko was sitting in front of the dozens of eyes that were watching him, still screaming out their final anguish.

"You coming up?" she murmured in his ear. "Let's get the hell out of here. I can't take any more."

He looked at her for a long time without answering, then stood up with a deep sigh.

Sharko pressed the light switch at the top of the stairs. The eyes of Mohamed Abane shone for a fraction of a second, before going out forever in the darkness of the basement.

Epilogue

The beach at Les Sables d'Olonne unfurled its great gilded crescent beneath the August sun. Her eyes hidden behind dark shades, Lucie watched Clara and Juliette as they carved elaborate shapes in the sand. Some seagulls spun overhead, and a tepid, calming roar rose from the ocean. All around her people were happy, sharing the slightest square foot of sand. The area was packed.

For the tenth time in less than an hour, Lucie looked back at the seawall. Sharko would be arriving at any moment. Since Coline Quinat's arrest, they had seen each other only three times, contriving quick round-trips on the TGV that led to furtive embraces. On the other hand, they called each other nearly every evening. Sometimes they didn't have that much to say; other times, they talked for hours. Their relationship developed haltingly and with plenty of awkward moments.

Even though they'd tried to avoid the topic, their last case had left an indelible stamp on their minds. Inner suffering would take time to heal. In the hours following her arrest, Coline Quinat had confessed everything. The names of military top brass, members of the secret service, certain politicians and scientists. An unofficial research and neurosurgery center devoted to Syndrome E and deep brain stimulation had been established in the hidden recesses of the army's health services, thirty feet below-ground. There, they studied the phenomenon, established experimental protocols, and performed surgeries. Slowly but surely, piece by piece, the think tank behind the operation would crumble. The case was far from closed, and the restrictions on military secrets didn't make it any easier, but those who should pay would soon be made to pay. Supposedly . . .

Lucie turned back to her twins, who were sitting in a puddle. Given the crowds, she had ordered them to stay nearby. The girls were playing a few yards away, laughing. Water, sand, and sun—all you needed for happiness. No more video games; Lucie had thrown out all the consoles. To preserve her daughters as much as possible from the world of images, their intrinsic violence, their harmful effects on the mind. Get back to the basics, those old wood or plastic toys, manual activities, paper and paste. Everything was being lost so quickly with technological advances. In some ways, Quinat was right: the world was running headlong into a wall.

In a week, the holidays would already be over. She'd have to go back to Lille, shut herself up in the apartment, and think. Think about the future, about making a better tomorrow out of a life that moved too fast. Lucie let some sand run between her fingers, telling herself yet again that she couldn't exist, that she couldn't reach her full potential if she wasn't a cop. Her job was like a gene, inextricably attached to her cell structure. It was her profession that made her Lucie Henebelle, that gave her her real identity. At the same time, she knew she could improve, be a better mother, a better daughter too. Deep down, she felt she could do it. It was all a matter of willpower.

Lucie's face broke into a wide smile when she heard that particular crunch of sand right behind her. She turned around. Sharko was standing there, in his incomprehensible linen trousers and white short-sleeved shirt, his eyes still behind those patched sunglasses. Lucie stood up and gave him a hug. They kissed. Lucie caressed his cheek with the back of her hand.

"I missed you so much."

Sharko removed his glasses, gave her a simple smile, put his backpack down on the sand, and nodded his chin toward the twins. He was holding a small package.

"They're so beautiful . . . Did you tell them?"

"Why don't you do it yourself? You're not *that* shy, are you?"

"It's your vacation, for the three of you. I don't want to horn in on your nightly games of Parcheesi."

"Oh, of course I told them. They're looking forward to welcoming you into our little rented cottage, on one condition."

"Name it."

Lucie pointed to the package dangling from the inspector's hand.

"That you stop bringing them candied chestnuts every time you visit. They can't stand them!"

Sharko raised the package as if to give the candies a good once-over.

"They're right. These things are disgusting."

He walked to a trash can, took one last look at the box of glazed chestnuts, and dropped it into the plastic bag. He put back the lid. No more chestnuts . . . No more cocktail sauce . . .

The two girls saw him and ran up to give him an affectionate hug. He kissed them on the cheeks and gently petted their hair. They wanted to play ball and he promised to come in a few minutes, warning them they'd better practice up before he got there. Then he sat down next to Lucie, rolling up the cuffs of his trousers.

"So? Your chief?" she asked.

Sharko's gaze was riveted on the girls. Lucie had never seen such intensity or such tenderness in a man's eyes.

"Finished. He handed in his resignation yesterday to the big boss. Falling apart like that, just eight years before he's eligible to retire. After all the sacrifices and tough breaks. The job finally got him."

"And what about you, your job in Nanterre? The two of us . . . Did you have a chance . . . to think about it?"

He picked up a fistful of sand and carefully watched the grains slip through his fingers.

"Did you know that a few years ago, I left it all behind to open a toy store in the north? Then I went back to school for criminology. And after that, I—"

Lucie's eyes widened.

"You, in a toy store? Are you kidding me?"

He rummaged in his bag and took out the miniature O-gauge Ova Hornby locomotive, with its black car for wood and coal. It shone in the sun.

"The store was called the Little World of Magic. It's not around anymore—a video games shop took over the space."

Lucie felt a lump in her throat. Sharko was speaking from deep emotion.

"'The Little World of Magic'—it's nice."

He nodded. The horizon now absorbed his attention.

"I wanted to create an interlude in my life. Take the time to watch my daughter grow up. I wanted to remind myself that I'd once been like her, and that the happiest memories we preserve are of our parents' faces."

He delicately put the train back in his bag.

"You know, something important happened during our case. I lost someone who used to occupy a very significant place in my life. Someone, I think, who was there for the sole purpose of telling me things I didn't want to hear."

Lucie felt nervous.

"You're starting to frighten me."

"Don't worry—that someone is somebody I never want to see again. And there's only one way to make that happen: keep moving forward. So in a few days, I'm going to go see the big boss myself, and tell him—"

Juliette ran up and asked if she could get an ice cream, interrupting Sharko. Lucie shot a quick glance at the ice cream man, about ten yards away on the seawall. She tried to stand up to go with her, but Sharko grabbed her by the wrist.

"Wait, let me finish. This all has to come out now."

Lucie handed her daughter some money.

"Go with Clara, but you come straight back, you hear?"

Juliette nodded. The two little girls ran off through the crowd of vacationers. Sharko started sifting sand again, while Lucie kept an eye on her children from afar.

"I was saying, I'm going to write my boss a letter of resignation. That is, if . . . if you want me. I don't know if things'll work out. I've got plenty of ingrained habits, and also . . . I'd need a special room for my trains, and the kids wouldn't be able to play with them, because—"

Lucie suddenly leaned toward him and squeezed him against her chest.

"So is that a yes? You're moving up north?"

He pressed his chin into the hollow of Lucie's shoulder, then let his eyelids drop.

"A guy can still try out new things at my age, don't you think? I'm not especially tactful, but I'm not such a bad businessman. And besides . . . I have a fair amount of cash socked away in my account, and I don't spend much. Do you think that bar in the old part of town is still for sale?"

Lucie slid her hands under his shirt and affectionately caressed his back. She adored these moments at his side; she needed to make them last, more and more.

"Franck . . ."

They were silent a few seconds, giving in to the sounds around them. Laughs, shouts, the rustle of the breeze. In this moment of pure happiness and caresses, Lucie glanced over toward the little ice cream wagon. Animated silhouettes constantly crossed her field of vision; the beach was jammed. She craned her neck, could see in the hubbub the five or six people waiting in line for their treat. No sign of her daughters. Lucie raised herself onto her knees, a feather of panic in her throat.

Sharko stood up quickly then, shielding the sun, his body frozen as he looked at the seawall.

"Franck, do you see the girls near the ice cream wagon?"

A breath between them.

"Franck! Franck, tell me you see them . . ."

Wind floated over the waves, carrying distant sounds of laughter.

COMING FROM VIKING
WINTER 2015

Bred to Kill

In the thrilling sequel to *Syndrome E*, Lucie Henebelle
and Inspector Sharko have reunited to take on another terrifying
case. When a promising grad student is found brutally killed at a
primate research center outside of Paris, the down-and-out Sharko
is called in to wrap up what's thought to be a straightforward
crime. And although the cause of death initially seems quite
simple—it is assumed a chimp attacked poor Eva Louts—it soon
becomes clear that her murder was staged and that far more sinister
forces were truly at play. Who would have wanted Eva dead,
and why?

Now Sharko and Lucie must strip layer after layer away from this
terrifying mystery before the person who killed Eva finds them
too. In a riveting hunt that jumps from the streets of Paris to the
heart of the Alps to the innermost sanctum of the Amazon jungle,
Franck Thilliez once again delivers an adrenaline-fueled story that
hinges on modern genetics, paleontology, viruses, and human
nature in its most essential form.

ISBN 978-0-670-02597-8

VIKING